A Very Inconvenient Scandal

Also by Jacquelyn Mitchard

The Deep End of the Ocean
The Most Wanted
A Theory of Relativity
The Breakdown Lane
Still Summer
Cage of Stars
Twelve Times Blessed
Christmas Presents
No Time to Wave Goodbye
Second Nature
Two If by Sea
The Good Son

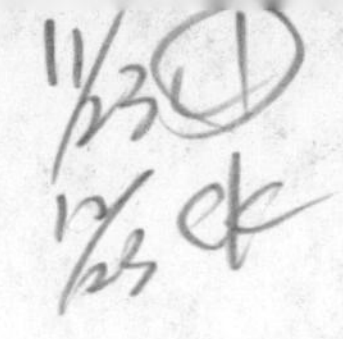

Jacquelyn Mitchard

A Very Inconvenient Scandal

Recycling programs for this product may not exist in your area.

ISBN-13: 978-0-7783-6937-0

A Very Inconvenient Scandal

Mira
22 Adelaide St. West, 41st Floor
Toronto, Ontario M5H 4E3, Canada
BookClubbish.com

Printed in U.S.A.

For Deb T. and Diana B.

And for Jeff Kleinmann

"The cure for anything is salt water:
sweat, tears or the sea."

Isak Dinesen

"He prayeth well, who loveth well all things
both great and small."

Samuel Taylor Coleridge
The Rime of the Ancient Mariner

1

Something terrible had happened, but Frankie didn't know what it was. In her rental car, she pulled up in front of her childhood home. Not a single light. Not a single sound. Was Mack already dead? Was he in the hospital? Please come home, read the text on her phone. Urgent. Today. Here is your ticket number. Her father had made her reservation and paid for her ticket. Everything about it was strange. Mack was not the type to say *please* nor to splurge on pricey airline fares.

And if you were on your deathbed, you didn't send your own message.

So…the *something terrible* must have happened to her brother, Penn. Or her beloved best friend since fourth grade, Ariel, as close as any sibling. All the texts she sent as she rushed through three thousand miles between airports went unanswered. On the drive from Boston to Cape Cod, she hit redial on everyone's number until her phone was out of charge. No one picked up.

She could not bear it.

The last time she'd been here, just over a year ago, was for the funeral of her mother, Beatrice, her rock, her mainstay, struck down overnight from strep at the age of fifty-two.

Oh please, no more, Frankie thought, remembering a line from an old poem her mother used to read to her and Penn. *So far? So early? So soon?*

Exhausted, sweaty, pregnant, thirsty, nauseated, her distended bladder a taut water balloon, she lumbered out of the car and stumbled to the place on the front steps where she knew a key was wedged under the bottom of a big stone planter.

But wait. Where…? The planter was gone.

Frankie went back to the car and flipped on the headlights, then the brights.

Two huge new bright metal planters flanked the entryway, overflowing with the gaudy bells and tongue-like flowers of fuchsia plants. She fumbled in one, then the other, until she located a slim metal magnetized key holder. (Didn't burglars know about these things too?)

The facade of the white house with its three wings and extravagant second-floor porches reared up before her, summiting a slight rise from the curl and boom of the surf. For the first time since Frankie could remember, the whole place was freshly painted, a door of marine blue and shiny black shutters jaunty as bright lapels on a tuxedo. Still, though the paint might be new, Frankie knew every cleft and corner of this old house, every change cobbled skillfully onto the main building by six generations of her mother's family. Despite her old grief and new worry, she nearly wept with relief. Much as she loved her work, which took her all over the world, there still were many nights when she dreamed that she was eight years old, running from the pond with her brother under the long avenue of smoke trees in all their pink summer finery to this house, which would always be home.

"Dad!" she called, as she noisily unlocked the door and

stepped into the foyer, reaching for the light switch, flinching at the glare from a new overhead fixture like a gigantic suspended gyroscope, bright white wainscoting, translucent blue floor tiles… What? More redecorating? From Mack, who had sweatshirts older than his children? He really did have a screw loose. Everything was different—walls, floors, furniture, windows! The only things she still recognized were a gigantic print of one of her own best-known underwater photos—the placid, bemused gaze of a manatee—and Beatrice's big painting that looked like the undulating hills of a desert but was actually a close-up detail of an Angular Triton shell. Such giant close-ups were their art in common.

"Dad!" Frankie shouted, louder. "Dad, are you here?"

No sound except the tinny exhalation of the air-conditioning.

Frankie made her way down the wide dark hall to the closed door of the master bedroom. "Dad! Dad?"

A cough, or a groan, issued from within. That was Mack. He really was sick! She'd arrived just in time. Pushing her way in, Frankie flipped on all the lights. Bare-chested, tanned and fit, Mack sat up. Next to him, pushing her white-blond hair out of her eyes, was Ariel.

Ariel!

The world slipped. A piano fell out of the sky and clanged to the ground, narrowly missing her head.

Frankie screamed. She screamed again.

Ariel rolled out of bed and stood up. Under her huge white T-shirt protruded her hugely pregnant belly.

Frankie ran to the hall bathroom, where she managed to get to the sink in time to throw up.

"Frankie, let me in!" It was Ariel's voice. "Let me explain!"

Frankie couldn't answer. She clung to the sink and sluiced her face with cold water. Ariel called, "Frankie! Answer me!"

"Get my brother," Frankie said, through the locked door. "Get Penn. I'm sick."

"She's sick," Ariel said to someone. "I told you that we should—"

Mack rattled the knob. "Frankie, come out right now." Frankie leaned against the door, trying to knit common sense with what she'd just seen. Ariel was, after all, the administrator, and its only permanent employee, of the Saltwater Foundation, the nonprofit organization for the conservation of marine animals, Mack's lifework. Had Mack forced Ariel... Frankie hunched over the sink in a fresh churn of nausea. Or had Ariel somehow... Was Mack suffering from some kind of dementia?

At last, it was her brother's voice. "Frankie, are you okay?"

"Help me," she said. "What the hell? What's happening?" She opened the door and poked her head out. With his curly dark hair stuck up like springs and his skinny legs poking out of his boxers, Penn stood there in his ancient gray T-shirt that read *Sorry, I Can't. It's Shark Week.* In her bare feet, just behind Penn, Ariel seemed even tinier than her five feet two, her long nearly white-blond hair pulled up in a toppling bun, purplish smudges of exhaustion under her eyes.

A few minutes later in the kitchen, Penn sat beside Frankie, ineffectually holding one of her wrists, while Ariel rushed around making her a cup of tea, giving her dry toast for the nausea, as if this were the set of some British TV show instead of her mother's kitchen on Cape Cod—her mother's very kitchen, from which everything Beatrice treasured had been removed.

"It's a lot, Frankie," Ariel said softly. "I should have told you."

"You think?" Frankie replied. "I'm having a baby. I'm getting married."

Ariel stopped. She blinked. Then she said, "How...how did you guess?"

What? Frankie was confused. "How did I guess what?"

"That I was pregnant."

"You mean before? Or now? Jeez, Ariel! I majored in biology. I have eyes. But, actually, I was referring to myself, you cow! Me. I am pregnant! Almost five months. Even before I got the big emergency text from Mack, I was already coming home, soon, to tell you my big surprise. I never thought you had an even bigger surprise, that you were screwing my dad." She cupped her hand and drank cold water from the faucet. "Is it his? Or, sorry, do you even know?"

"Don't you dare talk to me like that, Frankie, in my own—"

"In your own house? Right, all yours! Not everybody who sleeps with the boss gets a nine-bedroom beachfront house, and hey…that's my mom's twenty-fifth anniversary ring on your hand, not bad, Ariel. Trashy girls everywhere are going to get tattoos of you."

"Listen to yourself, Frankie! You should be ashamed of yourself. I already said I was sorry…"

"You should be sorry," Frankie said stoutly, but she thought, *she's right, I really should be ashamed of myself.*

"I'm not sorry for this. I'm sorry for not telling you. That was really dumb and wrong."

Now wearing a pink-and-navy checked shirt, his hair neatly brushed, Mack burst in to the room. "Girls, stop. Stop. I'm honestly sorry you found us that way, honey. But of course, Ariel and I are getting married."

"Dad! Have you lost your mind?" Frankie shouted. "You're… uh, with a twenty-seven-year-old? A-a girl your own daughter's age?"

"I don't think of it that way. Ariel is very—" Mack began.

"Yes, apparently."

"Cut it out, Frankie. You're being a bitch because you think you can get away with it," Ariel said. "But you can't. I'm not going to listen to this."

"Ariel is very dear to me," Mack went on. "We're going to have a baby."

Clearly, for Mack at least, this explained matters: Frankie's geriatric father had gotten a girl in trouble. He had to do the right thing by her. Mack turned to Ariel, reaching over to smooth her long summer T-shirt against her bulging belly in a gesture of such proprietary intimacy that Frankie, who thought she was finished throwing up, felt her stomach squirm again. She had to pass between them, their skin smells of soap and salt and something loamy intercut with a bright pin of scent—Joy, her mother's favorite—and then she hung over the sink, humiliated, retching, although there was nothing left in her to heave up. Penn passed her a clean dish towel.

When she could breathe normally again, Frankie said, "You're sixty years old. You're almost sixty-one."

"Plenty of men my age—"

"Creeps, sure. Creeps and narcissists. What if your ages were reversed? Would you think that was okay? Would Mom? Surely you remember her, Beatrice? Your wife for thirty years? Is she just nothing now?"

"Of course not. This is not about your mother."

"What are you thinking?"

"Honey, please, take a breath," Mack said. "This is not healthy."

"I'll tell the whole world it isn't! Dad, I can't look at you. Don't stand there patting her belly. I'll leave, but I have to rest for a while. I couldn't sleep all the way back on the plane. I thought one of you was dying."

"Frankie. Just stay for dinner tonight, so we can talk it over. I'm making steamers and corn. Ariel's making her famous olive bread. Lie down for a while, and later—"

"We'll all sit down for dinner like a nice family? What about you, Ariel? This is like if you caught me having sex with your mother."

"It's nothing like that!"

"You're right. It's like you caught me having sex with your grandmother! Your mother's a lot younger than Mack."

Ariel's eyes narrowed then, and she visibly drew back, her long graceful neck suddenly suggestive of a bird of prey. Frankie saw the face feared even by the mean girls back in high school. Ariel's long-vanished mother, Carlotta, was forbidden territory. Ariel blew her breath out, very slowly, then she said, in a low voice, "That's not how we see it."

"That's how everyone else will see it," Frankie pointed out.

Mack's face was reddening now, more stroke than blush. When he looked like that, she could tell he was running out of his famously short supply of patience and about to blow. She was, however, past caring. "Go ahead, Ariel, picture that!"

"Frankie, stop it," Penn put in. "This is out of control."

"You knew I was on the way here!" Frankie said to Ariel.

"You weren't supposed to get here until noon or something," Ariel said. "It's five in the morning."

"Did you want me to see you two going at it?"

"We were not going at it. We were asleep."

"So obviously you never really cared about Beatrice, who you supposedly loved so much. Do you even care about me?"

Frankie knew she sounded like a child throwing a tantrum, fury pushing her past reason. But the question was valid. Was she invisible? Was she inaudible? Did she know her own father at all? Or Ariel, for so many years her confidante and soulmate? Had she been crazy to think that her father, so eager to showcase his muscled midriff and full head of hair, would cherish her for making him a grandfather? Mack was nowhere near ready to bounce a grandchild on his knee: he wanted to prove that he was still man enough to sire a new line. Carefully, Frankie folded the towel in half and then folded it again. As if it were a weapon, she pointed it at her father.

"And how long has this been going on, anyhow? Was Mom still alive when you started this?"

Mack didn't reply. By the big wall clock, a full minute swept past.

"I won't even dignify that," Mack said, his voice dangerous. "Don't insult me. Don't insult Ariel."

"What about me?"

Frankie got up from her chair and slammed her mother's rose-colored teacup into the sink. It broke with a dry pop: she ended up holding only the broken-off handle. Horrified, she gasped. Then, well, *good*, she thought. They could buy new ones. Something tacky, maybe with cats fishing from rowboats. It would go with the rest of the kitchen, now slabbed with tile and stainless steel like an operating room. The huge double wooden shelves above the windows were still there, stripped of their historic amalgamation of odd objects—geodes, a delicate wire sculpture of the Brooklyn Bridge, a life-size velvet rooster Beatrice had made from old quilts. Now they were crowded with paintings of sentimental sunsets, antique Cape Cod Creamery bottles, an old trap with a papier-mâché lobster inside it.

She walked out, not even bothering to close the front door behind her.

"Frankie..." Penn's voice trailed after her.

"Let her go," Mack said. "Give her a moment by herself."

But she heard footsteps behind her, Penn following at a distance. The night was ending. Over the ocean, the first light bloomed from a violet seam in the clouds.

Crashing through a gap in the trees, Frankie veered off the drive and marched up Two Ponds Road, just half a block, to the door of the curious small house she and Penn used to pass every day on the way to the school bus.

No confusing planter on this little porch.

Right next to the bright yellow door was a keypad. Frankie

punched in 8-8-8-8, Gil's favorite numbers. He thought that eights looked like snowmen.

"Frankie, cut it out! I haven't seen those old folks for months, but there could be an alarm system or something."

"There's no alarm system," she said and stepped inside. As she expected, the place was redolent of lemon, freshly cleaned, the smooth old wooden countertops scrubbed, the windows sparkling. A long arch-backed dark green sofa faced the big picture window, and plumping up a couple of the old-fashioned embroidered pillows, she lay down.

"Frankie," Penn whispered at the door. "What the hell are you doing?"

"Take it easy," she said. "It's my house."

"Your house? Since when?"

"Since June. We bought it. Gil and I bought it."

"You and your boyfriend—"

"My fiancé."

"You and your fiancé bought the Barbie House?"

All the locals called it the Barbie House. It was a turquoise cottage built years ago by an artist, now in his late eighties. He'd decorated it with the fabrics and colors and furniture of his mid-twentieth-century childhood, right down to a bright red Kelvinator refrigerator that looked like two bubbles stacked one on top of the other, which he had commissioned a heating-and-cooling specialist to gut and modernize. During college, Frankie had made a series of photographs of the cottage for *Yankee Magazine*, among her first published pictures. Just after she learned that she was pregnant, Frankie told Penn now, she and Gil agreed that their home base would be in the United States instead of Gil's native Montreal. Only days later, Frankie happened across a story online about quirky houses, listed by state, two in Massachusetts. The one on Cape Cod was none other than the funny beach cottage. Astonished, because what were the odds, she read that the owner, who had no children of his own, was putting the place on the market after sixty years. Frankie pleaded with Gil: she could think of no better place to raise a child than the place she had grown up, close to the sea, close to Ariel, and if she were honest, close to Mack. Never much of a father, he might do better as a grandfather. There were some who did. The house seemed like some sort of sweet omen in service of that hope. Gil had never been south of Boston, and in Boston only once, but he trusted Frankie's stories and her photos. They were the first to make an offer, one Frankie knew was ridiculously low. But the old artist remembered Frankie and her mother, who had taken painting classes from him years before. He wanted Frankie to have the place. He knew she would cherish it. He was even willing to take a modest price for most of the furniture.

"We didn't want to tell anyone until we were sure about everything. We wanted to wait for the amnio results and make sure the baby was okay, and yeah, I know I'm too young to worry much about that stuff, but I also know too much about what can go wrong, so I insisted. And then, we were going to come and make this big announcement about the pregnancy and the wedding and the house, and it was all going to be great. So yes, at least for tonight, this is my very own vintage green couch. Which I must admit is very uncomfortable." She looked up at an old red-and-white tin sign advertising *Carnation Evaporated Milk, Tall Cans 10 cents. The Modern Milkman.*

"And now I guess we'll just sell the place."

"Frankie, don't decide that right now. Remember Mom used to say, one world at a time? So I mean…you…marriage? A house? A baby?"

"I know," she said, ruefully using the heels of her hands to press sudden tears from her eyes. "It was the impossible thing. And then it was all possible. You'd understand if you met Gil."

"It's not like I won't meet him."

"But this was all supposed to be so… After Mom, after everything…"

"You wanted the baby and Mack and this house to all be here and make it all better," he said. "Like one of your pictures."

"Don't make fun of me, Penn. I thought it was at least possible."

"I'm not making fun of you. But Mack was trying to make it all better too."

"That's different from here to the moon, Penn."

"I know it is. But it's still true." He added, "If you want it to be different between him and you, you have to start someplace."

"Do you want to see the rest of the house?" Frankie tried to distract him from his sermon. She pointed out how its toyshop appearance belied how sturdy and serviceable it really was, the solid floors and plain pale paint, with a huge bedroom on the first floor and two nice-sized ones upstairs, pristine views of the ocean, along with something no fifties house ever had: central air. Glass sliding doors opened to a small stilted open porch at the back, facing the beach. Two old Adirondack chairs, their oiled wood deeply scarred, were tucked next to the porch railings. They sat down together.

"It's great, Frankie," Penn said. "I've got to get my own place." Penn had a lower-level apartment in the big house, with a separate entrance. Especially since he worked and traveled with Mack, it had been an easy solution, the compensations including the presence of a full fridge and the absence of a utility bill, as well as the chance for Penn to spend time with his mother as he worked toward his PhD. Now, with Beatrice gone and Ariel in residence, Frankie could tell that unease outweighed the ease. "The sooner, the better."

"You never told me anything!" Frankie said then, unable to quell her outburst. "How could you? You lied to me."

"We barely talked the whole year, remember? What, four or five times? I didn't lie to you. I just didn't tell you."

"That's the same thing, and you know it. Did he pay you off?"

Penn flinched. "Who do you think I am?"

"A person with no integrity? A lapdog? The son of Mack Attleboro, famous marine conservationist and pervert?"

"That's harsh. I work for him. You don't. I have to live with him."

"Maybe you can tell me how you stomach it? You dated Ariel in high school."

"Hardly. For a few weeks," he said.

"Did you and Ariel...whatever? Back then?"

"Frankie, no way! I'd probably have to be in a psychiatrist's office right now, and I'm not sure that I won't anyhow." He added, "Plus, even when we did go out, it was always too much like she was another sister."

Which was true enough. When they were in third and fourth grade, Frankie and Penn and Ariel slept like siblings in a tent, on piles of quilts on the bedroom floor. Frankie rested her hot face in the cradle of her cold hands.

She asked Penn, "Do you think they thought she would get pregnant? Do you think she thought he was, like, sterile?"

Penn covered his eyes. "There are some mysteries in the world I never want solved. Imagine me talking dating strategies over with my dear old dad. He was the one who used to give me this stern advice about avoiding what he called *unforeseen consequences*...as if someone who artificially inseminates a manatee is too shy to say, *Hey, son, use a condom*."

"And now, a baby? He's sixty-one."

"Grandpa's eighty-seven, and he's still playing tennis. Mack's got a lot of go left."

"Evidently," Frankie said. She shivered. "I'm going to take a walk. I have to clear my head. I'll just be a few minutes. Do you want to come with me?"

"I'll wait right here."

"You sure you won't be called to do something for the happy couple?"

Penn said, "As a matter of fact, that'll be you, sis, so shut your fat mouth."

"What are you talking about?"

"You'll find out soon enough."

Frankie shrugged and stepped down the four steps toward the beach. The day was coming in essentially Cape Cod, hot but misty and moody, the kind of weather Beatrice had loved. On the beach, the fog still reigned, forming itself into cloud pillars and cloud skeins. When Frankie was small, seven or eight, Beatrice had told her that when the sea fret rolled up from the shore, it brought with it the ghosts of the drowned.

"Are they looking to take people with them?" Frankie asked nervously.

"Oh no," Beatrice said. "They're just looking for company. They want to smell pancakes again."

Oh, Mom, Frankie thought. *Come and haunt me.*

Tomorrow would have been her mother's fifty-second birthday.

Did anyone else even remember?

Life must go on, of course, Frankie thought. But she never expected that, just a year after her death, their mother would be quite so firmly consigned to memory, her territory reimagined, her life, like their childhood, bundled up like the cardboard boxes she'd glimpsed in the hall, with *Give to F* scrawled in marker.

Even Frankie could no longer summon up Beatrice's face. When she tried, she could sustain the vision only for a second, wavering like a single flickering frame from an old movie. A quick smile. A pleased widening of gray-green eyes. Then gone, evanescent, just like the fog on the shore.

Frankie walked into the surf, her ankles instantly numbed

by the cold, as always. How could anything so seductive at a distance be so punishing up close? The ocean beckoned land creatures and then showed them who was boss. Beatrice used to turn off their computers and chase them outdoors by telling them that the sea was never the same for an hour and what if something changed and they weren't there to see it?

Something had changed. And Frankie had not been there to see it.

Yet Ariel had been there, or right after. Of course she had.

Sailor Madeira, Beatrice's best friend, who'd been in love with her since they were in high school, was the one who'd found her. He'd dropped by for coffee, as he often did. With Mack so frequently on trips or lecture tours, she was too often alone and delighted by his company. She looked like a queen on her chaise, reclining in her slumbers, rain from the open glass doors spangling her afghan, her cheeks, her arms, her thick silver hair. She was dead, of course, not just sleeping. He couldn't reach Mack or Penn or Frankie, but Ariel had been in the office of the Saltwater Foundation.

That night, sobbing on the phone, Ariel begged Frankie's forgiveness: she had known Beatrice was ill, but Beatrice had played it down…a sore throat, a chill… She promised to see the doctor the next day. Instead, she died of strep, a treatable thing healthy people usually didn't die from anymore, and Frankie was furious, not at Ariel, or only a little at Ariel, but more at Beatrice, who would always put herself last. Beatrice dreamed big, never for herself, but for all of them. Without his tall, elegant, composed wife, and without her father's considerable money, Mack might been just another ill-dressed wildlife biologist with an unruly beard, looming awkwardly in the shot of the faculty picnic instead of posing on the cover of magazines, the American Cousteau. Beatrice sent them all off to ride those dreams, so that at the moment when her coffee mug had slipped from her fingers, Frankie had probably been underwater in the Red Sea, pointing her camera at the just-right tunnel of peachy dawn light, into the deeps where humpback whales three times the size of elephants bobbed like untethered parade balloons.

Who else would ever understand why she felt so privileged, almost anointed, by that sight that she began to cry, fogging her mask?

Only one mother.

The whole world over… She remembered the line from childhood poetry books. When they were children, Beatrice read poetry to them and forced them to recite from memory. They moaned, and she told them to put a sock in it. Whether you were a bishop or a bus driver, being able to recite poetry a little was like being able to play the piano a little: it made you sound smart. She'd insisted that they would be grateful when they were grown-ups, and they were. (Mack, on the other hand, being informed that Frankie wanted to minor in American literature, asked, *Why not basket-weaving?* And when she took an extra year to study photography, he told her that she could pay for that one herself. Beatrice ended up paying for it, not quite keeping the truth from Mack, not quite revealing it either. "He'll get over it," she said. "He'll be proud of your pictures.")

But would he, ever? And why did Frankie even care?

When Beatrice died, one of the things that Frankie thought was *Who will be proud of me now? Who will I have to impress?* There were other things she thought, not so selfish, about Beatrice's role in the community, her mother's small but serious reputation as a painter. But she couldn't recall them.

Slowly, her cheeks stiff with tears, Frankie made her way back to her brother, who was stretched asleep on the deck with the perfect relaxation of a newborn puppy—or a grown man. Frankie was no slouch at falling fast asleep wherever she had enough space, in a van or a tent or a hammock, but Penn slept like he owned the earth. Kneeling down silently, she whispered, "Don't move, Penny. That spider is huge!"

"Okay," he spluttered. "Okay, is it gone?"

"I think it's a brown recluse..."

He looked up at her. "You are a complete ass, you know that?"

"I thought you missed me."

"I did miss you, until you got here."

Frankie said, "I told you, I just feel so mean. Here I thought Mack was still suffering. He looks like a million bucks. What happened to the Mack who didn't speak at all after Mom died? Who didn't sleep? Who didn't work?"

"All true," Penn said. "But you'd know that if you ever bothered to come and see him, Frankie."

That was true as well. Frankie fought and failed to silence her inner harpy, which flapped out shrieking to make a rationalization. "Who knows? He might even have given a damn." She thought then, but did not say, this brand-new Attleboro baby might rival Penn's relatively exalted place in Mack's life, while Frankie would lose even the small wedge of his regard she'd always competed for.

As if he had heard her thoughts, Penn said, "I know you think Dad was all about me. But not as much as you think." They both knew that Mack had never really *needed* his children, per se. At best, they were a pleasant distraction, at worst a bothersome distraction. Needing Beatrice was another story. "When it came to Mom, we thought that was all on one side. Her side. But it wasn't."

Frankie scoffed, "She was Mack's minion. Remember when we were kids and he used to come home after one of his trips? He would be gone six or eight or ten weeks, and he would just walk in, no warning at all, and expect Mom to have dinner ready?" She added, "I told you, I can't help how I feel. I feel mean."

"She loved him," Penn said. "That was just their way of doing that. It wouldn't be yours, but it worked for them."

Mack would throw down his gear, sticky from the mud and the water, and bawl out a greeting, and Beatrice was supposed to come running to exalt him, patient Penelope to his Ulysses. She would quickly banish the children to Grandma Becky's for a week so that Mack could rest and regale her with his exploits, without having to put up with their antics and their chatter.

Only now did Frankie ask Penn what the first days after Beatrice's death were like for him.

"I didn't get any chance to grieve for Mom, if that's what you mean," Penn said. When news of Beatrice's death arrived, Mack and Penn made their way back from Costa Rica, where they were heading up a BBC documentary on the vanishing jaguar. On the plane, in the cars, Mack didn't eat. At home, he sat on Beatrice's chaise, facing the sea, not speaking. Penn had to remind him to shower and dress for the simple service that Ariel had arranged at the Quaker meeting house after Frankie got back from Egypt. In a gentle rain, Frankie and Mack and Penn had stood side by side on the stone bridge at Grace Point, so-called after Beatrice's maiden name, opening their hands to send a silty cloud of her ashes down to the surface of the sea. And then, Mack had gone home and had a breakdown, although no one ever said the actual word. He collapsed, like a wooden bridge in an earthquake. And Frankie simply left. A better daughter would have recognized how much Mack needed her. At the time, she couldn't wait to be away from him. She was too wounded to recognize anything except how much she wished that Mack had died instead of Beatrice. Let Penn, Mack's chosen one, look after him. A year later, Frankie could admit that on some level, she blamed Mack for Beatrice's death. She blamed his constant, self-centered absences that left her mother lonely.

But was she any better?

During those early months, Frankie called only infrequently. It was Penn who talked to her, never Mack. Even weeks after the funeral, Mack was like some kind of sick mammal. He could summon no more than the effort to sleep and breathe. He lost thirty pounds. Ariel postponed his brisk schedule of travel, lectures and university research. Mack was in no fit state.

But when he rebounded, it was with the vigor of a man half his age. It was always Mack's world. But he legendarily couldn't bear to be alone in it. He always had to have an audience, even if it was just an audience of one. "And there she was," Penn said. "I have to say, I don't know what's in it for her, really."

Frankie pointed at the roof of the big house. "All that. Everything."

"Give me a break, Frankie. That's not Ariel, and even if she were like that, it's hardly Buckingham Palace."

"Will he go back to the university now? The terms starts in what, a few weeks?" Penn shrugged. "I bet him going all catatonic didn't help his reputation there. Did they think he was even crazier than usual?"

"The other faculty? Not in front of me, obviously," Penn said. "But I know they did. They still do." Mack's snippier university colleagues tittered behind his back—envious of Mack's appeal, sure, and his ability to fill auditoriums, but also disdainful. They said he was not a scholar but a wacky cable-TV explorer, a scientific parvenu with his corny lectures and breathtaking slides, most of them taken by Frankie's own mentor, the British photographer Abram Murphy. They focused especially on the strange fable at the core of Mack's career: twenty years before in the Hebrides, Mack insisted that he (and he alone) had found an extinct species, the Regent Red sea eagle. There was no proof of this, and no one else—not even Mack when he returned with Penn—could locate the unmapped swamp where the creature supposedly lived. But Mack acted as if he had already claimed his spot in the history books.

"Do they all know about the wedding?"

"Everybody knows," said Penn. "There was a big announcement in the *New York Times*, and some reporter is coming here to do a story about the event. And Mack invited everybody he ever met."

"How did it not get around to me?"

"You weren't around, Frankie."

Frankie pulled a dour face. "Obviously," she intoned.

It was this epic wedding then, apparently next weekend, that was the reason for Mack's global shout-out. If she hadn't been so far away and so literally underwater in her work, if she'd had more friends and kept in closer touch, been a better daughter...maybe none of this mess needed to have happened.

All her work was freelance, so she could have come home again quickly. She'd promised to. She'd intended to, but *quickly* turned into weeks and then months. Hip-deep in rushing water in the Australian river highlands, or in the danks and deeps of the Everglades, pushing herself from job to job in a frenzy, she could almost forget. She let her work become her hermitage. Sealing herself off from everyone—even her beloved grandparents, even Ariel—she could talk herself into believing that Penn was on the case. Look how well that had worked out. Was she being punished for letting the time slide past? It was ridiculous to even entertain such thoughts, but despite all her training in science, she was as vulnerable to false assumptions of causation as any other human being.

She said aloud, "I want my mother."

Penn said, "Me too."

"I have to sleep a little," Frankie said. "Jeez, all those old sitcoms from the sixties when people would sleep on the couch after they had a fight and couldn't stand up the next morning? That all makes sense now."

"So come back up there with me. Just explain you want to have a nap and there's nowhere in here..."

"I'm not saying that."

"Okay, I'll say that. It's my house too."

"Are you so sure?" Frankie said. "That's Ariel's house now."

It slapped Frankie then, the really big fat joke on her and Penn. What she had said sarcastically was, in fact, true. The old house called Tall Trees, built a hundred and fifty years ago by Beatrice's great-grandfather for his family of ten children, added to by their descendants, with its arches of Maine granite and shingle siding and its widow's walk, its deep cold stone swimming pool, would never be hers or Penn's. Everything had been Beatrice's. It had all come from Beatrice's family and was meant for her children and their children. She would never have suspected such shenanigans from Mack. She would not have provided some clause in her will for another family if he survived her. A lawyer had written to Frankie, informing her that, on her thirtieth birthday, she would receive a substantial cash bequest from her mother's estate, as well as "within reason and with Macklin Attleboro's advice, whatever of my personal effects, including but not limited to jewelry, art, furnishings and clothing, each of my children should desire." But Mack was Beatrice's primary heir. So now the house would belong to Mack and Ariel—and to their child. She and Penn might not even be able to visit unless they were invited. She saw the same knowledge sweep over Penn's face, like water submerging a child's sandcastle. Then he shook himself, as if banishing a bad smell.

"Franny Frank, you know better than that. Dad may be having a midlife crisis—"

"Midlife? What, is he going to live to be a hundred and twenty?"

"You know what I mean. Even though he's obviously in the love undertow right now, he would never, ever take this place away from us. Mom would never have allowed that. I always knew we would come with our own kids every summer from wherever else we lived. That's still how it will be, even after Dad dies, which, like they say, God forbid...but he said as much."

"Don't be so sure, Penn. Where's Ariel in all this?"

"You know, I'm the executor for Dad's will, and when this all first happened, when they found out about the baby, he told me, 'I'll make a special provision for Ariel and this baby. I'm not going to take Tall Trees away from you guys. This isn't going to mean you and Frankie are out of the will or anything.'"

"What did you say?"

"I said, 'God forbid, Dad, but yeah, that's reassuring because we love this place, and it's our connection to Mom.' And he said he was well aware of that, and everything else was enough of a shock without that too," Penn said. "So he was thinking about us. And Frankie, you might as well stay for the wedding and the Saltwater banquet. You have your own place. If you ran away tomorrow, where would you go? It makes no sense." He added, "Why don't you talk to...what's his name, Gil? Tell him about all this. Plus, I haven't seen you for a year either."

"I'm sorry," Frankie said. "It all seems so pointless now. My little rebellion."

She looked at Penn, still a gangly, nerdy boy, with Beatrice's startling sea-glass green eyes. Penn was good with girls, probably as a result of how genuinely bemused he was by the actions of two-legged animals that couldn't fly. Women wanted to bundle him up and take care of him. Though only thirteen months younger, he was still very much Frankie's little brother. The night of Beatrice's funeral, Penn brought his pillow to her room and lay next to her while they both cried.

"Frankie, think about it. Sure, they kept their secret from you. But you kept this from them too, and maybe it's not the same thing, but you still don't want to burn any bridges."

"Maybe that's exactly what I should want," Frankie said.

"Well, I would give it a chance, at least. And you were going to tell me about how all this happened with Gil, and I don't mean how it literally happened, thanks very much," said Penn.

No, Frankie thought, the only person she ever could have told that, once upon a time, was Ariel. But thinking of gentle, brave, circumspect Gil, owlish in his glasses, was the first comfort she'd felt since her plane landed. She had something to turn to, a life of her own. Maybe it was time to let the past go—as Mack and Ariel had so clearly done.

Once inside, she leaned around the kitchen door and asked Ariel, who was alone eating oatmeal, "Do you think I could have a glass of juice or something? Plain water will make me sick to my stomach."

"It's your house, Frankie. You don't have to ask for—"

"It's not my house."

Ariel sighed and silently poured juice from a pitcher in the refrigerator.

On the glassed-in porch, she sat down on Beatrice's chaise and drank the juice, some wonderful concoction of mangoes and cherries so cold her teeth ached. She thought of herself, a little kid watching as Beatrice used her handsaw and chisel and sander to make the sign that read *Tall Trees* (for this had always been its name), then covered it with the paint she mixed on an ordinary rock until the glossy pearlized blue and purple of an oyster shell appeared. The sign was bolted to a small stone pillar at the start of the driveway. Frankie wondered when they'd change that, too, to something weird like *Seas the Day*.

She lay back and, at once, as if in her mother's arms, she fell asleep.

When she woke, it was with a shudder, to the sense of another presence, though there had been no sound or touch. Across from her in a big rattan chair, she could see Ariel, her silvery-blond hair backlit by the afternoon sun. Frankie must have slept for many hours. Someone had tucked Beatrice's afghan over her legs. Without a word to Ariel, Frankie went outside and walked, aimlessly, down the drive. Both sides were flanked by her mother's gardens, the big vegetable plots still producing the summer's bounty, the delicate decks of herbs interspersed with riots of annual flowers, blooming bushes, frothing hydrangea and stubborn rosa rugosa, as well as the occasional space of artful rubble, rocks and shells on white sand that Beatrice had assembled with all the allure of a Zen garden.

How could all this still be here when her mother was not?

Just as she could no longer picture Beatrice's face, she could no longer hear Beatrice's voice: *Francis Lee! Penn! Come in right now! It's bedtime!* They never listened the first time or the second or the fourth, not until the sky and sea had poured together into an ultramarine bowl stippled with stars. But it wasn't really Beatrice's voice Frankie heard with the ear of her mind. It was her own, in imitation. She was playing both parts.

Last year, just before she went back to the Red Sea, Frankie took from the garden shed an old cardigan that smelled of Beatrice's cologne, soil and something else, something ineffable, like linen baked in strong afternoon sun, and she slept in it every night, not caring if it was a horrible cliché, until somebody at Branha spilled paraffin oil on it. In one pocket she found one of her mother's lists: *Francis, new lantern? Mack, oilskin, repair or new? Return books, get tabbouleh, La Mer samples from Macy's?* Frankie took it out, unfolding it and caressing the handwritten words so many times that the paper softened like old cloth and eventually fell to pieces.

If even she was forgetting, how could she blame the happy couple?

If Mack were marrying someone else, some other widowed person perhaps, would she be half as shocked? Of course not. She'd be surprised at the haste of it but not distressed.

Penn was right. She had, if not expected, then hoped, that after she knew that her future with Gil together was sealed, Mack might welcome a new role as a grandfather—and as a father who loved her, perhaps not as Beatrice had, then at least with the understanding that he was now the only parent she had.

She kept walking and when she heard steps and a rattle behind her, she didn't look back. "Frankie! Wait up!" Ariel called. "Help me pick some vegetables. I can't bend over that well." She was pulling a child's old wagon, stopping at the garden that was tumbling with squashes, peppers and eggplant. After they awkwardly picked some of the vegetables, Frankie picked some mint leaves, some basil and a few strands of lemongrass. Inhaling the tiny, citrusy bouquet of the herbs calmed her. She crushed it between her hands and rubbed some on her wrists and even on her hairline. She watched as Ariel stood up from a crouch and kneaded her lower back, her face drawn down by the longing for sleep that was now so much a constant in Frankie's life too. Why couldn't they be sharing this time in their lives? Why had she so resolutely turned Ariel away during the first months after Beatrice died? Was it because of her jealousy, because Ariel had been there for her mother when Frankie had not?

Oh, Ariel.

She had imagined being close again, Ariel having dinner with them at the Barbie House, staying up late for a movie, fifty bowls of popcorn with brewer's yeast, maybe spending the night, snorkeling in the early morning, shopping for clothes for the baby, Ariel getting to know Gil.

Selfishly, she had imagined Ariel sharing her life—not her sharing Ariel's. The tables had turned with a vengeance.

As she helped Ariel arrange the vegetables in the wagon, Frankie said, "I drove past the middle school on the way here. They have this big new glass building now? It was lit up like a space station."

"It's a greenhouse. The Saltwater Foundation helped pay for

it. The kids use the vegetables in cooking classes and sell them too. There's even an orangery."

"That's so impressive. All we ever did was grow sunflowers. Anther, corolla, ovary. You memorized all the parts and then you could never just see it as this big beautiful flower anymore."

"Same thing with poems. Is this an elegy? Or an ode? Is it a villanelle?"

"Do you remember our banner?" Frankie said.

An eggplant in each hand, Ariel stopped and smiled.

"I still have it," Ariel said of the forty-foot banner they'd made from old bras, pantyhose, stiletto heels, garter belts and waist-cinchers to illustrate their final English project—*Discomfort or Why Feminist Poetry Was Written.* Swamped by history and love, Frankie opened her mouth on what might have been words of goodwill, but at that moment, Ariel said, "The way Mack is being, don't take it the wrong way. It's easier for him to talk to a thousand people than to one. He's socially awkward. And especially about you. And all this."

That was enough. Frankie said flatly, "Thank you for interpreting my own father for me."

"I'm not interpreting..."

"Ari!" Mack shouted.

"Your master's voice," Frankie said.

"Oh, shut up, Frankie," Ariel said. "This is boring."

"Could I have a shower before I leave?" Frankie asked.

"Leave? Don't be silly. You're not leaving! At least we should have a chance to talk."

"With my father between us in the bed. That should be fun," Frankie said.

"Fine. I'm not going to beg anymore. None of this was done to insult you, Frankie. Not everything is about you. Do what you want."

Inside, Ariel led her to Beatrice's studio, now a small guest room. Almost every room was transformed. Penn had his own quarters, downstairs, with a separate entrance. Frankie assumed at least that area hadn't been disturbed.

Ariel said, "Look. I knew you would be surprised…"

"*Surprised* hardly covers it. *Shock and awe* hardly covers it."

Ariel closed her eyes and pressed against them with her tapered and shelly pink-tipped fingers. She was always beautiful, but, except for her tiredness, the pregnancy had made her glorious. They'd spoken so seldom over the past year, nothing seemed changed. Now, she noticed, Ariel no longer wore short skirts and midriff tops with platform sandals, instead favoring jeans or a khaki skirt with plain tee shirts in muted neutral colors. Her makeup was subtle, barely visible, a touch of lip stain, a bit of mascara. Maybe that was what Mack requested. Her hair was still platinum, but that was stunningly real, like her mother Carlotta's. It was beautifully cut, swinging in thick wings that brushed her collarbone.

Why didn't Mack lust after Carlotta instead? Though he would have had to find her first. If there could be a more upsetting thought, this was probably it.

"Franny Frank, it's probably asking too much too soon. You need time to get used it. I needed time to get used to it. At first, it all felt odd, and kind of wrong. We both thought that."

Abruptly feeling suffocated in the bright, airy space, Frankie cranked open one of the panel windows and gulped the warm sea air. No other water smelled like the salt water of her Cape Cod home. Her own blood was part of its biome. If your work is your house, Frankie thought, she had spent more time underwater than almost any human being her age, maybe even counting Navy Seals, and she had observed how the texture of water was particular to place, almost the philosophy of a place. Now, that saltwater smell that once made her feel cherished would always remind her of what she'd lost. She tried to breath in deeply through her nose and out through her mouth although that mindfulness stuff never worked for her. "Oh, it's we now?" she said. "You and Mack are 'we'? So, who am I? You and Mack and your baby are the new Attleboros? Ari, you don't see this the way I see it! But only because you don't want to. Remember how we used to make gagging noises when Mr. Paderacki married the new art teacher, what was her name? Miss Simone? And he was maybe only ten years older? That's how I feel now. Except it's my own family."

Ariel picked up a heavy ornate silver frame, a snapshot of Ariel and Beatrice running together on the sand at Funnel Neck. Is she going to throw it at me? Frankie wondered. In the photo, Ariel looked like a teenager—maybe she was a teenager. How long ago was this taken?

"Did my dad always feel like this about you? Is he a pedophile?"

Ariel bowed her head, as if waiting for Frankie to lower the sword, and held the photo to her chest. "That's so stupid. You don't really think that. Frankie, when I came to work for the Saltwater Foundation, he said he was pleased to meet me. Pleased to meet you, he said! Your mom said, Mack, this is Ariel, Carlotta's daughter, and Mack sort of blinked and said, oh right, hello." This honestly made sense. "Mack wasn't what they'd call a very present father. But he was a father figure to you—but not to me." Beatrice's old friend, Sailor Madeira, she said, was more of what she imagined a father figure would be. He'd given her a brand-new bike and would bring homemade bread and rice pudding and fresh fruit and vegetables from the farmer's market to her and her mother and grandmother. A couple of years after Carlotta took off, Sailor fixed up an old Toyota for Ariel—even Frankie hadn't known this—and taught her to drive. He and Beatrice took her for her driver's test. "He was just a kind person who had no kids of his own. I guess he just saw how I was struggling. And he knew how much your mom cared about me. I'm sure your mother helped pay for some of the stuff, like she did for my big attempt at college. But none of it ever seemed to include Mack. He wasn't really anything to me when we were kids."

Mack and Ariel hadn't had any real relationship at all, except the abstract give-and-take of an employer and an employee, until Beatrice died.

"Your mom, when she left us," Ariel began. "Back then…"

"When she died. She didn't leave us, she died," Frankie said. She thought, *What an asshole I sound like! Is this really me?* "Your mother left us. My mother died."

"I didn't think I could live without her," Ariel pressed on. "Not that she cared about me the way she cared about you. But say what you want, Frankie, you were gone! I was here. I lived with her. I was there for her. Beatrice taught me to draw. She gave me the books she said that every person should read. She taught me to cook. She taught me, you're going to laugh at this, how to pack a suitcase and how to change a tire. She taught me to love and to trust after my crap upbringing."

"So how did that…"

"She saved me. Then she was gone. I wanted to be her. I wanted to live my life the way she lived her life. And Mack needed me."

In that moment, Frankie almost understood. Who would not have preferred Tall Trees, big as a ship, crisp as a maritime flag, to that tiny stinking gray ashtray of a cabin? Who wouldn't have chosen Beatrice as a role model, her paints and paella and poetry books and garden parties, her long legs and shorn curls—rather than the gorgeous and slutty Carlotta Puck, her boobs spilling out of her tight low-cut blouses, who flirted with everyone from Penn to Mr. Campo, the eighty-year-old guy who mended nets?

They stopped to unload the vegetables at the back door and dumped them into the big farm sink to wash. The sky was darkening, not toward night, but to some kind of afternoon weather event, the old oaks now snapping their bony fingers.

"You know that there have been five or six houses on this spot, Ariel? Beatrice's grandfather built this house right after the Second World War, and he even tore down the timbers from the first house that his father built and put them in this one." The same vast dry-stack rock fence wound around the backyard and gardens, she went on, the same walls continued plain and upright to the pearly cove ceilings with recessed lights that once spilled down illumination on Beatrice's paintings. The same old seashells were embedded in the gray rock facade of the fireplace. He made his living as a boat builder, but Standard Grace had been an artist in his own right. "His name is etched in the concrete at the top of the fireplace. Stan. And that was the name of his son and his son's son and then Beatrice. All this came from her family."

"I didn't know that whole saga," Ariel said. "But for the record, I told Mack we should build a place of our own."

"That's an excellent idea," Frankie said.

"But when I suggested that, he said, why should we? He said, remodel anything you want, but I want to keep this place. This is the kind of house that comes along once in a lifetime."

"That's what Penn and I always thought," Frankie replied. "Maybe I can take the old bridge sculpture that used to be in here? Up on the kitchen shelf?" Frankie asked then. "My great-grandfather made that too."

"Well, that broke when we took it down, but you could probably fix it. I think it's still in the garage."

"Well, great. Okay."

"Unless Mack moved it."

Frankie glanced out at the swimming pool built from rock that would never leak or need a patch. This was the most beautiful house she knew. What if getting our own place meant selling this house? Would that situation be better or worse than this one? Surely Mack had enough money to keep this place and buy another one in some other town? Might he not want

Penn to live here with his family? That would be good, with hers and Gil's family just down the way. Thinking of Gil, she unclasped the thin gold chain from around her neck and slipped her ring onto her finger: she still could not get used to having anything on her hands. Rings could get trapped inside a diving glove or snag on tough strands of seaweed. *But you have to wear it now, at least some of the time*, Gil told her before she left, *because that was my grandmother's ring, and you're* ma mariée.

"I have to go," Frankie said.

"Go where?" Mack boomed out, bounding into the kitchen. "Why are there windows open all over the place? I'm not paying to air-condition the whole cape! What say we have a later-afternoon dinner? We have to talk about the wedding."

"You don't have to do anything for it," Frankie said. "We'll just… His family's in Montreal. Now I think we probably should get married there."

"My girl, I'm talking about our wedding!" Of course he was. "It's next weekend. You're my only daughter. And I'm sure Ari wants you to be her maid of honor."

"I'm sure she has someone else in mind," Frankie said.

"*You* are who I had in mind," Ariel answered. "Nobody but you. I somehow thought you would agree."

"Why on earth did you think that?" Frankie said. "You're going to be my, uh, stepmother."

Mack drew Ariel close to him and reached out his other arm for Frankie. "My two girls. The baby's a boy."

"How did you know that? We just found out the other day," Frankie said and instantly cursed herself for thinking Mack was referring to his grandson-to-be. Of course he wasn't! This was like *Alice in Wonderland*.

"Here I am, come to find out I'm about to become a grandpa, and the last I heard, I was about to become a father! What a day! And what's Frankie's baby going to call you, Ari? You're way too young to be a granny."

I could think of a few things, Frankie said to herself. Why did Ariel suppose she would agree to any of this—especially to being part of a public spectacle?

"I really hope that you'll take the pictures," Mack went on.

"I'm not a wedding photographer," Frankie said. "I've never taken a wedding picture."

"Just pretend we're all fish. Why should I pay somebody else when you're already here?"

"You're so sentimental."

Frankie left the kitchen and located her cell phone. She texted Penn, ignoring how many times she'd mocked others for texting people in another part of the same building.

Let's go out for dinner, she wrote. Let's go to Cobie's. I'll buy.

We can't. They're cooking all this stuff, he wrote back.

She wrote, Can we just take a ride? I can return the rental car. Okay? I have to get out of here.

Within five minutes, she saw Penn outside the house, waving to her.

He followed her past the Brewster General Store, over the hill to the grist mill where the alewives massed in writhing silvery throngs every spring for the most munificent seagull brunch known to nature, past the cranberry bogs, their surfaces like pebbled pink piazzas, to the storefront in Orleans where she returned the car, then on to the Hot Chocolate Sparrow, where they'd been buying coffee since they first learned to like it. They sat on the hood of Penn's truck in the parking lot at Skaket Beach, watching the waves wrestle. Penn had to give her a hand up. "I'm going to have to start bringing a chair for you, like Grandma Becky," he said. Their mother's mother was hale in her late seventies, but barely five foot two.

"Did you hear me and Ariel?" Frankie said. "Talking?"

"People in Hyannis heard you and Ariel. That was hardly what you'd call talking."

"Well, she just kept insisting on normalizing everything, Penn."

"What else should she do? Really, Frankie? What choice is there now? It's, what…a week to the wedding?"

For the third time in twenty-four hours, Frankie started to cry.

"Wait, wait," Penn said. "Oh, Franny Frank, come on. Let's talk about something else. Tell me all about Gil."

"Do you have any food in the truck?"

"We have to have dinner. And you just returned the rental car, so I guess you're not leaving tonight after all."

"Can we at least go back to the Sparrow and get some chocolates?" They did, and skipping the caramels, which they both hated, Penn and Frankie ate their way through a full-pound box as she told her brother how, the first time she met Gil, he protected her looks, and the second time, he protected her life.

"Oddly enough, it all started with Dad," she said.

Frankie had been shooting sea otters at the Branha wildlife reserve in the Hebrides, where most of the coastal reserve had once belonged to a single family. The conservator, a man called Roaken, was the head of that family and had gathered as many wildlife writers and photographers as he could induce to visit for an all-expenses-paid ten days, to show off how the restoration of the coastline fauna and forest had paid off. All of them stayed with local families—crofters, fisherfolk, storekeepers—who were part of the effort, who also fed them, and, despite the Scottish reputation for horrifying food, Frankie learned that she never met a scone she didn't like. On the first Saturday night, Roaken learned that they were faced with a storm, but was unwilling to give up the cliffside-overlook feast he'd planned. He found someone to fabricate amazing, tall-ceilinged tents of some plastic clear as ice that somehow defended them from the gale, so thirty of them dined in a bubble of impossible romance, eating grilled venison, potatoes and turnips as a storm raged all around them and the waves frothed like giant meringues.

"I was sitting next to Gil, just by chance, and there was this wildlife writer from Montana. Apparently, she and Gil knew each other a little, even though he's from Montreal. He's spent a lot of time in the western United States. Anyhow, I could tell she liked him."

Penn said, "So? What does this have to do with Dad?"

"They saw my last name, and they wanted to know if I was related to Mack Attleboro. I said I was, and then Gil brought up—"

"The eagle."

"Yes, and I thought, Will I ever outlive this?"

The night went on, and when everyone had so much to drink that they felt as if they knew each other much better than they really did, several of her colleagues tried to convince Frankie to lead them to the drowned forest where her father said he saw the extinct bird. She pointed out that not even Mack could find it a second time. Then she heard somebody mutter, "Convenient." So she agreed to try. It wasn't as if she entirely believed Mack either, but she wasn't about to let anyone else openly lampoon him.

The next morning dawned hot and sunny, an almost apocalyptic event in that part of the world. People were walking around dazed and hungover, wearing ragged trousers they'd cut off to make shorts. Everyone played in the sun, in the cold surf. Frankie took photos. By three, Stella, the Montana writer, offered to help Frankie aloe up the worst swaths of sunburn on her back.

"Your hide is taking a beating. You're lucky you're not vain," Stella told Frankie. "I swelter wherever I go because I have to keep covered up. Can't risk it. I'm too vain. It's the worst thing about me."

"And I thought, No, it's not the worst thing about you," Frankie told Penn.

"You don't think of wildlife people being petty and mean," said Penn. "I always think they should be generous and above all that."

"Well, that was when Gil spoke up. He said, 'I think she has terrific skin. She looks healthy. Not all women have to look like a corpse bride.'"

"They're called wrinkles, Gil," Stella had said. And Gil gave Frankie the kindliest glance, as if to say, Who can account for people? Still, Frankie thought of Mack commenting that she was only in her twenties and she already had crow's feet and yes, he had been the same, but what made a man look wise made a woman look shopworn. After that night, she slathered up with SPF 100, always wore a long-sleeved top and, when she could without interfering with her camera, a hat.

Later in the week, Gil drove one of the green Branha vans on an expedition for six of them determined to find Mack's purported swamp. They asked every local they met about sunken forests, and they even found one, a beautiful, haunted place Frankie photographed. But so far as any of them could tell, the Regent Red sea eagle remained extinct. Still, Frankie made sure that she sat next to Gil in the front of the van, telling him about her otter commission for *Oceanographic*, asking him about his work for the huge Canadian organization, EnGarde, dedicated to purchasing and preserving unspoiled habitat, and his hopes for editing its lavish newsletter.

In the morning, Gil took off. He didn't say goodbye. Frankie thought she might never see him again.

"That's it?" Penn said. "That's not the ending I was expecting. So you had to call him to inform him of the blessed event?"

"That's not the end of the story, Penny!"

A few days later, the sunshine idyll was over, but at dinner that night in the dining room at Roaken's huge house, Frankie noticed that Gil was back. When the meal was over, and everyone else ran away through the pouring rain, but Frankie huddled under one of the eaves until Gil emerged, a tricorn of folded paper placemats held nerdily over his head. She thanked him for defending her and laid her palm against his cheek, surprising them both. He kissed her. They went back to their separate lodgings.

"And this is the highlight reel?" Penn said. "Can you hurry up? The chocolates weren't enough. I'm starving."

"It was the second-to-last night there, and we were looking for golden eagle chicks. Somebody said maybe we could see into the nests if we climbed up this big wooden fire tower."

"You guys know how to party."

"Well, that's how nutty wildlife journalists are, Penny. We go all out. Anyhow, this fire tower was right near the cliff. And it dropped off to rocks, hundreds of feet down. And somebody said to Roaken, 'Hey, guy, that thing doesn't look too stable.' He told them that the conservancy was going to replace it with something that had deeper footings, but that it had been there a long time. Then, this storm blew up from nowhere."

The wind increased to a gale. Suddenly, that wooden tower began to sway. Utterly quietly, Gil said to Frankie, "*Attends*. We are going to have to jump, but jump with me and jump for the mud, not the gravel. Look straight at the mud." And so Frankie had jumped, twenty feet, and landed filthy and bruised, but otherwise unhurt. Five minutes later, they watched the tower teeter and then walk itself eerily over the cliff.

That was the night that their son was probably conceived.

Frankie told Penn that much, but not all the details.

Gil's housemates had gone to a pub in town. He invited her to come to his quarters and have a hot bath. Still shaking from the sleety storm on the cliff, they climbed together into the big cast-iron tub, took an hour-long hot bath and calmly discussed birth control. Frankie heard herself suggest, "How about nothing?"

Not until later did she consider what an idiot she might have seemed, basically offering to have a baby with somebody based on one kiss and a discussion about sunscreen.

"I thought he was going to say, well, what a sane person would say. *We don't know each other. That's a huge deal*, something." Gil waited a full minute. Then he said, "I want to be a father. I couldn't wait to grow up so I could be a father. I was just afraid of not finding the right woman."

Frankie was not even surprised. It seemed entirely right.

Later she asked, "What were you looking for…in a woman?"

"I didn't have a list. I would just know who she was when we met."

"How?"

"Just as you did. You knew me. I knew you. True love, of course."

Penn said, "That's pretty damned impressive. I'll have to remember that line."

"What? *Jump for the mud?*"

"Think of that tower going over. If I had that kind of near-death experience with somebody, I'd probably think it was destiny. I would want to marry him too. In fact, I think I might want to marry Gil myself."

"It was epic, as they say," Frankie agreed. "I thought that was the strangest week of my life. But now I'm absolutely sure that this will be."

They headed back to Mack's house. Frankie was starving too, but all she wanted was Gil.

2

Because dinner was not yet ready, Frankie snagged a handful of cookies from the kitchen and then called Gil from the guest-room closet.

Awkwardly, she pulled down a big suitcase and sat her increased bulk on that, in the cedar-smelling recess she remembered from games of hide-and-seek.

Had there ever been a longer day? The day seemed to have swollen to contain a month at least, like Asteroidea, starfish, expanded their stomachs to engulf their prey. And it wasn't over.

"This is Gilbert Beveque," said his voice-mail message. "Right now, I'm finishing my new book, *In Praise of Snow*, but I promise to get back to you." He repeated the same thing in French and by the time he got to *J'aime la neige*, in her mind Frankie was screaming, *Pick up! Pick up! What if I were stranded at sea? What if this was the last call I could ever make?*

She texted him, Call me when you can. Soonest. Please.

Frankie came out of the closet and lay on the floor. She tried to do the little exercise she learned years before in a psychology class: if you're upset, when you ask yourself what's the matter, don't accept your first answer. Dig deeper. What is this emotion really? Are you angry or are you afraid? Are you hungry or are you tired? She wasn't really angry with Gil. But she was angry.

Forget the guest room. Frankie shouldered her pannier—which somehow had made its way from the rental car to the house. She slipped down the hall to her room—now a yellow-and-navy blue nursery where a border of boats and ducks bobbed along the chair rail—carried through to the adjoining bathroom. In one corner was a crib massive enough for six babies, and around the room all the things that people used to care for a creature no bigger than a cat: a changing table, a bassinet, a swing—two swings—a toy baby giraffe that would have fooled a real giraffe… Either Ariel was tearing through online retailers or a delivery truck had driven from FAO Schwarz in New York. Against one wall was a modest but plushy trundle bed with a navy blue chenille bedspread—Frankie recognized this from Penn's toddler bed—and a yellow one folded over the foot. That had been hers. On the mattress sat a handmade primitive cradle, with oak leaves and acorns carved into the head and foot, entwined with the letter *A*. Her great-great-grandfather Grace had made it for Frankie…although he was ninety-three years old at the time Francis Lee Attleboro was born, the first Attleboro of her generation.

And now here it was, done and dusted for the Attleboro-to-be… But no. That baby would never see this cradle. Frankie would rather burn it… Well, maybe not burn it, but she would hide it until she figured out how to smuggle it away. Her baby might not be an Attleboro by name, but a Beveque—but of course, he would be an Attleboro and, through Beatrice, a Grace.

Carefully, she placed the cradle on the floor, with her pannier beside it, and sat on the bed, pulling the navy coverlet up over her shoulders.

Her phone rang then, a recording of a cacophony of church bells from all over England.

"Sweetheart?" Gil said. "I'm so sorry. I must have gone out of range. What's so urgent?"

"You will never believe it."

"Are you okay? Is the baby…the pregnancy okay?"

"I'm just fine…but I have to tell you…" She launched into what Penn would have called the highlight reel.

Suddenly, Ariel stood in the doorway. "Your dad said—Mack said it's going to be dinner soon, so I'll just help you move your things over into the guest room."

"I'll sleep here."

"But it's the baby's room now," Ariel said wearily.

"I promise not to pee the bed or write on the walls. I'm completely house-trained."

"Still… Okay."

"And I really don't want to sleep with the head of my bed against the head of your bed, your bed with my father…if you don't mind. I'm still a little grossed out by the idea. Wait, no. That's not true. I'm still a lot grossed out by the idea."

Ariel sighed and sat down in the big rocking chair. In the gloaming, she was like one of those flat cast-iron silhouettes of deer and cats and farmers people used to stake in their yards. "You know, Carlotta mostly used to just stay out all night with the guys she met. But she went through this phase where she would bring men home. Did I ever tell you this?"

What fresh hell? thought Frankie. She said nothing.

"She'd bring men home, and I wouldn't know how to act around them. Did I put my pajamas on before I brushed my teeth? Did I eat my toaster tarts at the same time my mom and her new boyfriend were sitting at the table? I used to hate it, I wanted to kill her, when she would make me tell Bill or Jerry or Louis about what I liked to do in school and about my favorite music and what I liked to eat. She would make meat loaf with ketchup all over it like cake frosting, and she would whisper to me to ask them to read to me, and it wasn't like she ever read to me—she hadn't read to me since I was two. But she thought if we all sat down and ate together, maybe Bill or Jerry or Louis would stay and really be my father and take care of her. But most of the time, any interest that any of those men had in me was sick. And a couple of nights later, even before the whole meat loaf was gone, they were gone too, and Carlotta would have a black eye and maybe not as much money in the plastic sandwich bag she kept buried in the coffee in the Folgers can."

"What's this got to do with which bed I sleep in?"

"Nothing to do with it. Maybe Beatrice could only teach me so much, and my real ways, the ways I saw when I was little, are the ways of a slut."

Frankie said, "Oh please! Please spare me the big soul-searching thing."

"That's so hateful!" Ariel said. "You can be so goddamn hateful."

It was true, Frankie thought. She could be hateful.

Ariel could be hateful too, but Frankie *liked* being hateful more. It had been useful when she was younger, but as she grew older, Frankie worried about how much she liked it. Ariel was different, she thought. Ariel was sweet at the core. The truest friend.

Was it even possible that Ariel had completely planned her journey from downtrodden waif to environmental activist to chatelaine of Tall Trees, or was Frankie being paranoid? The most Frankie ever thought was that Ariel might be carrying a torch for Penn. As if. She'd had her sights set on bigger fish. They had all played together on the beach when they were little. Beatrice brought them sandwiches and thermoses of ginger water. They wore long-sleeved T-shirts that they took off so often that pretty soon, they were so tanned it didn't matter anymore, made pools and corrals with sticks for the creatures they imprisoned. Ariel slept over more often than not. Beatrice would call Ariel's mother to tell her that her daughter was staying at Frankie's house, but half the time Carlotta didn't answer, forcing Beatrice into the uneasy position of leaving a message.

Now Ariel said, "Ellabella Ballenger called."

"What? Why?"

"I don't know why. She said she'd call back. I didn't know you two were friends these days."

"We aren't friends these days," Frankie said. "I know her parents are friends with Mack. How about you? Are you friends with her these days?"

"When hell freezes over."

It wasn't until they were older that Frankie could analyze the reason that people like Ellabella looked down on her because of Ariel. Most of her peers would have considered Frankie solid second-tier, a science geek, but still pretty, the kind of girl no one would shun because her father was kind of famous. Ariel broke that calculus. Frankie knew it. Ariel knew it. An earlier generation would have openly called Ariel *trailer trash*, despite her ethereal beauty. So Frankie and Ariel had to cling to their friendship all the tighter. North Atlantic University High was a small place, two hundred kids. Frankie never questioned how Ariel managed the steep tuition. They survived the prey savanna that was high school by stropping their cruel derision of the popular girls to a sharp edge, starting by trying to see the four truly popular girls as they would have appeared to untutored eyes. By that point, those girls were legendary social executioners. From about the fifth grade on, even teachers deferred to them.

"I'll call her back later," Frankie said. "Thank you."

All the events of this day seemed to have shoved the long past and the recent past together with the near future. Frankie didn't believe in coincidences. She'd seen Ellabella exactly once in ten years, when they'd exchanged a cool nod as they passed within inches of each other at the Chatham Christmas Tree Walk. Beatrice had spoken up. "Oh, Ella! Hi, honey! You look beautiful! And this must be your new husband..." But Frankie just walked on, pretending to be riveted by a tree decorated all in tin cutouts of coastal marine life.

Unless much had changed, Ellabella must be up to something.

Frankie lay back on the trundle bed and thought about those girls—especially about Ellabella and how Ariel's craftiness had once turned the tables on her with a vengeance.

Ellabella Ballenger's clique were all pretty, all rich, all talented, but she was on a different tier, the apex predator. Smart to begin with, a finalist in the state math Olympiad, bound for Harvard, she played the violin and well enough to place in regional competitions. She was also easily six feet, maybe taller, a poreless buttermilk blonde, absolute man catnip in that she was a skinny girl with grapefruit boobs who ate pizza burgers and soft serve all day long (if she puked, it truly was invisibly) and understood the infield-fly rule. She seemed born knowing how to navigate the edges of middle school, that Mariana Trench of human unkindness. She staved off her parents' lifelong wish to send her to Choate and stayed at North Atlantic University High. There, she mocked Frankie and Ariel relentlessly. She called Ariel Teen Angel or Goth Barbie, because Ariel favored sixties mod clothes, including updos and black fishnets. She left messages on Frankie's phone, pretending she was underwater drowning or making porpoise noises, and she once spread buckets of dead alewives on Frankie's lawn and even in her car which, by midmorning, stank to high heaven. (Ever upbeat, Beatrice used the dead fish for fertilizer, although Frankie later heard her on the phone, reading Kitty Ballenger the riot act. Frankie's car was picked up by a body shop and fiercely detailed. Ellabella was forced to write a note of apology on her own stationery). At the height of the warfare, Ellabella's minion Theodora leaned out from the tallest tier of the bleachers and dumped a full bottle of sriracha on Ariel's head. Frankie wasn't there to see it, but Ariel thrilled everyone who did see it by not reacting at all, not even reaching up to wipe the sauce off her hair and her white sweater, not even looking around to see who had done it. She simply went on serenely watching the band.

Frankie and Ariel never knew why Ellabella singled them out for such elaborate indignities. They still didn't understand.

Then, with an inspired gesture, the memory of which still delighted Frankie, they asserted dominance over her.

On the morning of the prom, Frankie and Ariel, with three of Frankie's friends, polished off a pound of bacon and a dozen banana-oat pancakes, then took out their dresses to see if they still fit. They planned to go swimming and get dressed for the dance, then come back that night, maybe with boys, for a late cookout and sleepover.

No one locked doors back then.

And Frankie's dress was gone.

She had sketched the design herself and found the old pearly silk-crepe material in a Boston thrift shop. The style that year was crinolines stiff as cakes, but Frankie's dress was fragile and slip-soft, sewn by one of Beatrice's friends whose specialty was fabric-art sculpture. It showed up that afternoon, ripped and muddied, on the old ship's figurehead outside the Yankee tavern. Like a gleeful terrorist, Ellabella texted around a series of pictures of girls in dark hoodies pulling the dress over the head of the buxom long-haired angel in front of the pub.

As it turned out, Frankie went to prom, memorably wearing Beatrice's wedding dress, which the fabric artist shortened to fit the day of. But Frankie didn't forget. More notably, neither did Ariel.

A few weeks later, Ellabella received a twenty-second video of herself begging Cove Buckner to come back to her. "I'll never yell at you again. I swear. Not ever. You can sleep with anybody you want to. I'll do anything you want. I need you. I can't go on without you. And if you can't do it now, promise you'll give me another chance when we grow up..."

She never knew who took the video. Someone, Frankie suspected, that most people didn't notice.

Frankie texted Ellabella: I have this but I'm not going to send it to people.

Ten minutes later, Ellabella texted back: Why not?

Frankie replied, Because it's too easy. It would make me cheap and low. I'm not cheap and low. It would make me like you.

That night, Ariel texted from her own phone: But I am cheap and low. So watch your back. This could make the rounds anytime. Even on the night before you get married.

Oh my, Ariel, Frankie thought, when Penn called from the kitchen, "Pick up! It's Ellabella Ballenger calling you!" It was like stepping from a memory into a dream. "Ellabella Ballenger. Jasper Ballenger's sister. Kenny Ballenger's daughter. She says she called before."

"I don't need her pedigree, Penn! Get the number. I'll call her back." She swung her legs over the side of the bed. There wasn't going to be any sleeping, even though, having swept over a crossword of countries and time zones since the previous night, let alone all this sludge, she was hypnotized by fatigue. She had to instruct her eyes to move left, move right. "Don't give her my cell-phone number!" she called then, just as Penn shouted, "I gave her your cell number!" He added, "She had some questions."

About what? How did she even know Frankie was in the United States?

Frankie had nearly forgotten Ariel's silent presence. Now she said, "I'm not going to debate with you who's more proper, you or me. I live in a van most of the time, and it's not even mine, so I don't know much about fancy melon spoons—" she thought guiltily that she did, in fact, know about fancy melon spoons and exactly where they went relative to the napkin on a breakfast service "—but I'm going to sleep right here on this bed, no matter what you say."

Ariel replied, "Fine. I'll just get the cradle out of your way—"

"Don't you touch that ever."

"Huh?"

"When I leave, that's coming with me. My great-grandfather—Beatrice's grandfather, not Mack's—made that for me. Nothing will change my mind. It's mine, for my baby. Unless you want to cut it in half, like King Solomon."

"This is really hard on me," Ariel said softly.

"Well, you should have thought of that before you decided to marry my father and steal my family home."

It was only then that Frankie remembered that Gil was still on the line. She waved Ariel away and put the phone on speaker.

"Are you still there?"

"Am I still here? I wouldn't have put the phone down for good money. It's been a real piece of radio theater, like my grandma used to tell me they had when she was a child."

"And now you understand?"

"Oh, I would absolutely not go that far," Gil told her.

"Their wedding is not even a week away. And my father thinks I'll agree to be her maid of honor. And take the wedding photos."

"Did you agree?"

"I didn't agree to anything."

"Well, Frankie, just sit tightly."

"You mean, *sit tight*." She had to smile at the way that Gil's English, his second language, could desert him in an idiom when he was excited. It happened only with speech: in writing, he moved back and forth fluidly. Once, when they scarcely knew each other, Frankie asked him how he was that morning, and he said, "*J'ai la pêche*" which, in French, meant he was feeling great. Frankie pointed out that she wasn't fluent, and Gil said he was *pêter le feu*—which, she thought, at first was something pornographic. In fact, it just meant he felt full of energy.

"Yes," he continued now. "Sit tight. Don't fight with anybody."

The first time he set eyes on her, Frankie was yelling at somebody to please tell her just what kind of person would roll up a photograph image side out to put it in a mailing tube.

"When will you be here? I need you!" Even she winced at the screech in her voice.

"I'll leave Wednesday morning."

"It's only Sunday!"

"I can't get a straight flight to Boston sooner," Gil said. "You'll be all right. I'll be there for the wedding. You have the cottage."

"It doesn't have a bed."

"You can buy a bed," Gil said. "Buy the mattress at a store. The *d'occasion* kind might have bugs in it," Gil said, using the French for *secondhand*.

"Oh thanks. I usually do get the kind with bugs." As if Gil hadn't spent what amounted to years of his life in forests, with every kind of flesh-eating creature in his sleeping bag.

She agreed to buy a table as well. Even if they didn't end up keeping it, they would at least have some privacy while they figured out what to do. Houses on Cape Cod, vacationland, didn't sell very well in fall. Perhaps they might even find a renter for some income.

"Just be careful. Sit in the sun and don't—"

"Fight. I will. I mean, I won't."

"Can't you just make light of this, Frankie?" Gil asked. "Lots of guys, they fall in love with their secretary."

"Gil! Are you listening at all? She's my best friend. She was my best friend. A second daughter to my mother. Try to picture… Okay, picture your brother has died tragically. You're heartbroken. Then your father decides to marry your brother's wife."

"Jesus," Gil said. "That would be disgusting. But you and this woman, you have a long history together. Weren't you good friends? When you were little?"

"No," Frankie said. "I met her because she was sick and my mother forced me to read to her."

She told him what she supposed was her and Ariel's origin story.

"I guess there was never a time when I didn't know her. She played with Penn and me. She was nice, but so shy and almost… what, backward? We had lots of other friends…"

"Of course you did. Famous dad…"

"It wasn't like that," Frankie said irritably.

But was it like that? If she was a spoiled little jerk, would she have the courage to remember herself that way?

"When Ariel was eight, she got really sick."

"With what? With cancer?"

"No one ever knew what she had. But it went on and on." The mysterious illness kept Ariel out of school more than she was in it, and the upshot was that Beatrice forced Frankie to go to the house and read to Ariel.

At first, Frankie begged to get out of it; then, when that didn't work, she flatly refused. Beatrice turned up the guilt, telling her how Ariel could barely eat, how much the light hurt Ariel's eyes…and while Frankie was sorry for the other girl and liked her, she wouldn't tell Beatrice the real reason she didn't want to go to Ariel's house, the reason why they never played there, which was that she was afraid. She was afraid of Ariel's grisly drunk old grandmother, Sherry Puck, who pinched the flesh of Frankie's chin and called her Bea, and she was afraid of Carlotta, Ariel's beautiful wild mother, who one dark summer evening stood naked outside their cabin in the rain because she said rainwater was good for her skin, whirling around in the lightning and the downpour even when a car of drunk boys honked and slowed down and yelled. She was afraid of adults who didn't seem to notice children or that the cabinet only had one kind of cereal in a box that was almost empty and the refrigerator contained only the smallest size of milk with a past sell-by date, a package of Velveeta and some ketchup, as well as several pastel-colored bottles of wine.

The tumbledown cabin stood not far beyond the Barbie House. Inside, there were basically just two big rooms. One area, perhaps five by seven, was curtained off as a bedroom for Ariel. Behind that curtain was a twin bed. Just that. Ariel's clothes hung from pegs or were stuffed into cardboard boxes on the floor.

She remembered the huge-eyed girl, thin and pale as a candle, propped up in bed, rapturously hanging on every word Frankie read to her from *Where the Red Fern Grows*, sobbing with her over the deaths of the Redbone hounds who saved the boy's life. Even when Ariel got a little better, Frankie remembered Carlotta constantly calling her in to take a spoonful of medicine or choke down milkshakes to put on some weight (and even now as an adult, Ariel gagged at the mere sight of a milkshake).

Frankie hadn't thought about Carlotta for years, and why would she? Ariel's mother was gone, gone for almost twelve years now. She was like a concept. But now she remembered Carlotta stumbling through the door of Frankie's house, Beatrice plopping Frankie and Penn in front of the TV—which they were normally forbidden to watch, except on Saturdays—so they knew that whatever was going on was juicy. *The doctors say she won't survive! She's too weak! They're calling in specialists from Boston Children's!* Frankie's mother, patting Carlotta's back, looked out over Carlotta's head into the distance, as if she would see there the cause of Ariel's suffering.

What if Beatrice had let Frankie off the hook? What if they had never sealed their friendship, whispering in the dark about werewolves and sea monsters and nose-piercing and periods and boys, about Marianne Pease, the art teacher who used to be a nun and had the tattoo of a dragon from her shoulder blades to the crack in her butt; about Teresa, the mail carrier, who one day dumped all the mail in her truck in the middle of the beach and set it on fire and then ran away with a boy who was only a senior at the high school; about Kelso Kelly, whose older sister was really his mother and whose grandmother was really his mother's older sister? Ariel had the gift of silence: she knew things only adults knew. She had hearing like a bat, and she listened through the cracks in every door. In most ways, before her mother's death, Frankie's life had been abundantly lucky, but what if she had not known Ariel, doubling and tripling her curiosity, her laughter? All through middle school and high school, Frankie told Gil, Ariel had lived mostly with Frankie's family. By the time Ariel was in seventh grade, the illness had disappeared and so had Carlotta. And Ariel's grandmother devoted herself full-time to her own beloved Johnny Walker.

Puberty meant that the girls were no longer as much of a natural threesome with Penn, and there was no part of their lives they didn't share in secret whispers at night. She remembered that Ariel thought for a week she might be gay and so they experimented with kissing, but she said Frankie's mouth was as hard as a pencil eraser. One night in May, when they were fourteen, they watched from Frankie's window as Ellabella's oldest brother had sex on a blanket with Dinah Holywell one night in June, and they watched as he did it with Dinah's older sister Petra. When they were fifteen, they took Mack's car and drove to Providence to dance all night at the Mad

Mouse, parking the car in the circle driveway fifteen minutes before Mack came out of the house to drive it to work. When they were sixteen and Mack was out of the country, they took the car on the ferry to Nantucket and camped with a bunch of college students from a choral group. Frankie could still hear them singing harmony, see their upturned faces pale as shell in the moonlight. They drank cheap wine and kissed boys who were five years older. Ariel almost went on the road with them and would have if Frankie hadn't cried hysterically. Beatrice later told Frankie that she knew all about these adventures, but decided to let the girls learn their own lessons unless they got in real trouble. This fact astounded Frankie then and now, another example of Beatrice's wise reticence.

One night, struck by lightning, the old cabin burned to the ground. Firefighters brought Sherry Puck out in time, only to learn that she had apparently died some days before. Ariel knew she should feel awful, she told Frankie, but what she felt terrible about was that she didn't feel anything at all. The plot of land, with its slight depression where the cabin once stood, along with a couple of burned stumps, was still there. No one had ever rebuilt anything there, although the land had to be valuable now, and Frankie sometimes wondered who owned it.

For a year, Ariel went to Boston University, with a good scholarship and with Beatrice paying her living expenses, studying math and business. But she was miserable among strangers. She came home every weekend and finally came home for good. At first, the plan was for her to continue at North Atlantic University, with Frankie. It turned out, though, she was through with college.

"She used to say I was a lighthouse and she was a flashlight," Frankie told Gil. "But that wasn't true. Ari could have done anything she wanted. And I guess she did."

When she and Gil finally hung up, Frankie listened for voices. They were all chatting on the deck, presumably over dinner. *I would rather starve*, she thought and then thought again, *nope*. She longed for the clams, their fat centers pursed by lemon, but she didn't think she should take a chance on seafood. She would have buttered corn and baked potatoes and bread, bread, bread, all the bread in Massachusetts, if she had to fight for it… But first things first.

She slipped into the master bedroom and into the half of the huge closet that had been her mother's. On a sane level, she knew that all Beatrice's clothes would be gone, replaced by Ariel's, and they were. But now, despite what she had promised Gil, she was spoiling for a fight and wanted every paint-smeared smock and apron and poplin shirt, every cashmere sweater and velvet hippie skirt that had ever touched her mother's skin. Those that she would never wear, she would cut up; she would sew a quilt for her son, the genuine Attleboro, not the usurper, although she had never made even a potholder.

She marched out onto the deck, nearly swooning at the sight of all the butter and starch. "I want to go through Mom's things," she told her father, in what she hoped was a neutral tone, as she piled her plate. The potatoes had been grilled with some kind of cheese crisped over the tops and a dusting of za'atar. She took a bite. They were the best potatoes she'd ever tasted.

"Those boxes that Ariel packed are for you," Mack said. "Penn already has some things."

"What I'd really like are some of her pictures," Frankie said. "I have picked a few out, but they aren't the only ones I would like to have eventually. For now, the one of the Bullina virgo. And the one she called 'The Only Child.' Of the little girl in the distance on the beach? The one that was supposed to be me?" Mack nodded. Like Frankie's photos, Beatrice's paintings were at minimum, five by five, many larger. "And the one of the clam-stand sign at night? I think she called it 'Carnival Lights'?"

"That was always my favorite," Ariel said. Frankie ignored her. "I love that one."

Frankie said, "I am taking it." She added, "I want them to hang in my cottage, which you don't even know about. Yes, Dad. New England's own Hugh Hefner. I have to tell you about my cottage. But first, I also want her clothes. Her pearls. Her sable coat, even though that's not done anymore. The silver haircombs she wore. I don't mean all of them. Of course, Penn will—"

"You can look through the boxes," Ariel offered. "Mack picked out the things to give away. I wasn't involved in that."

"It's not really giving them away, Ariel. They were my mother's. They're not really Mack's to give. And Mack might not have picked the things I would pick. I don't want to be petty about this. But I will if I have to. Like I said, that ring you're wearing—"

"I told Mack that would be a problem."

"Well, that should have been mine. But I'm not going to make it a problem."

"What cottage?" Mack asked then. So Frankie told him.

It was two minutes by her estimate—and two minutes can be a long time—before he said, "You'll be nearby, then."

"Are you happy about that?" Frankie asked, hating herself.

"Are you?" Mack replied. He turned to Penn. "You're going to have to pick Grandpa up at the airport tomorrow. He says he can drive down. But he's almost eighty-eight. He's not used to that kind of traffic." Grandpa Frank, who lived in Myrtle Beach, was the only grandparent left on her father's side. Her grandmother had died just before Christmas more than three years earlier. With another gulp of guilt, Frankie realized that was the last time she'd seen her grandfather, Grandma Katherine's funeral and the hushed, cursory Christmas they'd observed a few days later.

Of course, they wouldn't be inviting Beatrice's mother, but perhaps a visit to Granny Becky was just what Frankie needed. And it would probably do Granny Becky good as well. Widowed at twenty-seven, with two baby daughters, when her husband, a Marine pilot, had died in the Vietnam War, she had taught American political thought at Emerson College and had staunch liberal opinions she never hesitated to defend. Still, her fierce light had faded after Beatrice died. *I've never felt old before,* she wrote to Frankie. *I've always been eager for more useful life to live. But now, that is in doubt.* She had moved in with Beatrice's sister, Imogen. Frankie longed to be near her mother's people, to hear what they had to say—and not only about Mack.

"I have to…go," Frankie said. "Thank you for dinner."

Clearly fed up, Mack said, "You're welcome. You aren't going to help clear up, then?"

"You can do that," Frankie said. "Penn has to help me."

Frankie scooped up the navy quilt from the nursery and took it into the basement laundry room. What would she need short-term? What should she choose long-term?

She located a lightweight sleeping bag, two sweaters she found in plastic tubs, her first wet suit—so heavy it felt like some kind of furniture—fins and a mask and a small woven basket she could use for grocery shopping. And maybe for liberating vegetables from the garden. All this she placed in the center of the quilt and, knotting it on top, she heaved it over her shoulders, Santa style. From a low shelf near the door, she took one of Mack's flashlights. Leaving the impromptu sack on the floor of her room, she slipped back into the master bedroom.

Her teeth chattering with nerves, she shone the light along the upper shelves. There was Mack's briefcase, his shoe boxes… and then, there, the green satiny surface of Beatrice's old jewelry box. Tucking the flashlight under her chin, she slid the box down. She needed to see it, needed to know that it was still here, that it hadn't been tossed away like so many other precious memories. She would claim this as her own, in due time, but for now seeing the familiar shade of green, feeling the satin under her fingers was enough.

She could still hear voices from the porch, the clatter of

plates. All of them would be inside within minutes. Snapping open the lid, she inadvertently tipped the box and moaned as half the delicate chains and random strings of bright beads hit the carpet. She made herself take care to put them all back in, banking on the fact that, if Mack ever looked in the box, he would not remember any particular order. Breathing deeply, she located the old red leather box she knew held Beatrice's wedding ring and pulled it out. She closed the jewelry box and placed it on the floor under the lowest shelf of what had been her mother's side. Just as she opened the box, she heard Ariel come humming into the room, and Frankie snapped the flashlight off and threw herself on the floor of the closet. But Ariel just called, "I've got it! I'll be right there..." and left, closing the door.

The storm that had threatened all day now hurled pebbles of rain against the windows.

Frankie slipped the band on the fourth finger of her right hand—Gil's ring was on her left—and aimed the flashlight at it. This wasn't part of the set that Mack had given to Beatrice for their silver anniversary, the diamond now on Ariel's hand. It was her old ring, a ring that had been in Mack's family. Tears clotted her throat again: crying was apparently a second job now. Reluctantly, she began to remove the ring, but it wouldn't budge. Breathing hard, Frankie crooked her arm at the elbow and held it up, then tried again. The ring was on as if welded.

In the hall bathroom, she tried soap. No luck. Perhaps in the morning. The day had been humid, so perhaps a cool night's sleep would reduce the swelling in her hands. Finally, the small of her back aching, she lay down on the rug in the nursery with a pillow under her spine. Just as sleep reached out to take her down, she remembered that she'd left the jewelry box on the floor of the closet.

3

A rough hand grabbed her shoulder. Still fuddled by sleep, she spun around like a break-dancer and kicked out.

"For God's sake, Frankie!" her brother cried, jumping two feet straight up so comically Frankie almost laughed. "You were sprawled on the floor, I thought you'd collapsed or something."

Frankie stood, her thighs cramping as they did when she asked too much of herself on a dive. The house was still wrapped in sunny Sunday-morning slumber.

"Are you better today?" Penn asked.

"I'm just hungry. And I don't want to think about them."

"Frankie. Face up to it. She's Ariel. He's your father. What are you going to do?"

"Stop defending her. And him. Don't ask me how she would act if our positions were reversed, because our positions would never be reversed. I would never, ever do something like this. Do you think they're really going to go through with this wedding?"

Penn laughed, snorting through his nose in a way that made

Frankie want to pinch him. "What do you think? She's about a hundred months pregnant. He's acting like he planted the flag on the moon."

"Oh God," Frankie said. "This is so goddamn humiliating."

"Yes, but you don't have to live here."

"Penn, maybe I do. Maybe you don't. Last I heard, you were investigating internships at Woods Hole."

"I got one," Penn said. "Two years with Nina Branetti." He didn't need to say more. Nina Branetti was the Shark Whisperer, the Carcharodon Contessa, who got closer to more big sharks, more times, without a cage, without consequences, than anyone else. "But now I have to decline—talk about humiliating—because Mack's all back in the game. Back at work. Lectures set up. Off to count the last vaquitas for a documentary."

"A documentary? When?"

"He'll let me know. After…all this…"

"What if there are no vaquitas left by then?"

Penn laughed ruefully, but insisted that it would work for Mack either way. As a steward of water animals and their predators, it would be personally appalling if they couldn't find a single one…but it would still be a moral tale. Frankie knew that the last count of the snub-nosed porpoises on the edge of the Baja California Desert showed about a dozen individuals. "Still, it's going to be a big deal, very heart-rendering." This was a shared phrase from childhood and Frankie smiled. "You have the vaquitas about to be extinguished, but kids need food and clothes so the Mexican fisherfolk are gill netting. The vaquitas are collateral damage. It's one of those both-sides-now things Mack loves."

As good as their father looked, Penn, Frankie now noticed, was thinner. How selfish she had been, Frankie thought, to discount how severely constrained her brother had been by the events of the past year. Not only did he live with Mack, he was

Mack's professional partner, and their father was one of Penn's two advisers for his doctoral thesis—a conflict of interest that was more or less ignored.

"I have to get some food," she said. "I'm not trying to cut you off."

Frankie pulled a dozen eggs, some milk and a block of cheese out of the refrigerator.

"Do you know how to make an omelet?" she asked her brother. He shook his head. Tentatively, Frankie began whisking eggs in a bowl, adding milk and salt and pepper, then another egg. She remembered reading something about Alice B. Toklas using half a pound of butter in an omelet, so she melted a full stick. "Do we have any truffles?"

Penn stared at her. "Sure. Right in there right next to the foie gras and caviar."

"Where?" Frankie said, confused.

"We don't have any truffles, Frankie. We maybe have a green pepper." He asked her then, "If you stay, will it be until the gala?"

The donor gala for the Saltwater Foundation, Mack's lifework, was coming up, but not for more than a month. "I don't know," Franke said. Almost sentimentally, she pictured Mack in his good charcoal suit and flashy orange tie, excited but shy-seeming, for this was his charm, as he described his and Penn's work with helping the humble wood stork establish outside the Everglades…and, oh, Frankie hoped not, inviting titters from colleagues and big-money donors about the Regent Red sea eagle.

"He won't miss me," she said. "Not if I take the wedding pictures for him."

"The two things are unrelated. He'll want you there."

"He has you, the better Attleboro, the male."

Mack had wanted a son so badly that he named Frankie after a man—Francis Lee Attleboro, her father's father—just as he was named Macklin after his own grandfather. Then along came Penn. But Penn, she was well aware, was named for someone who could do magic.

Well.

They heard a noise then, a sort of polite cough. Both of them looked up. Ellabella Ballenger was standing in the doorway from the front hall.

"I knocked," she said. "No answer. But the door was unlocked. So…hi."

"Hi," said Penn. Frankie said nothing, keenly aware that her mouth was stuffed with toast.

"So, I brought a present," Ellabella said. "For the happy couple."

"Thanks," said Penn. "They are still asleep."

"Well, where should I put it?" She hefted a package wrapped in gold foil. "But really, I wanted to see my old friend, here."

Aware that she probably looked as though she'd been kept overnight in a barrel of bacon grease, Frankie turned back to the stove. "I must say, this is news. You never wanted to be my friend," she said. "I'm probably being too blunt."

"No, you're right," Ellabella said. Frankie observed her hypnotic effect on Penn. Frankie considered herself decent-enough-looking, but Ellabella was spectacular, much lovelier than she'd been in high school. Part of it was the sheer nobility of her height and posture. Penn was of ordinary stature, maybe five-eleven, but Ellabella towered over him in her rope-soled flats. She must be six-one at least, Frankie thought, and she had the look that movie stars have, which Frankie analyzed the few times she'd photographed such people. They had slender bodies, but their heads were sculptural, all face. "It's true. I never wanted to be your friend, but hey, now you're famous." She turned to Penn. "Your old girlfriend's getting married to your dad. Don't they have a whole section about that in the *DSM*?"

"We've been talking that over," Penn said.

"I know," Ellabella said delightedly. "I was listening! I couldn't bear to interrupt you!"

"And so?"

"I wanted to give this to Ariel."

"That's very nice," Frankie said. "You can leave it with us."

"I'll just bring it to the wedding. Want to be my date, Penn? I'm currently single, as of May, the first divorced kid on the block. But you'll have official duties, I suppose. I'll just have to be a wallflower at the beach club. I'm a journalist now," she said as she turned to Frankie, "as you may know. I work for the *Coast Chronicle*. The magazine. Do you read it?"

"I was in Scotland. Before that, Egypt. I don't think they stock it at Al-Mahmal."

"I'll be the editor soon, when Liesel retires. If I can fucking bear that. Then *The Atlantic*...right? But at the moment, she wants me to do a feature about you and your art...well, your photos."

About to cut this off without an explanation, Frankie reconsidered. Publicity was publicity. In a wildly competitive media marketplace, the more people who saw her pictures, the better. How much of a scandal could Ellabella cause, even with her pen dipped in curare, writing a story about someone who took pictures of fish? A couple of months from now, the scandal of Mack's marriage, if scandal it was, would be stale gossip. Still, Mack was who he was, and his influence on her own career was undeniable.

"The problem with today is I have to go out and buy a bed and a table, maybe at a used-furniture place? I don't have anything in this cottage that we... This cottage we're staying in." That wasn't a lie. It wasn't the truth either, but it wasn't a lie.

"I'll go with you," Ellabella said. "I'll help you carry things, given your delicate condition, which I heard about. It will be colorful. The famous *Nat Geo* wonder child buying furniture at St. Brendan's parish store. So very...eco chic."

"Can we do this later? I don't know what's going on with me," Frankie said. "Suddenly, all I want to do is sleep." The omelet fixings, so tantalizing before, now smelled like cooked feet.

"Everybody I know who had a baby said the same thing. I'll go have lunch and come back," Ellabella said. "I don't have anything else on today. Want to go for lunch, Penn?" He was across the room like Usain Bolt.

In the nursery, Frankie drifted off. She dreamed. She stepped into the cottage, admiring the freshly whitened bead board and muted floors of mixed wide planking. When she opened the refrigerator, she found metal ice trays tucked into the freezer compartment. She was carrying her baby. She lay down on a big bed under the sloped roof where decks of recessed skylights framed a purple sky pocked with stars. Then she got up and, using just her bare hands, folded the whole house up and packed it into her pannier. She tucked the baby in last. He never even woke up. Sigmund Freud's secretary could have told her that she was mourning the home she lost before she ever had it.

She woke up then.

In the kitchen, she found Ellabella chatting with Penn, who still looked to be under an enchantment. She slapped some left-over bacon into a haphazard sandwich, devoured it indelicately, and then she and Ellabella took off in Penn's pickup truck.

What Frankie and Ariel once called *the chapels of thrift* were all in brisk operation. Every church on Cape Cod had its own parish store, where the women of the altar guild sold a combination of quasiantiques, outmoded clothing and knickknacks, from scallop-shell Christmas-tree ornaments to the ubiquitous crocheted tissue-box covers. The first thing they found seemed heaven-sent: a chrome kitchen table with four upholstered red chairs, only one of them the slightest bit bent, for a hundred and thirty dollars, along with a short bookshelf made of wood Frankie recognized as ebony. The price tag was a hundred and twenty-five dollars. "I think I should tell them that they could get a lot more for these," she whispered.

Ellabella said, "Please. They're Episcopalians. They have enough money."

The only bedside lamps she found were wonky, the shades handmade of laminated boat sails. Ellabella encouraged her to buy them anyway. They were conversational and gave good light. At St. Christopher's Resale, there was a lovely, nearly new bentwood rocking chair. They visited the mattress store and lay on each of the prepared beds. Ellabella said, "Me, I'd get a mattress in a box. They're pretty great. They're cheaper too, and it's fun to watch them pop open."

Frankie did just that, on the spot ordering a queen-size bed from a company called Jazzy. "So you think about price?" she asked Ellabella. "You're rich."

"I'm not rich. My parents are rich, but not really rich-rich," she replied.

"Every rich kid says that same thing."

"Well, there's nothing wrong with being rich. Anyhow, you're one to talk. Beatrice's family had old money, like from wrecking the lives of Indigenous people with mines and trains and stuff." She added, "Mack has money too, but he had to work for it."

"I didn't know people even said that anymore."

"Now who's being oh-so-coy?"

"Isn't one of the rules of being rich that you don't talk about money?"

Ellabella said, "Touché."

Over coffee, she asked questions and made comments, with surprising insight. "Collectors are acquiring Francis Lee Attleboros now. The curator at Paper Kunst in Vienna wrote, right here in the catalog, *what might be cutesy subjects in other hands, Frankie Attleboro exalts. She resists the temptation to anthropomorphize animals to make them more appealing to human eyes. She respects their wildness, entering into their world instead of drawing creatures into our sphere.* That's pretty heady stuff. Do you think you could get in some kind of emotional cross tie? I mean, you might start to feel as though your best work is behind you, when most people are just starting out?"

"I used to think about that," Frankie told her. "I guess some of the first things you do are always the best. Or maybe they just get the most attention. The picture I love most was one of the first ones to have a great publication. It's a cave photo—"

"I know that picture, where the fish are swirling around you in a big circle, like the sun."

"That's the one. In New Guinea. Those were barracuda."

"Barracuda? Yikes. That's terrifying. Those are huge. I thought they were little fish like perch or something. Don't they bite you?"

"Not really. I know that sounds weird. They don't bite people very much, and when they do it's awful, but I've been lucky. So far. Of course, that *so far* is not really very far…four or five years."

Ellabella laughed. "Your big bite might be still ahead."

They finished their coffee and drove back to St. Christopher's. With twine and mixed results, they tied the rocking chair to the table so it would all fit snugly into the truck bed.

Once they had, Ellabella asked, "Who do you want to be?"

"Oh, I want to be everybody!" The obvious heroes, she said, were her own mentor, Abram, David Doubilet, Jennifer Hayes and others, brave, intrepid and constantly surprising. "What you go for is to be identifiable as an artist, if that isn't too chichi to say. You see an Annie Leibovitz photo, and maybe ten other photographers have made a picture of that person, but only one is an Annie Leibovitz. You see an Ansel Adams landscape that could only be an Ansel Adams. It's not just the technical way of doing it, it's the artist's vision. I don't know how to say this exactly, but I think it was Richard Avedon who said that a photograph is not a likeness, it's an opinion. What you put in the frame and the way you take it, you're taking a picture of the way you feel about something, not just the thing itself."

She told Ellabella that her biggest influence was Joel Meyerowitz and not just because of his photographs of Cape Cod, although she loved those too. "They're like Edward Hopper paintings," Frankie said. Meyerowitz loved color, and he fought against the notion that the only art photography had to be made in black-and-white: he fought and won. He made his reputation as a street photographer rather than as a studio portraitist, taking pictures of people he saw. "And that made me bold to use color too and not to be afraid that it was somehow cheap. I like to think of myself as a street photographer. But my street is the water, and my people are animals. I go to a place where I know there are otters. But I'm not taking pictures just of one otter, with one expression. I know it sounds like I'm sentimental when I say that animals have expressions, but they do. All creatures have expressions. Porpoises definitely. Even fish have expressions. Maybe not shrimp." They both laughed. "But the thing I love most about his work is that it's so emotional. In every picture, there is some little thing happening that is just so moving. You know he saw it that way."

She added that Meyerowitz was her hero for another reason: for making a record of things too, Frankie added, the biggest thing of all. "He was the one who was at Ground Zero right after 9/11 and took pictures of the search and the salvage. That was a war zone, like any other. No one was allowed in. No one. But he got in, talking his way in, sneaking in if he had to. He set up his large-format wooden view camera, and he was there for eight months, until nothing was left but a clean and empty hole." From his studio, Meyerowitz had taken photos of the World Trade Center intact, of its burnished grace and architectural glory…and when it was destroyed, he was drawn into its chaos, its spectacular collapse.

"The workers there were heroic people, like statues, and there were ordinary, fragile people too, like a father and a son searching for the boy's lost brother. He doesn't usually take pictures of people, but he did of them. Meyerowitz cried with people on the site almost every day, and some of them he never even knew their names. He didn't want to presume. But he shared their grief. He was known for his serene and beautiful landscapes. His book about the site, that could be his greatest work."

Both of them sat silent for a moment. Then Frankie said, "We were so young when it happened, but those pictures go so deep in me it almost feels like they're my own memories." She added, "That's what great pictures should do."

Then Ellabella asked, "For you. Why underwater?"

"Why underwater, I'm not sure. That's my habitat. It always has been. You know what Jacques Cousteau said about human beings, bolted to earth, but that you only have to sink beneath the surface of the water and you're free? That's how it feels to me."

"What's something about that choice that you've never said?"

"I'm afraid of water where I can't see the bottom. I'm terrified of it. I always was. My whole job is probably to overcome that fear."

Frankie told Ellabella the story about her first real encounter with the invisible world below the surface. She and Beatrice were rowing their big kayak where the Bass River meets Nantucket Sound, in maybe thirty feet of water, maybe a hundred yards from shore. Suddenly, there came a bump to the port side, just a little under the boat—but not the kind of bump that meant you'd hit a sandbar. It felt animated, intentional. Beatrice's face went as still as if she were sleeping. Again came the bump, this time harder; the front of the boat lifted out of the water. And Frankie saw the giant head of the great white shark slice the water inches from her arm, the rolling lifeless eye, close enough to touch, regarding Frankie like a corned beef sandwich. She slipped out of her seat and huddled on the floor next to Beatrice's legs. "And I remember thinking, I will not let myself feel like this forever."

She thought, then, of Ariel, who was worse. Raised on a beach, named for a mermaid, she was not only scared to death of water, she couldn't swim and wouldn't even go into the pool past her knees.

Ellabella interrupted Frankie's thoughts, asking what she loved best about the job, other than taking the pictures. Was it travel? All the places she got to see, off the beaten path?

Without hesitating, Frankie said no, it was the stories.

"It was telling the stories to people, but mostly telling them to my mother," Frankie said. "She was my first audience. She was the best audience. I mean, she was like any mother, sure. She thought whatever I did was amazing, because I was the one who did it." Frankie told Ellabella about how, when she was a child, maybe in first grade, she would bring home some kind of craft project, like a picture frame made of Popsicle sticks stuck all over with plastic jewels and little tongues of purple felt, a picture frame exactly like the picture frame of every other child in the class.

"Just like mine," Ellabella said, although she'd gone to the Land School instead of North Atlantic Elementary School "What would they have done without Popsicle sticks?"

Well, Frankie went on, Beatrice would be amazed. At least, she would act amazed, and do it with panache, not settling for simply saying *Oh, how pretty!* but commenting on the creative choices Frankie had made—like gluing two strips of rickrack in each corner instead of just one. When she grew up, her photos and stories were those Popsicle-stick projects, carried to her mother like wine in a chalice.

"Not every mother is like that," Ellabella murmured and went on, "So tell me one of those stories."

"Okay. One of the great things about my mother was that

she was so self-possessed. And so generous. Like, you wouldn't normally call somebody at two in the morning, but I knew I could do that. Beatrice answered the phone at two in the morning the same way she did at two in the afternoon. She was composed, she was polite, even a little eager."

"Okay, so you did this regularly?"

"Not regularly, but I knew I could," Frankie said. "You know how on TV, there's the character, the sexy detective who's so intense that he throws himself so deeply into every case that he forgets to eat, he only drinks whiskey, and when he gets home, he just falls on the bed facedown still wearing all his clothes? And then, somebody calls. So he fumbles to grab the phone and knocks it on the floor and just mutters, 'Ugh... yeah, yeah...huh.'"

Ellabella said, "Sure."

"Well, she was the opposite of that," Frankie said. "You could wake her up and boom, she would be right there with you. It was like you'd just left the room five minutes before. So one night, a few years ago, in the spring, I was in Washington State, out in the straits of the Salish Sea. My friend Lupe—she's a photography teacher at the college there—she was driving the boat. We got to this place, a good dark place where I knew that I could sink down to take pictures of juvenile surgeonfish because they glow this gorgeous fluorescent green."

"Why? Is it because of predators?"

"Nobody knows why. It's only when they're really young," Frankie said. "So I'm out there. I know I'm going to have to go deep, they're down, like, sixty, eighty feet, but before I do, I suddenly notice that I can't see anything."

"You were blind?"

"No, I could see the sky overhead, but I could not see Lupe or the big motorboat we were using. *What?* Did you ever have something happen that was so strange you didn't even know how to ask the question? And so my mind starts spinning. Was

I caught in some kind of crazy current? I couldn't feel anything special." Frankie swam forward, on her back, looking up at the sky, but to either side of her were these sort of walls, dark with light patches, wet and glossy. "Then I realized the walls were moving."

"Whoa. What?"

"The walls were orcas, killer whales. Three of them, four of them, six, more of them in a pod, close enough that I could have reached out and touched them," said Frankie.

"But they won't hurt you, right?" Ellabella said.

"Well, sure, they can hurt you if they want to. They're apex predators. And the ones in captivity, the way they're kept isolated and other stuff, that makes them psychotic. They definitely have hurt human beings, they've killed people, even the keepers or trainers who fed them every day."

"So what did you do?"

"Well, I started to cry. I was terrified."

"Then what?"

"Then I started to take pictures."

"Really?"

"The best I could do was to hope they were just curious, the way all whales and porpoises are curious."

"I don't think I could have done that. In the dark, in the middle of the night."

"I was scared out of my mind. Lupe was yelling, banging on the side of the boat with a big pole, sounding the air horn, trying to get them to scatter. But they didn't care, and why should they?" Frankie said. "They were the lords of that realm. That was their dominion. They weren't going to leave until they were ready. They let me in close. I could hear the sound of their breathing. They didn't harm me. They had their reasons."

These turned out to be some of the most spectacular pictures she'd ever made, the pliant powerful bodies, the giant-toothed mouths, the intelligent black eyes. When she got home, she couldn't wait to tell her mother. Beatrice was thrilled by the story. "And I'm sure she was terrified by it too. Her child, in the dark night, in the deep water, surrounded by killer whales? But she didn't say that. She just kept asking for more details."

It was the same way her mother had reacted to the picture frames made of Popsicle sticks, so many years ago, enthralled, engaged and loyal. What if the universe were not only limitless but also many-layered like an onion? What if it were made of translucent plates sliding and colliding, superimposed one upon another so that the fragile rubric of time was no more than what physicists believed it to be, a way for simple minds to try to comprehend infinity? Could the essence of what had been her mother still reverberate in the way that, theoretically, every word ever spoken on earth still tumbled out in deep space? Could some part of the essence of Frankie spin or climb or sink fast enough or high enough or deep enough that she would cross her mother's path?

Without thinking first, Frankie said, "I would give up all those moments, even though I love them, if I could just see her once more."

"You should write those stories down so everyone can experience them."

"I think about that sometimes. Then I think, who would care?"

What was Frankie up to right now? Ellabella asked.

She talked about choosing six prints for a collector, a Japanese-Italian woman from Chicago who had a gallery with eight rooms built onto her own house in Umbria. There, she displayed only photography by Americans, among them an original Man Ray, Steve McCurry's picture of herdsmen dancing in Sri Lanka, the iconic image of the ballet dancer Vita Swallow taken by Annie Leibowitz. One entire room was dedicated to water images, including several pictures David Doubilet made for his first book and the photo of giant river catfish that Leah Jones took from an overhanging tree branch. When she completed the work, Rita Sasaki would fund Frankie's trip so she could hang the photos herself. When Sasaki died, the whole house would become a gallery.

The veer came fast. That was probably the only way, Frankie thought later. Some topics were like that dark water: the only way in was in.

Ellabella said, "So Frankie, your dad marrying Ariel. Could you have imagined? I mean, your dad marrying anyone? After Beatrice?" Alert to the possibility of the razor in the apple, Frankie moved slightly to study Ellabella's face and took her time. Nothing in the other woman's expression suggested anything but a somber gentleness. Was she just an interviewer wise to the usefulness of compassion? Or had she been declawed somewhere along the way?

Frankie said, "I really don't know. It's not really my place to talk about it. It's their life. They have their reasons, I guess."

"I smell an evasion."

"Yup," Frankie said. "How well did you know my mom?"

"Mostly through Kitty." Ellabella's mother was striking and strikingly status-seeking. Kitty and Kenny were Cape Cod's peculiar version of society people. "You asked before how it is to be me. You asked me why I didn't like you. Why I was a kid who put so much effort into putting people down. You asked me why I changed. One answer is you had Bea for a mother, I had Kitty." She added, "Please don't think I'm blaming Kitty for my behavior. That I'm putting her down. She loves me. She loves all her kids. She's just ambitious. There's nothing wrong with that either. But the way she's ambitious, it can hurt. I didn't want to be that same way."

"I think I understand that," Frankie said. She wasn't certain that Ellabella had heard her. The other woman seemed to have wandered off for a moment. What, she wondered, had happened to the picture frame that Ellabella had made from Popsicle sticks?

Then she asked, "Could I shoot you?" Ellabella raised her eyebrows. "With a camera."

"I guess…"

"Everything underwater. Would that be okay? It would be the equivalent of you interviewing me."

"Sure. Why?"

"So, don't think when I say this that I'm making a pass at you, Ella. But you're just too beautiful to be mortal. And they say that women at your age, well, our age, it's the most beautiful they'll ever be. So for art's sake."

"That's a sobering thought," Ellabella said. But she nodded. "It could be fun. I can wear clothes, right?"

Frankie said, "Nope."

"Well, that might be fun too." After a moment, she said, "Okay. You're not going to pull me off the narrative here. I'll bet you're pretty mad at Mack. And Ariel. But what I think is—and you didn't ask me—life is short. Don't spend time on a grudge. I have done that a lot. It feels great for about ten minutes, and then, it's just a waste of concentration. What is already is. Go on, just go on and keep on rocking."

Back at the cottage, Ellabella helped Frankie off-load the furniture.

As they began to hump the table over the threshold, she stopped, confused. In the bedroom were bleached-white wooden nightstands, each with a mercury glass lamp, flanking a brand-new queen-size bed crisply clothed in fresh linen sheets, a white comforter and… Beatrice's cornflower-blue afghan thrown across the foot. Tears sprang to her eyes.

"I can cancel the box bed," Frankie said, "but I sense coercion."

"I sense an olive branch," said Ellabella. "Take it."

After Ellabella left, having secured a second interview to be scheduled later, Frankie lay gratefully on the bed, looking up at the coved ceiling, now swept of cobwebs. Then Ariel tapped at the window, and Frankie beckoned her in.

"Tell me that wasn't who I thought it was," Ariel said.

"She's actually okay," Frankie said. "She's doing some feature thing for a magazine. And I'm going to take her picture."

"You are not."

"I really am. She's maybe the most beautifully proportioned human being I've ever seen."

"I can't believe you would do that."

"You're the one who asked her to your wedding."

"Not me. Your dad. I guess he's known Kenny a long time."

"Well, anyhow, welcome to my beautiful little kingdom. And whom do I thank for all this? It's pretty great."

"It's a gift. From your dad. He really wants you to feel better. He really wants you to be happy, not just happy for us. It wasn't so very expensive. Mack knew a guy." Like an old-time Chicago gangster, Mack was inordinately proud of always knowing a guy. "Your grandpa's here. Mack wanted you to come over and have lunch. I made sandwiches and cold pasta with artichokes. Do you think it will make you sick?"

"I never get sick," Frankie said. "Well, that's not true. I do all the time, but I like to say I never get sick." They grinned at each other, and for a moment, real time fell away. Frankie rolled to her side, her center of gravity still alien to her. Ariel extended her hand, and after a moment's hesitation, Frankie took it and let Ariel help her to her feet. Together, they walked back to the house. Just before they got to the door, Frankie said, "I'll take your pictures too." Ariel squeezed Frankie's hand.

Mack's father, Frank, swaddled in a bulky cardigan, though it was seventy-five degrees outside, was in the kitchen, guzzling a huge mug of black coffee and eating a cheese-and-watercress sandwich. Why did old people drink black coffee with everything? "It's my name saint," her grandfather said, wiping his hands on a towel and then pulling Frankie close. "Remember when you were a little kid and you used to say that?"

"I do! Oh, Gramps, it's so good to see you. I'm so, so sorry, sorry I haven't been there..."

"But I get all those photos and letters from Florida and Scotland and Bermuda. I'm the only grandfather in my neighborhood who actually gets handwritten letters. So that part's pretty sweet. Maybe you can come down to that nice beach sometime with the bambino, huh?"

"Which bambino?"

Frank's eyebrows jigged like caterpillars on hot tar. He shrugged elaborately, turning his hands palms up, *What are you going to do?* With the soft lilt of his native North Carolina, an accent Mack had entirely lost, Frank said, "I meant yours, and yes, I'm the one who should apologize because they kind of jumped the gun on your news. I couldn't be happier. Hope I live to meet him. As for the other little one, I can probably make it until next week...seeing how the bride looks."

"Oh please, you will! You're indestructible, Gramps." Seriously, she added, "You're becoming a grandfather and a great-grandfather in the same year. Don't you get some kind of certificate?"

"I think you get a free dinner at the steak house."

"I bet they don't have to give out that award every day."

"I bet not that many people still have enough teeth for the steak."

She wished that her grandfather would give her a sign of solidarity, but how could he? Mack was his son, his child; it was to Mack he owed his first loyalty, for whatever he did that wasn't a crime—or even if it were a fairly minor crime. But as if he understood, Frank said, "Macklin could never be alone, Frankie."

"That's what Penn says."

"Even when he was little. He wasn't one of those kids who

got lost in their own play or in a book. He had to be right on your heels, he had to be doing something you would notice, and I don't mean something bad. It was like those poor folks standing by the side of the road with their signs that say *Will Work for Food*. Macklin's would say *Will Work for Praise*. Banner was another story. He didn't care what you thought." Banner was Mack's brother, five years younger, who was coming the next day from Raleigh with his wife and Frankie's cousin, Melody, still in college. "The press likes to think of this lonely explorer, out on the sea, who never gets tired, this sort of solo knight in shining armor. But did you ever think when you see those things—of course, you do, you know all the tricks, there's five other people there! Cameras! Sherpas!"

"Not Sherpas…" Frankie said, laughing.

"Do you think he just couldn't bear to face life without our Bea? And so…"

"You know all about that."

"I do," her grandfather said. "Still, Kathy and I had sixty years of everything two people could experience, all the highs and all the lows. We were just kids when we got married, and we didn't have the proverbial pot to piss in. Please pardon me, I'm an old man. But we built a great life together, and I could not have asked for a better friend. But Macklin, he was right in the middle of that with Bea, wasn't he? They didn't get to see around the next bend, together, so maybe what he's doing—"

Gently, Frankie interrupted. "I just can't talk about it anymore, Gramps. My head is going to blow up. You're going to stay a while? Say you will. Not just for the wedding? I would love you to meet my fiancé, Gil. I don't know when we're going to get married, but it will just be a little thing. Not like this extravaganza. Could I have one of those sandwiches? Pasta too?" She held out a plate and tucked in. "He's Canadian. From Montreal. Gramps, could I have that pickle if you're not going to eat it?" Her mouth crammed, Frankie went on. "And he would love Myrtle Beach, all this heat stuff is still exotic to him. Southwestern Canada is still the great north..."

"I'm sure I will like him," Frank said. "*Mais oui.* Maybe the baby can be Frankie the Third. Huh, Gil? Oh, forgot to mention. We ran into this guy at the airport, Frankie."

And just as Frankie began to chew the full third of a sandwich she'd stuffed into her mouth, Gil ambled into the room. *"C'est une fille délicate,"* he said.

Her face against his soft white shirt, which she then checked for mustard stains, Frankie said, "*Tais-toi.* I'm eating for three."

"Trois?" asked Gil, his eyes widening in shocked.

Frankie laughed at her own joke. "Serves you right." But she hadn't felt so safe since the tower went over the cliff.

4

Even for the wedding rehearsal, held the Thursday night before the wedding, Ariel looked resplendent. She had gone all out. The stylist had wound seed pearls and stephanotis into her upswept hair, now nearly white from summer sun, and while Frankie was suspicious about the long pearl drops in her ears, before she could say anything, Ariel assured her that they were old, an antique-shop find. Frankie had supposed that the *something old* was Beatrice's twenty-fifth anniversary ring, which was not in fact at all old. The flowers would be cornflowers, Mack's favorite, and white roses, Ariel's choice. Mack had given Ariel a brand-new sixpence to wear in her shoe, as the old rhyme stipulated. *Something borrowed* was a puzzle. Ariel turned to Frankie asking, in front of all of them, if she had any ideas for fulfilling the penultimate tenet of the old tradition. Relenting, Frankie lent her the gold necklace with the initial *A* that Beatrice had given her for her birthday the year before last. The second it was nestled against Ariel's collarbone, a tribute to her first name and her new last name—

the same as Frankie's own—Frankie's urge was to pull it off with a decisive tug. Instead, she did what she thought would be the next worst thing, which was to tell Ariel that she could keep the necklace. When Ariel was touched rather than offended, Frankie wanted to stomp through the floorboards like Rumpelstiltskin. Ariel showed everyone a photo of the *something blue*—her dress, a Violet Lang tube of periwinkle satin that would hug her body closely down to the puddled train of fabric. Her immense belly would be displayed like one of the antique-ship figureheads that popped up everywhere on Cape Cod. And while the wedding dress was exquisite, it gave Frankie dark thoughts about women from olden times who got in the family way, as they used to say, before marriage and had to keep to the shadows wearing large tentlike garments. Was that entirely a bad idea?

With large tents much on her mind, Frankie set out on Friday morning to find a frock that would bring the total number of dresses she owned to one. She was of ordinary height and normal proportions, so surely something would fit and preferably be elegant and simple and inexpensive. Gil offered to accompany her, but while an entirely reasonable and compliant man, he was a man, and Frankie knew that this enterprise would not be the work of a moment. On top of this, to her immense annoyance, Gil, Mack, Penn and Frankie's grandfather apparently had discovered that they were brothers separated at birth. It was like summer sleepaway camp. They went fishing. They went to the Yankee pub to play pool. They went golfing. They threw great slabs of meat on the barbecue. Mack couldn't find enough good things to say about his son of the north country. Of course, Gil had no shopping to do. In the spirit of all this camaraderie, Penn had lent Gil a gray blazer and a crisp blue shirt. Even a pair of Penn's black loafers fortuitously fit. And the photos would be their present. In Chatham, she was thrilled to find a shop that rented formal outfits. What a great idea! Enterprising women had hit upon a plan. After all, who except Ellabella's mother needed to buy and keep evening gowns? The place was airy and bright as an atelier, with clothing hung like art. An hour later, sweating, Frankie fled. Everything short canted up so much in front that she couldn't raise her arms, as she would need to do to shoot. Bending over would have been pornographic. Everything ankle-length, however, was so spangled and beribboned she looked like a Fourth of July display window. By then resigned to buying, she found a consignment store with a great reputation. Forty minutes. No hope. Frankie wondered, are my standards too high? So she determined to lower them. Expensive Cape boutiques came next. Another doomed errand. Frankie learned she could pay hundreds of dollars to look like a turtle stuffed into an oven mitt. She finally went home discouraged.

No one will be looking at me, anyhow, Frankie consoled herself. Even as the thought unfurled, she knew that it was wishful silliness. At the wedding, people would wish they had more eyes and ears than the pairs that nature had given them to snuffle up truffles of gossip, morels of impropriety. Guests would search her face for traces of the rage they knew must be bubbling and Mack's for evidence that he was headed the way of King Lear (to Penn's more hopeful Hamlet and her kinder, gentler Lady Macbeth). They would assess Ariel's face for proof that all she really wanted was her own reality TV show. The only thing that could possibly make this performance more unbearable would be the reviews. Being humiliated was one thing, having witnesses made it legend. At least—please, please—what they disparaged wouldn't be her looks.

Wistful, she found the box marked *Give to F* and lifted out her mother's long string of pearls. Pearls were alive, Beatrice used to say; they needed to be kept close to your skin. That wasn't true, but holding them close to her cheek was like holding her mother close. *At least,* Frankie thought as her throat filled with tears, *I can wear these. Would you forgive him, Mom? Would you already have forgiven him? Would you understand how Ariel feels? I'm trying my best. I'm trying to be as decent as you were. I'm not, though, Mom. I'm no Beatrice Lee Grace Attleboro. I'm just a bundle of sparklers all burning at the same time.* Then, deeper down, Frankie spotted a fold of palest yellow silk, what Beatrice would have called *jonquil.* She drew it out. It was the dress Beatrice had worn ten years earlier to the inaugural banquet of the Saltwater Foundation. Frankie remembered it now. Even as a teenager, she'd delighted in seeing her parents so good and glittering. She'd appreciated the Saltwater mission and their boldness in creating it. Frankie laid the smooth fabric over her lap. Then she stood up and slipped it over her head. She was shorter and smaller in every way than her mother had been, but the new fullness in her middle and her breasts filled out the contours of the dress, and while the fabric pooled on the floor, it did so artfully, as if on purpose.

There, Frankie thought.

Slipping out of her T-shirt and jeans, she put the dress on properly. The neck was square and the back dipped low, the dropped waist fell to a panel of lazy pleats. She remembered that night—Mack kissing Beatrice's hand. A moment that belonged to her that no one could touch. *Now, it is mine. It is mine to wear.*

All she needed was a pair of shoes, maybe some kind of ballet flat…and certainly, she could find those.

The only mirror in the cottage was in the bathroom, and Frankie didn't feel equal to balancing herself on the edge of the tub. Holding her phone high, she snapped a picture and sent it to Gil. Ten minutes later, he was at the door, admiring extravagantly the way the dress suited her dark hair and the tan she still couldn't avoid, spinning her around the tiny kitchen so that the dress swayed and billowed. "You look grand," Gil said. "*Tout à fais*, your mother would love to see you wearing this."

He then insisted on helping her take it off.

Later, after they gave themselves the respite of a brief nap, Gil told her the news. Mack and Ariel had relented about the maid-of-honor business. In part to be sensitive to the fact that Ariel had no family, at least none that she could find, and had invited only two friends, while Mack had a contingent. They decided that Mack's college pal, a Massachusetts Supreme Court justice, would simply stand with them in the middle of the ballroom for the exchange of vows. Instead of the traditional questions (*Who gives this woman to be married…?*) the ceremony would conclude with everyone in attendance speaking out a good wish to the couple, which, sometime during the evening, each of them would inscribe in a keepsake book of handmade paper that would later include some of the best of Frankie's photos.

With no choice, Frankie decided to up her game on the photos. The next morning, she inventoried the camera she used for land work, a Canon EOS 5D Mark IV DSLR that had been a splurge the year before. For work, she never went anywhere without all eight of her cameras and wondered, for the wedding, if she should pack a spare to be sure. She decided on the one that Beatrice and Mack had given her for her college graduation, the second one she had ever owned.

The ceremony would take place on Saturday at five, so Frankie beseeched the stylist to come early that day and help her prepare before attending to the bride. She had a photographer's good eye for makeup, but her formal occasions were so few that she barely owned any. Her guilty secret was that when she had a meeting with a sponsor or an editor or a collector, she went to the nearest mall and had herself made over by a bored young stylist only to end up buying—maybe—a lipstick.

Like a TV chef, the stylist set up in the kitchen. She brought lights. She brought cases of brushes and paints and scissors. She circled Frankie like prey. Finally, she asked, "When was the last time you had a good haircut?"

Frankie thought it over. "Not that long. Three years? Four?"

The stylist considered this, inspected her arsenal.

Frankie asked, "What do you want me to do with it today?"

"I don't know. What do you do now?"

"I brush it and tie it in a ponytail."

"Hmmm," the stylist said. "Do you condition every time you go in the water?"

Frankie said, "Sort of." She amended, "No."

Swiftly, the stylist bent in and grabbed a length of Frankie's hair. "Because it's really damaged."

"I don't color my hair. I never use a blow-dryer."

"Coloring wouldn't do this much damage. It's the salt water."

"Salt water's good for you."

"It's good for skin. Not hair. It opens the cuticle and leaches water out of your hair, and it ends up…like this. Here, do you have a credit card? Why don't you come with me?"

"I have to get ready to start the photos…"

"Okay. Well, then I'll go, and no, I'm not going to run off with your credit card. I own my own salon, five minutes from here. I need my scissors and…a bunch of other stuff."

She was soon back with a big bag and a big plan. A capful of this before going into salt water. A cap of that before she went into a pool. Wash your hair when you get out, even if it's just with bottled water. Wear a bathing cap. Frankie thought, a bathing cap? She protested feebly.

"Only if you want to have hair for most of the rest of your life," said the stylist.

"What can you do right this minute? Can you heal it?"

"I can't do anything. All that stuff is for when you're starting over. Today, I can cut it until most of what's left is healthy."

Snick went the scissors as the stylist murmured, "Lots of texture, not too chunky, cropped close so it grows out well, and then this dramatic piece." When at last Frankie looked in the mirror, she was transformed. One long thick triangle of hair fell from her crown to her chin; the rest was no more than a couple of inches long around her ears and nape. When the long piece was swept back and to one side, she looked architectural, impossibly urbane and elegant. After tipping the stylist extravagantly, she put on her dress and shoes, and at the stylist's suggestion, arranged the long rope of pearls to hang down her back. The stylist then headed for the beach club, where she would help Ariel make ready for the ceremony. Frankie and Gil packed the car with her cameras and drove the small distance to the big house, where they would pick up Frankie's brother and grandfather.

In their shirtsleeves and tuxedo trousers, Mack and his father stood at the kitchen island drinking orange juice.

"You…look stunning," said Frankie's grandfather.

Mack said more slowly, "You look just like your mother." He added, "Your hair is short like hers. And that's her dress." Frankie expected him to pull her in for a hug, but instead Mack said, "How could you do this?"

If Frankie had realized the potential for wounding Mack by bringing Beatrice so fully into the wedding ceremony, she might have considered doing just that. But it hadn't even crossed her mind. Now, she said, "You mean, wear my mother's dress?"

"Yes."

"You gave it to me. It was in the box…"

"I know, but today?"

"I looked everywhere for another dress, Dad. I couldn't find anything. And this just— I love this dress. What could possibly be wrong with my wearing my mother's dress?"

"To my wedding?"

"Now that you mention it, that wasn't one of the occasions that I would have predicted. Which I also didn't know about until three days ago."

"Mack, your daughter looks wonderful," said Frankie's grandfather. "She looks wonderful, Gil, this sweetheart of yours." Gil nodded. No one said anything. Slowly, Mack turned to his father. Frankie saw her dad's hand tremoring so much he had to stare at it to securely set down his coffee cup. She thought, he's not old, but right now, he's too old for this. Is this too much for him? Am I the one making this too hard for him? Or...is he the one doing that?

"She's invoking my dead wife, on this day of all days. She's making me think of Beatrice."

"And probably you should," his father continued. "I don't mean you should think of her every minute, particularly today. But this is your daughter, she's right here, and your son is here. This is your family. You couldn't pretend that nothing came before today even if you wanted to."

Mack said, "We should have just gone to Vegas."

"Well, yes, you should have. But it's too late for that now." To her ears, Frankie's grandfather sounded every inch the starchy Southern actuary he'd been all his adult life, reckoning things on the percentages of a good outcome. He didn't seem to think that eloping would have been a bad idea, but ever pragmatic, reasoned that the only prudent course left open was to salvage the occasion as people with good manners did.

He turned to the room and said, "Mimosa, anyone? Frankie, you can have one with ginger ale."

Frankie had decided to make a portrait in the round of her father and Ariel, which meant circling them while she fired off dozens of shots that would show up in the print as a beautiful blur of the guests with the floor-to-ceiling windows showcasing the summer sunset over the harbor. She asked if she could do this quickly, as everyone gathered for the ceremony, and Ariel agreed, delighted. When she finished, Frankie stood back with the rest of the assembled guests, Gil bringing her a tall chair she could clamber upon, while he held her secure, to shoot down on the couple. Penn handed Mack the rings, and Frankie listened as her dad and her best friend repeated the words everyone knew, about loving and honoring and cherishing from this day forward. Immediately as they finished, waiters circulated with trays of champagne flutes. Frankie spotted Ellabella in the group, giving her a covert wave. She wondered if her old nemesis was trying to decide if the tears Frankie helplessly shed were prompted by joyous surrender to the occasion or by hormones or by bitter rue—as she wondered herself. Grateful she was, however, for the camera that gave her a shield.

The leader of the string quartet called for the new Mr. and Mrs. Attleboro to dance their first dance. Mack sang along to the old tune, "I'll be loving you…always…" Her parents' song. If that didn't invoke Beatrice, what did? Frankie tried to feel charitable; she knew that the song reminded Ariel of Beatrice as well. Perhaps they were both trying to acknowledge her, perhaps it was as simple as that. When the song ended to applause, Mack held his hand out to Frankie, and the band struck up the cloying old tune "Thank Heaven for Little Girls." Dissonance clanging in her head, Frankie took her father's hand. She had loved dancing with her father: he was an expert dancer, agile and elegant. Now Frankie didn't know where to put her feet or her eyes. "You know, I never thought I'd be happy again," Mack said. "I love you so much. And I love this song," he added.

"And the irony is lost on you?" Frankie wanted to bite her tongue. She thought of the old fairy tale and how hoptoads and snakes leaped out whenever the girl opened her mouth to speak.

"You're my little girl."

"And so is your new wife! Come on, Dad. This song isn't really about having a daughter. It's about thanking heaven for little girls because they get bigger every day and pretty soon they're old enough so that you can have sex with them."

"That's a sick point of view."

"Oh gracious," Frankie said elaborately. "I'm sorry for that."

"Why do you want to ruin this?"

"Why did you want to ruin my family life? Why didn't you care that I'm having a child and I'm getting married and instead you only care about yourself?"

"I think if you asked most people, they would say I care about a lot of things beyond myself."

"Oh sure! Saltwater donors. And vaquitas. But what about your own kids? What about Penn, who's so embarrassed by all this that he—"

"People make choices about their own feelings, Frankie."

Frankie began to cry, again. She had cried more in the past two weeks than in the previous two years combined. "I'm doing my best, Dad. And the worst part is that you don't seem to realize I'm doing my best. You're acting like this shouldn't be traumatic for me."

Mack made a shushing gesture, and Frankie's grandfather thoughtfully cut in to whisk her away. She peered over his shoulder as Mack and Ariel danced with various guests to the old Etta James tune about her love at last, had come along… It was, Frankie thought, as if Beatrice had never existed.

Then the quartet leader called out, "Time to start the circle of wishes for the happy couple! We'll be recording them, should you forget what you said."

Kenny Ballenger raised his glass and went first.

"I wish for Athena—"

"Ariel," his wife Kitty corrected him, in a loud whisper.

"Okay, I wish for Ariel every happiness life can bring, even if it's life with Mack. Maybe Mack will finally grow up this time around."

Frankie saw her brother close his eyes, pinch the bridge of his nose with two fingers and then look up, smile gamely, and motion for more champagne.

Frankie's grandfather took the microphone. "I wish peace to this family who has struggled with a loss. Love is the great healer. To Mack and Ariel, joy. To my granddaughter Frankie and her fiancé, Gil, joy. To my grandson, Penn, comfort and joy, in hopes that his love will come along soon too."

Applause scattered around the room. Next came Simon Land, scion of the huge food cooperative Land Ho!, a major sponsor of Mack and Penn's work and the Saltwater Foundation. He sent a wistful glance at Frankie; although ten years older, he'd always had a crush on her. "Mrs. Hobbes at North Atlantic University High would be proud of me right now, because I'm going to quote from the Bard—Shakespeare, that is—from *Twelfth Night*, actually. Mrs. Hobbes, wherever you are, I really was listening! Mack Attleboro has traveled the world, only to find the great love of his life, both of the great loves of his life—if you will excuse me, Ariel—right here, literally in his own backyard. 'Journeys end in lovers' meeting—Every wise man's son doth know.' Maybe he'll settle down for a while now, and I won't have to sell so much popcorn!"

He was followed by a few of Mack's university colleagues, including large, sedate Charlotte Salazar, like an image of justice in a waterfall of ivory jersey, who toasted the couple, "Mack and Ariel, I'm sure I'm not alone when I say that this occasion reminds us that life is full of surprises."

Into the ringing silence that followed, Penn stepped forward manfully and said, "I'm going to quote from *Star Trek*, Dad, and say that you have given me a great example to boldly go where no man has gone before… I mean, out in the field, not here in this context… Wait, that's not quite what I meant. Long life to you! That's not quite what I meant either."

Everyone was reaching for a spinach puff when a final voice, from near the door to the ballroom, rang out. "Let me just say this. I hope that this generation of Puck women is luckier than the previous ones. Just looking at you, Ariel, I'd say that you probably have a pretty good start on that!"

The room turned as one. The woman in the doorway hoisted

an imaginary glass of champagne. *Radiant* was the word that came to Frankie's mind. She looked lit from within, her white-blond hair swept up in an artful mess, a cream-colored satin shirt open to reveal a black lace bustier, much like what she had once worn to tend bar at this very club. The years had not changed her. Four hundred years ago, Frankie thought, the Bard that Simon Land referred to must have known someone like her when he wrote "Age cannot wither her, nor custom stale Her infinite variety." Plenty of people are pretty, Frankie thought, but the woman's aura betokened something else... some sort of power that sapped the resistance of ordinary people. Without thinking, she took her camera from Gil and tried to take a picture that would capture that quality.

Unsteadily, Ariel said, "Hi, Mother."

5

If some people had come to the wedding out of genuine affection, and others out of obligation, the truest reward went to those who had come out of curiosity: months and years later, wedding guests would still dine out on the Attleboro affair, and the return of Carlotta Puck, after more than a decade of absence, was one of the spiciest ingredients. Like the Wedding Guest in the old Coleridge poem, they got more than they expected, two melodramas for the price of one and, counting what came afterward, a trifecta.

> The Bridegroom's doors are opened wide,
> And I am next of kin;
> The guests are met, the feast is set:
> May'st hear the merry din.

But then, the guest was waylaid by the Ancient Mariner, whom no one could get to shut up. He would not be stopped until he could tell the story of the albatross that was supposed to bring good luck to everyone on the ship that it followed, but instead, when the Mariner shot the bird with a crossbow, brought down with it an ancient curse.

Farewell, farewell! but this I tell
To thee, thou Wedding-Guest!
He prayeth well, who loveth well
Both man and bird and beast.

Even if she never got to say the words aloud, Frankie was never gladder for her poetry.

If Mack worried that Frankie, wearing Beatrice's dress, might somehow distract from or upstage the bride, he could not have been more mistaken. That honor went to Carlotta. Frankie might have been naked under a fishnet for all anyone noticed. Carlotta danced like a dervish to the fast songs and zephyred through the slow numbers. She asked the band to play a country line dance, but…it was a string quartet and, of course, the leader said she didn't know any suitable songs. Then, inspired, the violin player broke into "Blue Moon of Kentucky," and Carlotta galvanized the room. Even Simone Salazar, who outweighed most of the men by fifty pounds, was stomping and singing and spinning on her heel. As she swept past, Frankie heard Simone say, "I used to love to go to cowboy bars in California." Life was indeed filled with surprises. Carlotta danced with every single man…but then, she danced with every one of the women too. Perhaps not surprisingly, she danced like someone who'd been trained by an agency called Life of the Party. Even her hair seemed electric, like the sparking-wheel toys Grandpa Frank gave Frankie and Penn when they were kids, that they operated with their thumbs and forefingers. Those toys could burn your fingers: Carlotta looked that way now, alluring and hazardous. Mesmerized, Frankie stopped counting the glasses Carlotta polished off.

Strong men would have been prone on the floor, but the booze seemed to have no more effect on her than ice water. When Carlotta offered to bring her something to drink, and at the same time refilled her own glass, it was then Frankie realized that she really was only drinking water. When Carlotta asked Gil to dance, Frankie made herself grin and say, "I won't let him. He has to stand right next to me all night. For his sins."

"Are you preggers too?" Carlotta asked without skipping a beat, wiggling in place to the mambo.

"I, uh, yes, I am," Frankie said as Gil's face reddened with the effort to suppress laughter. "But now's not the time."

Obligingly, Carlotta continued her progress through the room, cha-cha-ing with Frankie's grandfather, who had been an admirable dancer, like all the Attleboro men, and still was no slouch. Guests lost track of their own partners as they kept their eyes on Carlotta, who apparently had the lungs of a triathlete. But Frankie watched Ariel: she almost forgot her own plight as alternating waves of elation and dismay broke over Ariel's face. She tried to imagine her way into Ariel's emotional state, but tripped over the threshold of it. How would it be to see your mother for the first time in twelve years at your wedding to a man so old that he made your own mother look like a spring chicken, by whom you were also hugely pregnant? Was Ariel delighted? Was she bemused? Was she humiliated? Was she all of those? She hadn't seemed the least bit abashed before Carlotta showed up, but had that been bravado, putting a good face on what might seem to be a situation that otherwise begged for eye rolls and titters? Did her mom's sudden presence bolster the idea of family—or burlesque that idea? Did everything seem to her a fever dream, as it did to Frankie? Carlotta hadn't even come home when Ariel's grandmother died. The lawyer who supervised the sale of the cabin, or, more correctly, its land, said he was acting on her grandmother's wishes. Ariel used the money to buy a condominium in Orleans. She had never lived there, anchored as she was to Beatrice and Two Ponds Road, but she'd found a stable renter and prudently banked the revenue from the place. A few postcards came from Carlotta at first, picturing destinations that ranged from Banff to Puerto Rico. Then those stopped. Ariel didn't know whether her mother was alive or dead.

Later that night, as they lay in bed with the screened skylight open to the stars above them, Frankie tried to explain. "We were maybe fifteen? Yes, fifteen, and Ariel lived with her mother and her grandmother in this rickety little cabin… It's not even there anymore. One night, Carlotta went to the store and never came back."

"I don't understand. Ariel's mother just deserted her?"

"This is because you're Canadian. Canadians are too nice to just up and leave their kids. In my wicked country, it happens all the time."

"She had her grandmother, though," Gil said. Frankie didn't answer. She was remembering something she had not thought about for years, of her mother calling Carlotta a *narcissist* even before Ariel's mother disappeared. "Attention is her drug," Beatrice told them. This was uncharacteristically harsh talk coming from Beatrice, who always counseled Frankie and Penn against gossip. "Don't ever laugh at somebody who's sharpening pencils on the curb. Everybody has a story." She wondered now if Beatrice and Carlotta had a history from girlhood, but how could they have? Although both of them had grown up more or less where they lived their adult lives, Beatrice was maybe five or six years older, a negligible span for adults, but the equivalent of the Mesozoic for teenagers. A woman who had her firstborn at the age of twenty-four was a young mother; but Carlotta, a mother at barely eighteen, was a child. Still, Beatrice would never have judged Carlotta on that score. There had to have been something else, and Frankie would never know what it was. Although the grandmother, Sherry Puck, lived on with

Ariel, she suffered from bad luck as well as bad habits, Frankie told Gil, and was nothing more than someone who signed a report card. That was why Frankie and Ariel grew closer than friends, why all this cut so deep.

"You aren't suggesting that Mack had eyes for Ariel when she was a kid, are you?"

"Oh, no," Frankie said. "Oh, Gil, no. Whatever I think he's capable of, he isn't a child molester. Ariel and I talked this over. When he was around, which was maybe nine, ten weeks out of the year, he barely even noticed me or my brother. He would have said that Ariel was just one of Beatrice's hatchlings that fell out of a nest."

"So your father and mother didn't have more kids, and yet she loved kids."

"She wanted to. She really wanted to. My dad said no. He told her—and I can't believe she ever told me this because it sounds almost disloyal to my dad, and she would never, ever speak badly of my dad—that they had come up with two normals, genetically speaking, and he didn't want to push his luck. Two *normals*, my God."

"Do you only want one?" Gil looked either optimistic or fearful, Frankie couldn't tell.

"I could change my mind after this one is born, but right now, no, I think I want more than one." She studied his face. "What about you?"

"I loved being one of three brothers. I still do. My brothers mean more to me than anyone on earth."

"Gilly, I can't wait to meet them."

It would be soon: their wedding would take place sometime in October, perhaps one more use for the pale yellow dress, though by then Frankie would also need a shawl—or a tarp. She would have chosen Beatrice's slender wedding dress, the one she had worn to the prom, but it would never fit now. All the Beveques would come, Gil's mother and father, his brothers and their wives, his two little nieces, Madeleine and Simone. Mack had generously offered to host a lavish dinner after the late-afternoon ceremony. Their baby would be imminent, but not quite that soon, and Frankie and Gil's son wasn't due until just before Christmas. With her father's wedding now mercifully past, although she still had the task of a last polish to do before delivering the Sasaki commission, as well as the wedding photos—and those needed no particularly hurry—Frankie could feel herself beginning to relax into what felt like a resigned peace. Certainly, it had a hormonal impetus, but she would take it; she would take it. How strange it was to contemplate sheltering rather than moving on to the next seascape and to do this with a vast calm.

Indubitably now, she had her own life to live. She was, and now gratefully, less a daughter. Every day, she moved further out of Mack's orbit, even as she settled into a physical proximity with her father she hadn't known since she finished college.

Once she was satisfied with the Sasaki photos, Frankie assured Gil that she would be absolutely fine taking the photos to Italy on her own. He was not convinced, however, and Frankie readily gave in. They would stay on for a few extra days in Italy, a sort of honeymoon before the fact. "Like a prequel," Penn said. Penn would be on his own with their grandfather Attleboro for a while, since Mack and Ariel were visiting the Chanler in Newport for ten days, Ariel bitterly disappointed that the hot-chocolate bar didn't operate in the fall.

After they left the home of Frankie's client, they traveled to Gubbio, where they stayed at a former Cistercian monastery turned resort and spa. Transfixed by the bleached heat, Frankie lay outside on a linen-draped table for a prenatal massage. Gil wheedled until Frankie gave in to the idea of riding the Funivia Colle Eletto—a small cable car that looked like a birdcage that slowly lofted them to the top of Mount Ingino. The rattly contraption terrified Frankie, who kept her arms clutched protectively over her belly.

"Oh come, now, *mon chou*," Gil protested. "You swim with sharks!"

"That's different."

"Yes, more frightening."

"You don't get it at all. When I do that, I'm in control of everything. I'm the one who checked the equipment. I've scouted the environment. I know what all the risk factors are."

"And the shark knows this too? That you're in control of the encounter."

"Well, true, there's that. But who knows what the safety standards are for this thing? When were those cables fortified last? They look like they're from the Second World War."

"It's the romance, Frankie. You're not supposed to think about things like that. Beauty asks us to risk everything."

When they gazed down on panorama of the city, she had to agree. But she was still acutely aware of her sleeping passenger, an awareness that astounded her daily with its intensity.

They visited the Basilica of Saint Ubaldo, which dated back to the thirteenth century, and as they paused before the glass case that held the preserved body of Ubaldo himself, patron saint of Gubbio, which didn't really look that bad for being eight hundred years old, Gil whispered, "That's the name, Frankie! I knew it as soon as I heard it... Ubaldo! He'll be the only one in his school..."

They visited some scrawny saints and after they visited them, they ate and ate and ate. They ate every variation of a truffle, and Gil consumed the creature that consumed the truffles, regional pork, three times a day—pork simmered with onions and peas in a pastry crust, pork meatballs over linguine, flatbread crackling with crisp fried pork. Forbidden from it because of the pregnancy, Frankie decided she would never touch pork again. She thought of the pigs innocently snuffling in the forests for acorns and truffles, suddenly in their death agonies… Gil said, "They died doing what they loved. That's what they say about bullfighters…"

Frankie said, "But not bulls."

"Meat is one of those things that you should just enjoy without thinking about too much."

"And I always have. But now, maybe I'm destined to be a vegetarian."

She lived five days on variations of hot cereal, vegetable soup with *strozzapreti* dumplings and renowned apples. They came home replete, happier than each of them had ever imagined being.

Once back, Frankie slipped into her bed and slept a nearly unbroken forty-eight hours, which along with lots of ginger ale, was her never-fail jet-lag cure. When she got up, she wished she had a chessboard to figure out how she fit into all the new and transformed alliances around her.

Carlotta was living with Penn and Grandpa Frank at the big house. Frankie noticed that her grandfather was in no hurry to get back to Myrtle Beach now that Carlotta was in town. And who could blame him? Carlotta sunned herself at the pool in a black bikini, to the delight of her grandfather, Frankie thought…and privately considered how the apple didn't fall far—although Mack would have been the apple and Grandpa Frank the tree. She hosted cocktails, concocting pineapple margaritas and espresso martinis, although she never drank them, but served them with pickle crackers toasted in the oven with garlic and cheddar. She told stories of cooking at a training camp for Alpine climbers ("Male, female, antelope, they didn't care, especially the Swiss guys") and of picking beets in Idaho and dealing blackjack in Reno. At a luxury hotel in San Diego where she worked as a concierge, she'd found extraordinary things in some of the rooms: in a hollowed-out Bible, a satin bag filled with what turned out to be diamonds, a bag no one ever claimed; a Saint Bernard with six puppies; four frozen turkeys in the tub. She told of crewing on a fishing boat in Canada; working briefly as the personal assistant to a famous and now-deceased suspense author who may or may not have murdered his wife, but who wept as he lit a votive candle every night in front of her portrait. The man fell in love with her, and Carlotta once thought she'd stay with him the rest of her days, but he wasted away from a mysterious undiagnosed disease, and Carlotta had to move on, this time to the place she thought was her true destiny, at first. She stopped short of ever saying what or where that was. Carlotta deflected the implicit question of why she never came back as if someone had told a racist joke. All this came back secondhand to Frankie, who heard it from Penn and her grandfather when they crossed the great divide between the two houses, since Mack was still aggrieved by all the things Frankie had unloaded at the wedding before Carlotta showed up.

When the newlyweds returned, Carlotta made noises about leaving, but Ariel insisted she stay, at least until the baby came. At first, Mack obliged readily: he probably didn't remember having a newborn and had never much taken care of one of them.

Penn was also pretty amiable about it. "I've been everywhere in the world and stayed in every kind of place with every kind of family. And I think people cook up their own awkwardness. However you feel about this will be the way other people feel." After all, the big house had three wings and nine bedrooms, each with its own bath, not counting Penn's lower-level studio. On this footprint, Standard Grace had once lived with his wife and ten children and his brother and his four children. Another thing that Penn had observed in his travels was that modern Americans were spoiled by an embarrassment of space. And now she was, technically at least, family, the mother of his father's…wife, so his fortysomething stepgrandmother? The very concept, said Penn, made him want to lie down.

So Carlotta fixed up one of the rooms entirely for herself, which was probably not quite what Mack or Penn had in mind. She made an environment for herself that was spare and yet elegantly feminine: gilded golden walls, rose-colored bed curtains draped down from a hoop in the ceiling, matching the rugs and a thick stack of towels in the small en suite bathroom. Instead of the full-length mirror, she uncrated one of Frankie's photos from the basement and gave it pride of place.

"This whole place reminds me so much of Beatrice," Carlotta told Penn. "Everyone loved your mother. I think I made her nervous. I was a reminder of her wild youth. I did some crazy things and some things that were probably even illegal. You have to live, you know? But you know, even Beatrice wasn't a saint all the time." Penn also related this to Frankie, who scoffed. Beatrice and Carlotta may have known each other, sure. But they were hardly peers. By the time Beatrice was married, Carlotta was still a teenager. Further, to Frankie's knowledge, Beatrice hadn't even had a wild youth to speak of—although, now her curiosity was piqued. For his part, Penn was pruriently curious about where Carlotta had been all those years. When he asked her, in a way meant to land as an offhand comment, Carlotta murmured something that was either *a cult* or *like a cult*, but then laughed dismissively and made a slighting reference to corporate greed. "She's leaning in, leading up to something, she's confiding in you and so you feel like she's telling you a secret. And then you realize she isn't. Zero sum shit," Penn said. "She's like the Sphinx."

"If the Sphinx never stopped talking," Frankie replied.

And yet, if she were honest, she was far from immune to Carlotta.

Not long after Frankie returned from Italy, Carlotta brought Frankie a simple necklace made from a raw pearl and a tiny shell on a cord of braided leather so slender it looked to have been woven by the fingers of a fairy. She also brought cookies in a tin. "I didn't make them," she assured Frankie. "You don't have to worry. Kitty Ballenger made them. Ellabella brought them when she came over to talk about you with your dad." She looked around. "Where's the kettle so we can have some tea?" Frankie had to grab her reserve with both hands to resist asking what her father had said about her. Before they could sit down, Carlotta caught a glimpse of some of Frankie's pictures, including a few from the wedding, some test prints that had just arrived from the printers, Merlin and Melville (Frankie loved the service, but was pretty sure that there was no one in the lab named either Merlin or Melville). When Frankie returned from the kitchen, she saw Carlotta regarding the image of herself, dancing, the other guests around her fading to a blue blur of color and motion. "I look pretty," she said softly. "I would never have thought of myself as pretty. I don't think I have two pictures of myself in the world. Could I have… Could I buy a copy of this and…maybe, a copy of one of Ari?"

"I'll give you copies of those, of course," Frankie said. "I'll give you prints of any of them. If you want a bigger size, I'll have that made for the price I pay. You've always been so pretty, Carlotta. I know enough about the way people think about themselves that it doesn't shock me, but you don't conduct yourself like someone who's self-conscious."

"All an act. My mother told me I better make the most of these boobs because I sure wasn't going to light the world up with my brains." For the rest of her life, Frankie would remember the look on Carlotta's face when she said this, the naked plea with its slick of shame that seemed almost to darken the woman's skin.

"That was a cruel thing to say."

"No one ever said anything like that to you."

"No. I was lucky."

"And you would never tell a child such a thing."

"I can't think of what would make me do it."

"Sherry was a crazy old witch," Carlotta said. "I don't know what makes some parents so twisted." Carlotta honestly didn't seem to grasp the irony in any of what she said. She simply seemed to presume herself forgiven. "Then I had to trust her with Ariel, and I hated doing that." Frankie made a noise of what she hoped was assent. It occurred to her that this was the only time in her life that she'd ever actually talked to Carlotta. She'd picked up the phone to hear Carlotta say flatly, "Tell Ariel *get home now.*" She'd heard Carlotta screaming on the road at Sherry. She'd listened to her purr at Mack when she brought Frankie's family to their table at the beach club. Once at the beach-club pool, Frankie saw a few college boys pick up Carlotta and the tray of drinks she was delivering and toss her into the pool. The boys were thrown out, and Frankie and Ariel cringed as the manager, in a low voice, argued with Ariel's mom, who stood there, soaking wet, protesting, "Why are you asking me? It wasn't my fault!"

And it had not been her fault. Carlotta was just another Cape Cod floozy, working in service jobs, hitting the nickel bar at the Yankee, flipping back hair just a little too big, laughing just a little too loud, wearing jeans just a little too tight.

What about her had so vexed Beatrice?

As if she divined Frankie's thoughts, Carlotta said suddenly, "You had a pretty cool mom, Frankie. I didn't know her very well, but she told me once that the wisest people always acted as if somebody were watching them, even when they were alone." Frankie put her hands over her eyes. The sun through the window shone directly behind Carlotta's head, lending her an otherworldly oracular aspect. "I'm indebted to your mom, Frankie. She did so much for Ariel when I couldn't."

"Why couldn't you?" Frankie heard herself say. Carlotta busied herself with the tea, pretending not to hear.

Penn was right. Carlotta was a sealed package. This perversely made Frankie all the more determined. She pressed on. "Did you talk to Ellabella?"

"A little."

"About me?"

"A little. All good things." Carlotta added, "I'm sort of an old friend of their family." She had a great deal to do before her grandson was born, she said. Ariel prepared for all the practical stuff, but not the spiritual. She was going to have Ariel's numerology done, for example. "I know, it's all claptrap. I'm not stupid. But don't you think that there are forces in the universe beyond the things we can measure and see?"

"I guess I don't," Frankie said. "I respect other people's ways of seeing things, but I believe that everything that's really there can be proven somehow. You can't really see an atom, but you can prove it exists by seeing where it's been." It was another moment between them she would later remember and apply to Carlotta, a woman no one really knew except by the path she left.

"I don't get all that stuff. You're one of those genius kids."

"Hardly. I had to work hard for every grade I got, Carlotta."

"Wonder is wonder. Maybe scientists just call it one thing, and saints call it another thing."

"That's possible," Frankie said.

"It's nice of you that you didn't get insulting on me. When people believe something you don't believe, they insult you. When they have a dollar more than you have in your jeans, they insult you. I've had it happen more times than you can shake a stick at. I think it makes them feel powerful." She added, "People must say you are like Mack. But I would not say that. You're like your mom. She had a graceful spirit. That was it, a graceful spirit to all the strays. She was above the pack and she could have acted like that, but she never did. There was always room at the table."

It was a pretty insightful thing to say. There was just something about Carlotta… Frankie guessed that this was what people meant by charisma. It was more than looks or brains or sexual alchemy, more even than charm.

"Ariel says you stayed right at her side all those years."

Aware that the door was again ajar, Frankie said, "I hope so."

"But now everything is tied up in knots for you two."

"Things have changed."

"But Ariel hasn't changed. She's the same girl she was before the wedding."

That was precisely what Penn had said; but that simple-seeming affirmation ignored a whole universe of choices and emotions. "That's like saying nothing we do changes us. In those stories, they always say, *he was a nice kid, he was quiet and polite, he kept to himself*, but then one day, he kills his whole family. Was he still that quiet, polite kid the day after?" Carlotta looked down at her hands, turning palms up, palms down. There was nothing she could say. The prudent choice was to let Frankie double back on her own absurd comparison. "It's not as though she did anything bad. But she did something wrong. And she didn't have the decency to tell me. So now I can't trust her."

"What would happen if you do?"

"It's too big a risk."

"So if you trust her again, she could hurt you."

Frankie said, "Exactly."

"But she already hurt you. You already don't trust her. All you risk is finding out that you were right."

Frankie shrugged.

As Carlotta left, she turned back to thank Frankie for the promise of the photos. "Could I come back to visit sometime?" she asked, and Frankie told her of course.

After she left, Gil emerged from the bedroom. One of his greatest joys on earth was to sleep in the sunlight, and he had been doing just that, supine on their bed washed in the honeyed light of the eastward-facing window. "I don't mean to eavesdrop, Frankie," he said. "But around here, you'd have to be standing out on a sandbar to avoid overhearing some domestic melodrama."

"I forgot you were there."

"Not to mention, if she had been here five more minutes, my bladder would have burst."

"What are you up to?"

"Actually, I don't know if you remembered, but my mother is coming on Tuesday… I didn't know what we should do around here…"

To her shame, Frankie had indeed forgotten. For their wedding, it had once been understood that Mrs. Beveque would stay in the bigger house, but with Carlotta hosting barbecues and Frankie's grandfather now staying on for Frankie's wedding and the upcoming birth of his grandson, Tall Trees seemed to have shrunk. Their cottage did have two small bedrooms upstairs, which would give Mrs. Beveque more privacy. But Frankie now worried aloud about the stairs, how long the water took to get hot in the bathroom up there, her having to come down whenever she wanted a cup of tea… Mrs. Beveque—Frankie realized she didn't know her first name—was staying just over two weeks with them, while the rest of the family, his brothers and a close cousin, would arrive two days before the wedding and leave two days afterward.

"She's Canadian, Frankie. She's used to a bit of a chill," Gil said. "And she's only sixty years old. Her knees are better than mine. I'll go get one of those electric kettles and a box of Builder's tea and some biscuits and put it all on a tray up there. She'll be happy as a queen. I actually prefer to have her here. I would have asked you sooner, but I didn't know if Americans thought family staying with them was too much…"

"Not at all! And if other Americans thought that, I wouldn't.

But you're okay with your brothers and their families being at the beach club?"

"Luc and Jeanne say the little girls are making all the children at school hate them saying, *we are going to stay in a grand hotel by the sea.* If we put them anywhere else, they would consider it child neglect."

"And they know that my dad is picking up the tab..."

"The tab?"

"Paying for it." Gil nodded as Frankie said, "That is, in fact, something Americans do. The bride's family provides for the guests."

"They're grateful. These boys aren't surgeons. Luc's a primary-school teacher, and Olivier runs the bakery with my father and mother." Since the Boulangerie Beveque had recently expanded to a second store, Gil's father, Thomas, regretfully remained behind, promising to join them for Christmas and the birth of the baby. One of the brothers would phone him in for the ceremony, so he could at least make a toast.

"So you're the big success story."

"That's what all the girls say."

"When you're out, buy her...flowers and something pretty... a pretty robe or...not one for a lumberjack, not flannel, something silky, ivory or lavender. Get some big fluffy bath towels. And get things she likes for breakfast, because most of the dinners will be at restaurants or some fish-boil thing my father has some caterer coming to do. And make sure you—"

"I've got it all under control."

After he left, Frankie called Ellabella and asked if they could possibly do their photo shoot the following day, since she was preparing for guests. If she waited any longer, until after their wedding, the weather was sure to turn on them. It was benevolent now, low in the seventies with a powder-blue napkin of sky. She would be happy, Frankie thought, to get back in the water however briefly. Though she paddled in the pool daily, she hadn't been in salt water since she arrived back home the month before. Ellabella agreed to let Frankie photograph her glorious bod, both in the pool and in the salt pond, in exchange for the completion of their chat. She told Frankie she'd spoken about her with some of her professors, to several collectors of her photos, to one of her grade-school teachers (Mrs. Firth, fourth grade), to her aunts and grandmother. About this last Frankie knew because Granny Becky had called to complain. "She's very inquiring all right. That's Kitty Steinway's daughter, isn't it? I turned it around on her. I asked her if she thought your work and your father's work on behalf of ocean creatures was valid, when human children are hungry."

On a day so still and hot for fall that even the birds seemed breathless, Ellabella showed up, announcing herself ready for her close-up. "Will people be able to tell it's me?"

"Yep," Frankie said.

"Oh good. So it's not going to be, you know, pornography?"

"High art," Frankie reassured her. "But I will let you see the photos and most of the time we can eliminate anything that makes you uncomfortable. I say most of the time, because if I really love something, I might fight you on it, which is where you have an advantage over a Royal gramma fish or a reef shark. They have to take what they get. This is the real reason that I don't photograph humans. I'm going to pretend you're a mermaid."

That was how she looked underwater. In traditional merlore, mermaids were supposed to be fierce and bloodthirsty predators, who wanted sailors not for kissing but for devouring, anything but the sexy little jollypops of Disney movies. Still, Ellabella looked like a creature of two worlds, a long pale petal of light poured into the darker medium, her blond hair arrayed around her head like a coronet. Sinking beneath her, Frankie focused upward at Ellabella's arched and outstretched form, betting on the position of the sun, which, in the later images, seemed to burst from the woman's shoulders, as if she were falling from the water into the sky.

She felt good to have her trusty Sony A7R back in her hands. In its Nauticam housing, it was the best combination of camera and protector she had ever used, including all the ones she'd borrowed for an hour to try. Some of her cameras were older, some newer, all except one secondhand, and she always brought at least one extra, both so that she could switch to wide-angle shots, but also in case something on her primary rig failed. When she could, she employed a local dive guide to carry extra gear, her snoots and fluorescent filters.

No race car driver ever babied his rig more obsessively. Her small climate-controlled dry cabinet went with her everywhere she traveled and, though she jumped from boats into freezing water, was tossed end over end by waves, beslimed in mud and sand, when she finished each day, no matter how exhausted or even bruised she was, she went through the obsessive ritual of swabbing and housing her camera and paid to have it lab-cleaned every couple of months.

It took Frankie forty minutes to get what she wanted, and then the two of them just drifted, lying splayed across floats, Ellabella naked and Frankie in her underwear. Frankie wanted to know when the story about her would appear and Ellabella said it was scheduled for the magazine insert cover in two weeks' time. "I have to ask you about your father and Ariel, you know. You can just refuse to talk about it if you want, but, honestly, if I were you, I'd just say something plain that wouldn't open a can of worms."

"That's not fair, though. That's about my father, it's not about me."

"But your father is who he is. And strictly speaking, you wouldn't be who you are if he wasn't who he is."

"The jury might still be out on that."

"I want to say that you would not be who you are without Mack."

"I had Beatrice too," I said. "And she was really the force behind the Saltwater Foundation and all the grassroots projects and community-based research that it pays for. She loved the sea and sea animals."

"But she was primarily a painter. Not a wildlife biologist. Not someone who could put together what people could really do for the animals in their rivers and oceans."

One of Saltwater's defining characteristics had always been the small grants it awarded to unlikely activists. In Bangalore, the so-called crane keepers were children who quietly reported on tourists who might put too much photographer's pressure on the revered Sarus cranes: the keepers could redeem their tokens for books and bicycles. Saltwater donated lavish kits for elementary-school teachers to study sea-otter awareness and then sponsored field trips to aquariums and other marine institutions vested in protecting the creatures. The organization gave stipends to Mexican fishermen to take several seasons off and allow populations of rare porpoises to recover. The companies that supported Saltwater, many of them family-owned businesses, liked the small, specific, hands-on nature of the projects and the fact that the efforts could be self-sustaining once they were set up. Ariel's gift for connecting the right people with the right cause was in no small part to thank for the foundation's prospering. That was much on Frankie's mind as she tried to shape an answer to Ellabella's question. "How much does anyone understand someone else's marriage? It's certainly easy to see that my father and Ariel are happy. And I suppose that there are plenty of relationships where the people don't have as much in common."

"Good," Ellabella said. "That's what I meant. People can take from it whatever they want. You could be saying the same thing about peanut butter and jelly." She lay still. "What do you find underwater? Give me one word. Two words."

"Silence," Frankie said. "And color. You know how it is when you see a shell and it's silver and lavender and orange? Then it dries out and it's just a shell? That's what I mean." She added that it wasn't really silent underwater, telling Ellabella that sperm whales made clicking noises so loud that above the surface they couldn't even be processed by your ears as sound: some said those clicks could blow out a human eardrum.

At that moment, Penn came trudging up from the pier with a load of muddy slickers and boots slung over one shoulder. "Whoa! No!" he cried when he caught sight of the two of them. Both women quickly rolled into the water neck-deep. "Think about it, Ellabella. You go your whole life trying not to be a pervert and think about other people's sex lives, so then, in a couple of weeks, the sex-lives smorgasbord is delivered straight to your own backyard."

"I can quote you on that, right?" she said. "Come on, Penn! I'm a divorced woman now, and you know what kinds of shenanigans they get up to."

"Not to mention the other person in the pond is my sister."

As Penn began sluicing the boots and coats with the power spray from the hose, Ellabella said, "I hear that Ariel and Mack and Penn have a new roommate."

"How the hell do you hear news like that? And who would care?"

"Don't be silly, Frankie. Ariel's mother is kind of a celebrated character even among a big cast of characters around here." Ellabella swam to the edge of the pond and hoisted herself out with toned shoulders, flashing Penn before she pulled one of the ragged beach towels around her like a sarong. He pointed the power nozzle of the hose at her before shaking his head and turning back to his task. "He's so cute. Maybe I should… Would you mind?"

"My brother's romances are entirely his affair. As it were."

"She had an affair with my father."

Frankie had to briefly orient herself and backtrack through that cast of characters. So far as she knew, Kenny and Kitty had been married since people lived in trees. Ellabella had two older brothers and one younger brother indistinguishable from Kenny and from each other, all chiseled from the same block of New England granite, and then this swan.

Ellabella added, "And with your father."

Frankie rolled on to the bank, toweling herself thoroughly and roughly, slipping quickly into her sweatshirt and the pair of Gil's jeans that would still close around her middle. She shoved her feet into the ragged sneakers she'd cut open to fit her swollen feet. "That's not even remotely possible, but before I say anything to you, or even ask a single question, you have to promise me that not one word of this is going into some article that is apparently only incidentally about my work..."

"I would never..."

"Because even if all of that was just a rumor, if it got out, it would break Ariel's heart."

"And you so care about breaking Ariel's heart."

Frankie leveled her eyes and drilled into Ellabella's. "I think you need to leave now. You had me fooled for a minute there. But you haven't changed. Small-town gossip. That's the perfect medium for you, Ellabella."

Ella literally reached out and took Frankie's arm. Frankie shook off her hand.

"I apologize. First of all, I give you my word that none of this gossip, and it is gossip, would ever go into anything I write. But not because I want to hide it, or because I'm sucking up to you. It's because it's not relevant to this story. I take this seriously. I'm going to do it for my life, hopefully not stuck on this suffocating little island. Second, I have changed. I'm not that mean, spoiled girl I was when we were in high school.

And third, maybe most important, would you really prefer I not tell you the things people say, Frankie? Like, if I don't say it, it won't be true?"

"I just don't care."

"But you do care," Ellabella said staunchly. "If you didn't care, you wouldn't be mad."

"You have such deep insights now. Who would have thought?"

"You're just killing the messenger."

Frankie turned away to look out across the ruffling surface of the ocean...*never the same for an hour*...and what occurred to her was: Why did she think that Gil would be unlike these other men? Why did she believe her own story would be a different story? Ellabella was speaking and Frankie turned back, ashamed for snapping at her. As it transpired, the Ballengers had separated when Kenny wanted to sell their Boston town house and build a bigger place here. Kitty thought it would be a living death. Kenny was sick of Kitty's status-seeking: he told her that she could not will herself into being Back Bay no matter how hard she tried, she would always be a girl who grew up in Dorchester. The standoff lasted a long time, which was why Ellabella's two brothers were so much older. She was the symbol of her parents' reconciliation, followed closely by one final brother to seal the deal. But while Kenny was on his own, living at the beach club, he'd eaten dinner every night in the bar where the fiery bartender kept everyone's spirits up, singing Patsy Cline along with the jukebox as the night went long.

A friend of the family.

"Okay, you're right," she admitted. "So what happened with my...with Mack?"

"I don't know if this is true, but according to her—"

"You asked Carlotta?"

"She volunteered it, Frankie. Can you imagine a situation where I said *Hey, did you ever happen to sleep with the old man your daughter just married?*"

"That is so, so, so creepy when you put it that way," Frankie said. "And how could it be, anyhow? My mom was just out of college when they got married."

"Same setup. I guess he was just getting started at the college, young professor, ate at the beach club on Saturday nights when he couldn't stand the cafeteria food..."

"Why in the hell would she tell you? Do you think she wants Ariel to know for some twisted reason?"

"Beats me. Mack would have been early thirties when he came here from...where is he from?"

"North Carolina. Years ago, though," Frankie let the numbers roll around. "How old could she have been, though? Twenty? Not even. Eighteen? Nineteen?"

Ellabella sat silent, the import of the assertion swinging like a weight between them. Then she toweled off and slipped into her black linen pants and top. "I love my dad, and you love your dad, and the past is the past. As far as I'm concerned, this stops here."

Impulsively, Frankie leaned over and hugged Ellabella, another unforetold moment in a day of them. Though nausea churned her stomach, filling her mouth with saliva, she had no choice but to fake much more sangfroid than she felt. In parting she said, "You know? We should have raised our parents better."

6

White roses, tangerine dahlias like the sun-kissed faces of children, tiny ropes and spikes of elegantly twirled greenery. Her bouquet pleased her so much that she got up twice the night before the wedding to open the fridge and hold it heavy in her hand, then nestle it back beside the corsage of cymbidium orchids Gil would wear. Neither Frankie nor Gil had elected someone to stand up with them since, in ordinary times, Frankie would have chosen Ariel as maid of honor and Gil would have had to single out one of his three brothers for best man. The judge who'd agreed to come to the backyard pergola for the ceremony said that anyone nearby might volunteer as a witness. The previous evening, Gil and his brothers had strung fairy lights over the eaves and placed a giant copper bowl of football cremones and coppery cushion mums with sprigs of thistle in cornflower blue on the mantel of the giant fireplace where the young Frankie and Penn used to hang their Christmas stockings. If she looked to the right from her window, she could see the delicate sparkling.

The next time she looked out of this window into the night, she would be a wife.

That girlhood playhouse dream was coming true, in exactly the spot where Frankie had dreamed it. She had not imagined that the prospect of domesticity, of putting down roots, would bring her so much happiness. Even with all the bumps in the road, she relished the idea. When she looked around her at marriages she knew, as she sometimes did, they seemed unequally weighted. Maybe the husband extravagantly adored the wife, but she still shouldered most of the work of home and hearth. Maybe the wife presented a merry face in public, but in private, she disdained the man she'd once loved. Maybe what the husband and wife had was no more than a lifelong friendship that grew green from the ashes of passion. And yet, here she was on the selfsame cliff, about to jump, certain in the way that some eager brides must be certain that they were a delicate and perfect pairing, like how the Amarone della Valpolicella in Italy, of which she took a single sip, belonged with asiago cheese, like a sailboat in yellow and blue, like pizza and beer, like macaroni and cheese, like Chandler and Joey, like Holmes and Watson, like Marvin Gaye and Tammi Terrell. She would never disdain her Gil. He would never try to make her into a domestic. And…at the end of the day, what was wrong with a lifelong friendship and the memories of a grand passion?

At that moment, for the first time, Frankie felt the baby kick.

It was unmistakable, not a flutter or a nudge, but an assertive thump. She'd been worried. People said you felt strong kicks all the time, certainly after the fifth month. But although the baby's heartbeat was strong (and Frankie, guiltily, had purchased a stethoscope to be certain), he had been an otherwise quiet traveler. While she had seen the baby in otherworldly ultrasound pictures, these had seemed more alien to her, and not because of the outsized cranium and spindly body. The pictures were like a translation of motherhood, a clinical surveyor's map.

This was something else. "Hello, stranger," Frankie said, and, like the cliché she was more each day, she burst into tears. She called Gil's phone and shouted out the news, but he was with his brothers (and her brother and her father and her grandfather) at some fishers' dive where it sounded as though the primary occupation was breaking glass.

"That's thrilling, *chérie*!" Gil called out. "It's thrilling! I wish I were there. But I'm afraid I would not be able to walk through the door if I were there because these men drink too much alcohol."

"Why does their drinking alcohol affect you?"

"Because I am what Americans call a good sport," Gil retorted. "They buy drinks for me, and I drink them."

She said, "I see."

Although Gil had planned to come home that night, his mother was adamant. "*Pas avant le*...the wedding!" she said. Somehow, Madame Beveque, whose given name was Giselle and who insisted that Frankie call her *Maman*, which also brought a flood of tears to Frankie's eyes, imagined that the wedding was being held in a church. A cradle Catholic, she further assumed, Gil translated rapidly, that Frankie would lay her flowers at the feet of the Virgin, and that she, Giselle, would walk Gil down the aisle before Mack walked Frankie down the aisle, as French mothers did. She also expected that, instead of "I do," Gil and Frankie would repeat *"Oui, je le veux,"* which translated sort of as *I take you*, and she had found a patisserie which assembled a pyramid of cream puffs nearly three feet tall, the traditional *croquembouche*. "You don't have to agree to any of this," Gil assured Frankie, who agreed to all of it, particularly after Giselle placed her light hands on either side of Frankie's face and exclaimed, "*Si belle* and *si intelligente!*" There was no aisle, so Mack would walk with Frankie from the door of her house to the pergola, as brides did in French villages. Gil then asked if Frankie happened to have a statute of the Virgin Mary around anywhere… It didn't seem to be the kind of thing you could rent. Gil did find one, however, and when Frankie, astounded, asked, "Where on earth…?" Gil answered, "You don't want to know," whereupon she realized it would have been at a place that sold tombstones. ("We're called *memorial masons*, these days," the proprietor assured Gil, when he balked at taking the man's card two days before his wedding.)

That night, after Gil hung up, Giselle made her way down the stairs.

"I hope you don't think that I am busy," she said and Frankie knew she meant *nosy.* She'd overheard Frankie shouting the news of the baby moving into the phone, and Frankie apologized for the interruption. "I won't touch you," she told Frankie, but she held her hands in the vicinity of Frankie's belly and murmured what Frankie could not help recognize as a blessing. She gazed at Frankie then and said, "It is so cruel that your own mother is not with you. Isn't it? I can't be your mother, but I promise this to you. I will be as a mother to you whenever you want me to be. And I will never take Gil's part against you, which my *belle-mère* did to me, and she still does. Yes, she is still alive, she is the age of your *grandpère*, sadly, and you will meet her. She will never die. She is a cow."

And then Frankie couldn't sleep, because she kept laughing. ("She is a cow," she kept saying to herself.)

When the sun splashed over the sea, she finally slept, waking to noon light and a shadow over her bed. She said, "Gil?" But it was Penn.

"I have to tell you something," he said.

"Grandpa died?"

"Grandpa's fine. It's…it's Dad. And Ariel."

Frankie sat up, clutching the white star comforter Giselle had hand-quilted for a wedding gift, along with a duplicate in a smaller size for her unborn grandson. "What's the matter? The baby?" Indeed, the baby was late, but only by a week or a little more. "Penn, whatever this is, you're making it worse by not telling me right straight out."

"Ariel just went into the hospital," Penn said.

"She's having the baby today?"

"That's the idea."

"I don't get it."

"The labor is being induced."

"What? Why?"

"Because the baby is supposed to be born today. Carlotta did Ariel's chart…"

"Her chart?"

"Her numerology numbers, for her and the baby. And it has to be today because otherwise, I don't know, there's some ancient Celtic curse that will come down…"

Frankie tried to smile. "Okay, I know you heard her talking about doing Ariel's numerology." She studied Penn's face. "So you are joking. Not funny. Cut it out." Firstborn babies were often late to arrive, Frankie added, and this baby was just a week or so overdue, from what Ariel had said earlier. She went on for a moment, then noticed that Penn was still standing silent and apparently mournful. "Frankie, I'm telling you the truth."

"You are," Frankie said. "I should have known better. You're not kidding."

"They wanted me to tell you that they couldn't come, but that Dad would still pay for the wedding dinner—" Frankie rolled over and grabbed her phone. "Franny Frank, don't. It's your wedding day. Don't upset yourself."

"So it's me, upsetting myself? That's how you see it? They sent you to tell me?" Into the phone, she shouted, "Dad! Pick up! Pick up right now or you'll regret it." She immediately dialed back. "Dad!" There was a click as Frankie switched over to speaker, Gil and Giselle watching anxiously from the door. "Penn is under the impression that you're using some numerology thing to have the baby today."

"I'm so sorry, Frankie. Please forgive me. I can't talk. They're just taking us into the labor and delivery—"

"Wait. This is real?"

"I'm so sorry, honey. I'm so sorry. If it were any other day..."

"Any other day? Except your only daughter's wedding day?"

"Ariel was afraid something bad would happen if she didn't. She was going crazy with anxiety. I know it sounds ridiculous, but Carlotta insisted, and she has more hold over Ariel than you know, Frankie. You know, I don't believe in this stuff at all but...what can I do? I'll make it up to you, Frankie. I promise."

Frankie said softly, "You can never make it up to me."

"But I will." He dropped his voice. "Frankie, she's young, and it's her first baby..."

Frankie yelled so loud that all three of the others jumped. "Do you even hear yourself? Do you even hear what you're saying?" She added, "Do doctors just let you have your baby anytime you want?"

"Sure," her father told her. "If the baby is healthy, and they were going to induce soon anyway, like tomorrow, given that Ariel is already late. And you know some people have special reasons for having the baby right then, like the husband is deployed overseas or..." Mack was still talking when Frankie pushed the button, disconnecting him. She turned off the phone.

"I should probably go. He wants me to go back there," Penn said miserably.

"Go ahead. But if you do, even for five minutes, I swear to you this. I will never speak to you again in my life. That's nonnegotiable."

"Frankie," Penn said.

"In my life. Ever."

She heard Gil's voice. "Frankie, you're putting Penn in a hard place." To his mother, he said, "Don't worry, I'm not coming in."

"I'm Penn's sister. I'm his closest relative. It's my wedding day. If he leaves me too, it's for good."

From the front door, Gil's brother Luc said, "She's right, you know! She's absolutely right. Have some balls, Penn."

"I know you're well-meaning here, but you have stay out of this," Gil told Luc. He didn't walk into the house, but his mother chimed in along with two of his sisters-in-law, all in agreement with Frankie.

"Perhaps we should all go to this hotel for breakfast," said Giselle. "Not you, Gil. You should have some coffee and a sleep because you look very sick. We could go to this hotel and have some coffee and a pastry."

They went, Penn stopping to collect Grandpa Frank, who also, blessedly, pronounced this turn of events *preposterous*. In a state of unnatural calm, Frankie studied the table, the little girls leaping up to run to the plate-glass windows and look at the ocean, the sisters-in-law smoking in the nonsmoking dining room, gossiping in French, their updos as perfect as if they'd walked out of salons, Gil beside her, offering the pale-cheeked Penn a dry toast and a glass of champagne with his coffee. *This is my family now*, she thought. *They are loving people, and I will get used to them. In time, it will feel as though I've known them always. In time it will be as if I never knew Ariel. And as for my father, well, anger will keep me going for a while, and then something else will take its place. He doesn't deserve me.* To her shame, she felt tears gathering on the cliff of her chin, dropping on to the scrambled eggs she couldn't swallow.

"Now this bride should have a quiet nap," Giselle said. "Then she will be ready to take this step. There is plenty of time for other kinds of thinking another day." They headed back to the cottage, and Giselle laid a cool wet cloth over Frankie's eyes, and she lay down to rest.

When Frankie woke, it was late afternoon. She showered and was ravenous, consuming half a coffee cake while the stylist fussed with her hair, sculpting tendril after tendril, then she started in on the bacon. "Now, no more bacon!" the woman scolded, as she cleaned Frankie's rugged hands and nails with pumice and touched the small ovals with pale gloss. "Relax your lips," said the stylist. The photographer showed up, the one-hour shoot a surprise gift from Ellabella, a local woman, intimidated, whom Frankie kindly reassured. Soon she was slipping her dress over her head, stepping into her shoes, with Giselle helping her fasten a small ruby on a light gold chain, which had been Giselle's own mother's. When Frankie thought of Mack or Beatrice, she forced herself to breathe in deeply and out slowly. *Another day. Another day.* She came out into the living room, where her grandfather and Penn were waiting, resplendent in morning suits.

"When I came to visit I never imagined that I would have the chance to walk a bride down the aisle," Grandpa Frank said. "You know, I had sons. I never got the chance to do this."

"Obviously, me either," Penn said. "Franny Frank, I'm so sorry—"

"You don't have to apologize. You did the right thing."

Frankie scanned the small population that would comprise the bride's side of the aisle. Granny Becky and Beatrice's sister Imogen had at first happily accepted, but Grandma had sadly reconsidered a few days later. The sight of Mack and his teen bride, she told Frankie, would be repugnant to her. "I know that this is not what Bea would want me to do. She would want that old fool to be happy, because she thought he hung the moon. I, however, reserve the right to my disgust for this nonsense. I'm afraid Imogen feels the same, although we absolutely grieve to miss seeing our Frankie on your wedding day." Frankie and Gil agreed to come for Thanksgiving with Penn and to stay for a day or two in the big house in Concord where Grandma lived with Aunt Imogen and her pilot husband, Corbley. Frankie's two cousins, both in the air force, would be home for that holiday as well. And that would have to do.

Taking her flowers from Giselle, Frankie waited for Madame Beveque to go outside and join Gil. Then she linked her arm through her grandfather's, and Penn walked beside her too. The sun was just beginning its descent, setting torches to the resplendent red leaves of the trees… October, the extravagant sister, as Oliver Wendell Holmes Sr. called it. Not spring but fall, Frankie thought: that was really the season of beginnings—new sweaters and school shoes, harvest and holidays.

Then it was of Mom she thought, as she gave herself into Gil's arms. He swung her around under the roof of the twinkling little hut, his brothers teasing him that he had to wait for that until they were pronounced man and wife.

I can do this, Frankie thought. *All on my own.* She glanced at Gil. *Except I'm not on my own. This is my family now.*

An older and portly version of Gil, Thomas Beveque appeared in a video call, hurriedly adjusting the top button of his crisp white shirt. He told the couple, "Old saying. *Mangez bien, riez souvent, aimez beaucoup. Félicitations*, Gil! *Bienvenue*, Frankie!"

She made the promises in English and in French. She kissed Gil, whose eyes were bright with tears, then her grandfather and her brother. All around her, faces were soft with joy. Without explanation, as the others stood quietly, she plucked a single blue cornflower from her bouquet and carried it down to the edge of the pond where, in a single breath, she released it to her mother's memory. Then she laid her bouquet at the feet of the tiny stone Madonna that would stand in the same spot for the rest of Frankie's life. As she and Gil made their way to the car, her new sisters-in-law and nieces threw bird seed that felt like the dripping of leaves in the rainforest. *So far? So early? So soon?*

At the Sandpiper, they dined on salmon rolls stuffed with lemon basil ricotta, grilled street corn and raspberry sherbet punch. Frankie fed Gil one of the crispy cream puffs, and she did the same with him. As they drank their tea and coffee, Penn abruptly excused himself to take a phone call. Sensing news, Frankie followed him outside. When he saw her, he held up one palm, pressing the phone to his ear. The wind was kicking up for a storm. Finally, he was finished and returned to Frankie, hugging her shoulder with one hand. "Baby Jesus," he said.

"What are you now, brother? Like, the ex-scion of the Attleboros?"

"Mack's very excited. He said to tell you the baby was eight pounds and seven ounces, but that Ariel was doing fine."

"You must feel the way some of those Fitzroy sons of Henry VIII felt. Maybe he'll give you one of the canoes, because the young prince will have to have the Regent Red..."

Penn pushed away from her, his mouth a compressed line. "What are you needling me for, Frankie? Do you think I'm not upset enough? Do you think I should break something? Would that prove it to you, that your feelings aren't the only feelings?"

He was right, and she was sorry. Her rage was now like a small pet she carried in her arms, protecting it from the elements. But she really had no just cause: she had married without her mother, without her father. Oh, boo-hoo. What a middle-class problem to have. The cost of the single meal they were eating in the restaurant would have fed a third-world village for a month. And yet, the things that wounded a person couldn't be soothed just by relativism. After all, in that third-world village, a girl was getting married tonight, with both her parents beaming at her side.

"Penny, I didn't mean it," she said. Penn didn't look up. "I'm really sorry. I was being an ass. I'm glad the baby's healthy, I guess." Penn widened his eyes, horrified. "I didn't mean it like that! I meant that in spite of all this, I'm glad there's nothing wrong with the baby. Is Carlotta over there?"

Penn nodded. "And I have to face her too? Our lovely permanent houseguest? After this? How are we going to get around this one?"

"I don't know. What did they name it?"

"No name yet."

"Maybe Nemo! That would be good. All seafaring and fishy."

"You can't stop yourself, can you?"

"Well, what? Her mother named her after an animated mermaid! It could be a new tradition."

Penn's mouth twitched with a phantom smile, although he tried to suppress it. "Maybe Simba."

"That's even better," Frankie agreed. "It's the circle of life... Well, I'll name my baby after you."

"Please," Penn said, "one baffling name per family."

But he loved his name and its origin. Once a year for several years a long time ago, Mack took his vanishing-water-wildlife show to Las Vegas, where it gathered a loyal if bemused following in a small theater tucked into the corner of a vast casino next to a coffee shop. With the staccato bells of slot machines chiming and the anguished shouts from the blackjack tables as his background, Mack talked about swordfish and wood storks. One night, he caught sight of the great magician philosopher Penn Jillette in the audience. They met afterward and had dinner, Mack enormously gratified to learn that the admiration was mutual. Mack actually took selfies. A few months later, Mack's son was born, and to his delight, Mack introduced the two Penns when Frankie's brother was a child. Now, Penn recalled, "My own namesake has nothing on me. He named his kid Moxie Crimefighter."

"Gil's fond of this patron saint we heard about in Italy. Saint

Ubaldo. Do you like the ring of that? Ubaldo Attleboro Beveque?"

"It sounds like a swear word. Like, *go Ubaldo Beveque yourself.*"

"Maybe Penn Regent Red Eagle Beveque instead. Like some fur trapper from Marquette and Joliet times."

Penn said, "That sounds like cultural appropriation."

As they chatted, Frankie decided she would definitely have another child after this one, all things going well. Maybe another after that, since she and Penn had often considered what it would be like to have a backup sibling to bitch to when you were mad at the other one. The prickles and snapped threads of jealousy and annoyance were a small price for the essential ease she felt only with Penn, the keeper of her complete history, the one person she could speak to without a need to check or edit herself. "Are you actually jealous?" she asked then.

"Well, if I admitted that, it would make me a small-minded jerk, wouldn't it?" He added, "We'll have to go to see the baby at the hospital. Or, I imagine they let them go home right away these days. Maybe they'll be home in the morning."

Frankie said, "That I won't do. Not now, at least. I have to let things settle first. I don't want to make it worse by pretending I want to make it better."

That night, the wind having lessened, they made a bonfire in the big rock ring behind the cottage. Luc and Olivier sang "O Canada" in French and in English. Madeleine and Simone had their first s'mores, Simone asking suspiciously in French why Canadian children didn't get to have these treats more often and Giselle telling her teasingly in English that Canadian children had lovely real desserts that were never burned, like *Grand-mère*'s *Mogador Saint Honoré* and Uncle Olivier's opera cake…

"You are a pastry snob," Gil told his mother. "I like graham crackers and Hershey bars. I like hot dogs and pizza."

"Please, no," said Giselle. "I'm old. I can't hear this."

Frankie nearly fell asleep leaning on Gil's shoulder as the little girls blew soap bubbles toward the moon.

The next day, Frankie went to Chatham in a group of all the Beveques, who had promised souvenirs apparently to everyone they knew. They would all depart the next day, but Giselle was coming back for several weeks at Christmas. They had lunch at the Yankee, where Frankie wistfully regarded the figure-head angel in front and thought of Ariel. Not ten minutes later, Ariel texted a picture of a swaddled little baby with a great deal of dark hair, healthy-looking and rosy. Frankie texted back an emoji, having to search for one because she never used them, the most generic thumbs-up she could find. The next photo was of the baby flanked by Mack, looking haggard, and Ariel, looking serene and triumphant. That time, Frankie texted back nothing. No third photo arrived. No further apology or rebound congratulations on her wedding. Many people, she knew, believed that even to raise a sore subject was to exacerbate it, but the lapse felt cruel and deliberate. In truth, they hadn't ruined her day at all. In every respect but this, the day had been everything Frankie wanted. She understood that Mack was selfish—he had always been selfish—and that Ariel was enthralled by the mother she thought she had lost so long ago. Under stress, people did incomprehensible things that made no sense to anyone other than themselves. Still, it was as if she had emerged from her shell and shaken off her feathers to become a different creature. While she wished Mack felt more of an attachment to her, in that moment, she felt almost none to him.

Waking with Gil in their own small home, falling asleep with him at night, watching as he researched the next article for EnGarde, as he put on his glasses and then removed them, as he made his tea and then let it grow cold and made more, she brimmed with contentment. If she had expected to become restive, after years of snatching up her camera bag and pannier and arranging a ride to the next airport, after years of rolling up the same three sets of clothing in plastic zip bags, her water-proof layers, her flexible wet suit, she liked having possessions to choose from, drawers that held nightgowns and sweaters and underwear. She liked buying more of them, though, on a daily basis, she still wore forgiving leggings and sweatpants.

Walking the roads and the beach, cocooned in her light puffy coat, she auditioned ways to compile an account of her first roaming years, the loneliness and the dirtiness and the occasional terror, the exaltation and tenderness. A memoir with photos? A coffee-table photo book with cursory stories? If she wrote a memoir, she would be one of those silly people who hadn't lived long enough to justify a memoir, but wrote one anyway.

Still, she knew she had stories to tell.

Once, deep down in the Bahamas, she came upon a full skeleton wearing diving gear. She panicked and almost arrowed for the surface but forced herself to slow down and do her decompression stops. It was, after all, a skeleton, so it had been there a long time, her mind kept lecturing her. Whatever accident or mishap had killed him was long gone. She would later learn that the man, an American, was a suicide or a murder victim, as his oxygen was turned entirely off. Another time, during her one and brief trip to Alaska, she surfaced nearly face-to-face with a polar bear. Deep in a cold Scottish lake, her headlamp suddenly revealed four figures seated at a table with a teapot and cups. All of them were mannequins. How, she wondered, did the person who elaborately arranged this scene enjoy people's reactions? Did he just think about it, or was there a camera in a housing somewhere that detected motion? If so, it could not have been human motion too often. The thought of that, in the depthless darkness that extended only to the penumbra surrounding her flashlight, made Frankie's breath come faster. These lochs sometimes were home to giant eels, and Frankie didn't like even the small kind. Eels were monsters: they comprised everything that was upsetting about dark water. She'd spent four delirious days in a New Zealand hospital after being stung by a ray...and two more after an encounter with a hundred-and-fifty-pound catfish in the Rhône River. Once, she and an acquaintance splashed joyously into the water off the storied beach at Waikiki, and within seconds, the other woman was stung by a jellyfish and went into a coma from which she died, days later, the most evolved creature slain by the most elemental. A jellyfish had no heart and no mind: it was ninety-nine percent water.

Occasionally, her bad luck was her own fault. Wading out from a beach near Savusavu in Fiji, she wanted to take pictures of the same scene, above and below the water line. Slowly, she went deeper and still deeper, entranced by the drop-off from the white sand with its cartoonish bright blue starfish to an abyss where huge creatures drifted, what she thought was a dogtooth tuna, something silvery with a fin...a marlin? She was alone, violating every rule of diving, but she wore only a mask and snorkel, she wasn't going down deep, and what could befall her in water barely up to her chest? The current took her, hard and unexpected. Struggling to protect her camera, she fought to find her feet and bully her way back to the beach, but she was going fast, shockingly fast, scraped by coral and boulders. Finally, she was able to cling to a clump of floating vegetation, almost like a three-foot island. There was no way back except to work with the current and hope to get close enough to pick her way to the shore. When she was a child, she'd been afraid not of the comfortable exposed basement with its plushy rec room but of the cellars behind it—hardly a dungeon, but to her child's eyes, a cavern lit by weird blue fluorescents with storage shelves and the washing machine. When she had to bring laundry up, Beatrice would obligingly wait for her at the top of the stairs, playing out her voice as a guide line. "Go, Frankie, go!" she would call, over and over, as the little girl scurried, "Go, Frankie, go!" And that was what Frankie had done. She steeled herself, repeating that childhood cheer, until, battered and breathless, she was able to drag herself up on an inhospitable pile of black rocks a quarter mile from the beach. For hours, how many she didn't know, she slept on those rocks, waking when it was nearly dark, stumbling back to the guest house.

Her encounters with land creatures also could be harrowing. When a group of feral teens in Brazil along the Amazon stole two of her best cameras and backpacks, she had to buy back her possessions as they threatened her with poison darts. Lost, on that same trip, with no more than half a cup of water in her canteen, she pulled branches over herself, making a cursory shelter for two miserable days of stupefying sun, two nights of stinging ants and unblinking yellow eyes in the darkness, as she set off flare after flare, finally attracting the attention of a group of local women. She'd been frighteningly cold, dizzyingly hot, so filthy she would not have recognized her own face in a mirror, so lacerated and swollen with infected bites that her nerves sang with fever and pain. She considered herself a fastidious person, one who jumped if she saw a mouse in the kitchen, who liked the smell of pomegranate shower gel and soft sheets dried in the sun. After every one of those encounters, she would say to herself, *That's it, I'm finished. There has to be a safe and marginally more comfortable way of making a living.* After weeks away from the water, she had to talk herself into getting back in. But once under, the romance reclaimed her. She was captivated; she would wonder how she had stayed away so long.

There were the many events that were phenomenal in their tender majesty, among them her witnessing a sea otter giving birth underwater off the Monterey coast, or fleets of newborn turtles flying through the deeps at the Great Barrier Reef.

Now she was faced with a stretch of landlocked time. How could she tell those stories?

Words for what she meant to do with her pictures tumbled over and over in her mind. Although as a documentary photographer, she tried to stay away from playing with effects, photography was the art of capturing light. She crisscrossed the world doing that.

She traveled.

She worked with what light was available.

Available light, she thought. *Available Light.*

If I write a memoir, I will call it that.

"I'm going to write a book," she told Gil that night.

"Brilliant," he said. He didn't look up.

They'd recently had the cottage equipped with Wi-Fi, instead of pirating off the library or the main house. Since the moment it went live, Gil had hunched over his computer, making notes for his article on the conversion of foreclosed farms to wildlife habitat. He would leave for two weeks around Thanksgiving, an interval Frankie dreaded now that their community had shrunk to two, sometimes three with Penn or four with Ellabella, who actually was casually dating Frankie's brother, and sometimes including Grandpa Frank, who would be leaving in a week. His leaving was an occasion Frankie also dreaded, for would she ever see her grandfather again? He was absolutely hale and strong, but how long could a person live? It would not take much to take him out, as she had learned from the loss of her mother. Terrors concerning the health of their son were piling up too. It amazed her that anyone survived to be born, much less grow to adulthood. The world was mined with perils of every description. She could go with Gil, but it might be too late in the pregnancy for her to travel. Giselle would return, from just after Thanksgiving for their baby's birth, to be at her side, but still Frankie was not comforted. Sleepless and fretful, she indulged herself in dark fantasies of birth accidents, hospital viruses, catastrophic weather.

Centering her mind on real perils she'd already survived might help, she thought. Along with her images, a book might be another way to seize the hearts of those who could make a difference to the health of the ocean and its creatures.

She wasn't a writer, though, she reminded herself.

But Gil was. He would help her. Perhaps she could give it a try.

"I really am going to write a book," she said.

Gil said, "Good. Good idea."

"I've decided on the title. I'm going to call it—here is the title—*Shove This Battleship Up Your Ass*," Frankie told Gil, who clearly was not listening.

"Brilliant," he said.

Frankie sat down that night with her laptop. Write a couple of pages. Commit only to that, she suggested to herself.

It began with terror, she wrote.

I was seven years old, and my mother and I were piloting our big kayak on the Bass River. We had a sturdy tandem kayak, the kind with actual seats instead of slots, what you call a sit on top *kayak. They last forever. I still have it. My mother was teaching me the pace of the paddling motion when suddenly there was a hard bump, and the bow, the place where I was seated, lifted out of the water. It was just an inch or two, and we plopped safely back down into the water. But still, a feeling came over me. There was something nearby, something big and wild and alive. "Did we hit a rock?" I asked my mom. She put one finger against her lips and motioned for me to take my paddle out of the water. Then I saw the huge pale body glide under our craft. Our big and sturdy kayak felt as frail as a paper envelope. "What's that?" I said. But I already knew. I've never seen another great white anywhere near that place…*

She would pair the writing with a photo Abram Murphy

had taken long ago in Hawaii of her shooting a great white shark while swimming a few feet under its enormous belly.

Slowly, each night, she added a page, then another. Her first dives. Her first photos. The growing conviction that this way to see the sea was a vocation rather than a hobby. Her first publication. Her first assignment. The first time she was invited by a gallery. The way that the size and shape of her pictures evolved, inspired by her mother's paintings. The urgency to tell it consumed her. Being a first-time mother would be a full-time job. She didn't want to run out of time.

As she left for a walk one dark morning, Frankie found a large cream-colored envelope tucked into the back door. Inside, on engraved stationery, was a note. Signed by her father and Ariel, it thanked her for the large framed print and the file of all the photos from the wedding they could choose to have copied for a book. That was it—no congratulations, no acknowledgment of her wedding in any way. She guessed Mack was more upset than Frankie realized. But then, so was she.

Mack also reminded Frankie that she was expected at the annual donors' banquet of the Saltwater Foundation the following week. Frankie had, after all, taken Beatrice's place on the board of directors. No matter how she was feeling, Mack wrote (how she was *feeling*, Frankie scoffed in her mind), to absent herself from the event would be to cause talk, and that kind of talk could only damage the mission of the organization to which he (and Beatrice) had given so much of their lives.

"You have to go," Gil said, reading over Frankie's shoulder. "You'll just have to take a break from writing *Shove This Battleship Up Your Ass.*"

"You heard me!" she chided him.

"Of course I heard you. I like to foster that image of me being the woolly-minded researcher."

"If I have to go, you have to go with me. It's a husband's duty. You're the one who insisted we get married. Promise!"

Although he famously hated dress-up occasions and had told anyone who would listen that he next intended to wear a suit to their child's wedding or his own funeral, Gil agreed. They would share a table with Penn and with Frankie's grandfather, his last night on Cape Cod.

Even the yellow-colored dress was an impossibility at this point so Frankie turned to Irene, the friend of Beatrice's who'd designed her prom dress so many years ago. There was no time, Frankie apologized in advance. She knew there wasn't enough time, but perhaps there was something Irene already had? Some costume or… But though there was no way to do it in a week, Irene made Frankie a knee-length, long-sleeved dress in a stretchy, but not tacky, silky silver-green fabric, with a dramatic draped panel that dropped from one shoulder to the floor.

As she and Gil walked into the banquet hall with her grandfather, she saw the room transformed. To the strains of Saint-Saëns's "Aquarium" from *Carnival of the Animals*, four wall-sized fabric screens displayed a slow rotation of images. To her shock, they were all hers, not Abram Murphy's. The expert enhancement and quality of the fabric screens was such that the photos seemed softly to undulate. In huge blue bowls of sand and shells were flickering candles mounted in glass columns. Attached to each centerpiece was a sign that read *Photography by Saltwater Foundation Trustee Francis Lee Attleboro*.

In the full knowledge that she was being manipulated, Frankie could not help but respond. The setup was beautiful and the innocent joy on her grandfather's face transforming. As had always been the case in recent years, the master of ceremonies was Simon Land from Land Ho! Foods, one of Saltwater's major supporters. When he saw Frankie, he walked over, shook Gil's hand and kissed Frankie's. "I see you've managed to get yourself in trouble, but I'll still marry you," said Simon.

For a moment, Frankie, who'd always had the slightest crush on him as well, thought this might not have been a bad idea.

"Do you think Gil would mind?" Frankie said. "Simon, this is my husband of one month, Gil Beveque, and Gil, one of my oldest friends, and your rival, Simon Land. You see, the thing about Simon is you may have wooed me with words, but he can give me gold doubloons."

"And seltzer!" Simon added. Gil looked hopelessly confused until Simon Land explained that Land Ho!'s signature products were Gold Doubloons, a cheesy popcorn, and Rum Good Seltzer. "I'm giving the baby a lifetime supply, and you can probably have some as well. Seriously, Frankie, I couldn't be happier for you...and I actually do have a gift for the baby." He handed Frankie an envelope, which she later learned was one hundred shares of Disney stock. Simon then called the audience to take their seats and began his introduction of Mack with a reference to Frankie's extraordinary photographs. "This is why a picture is worth a thousand words, folks. You can yak all you want, but bad or good, a picture communicates everything. This," he said as he gestured around the hall, "is what we're fighting for and what Mack Attleboro has fought for all his life. And I want to announce that this year, for the first time, Land Ho! is giving a four-year scholarship to a student in the natural sciences, the Beatrice Grace Attleboro Memorial Scholarship." He paused and smiled at Frankie. "If God created the great creatures of the sea and every living thing with which the water teems, as the Bible says, and saw it was good, then surely heaven blessed the Saltwater Foundation with Beatrice, who made it her family's mission to protect those creatures from harm. We know you are with us tonight, Beatrice." Frankie pressed her napkin against her eyes, and Penn squeezed her hand. "When the hat passes to you tonight, give generously in her name."

Mack got up and thanked Simon. He began his talk with a few tales of past deeds of the Saltwater Foundation...helping to outfit boats for the Sea Shepherd Foundation's campaign against whale hunting, enlisting whole communities to protect nesting seabirds from predatory cats and rats, the foundation's role in the reintroduction of Greater Splashspeck cranes to waters from Florida to Rhode Island.

Then, as Frankie had prayed he would not, Mack once more recounted his own twice- (thrice-?) told tale of the Regent Red sea eagle.

"Now, they call this my windmill! Yes, I'm not stupid, and I'm not senile. I know what they say. Twenty years ago, I met an old man in the Hebrides, Bryon Adair was his name, and he swore that his father visited the Regent Red sea eagles in a drowned forest. Like everyone else who's sane..." laughter rippled "...I knew that the Regent Red sea eagle had been extinct since the turn of the previous century, but he was a nice old guy and he brought me tea and a sausage roll, so I put on my wellies and followed him. Followed him through some of the hardest track I've ever tried to cross in my entire life. He was as sure-footed as a little donkey, but I hit my knees at least ten times, and this eighty-year-old guy who's about five six had to help drag me up to my feet. Then we got to the drowned forest, and it was worse. A drowned forest is just what you'd imagine it would be, a woodland that's living almost entirely underwater at least half the time..."

On Mack went. The thorny marshland that was nearly impassable, even in winter, the deep craters of muck he sank in up to his chest, but how it was all worthwhile because "Then, all of a sudden, there they were. Like a dream. These huge beautiful birds with their huge nests in the tops of those trees, two of them circling to go in for fish..." No, he'd never been able to get a photograph: this was before the days when he could have just whipped out his iPhone. By the time he went back, Byron Adair was long gone. Mack said then, "But I'm not finished yet. I'll see that eagle again, and this foundation will help bring that species back from the brink. It's one of the largest eagles to have ever lived. A magnificent creature. What a gift if more people could see it. Next time, I'll bring back slides of one of those bad boys to this banquet, and then who'll be laughing last?"

The bemused looks Frankie had come to dread were now passed from table to table like handshakes at a church service. Mack continued. "Now, if all of you were kids, you would have no trouble believing me, because you'd still think science is magic. And that's what I believe too. What makes me happiest is seeing how excited children get at these lectures and school visits when we tell them that these creatures' future is literally in their hands, that they are the guardians and protectors. As I said, I'm not finished yet, but it gives me great pleasure to tell you that I've done my part to ensure the stewardship of the Saltwater Foundation. You know Ariel Puck as our incredibly capable and personable administrator. But now, she has a new name… Mrs. Ariel Attleboro…"

Frankie wished she would dissolve into her seat like sand or salt when she heard one of the donors whisper, "She married Mack's son? I didn't know that!"

"Ariel isn't here tonight, for reasons I'll soon tell you, but she sends her best to every one of you. I hope you'll help me with our next goal for Ariel. That is, to get her into the water. She curates one of the foremost marine-conservation organizations in the world, and she's named after a mermaid, but she's terrified of water. Maybe she never had anyone to push her before, but trust me, I'll soon take care of that!" There was a slow spatter of applause as the meaning began to sink in for those who didn't already know. He pressed on. "And, as I say, even though I'm not finished yet, by far, I know the future of the Saltwater Foundation into the end of this century is assured by this fellow." Penn looked up with a shy smile, but then, the screens displayed photos of Mack and Ariel's first dance at the wedding, and then of Ariel with the new baby and of Mack and Ariel with the baby. "I want to present the heir to the Saltwater Foundation of the future, my newborn son, Banner Benjamin Attleboro!"

As Mack took questions, Penn quietly set his board of directors' badge on his napkin and slipped away. When he didn't return, Frankie followed him, and Gil followed her. They found her brother standing in the parking lot, smoking a cigar. Miserably and without speaking, they got into the car. Inside their cottage, Gil poured Penn a whiskey. After a long while, Gil asked, "Do you think he even realizes what he's saying?"

"That would mean he wants to hurt Penn, and I'm sure he doesn't want to do that at all," Frankie said. "He's on the outs with me, not Penn."

"He's an asshole," Penn said. "Once you understand that he isn't thinking about the effect of what he says, because he doesn't give a shit, a whole lot falls into place."

"He's thinking about what he says, but not the effect of it on people," Frankie said.

"If you were me, he wouldn't have said that. I mean, if you were the one who works with him," Penn added.

"What?"

"Because you're just like him," said her brother.

"Please don't say that!"

"I mean, you're like the good part of him, the bold, adventuring, save-the-world guy, the one who says *Don't tell me I can't do that! I'll do that just to prove I can!* He'd have been talking about you being the future of the Saltwater Foundation. He wouldn't have had to bypass the second born. Because I'm like Mom. I don't need to be the center of attention every minute of every day. I wanted to be a kindergarten teacher," Penn said, and Frankie remembered, long ago, Penn saying that more guys should teach little kids because they didn't have enough good male role models. "When I told him that, he said, 'People will think you're gay.'"

"Wait. Why would you care if they thought you were gay?" Frankie asked him.

"I wouldn't necessarily care. But he would care, don't you get that? He would think it was a failure if big, brave Mack had a sissy son. So I spent the last five years crashing through the fucking underbrush and freezing my nuts off in swamps and dissecting animal shit just to prove I wasn't. And why'd I do it? For this, right? I will say, he's got the perfect wife in Ariel. She's just like Mom. She worships him. They're both in love with the same person."

After Penn left, Frankie sat up late, huddled in thicknesses of quilts she'd liberated from the big house by slipping into the basement storage closets while Penn was taking a walk with his grandfather, and Ariel and Carlotta were off somewhere with the baby. Like many other things she intended to snag in due time, including her mother's big ceramic soup pot, the quilts Beatrice had made were rightfully hers. Every time she went to sleep under the caress of silk and velvet, she was happy she still had a key. That night, however, sleep would not come to her. Was what Penn said the truth? Was she really Mack's image? How could that be? Genetics only went so far. As a child and a teenager, she barely knew him. The combined total of weeks she'd spent with him this summer seemed to be about half of what she recalled from the previous twenty years. Mack would return for a glamorous few weeks and do all the things other fathers did as a matter of course, as she and Penn were ping-ponged from a fishing boat to the zoo to the tennis courts, and then he was gone again.

He'd still never asked her what she thought. He'd never asked what frightened her or what she dreamed of. He'd never asked how she was doing in school or met a single one of her teachers. When her first photos, of the kind of common snapping turtle that Texans illegally used for turtle soup, were published in *Smithsonian Magazine*, he sent her a congratulatory note and a check for a hundred dollars. But the note had been in Beatrice's handwriting.

In the morning, Frankie and Penn took their grandfather to the airport. Saying goodbye to Mack's father was a wrench for Frankie. She found herself asking, "Why don't you move here?" forgetting that Frank lived not far from Mack's brother and his family. But her grandfather assured her that he would come back to see her baby and further urged her to mend fences with her father. "Life is long, Frankie, but not patient," he said, just before he headed to the gate.

Before they left, Frankie asked her brother if they could go on to visit Beatrice's mom, Granny Becky, and their aunt Imogen in Concord. Frankie hadn't visited since she'd been back, and she could nearly forgive herself for that because of the tumult of events right here. They were expected at Thanksgiving, but Frankie wanted to cherish her mother's family right now.

"Should we surprise them?" Frankie said. "I like surprises."

"I hate surprises," Penn said. "I would especially hate a surprise that involved cleaning the house and making dinner for three more people."

"Live a little, Penny," Frankie said. "Gil, would you mind if someday your only granddaughter and her new husband dropped by unannounced?"

"I'd be furious," Gil said. "And your *grandmère* is a professor. She's not sitting in the house waiting for you to show up!"

But she was.

As it happened, Becky Grace had no classes that day and was literally sitting in the bay window of the house on Monument Street, just blocks from where Louisa May Alcott wrote *Little Women*, when they pulled up.

Now Frankie's grandmother, tall and slim and strong like Beatrice, came running out of her front door, pulling a thick sweater around her shoulders and laughing. "I thought, that girl looks just like Francis Lee, but…what would she be doing here? What a wonderful surprise. I love surprises!" Frankie could not help but cock an eye at her brother. "Now, you're going to stay for dinner, of course. I won't hear otherwise. And do you really have to go back right away? I don't have a thing to do until Monday, and even then, I have everything I need for my classes branded on my brain after all these years! Imogen will be home in a few hours. I'm going to let it be a surprise for her too."

After a ridiculously Yankee meal of roast chicken, green beans with almonds and peas, and baked macaroni (Gil said, "This is why I love America!"), Gil and Penn helped their aunt clean up, and Frankie's grandmother motioned her into the library. "Let's have a visit," she said. "Just us." She asked if Frankie wanted coffee. "Are pregnant women supposed to have coffee these days? Everything keeps changing. I think people had gin and tonics back in the day." Frankie said she could certainly have a little coffee with lots of milk and sugar.

"I can get it!" she said.

"Oh, no, Imogen and I have this new espresso machine, and I use it every chance I get. It takes literally minutes."

Frankie sat quietly in the low-lighted room, studying her grandmother's neatly alphabetized shelves of books, including two that Becky had written, her odd jumble of keepsakes, from a huge crystal paperweight with the word *Grace* in blown-blue glass inside it, a stand-up paper doll of Marie Antoinette and one of the singer Beyoncé, an intricately carved wooden door-knob, a miniature oil painting of a sinking car, and a purple ceramic octopus that Frankie had crafted when she was ten.

Then her grandmother was back with two small mugs. "I did tea," she said, "to be on the safe side. But it's Builder's!" As her grandmother began to apologize for missing the wedding, Frankie gave her the small book of photos she'd ordered from the photographer. "Look at you!" Granny Becky said. "Look at that dress! Did you get it in Paris?"

"I got it in Hyannis," Frankie said and told the story of Beatrice's friend who'd come through for her.

"That was what Bea inspired," Granny Becky said. "I know that when someone dies, it's a cliché to say *Oh, everyone loved her,* but that was true for your mother. She endeared people to her." Granny Becky pressed her thumb and middle finger against the outer corners of her eyes, but couldn't stop the tears. "I never forget for a whole day. But I forget for a whole hour. And then I catch myself saying, *Oh, I must tell Beatrice, look what that rascal senator did now...* But I'll never see her again. What kind of fate is that for a mother? I know, people have faced much, much worse. I just imagined we would have time together, with you and Penn...a time of fulfillment, with grandchildren. She was fifty-two years old! She had years before her...but Frankie, I'm sorry. All this, on top of your loss..."

"It's probably even worse for you," Frankie said. "I'm not even a mother yet, and it's unimaginable."

"Let's talk about Mack and his mischief. I need to get my spine back."

Unexpectedly, Frankie found herself wanting if not to champion Mack at least to offer him a shred of defense. "To be fair, he was just distraught about Mom, and he's not the type who could ever really function on his own. We think he had a sort of breakdown. He lost weight. He couldn't teach. He barely left the house."

"That is what grief does, Frankie."

"I know."

"That's why people in times past observed a period of mourning, a year, to help them make a transition from one way of life to another. Instead, what is this girl who's expecting in a few months?"

"Oh, Granny, you've missed a couple of episodes."

Over the course of the next hour, Frankie told her grandmother about the baby's birth, the Saltwater Foundation donor gala and Mack's speech describing the organization's future. "Poor Penn! How humiliated he must have been. How angry!" Granny Becky said.

"I don't think my dad meant it to sound that way. I think he meant…in the far future."

"But that's not what he said." She told a story about Abraham Lincoln and his fractious, probably mentally ill, wife, Mary Todd. "By all accounts, she behaved like a witch most of the time. She was very jealous. She was rude. She suffered from terrible headaches, probably migraines, and some medical scholars have suggested that she had symptoms of anemia and of bipolar disorder, of profound depression at the very least. Of course, three of her children died before she did." Becky got up and carried her cup to the mantel of the fireplace that, while impressive, had never worked. "Lincoln used to say about his wife, 'My old father had a saying, *If you make a bad bargain, hug it all the tighter.*' And that's what I think Mack is doing. He's embarrassed. He should be embarrassed. So he's pretending that everything is all Jell-O and pudding to try to normalize a situation that is… Well, maybe it happens all the time in California, but not here." She added, "I don't want Beatrice to be a symbol. Or a name on a scholarship. I want her to be my child. Are you going to remember her when you name the baby? Maybe give her the name of Grace as a middle name?"

"It's a boy. Do you think people would be weird about it if I gave him the middle name of Grace?"

"I do," Granny Becky said and almost laughed.

"But I think there might come another baby one day. I'll have more time to think about that. What's your middle name?"

"It's Rowan. After the tree. My grandfather Stan wanted to name me after his favorite song, the old song about the ash grove, but thought Ash was not a very nice name for a girl."

"Well, there. That's a perfect name. Doesn't have to be Ubaldo after all."

"Ubaldo?"

"This guy we met in Italy," Frankie explained.

"I'm tired," Becky said. "Do you mind terribly if I turn in? Imogen has the green bedroom made up for you and Gil, and the small white room for Penn. Are you going to leave first thing? I hope not. I don't have to teach tomorrow."

"I'd actually like to show Gil some of Concord. They don't study Emerson in Canada that way. But I know he loves Thoreau. He's a nature writer, you know that, and he's always quoting, *I went to the woods because I wished to live deliberately*, although Gil would only be happy if the woods had cable, and Canadiens hockey. I don't think he's read *Little Women*, but he's a big fan of Hawthorne, although I'm not, Granny, I'm not."

"Ah, yes. Hawthorne. Hated women, so far as I could tell. Especially the Brontës. I think he knew they were better than he was. And never one word where fifty would do... Maybe I'll come along with you."

"Oh, I'd like that," Frankie said, and then she asked, "You knew Ariel. Did you ever meet her mother?"

"I did," her grandmother answered. "Charlene? Carla?"

"Carlotta."

"Yes, now I remember something... Beatrice had no use for that woman. My sweet girl."

"Because of the way she treated Ariel."

Granny Becky shrugged. She got up and collected the mugs. "You're going to have to take some of these books, Frankie. There are some first editions here."

"I'm actually thinking of writing a book, Granny. Do you think that's crazy?"

"Of course not. A photo book?"

"Well, it would have my photos, sure. But it would be more of a memoir about the things I've seen, above and below the water, and why the way you see the sea is not just beauty, it's important for human beings, as a species, to see under the surface. Otherwise, we can miss so much. I'm not entirely sure what the meaning would be. I think all the time about how I was inspired by my mother's paintings to make a big deal out of small things."

Such a book might have crossover appeal to women interested in adventure and to armchair ecologists, Becky said. That would be her dream, Frankie agreed. She told her grandmother about Gil's first book, *Hoofer*, the triumphant story of the salvation of the wood bison in Canada. That, in part because of Gil's lyrical writing, but also because he was so captivated by the subject, had been an unlikely bestseller.

Becky took the mugs and plates to the kitchen, and Frankie heard the water running as she rinsed them. A momentary wisp of nostalgia brushed her as she thought of her mother's clean-it-up-now dictum, and then Becky said, "It wasn't just the way that she treated Ariel. It was something else. Wait! I remember now. It was something about that old boyfriend or friend of hers, that dear man who found my poor Beatrice, Sandy Madeira… Sailor, they called him. Something Carlotta did to that man, who was such a great friend to Bea. I'll think of what it was. Or maybe I won't! But it really got to your mother. I mean that it still bothered her, even though it was probably thirty years ago. No idea what it was. I really am going to bed now, darling. Sleep tight." As she left the library, she turned back and asked if Frankie had seen her father's baby.

"Not yet," Frankie said. "I know I should."

"When you're ready." Soft as flannel, Granny Becky touched Frankie's head. "I'm not suggesting you bear a grudge, but listen to your own instincts. They're never wrong."

7

On the way back, Frankie called Ellabella Ballenger to tell her that sometime in the coming week, she could choose from the photos Frankie had taken and Frankie would make a huge print that was her trademark.

She also told Ellabella she had a favor to ask. She didn't leave a message because she wasn't quite sure of all that favor would entail.

When Frankie got home, she wanted to do nothing but sleep, and she did just that, for the best part of a day. Then she got up to study the proofs of her session with Ellabella, which had arrived while she was away. As she pored over them, she wondered for the dozenth time if she should have a darkroom of her own, as people used to in their basements—even though she had no basement and no real inclination to do her own printing.

As for the pictures, they were, Frankie had to admit, splendid.

Ellabella's body, insubstantial as myth, seemed to have bloomed from the water itself. One series of three was so ravishingly synchronous that Frankie decided to print it as a triptych for a huge upcoming invitational exhibit—although the exhibit, part of CartaArts at the Cigno d'Argento Gallery in Rome—was not slated until the following year and her submissions not due for five months. It was a big decision, because she could choose only seven photos.

Under the quilts that night with Gil, she said, "I'm getting better at this."

"Pregnancy has improved you," Gil said. "And you were always pretty hot. Now you are *epicée*."

"I'm like hot sauce." Her French was still childlike, but it sounded just like *spicy*.

"I mean you are wanton," Gil said agreeably.

"I'm surprised you didn't say *won ton*."

"That too, little dumpling."

"I don't mean any of that. I mean good, at pictures. I was always pretty good, but I'm getting better." She added, "I'm not bragging. I have always thought people believed I was better than I was. And I thought they were reacting more to what I took pictures of than to the pictures themselves. But you should see the pictures of Ellabella."

"I did. Speaking of *epicée*."

Frankie punched him. *I am happily married*, she thought. *I don't want to run away.* Okay, it had been just a short while, less than a year, and anyone could be happy for a year. But with Gil, she was safe and adventurous. She knew that he would never hold her back, only hold her close. She would protect him because he was Canadian and too trusting. He would protect her from her glooms and the temper that could flash up, unlooked-for like those sparking-wheel toys she'd thought of at the wedding—the first time she'd seen Carlotta again.

The next day, after Ellabella, fascinated, chose her image, she said, "Imagine me someday if I have this picture on my wall and my child, who's, like, twelve years old, comes in with his friend, and the friend says, *Is that your mother?* What am I going to say?"

"You don't have to display it in the living room."

"No, I really do have to display it in the living room. It's completely beautiful, and you can't really see…that much. But this is all theoretical anyhow. Here I am talking about my living room of the future and worrying about embarrassing my twelve-year-old son of the future…when I was married and divorced by the time I was twenty-four and I'm currently living with my parents."

"I think your twelve-year-old of the future will be fine. He'll have progressive views about art."

"And I'll be fat and fifty by then, so maybe I'll just say, *No, of course not, it isn't me!*"

"You could do that too." Emboldened by the moment, Frankie asked then, "Why did you hate me when we were kids?"

To her credit, Ellabella didn't even try to deny that she had. She said only that there were several reasons, and that she needed a moment to put her thoughts together coherently. Finally, she asked Frankie to remember how her parents, all parents of kids who came home crying because someone was cruel, tried to comfort their children by saying, *Oh, she's just jealous.* "And I was jealous, but not in the sense that you usually think of. It wasn't because you were smarter or prettier. It was because you seemed to know what you wanted and you didn't need a boy to get it."

Frankie said, "Huh."

"And I was also jealous of you because of Ariel."

"Ariel? You…your tribe… If you hated me, you thought Ariel was practically invisible."

"My tribe? My so-called friends would have copied my test papers or slept with my boyfriend without thinking twice. They were about as loyal as minks. They were only friends if you didn't have something they wanted. But Ariel would have walked through fire for you." Frankie looked down at her hands and realized she was smoothing the skin first on one and then the other, as her mother had done. "I was never much of a reader, but there was this novel called *The Member of the Wedding* by Carson McCullers. The girl in it, she was excited about her brother's wedding, but she almost thought that being part of the wedding meant she would always be with her brother and his wife, I think. She'd go on the honeymoon with them and stuff. She talked about wanting a 'we of me.' That's what you and Ariel have, a 'we of me.'" *Not anymore*, Frankie thought. "And the girl in the novel, she was named Frankie. Did you know that?"

Frankie shook her head.

"It's an old, old book," Ellabella said, who had no idea what had really happened between Frankie and Ariel, only the outlines. "How's the baby?"

"Good," Frankie said. "It's a boy."

"So I read in the newspaper. Banner?"

"Banner Benjamin. They call him Ben."

"He must be cute. Ariel is so beautiful. It'll be nice to get in some practice with him before your own arrives."

"Yep."

In the sudden discomfiting stillness between them, which Frankie wanted to relieve but couldn't, they drank the coffee Frankie had made and talked, the way Cape Codders do, about how all-of-a-sudden cold it had become, as if this was something impressive that had never happened before. Last night, it was summer, and the screens were open to the long night, and then, as if a light switch snapped off, the windows still dusted in the corners with summer pollen were wiped down, closed and locked. Winter flayed the trees and steeled the ocean. *So far? So early? So soon?*

Frankie told Ellabella about the show in Rome. Ellabella

closed her eyes and laughed hard. "Kitty Ballenger will blow an aneurysm. First, I divorced the dream son-in-law and now I'm posing nude in public. Some Puritan girl I've turned out to be!"

It was only after she left that Frankie remembered what she wanted to talk to Ellabella about. As most people imagine about journalists, Frankie thought that Ellabella had access to some hidden database of information on just about everyone, and she wanted to know more about her mother's old friend, Sandy Madeira. She made up her mind to call Ellabella the next day. But then she and Gil went to the hospital twice a week for a birthing class, which Frankie considered a waste of time, and after that, Thanksgiving was upon them, and then Gil was to leave the next day.

That afternoon, she helped Gil pack—annoyingly, according to him. "I hope this makes you feel wifely, because you're driving me nuts," he said as Frankie insisted on double-wrapping his shaving cream and razors in plastic bags, then took them out altogether and went to get a good-size flowered waterproof makeup bag, one of many in which she'd always carried her few travel essentials, and packed his things into it. "Oh, that's nice," Gil said. "Now I'm expressing my feminine side."

"Well, I never met anyone before who travels for a living who doesn't have a dopp kit. What kind of barbarian are you?"

"I don't have time to mess about with little matching packing cubes and things. Especially those with posies on them."

"I bet you mess about when the top of your toothpaste comes off and gets all over the front of your shirt." The open, proud look on Gil's face told her that this was exactly what had happened. "Anyway, who's going to see them? The bears?"

Gil was on his way to do a story for EnGarde about the so-called bear girls in the Great Bear Rainforest, trained to guide tourists in inflatable boats to observe wild grizzlies along the Atnarko River in British Columbia. She would drop him off at the airport, then again spend the night with her aunt and grandmother and pick Giselle up the following day. Granny Becky had insisted that she bring Giselle back for dinner and a sleep before returning to Cape Cod. While Frankie thought Giselle might be exhausted and jet-lagged, she also knew her mother-in-law would be horrified at the thought of refusing an invitation from the matriarch of Frankie's family.

"What if the bears want to eat the tourists?" Frankie asked Gil.

"I guess they would if they wanted to badly enough. They prefer the salmon, though."

"That's a comfort."

"They eat forty salmon a day, especially now, right before hibernation. I could eat forty myself. They cook up some fine salmon in those lodges."

"Another talent of those bear girls? I'll be they have lots of talents. Keep you warm at night."

"Yes, they're wild animals," Gil said. He stopped. "You're not on the level, are you, Frankie? Because I would never, ever betray you. I hope you are the same."

"I don't think the kind of guy who'd want to mess with me now is the kind of guy I'd want," she answered, laughing. But then she saw he was serious. "Of course I would never. Not even if you...looked like a polar bear." Gil pulled her close to him.

"I'm going to take that as faith, if you don't mind."

"On faith," she said.

"I agree."

"No, the phrase is *on faith* not *as faith*."

"Oh, of course, the great writer speaks."

"Did you read anything I wrote?" she asked him tentatively.

Gil said, "I did. Frankie, I'm not sure how to tell you this..." She inhaled sharply. Gil loved her, but he would be honest, if only so that she didn't humiliate herself in front of people who admired her work…not to mention those who admired Mack. There was nothing feebler than the ambitious offspring of someone well-known trying to ride on their coattails to some kind of reflected fame. "I hope you believe me," Gil went on. "Your writing is good. It's simple and clear, and it shows the reader the scene, clearly. I found myself absorbed in the story, even though I knew you. I really think you should finish this. I think people will read it. My only hesitation about telling you sooner was because you might think I was just being kind."

"I'm thrilled by this," Frankie said quietly. "I guess I didn't realize how much it meant to me until—"

There was a knock, but disconcertingly, at the front window rather than the door. As a child, Frankie had a recurring nightmare of waking and looking out the big window closest to her bed and seeing a face peering back at her. It was like that now. The darkness and the distortion of a flashlight ringed the eyes of whoever it was in shadow. Frankie nearly screamed. Then she recognized Carlotta.

She opened the door, but said quickly, "A visit here is not a good idea. We really have nothing to talk about."

"Frankie, give me five minutes."

"I really don't want to be rude. But this whole mess was your—"

"It was completely my fault," Carlotta said. "I just want a chance to apologize. I was foolish, and I made a terrible mistake. Now I'm so regretful, and Ariel is heartbroken. Mack is furious. He's looking back at it now, and he thinks, well, he thinks that doing Ariel's sacred numbers was a silly superstition and—"

"Gee, he's a scientist. Why on earth would he think that?" She felt a surge of pride for her father. While he was leading with his dick, he still had residual character.

"Some beliefs predate science, Frankie. I've said that before."

"Right, but these days, we have science."

"That's not the point. They're not speaking. He's leaving."

"He's leaving?"

"He's going on a research trip the week after Christmas and... Couldn't I just come in for a moment?"

Frankie finally let Carlotta in, making no move to sit down.

"Please let me explain," Carlotta said.

As it transpired, it was really Ariel's idea for Carlotta to go on living with the newlyweds. Ariel was comforted by having her mother after so long apart, particularly because she didn't have Frankie. While Carlotta knew how fortunate she was that Ariel's nature was to move forward rather than judge her mother for what she called *those lost years*, Mack was increasingly irritated with what he saw as Ariel's divided loyalties. He wanted Ariel with him at all times and expected her to care for the baby entirely on her own, even when she was exhausted after a sleepless night. Beatrice had done that, Mack said, which made Ariel cry. Because he was to leave on his first research trip in a year right after the holidays, Mack was preoccupied and tense, busy with his own reading and with preparing for the seminar at the university, on the interesting subject of the conflict between species preservation and the rights of Indigenous people, a favorite subject for the Saltwater Foundation and an age-old ethical dilemma. From all over the world, Mack had invited cultural experts, agricultural activists, writers and even commercial fishers to speak to small and large student groups in a series of lectures and panels. Because Ariel also was the administrator of the Saltwater Foundation, making those contacts, sending those invitations and making travel arrangements also fell to her. Carlotta was caring for the baby most of the time.

Just the other night, Carlotta overheard them quarrel. Ariel was pleading with Mack not to go away again so soon. Yes, she knew how important his work was, but she was overwhelmed, Ben was barely sleeping, and she needed him to be with her.

At first, Mack soothed her, pointing out that he wasn't leaving until early January and that Ben's schedule would probably be sorted out by then...and that when he did leave, it would be only for eight weeks, or a little more. Ariel wailed, "Eight weeks?"

And Mack roared, "Look, I'm not your father! You're not a child, are you?"

"Ariel needs you," Carlotta went on. "I was completely wrong. I still believe that numerology is very powerful, but nothing should have mattered that day except your wedding. I even told Ariel that, but she was terrified."

"Well, congratulations. You terrified her. She probably thought the baby would die or something if she didn't give birth right then."

"I tried to explain to her that the sacred numbers are only indications. But she was too afraid by that point..."

"Well, you're back in her life now and welcome to her. I'm busy. Have a good evening."

"Please, Frankie, don't do this. Ariel admires you so much. She says you're her light. You never looked down on her."

The woman was exasperating. Penn was right. How could she stand here and plead for the remedy to a breach she had herself caused? "Why would I ever look down on Ariel? Ariel is one of the smartest, bravest people I ever knew."

"That's as may be. There are people who don't need a reason to look down."

"That has way more to do with them than the person they're looking down on."

"That's something Ariel would say." It was, in fact, something Ariel had said, multiple times, as they guarded their vulnerable flanks against the attacks of the alpha females. *Ariel!* The longing for her mother and for Ariel fused into a pure cry of grief that all but escaped Frankie's lips. It was unwise and even unhealthy to get them mixed up in her mind, but she was powerless against the effect of this place, this season, this gathering of all those who represented her past and her future. "This is not just about my wedding day, as you know. It's about everything..."

"But a great friendship is rarer than a great love. And you and Ariel have a friendship that is legendary. Your friendship is the most important relationship in Ariel's life. And I mean counting everybody. She made a choice, and she made other choices, but I know she is heartbroken about losing you. Don't tell her I said this, but I'm asking for myself. Can't you just try to get past it?"

"Just...get past it?"

"Like, if you think she's so great," Carlotta added, "then how can you give her up?"

More to the point, Frankie thought and almost said, *How did you give her up?*

"You need to leave now," Frankie said. She opened the door. It had begun to snow. As Carlotta walked away, Frankie noticed the woman was wearing rubber flip-flops. Carlotta stopped then.

"You aren't jealous, are you?" she asked Frankie.

"Of what?"

"Because everything you used to have is Ariel's now."

"Forgive me, but that's kind of blunt, and it's assuming a lot."

"I just meant, I might be, in your position."

"Well, I'm not," Frankie said, closing the door, as if that exact ungallant emotion were not even then seething from her very pores, like a smell. She wanted to slap Carlotta, but for what? The woman was only stating openly what Frankie was feeling.

There were other emotions, however.

Oh, Ariel, she thought! *I'm a fool. You would not do this to me if our positions were reversed. You would find a way to make it right.* At that moment, she picked up her phone and hit Ariel's number, but before the ring, she ended the call. She thought of the banquet, of Mack's jovial cruelty, ham-handed if unintended, of Penn's interrupted grin, his blasted eyes.

No.

She knew that in the kitchen, Gil, who had overheard everything, would counsel remediation and patience. But the high road was too lonely a place. Let Mack take his turn walking it. Let him see outside himself, as he never had, for if he did not now, he never would.

The next morning, she was holding Gil close at the airport as they said goodbye, then collecting his mother to take her to Grandma Becky's house. For Giselle and Becky, it was love at first sight, which Frankie had suspected might be the case. Except for commenting on her enormous girth, they essentially ignored her, which was fine by Frankie. She finally called Ellabella to ask what her resources were when it came to finding out deep secrets. Ellabella said she did know a few tricks, to the extent that she could summon up their bona fides and their criminal records, with the help of a few records clerks and some police public-relations officers who had fallen victim to her charms. Before Frankie could reveal her mission, Ellabella was called away but promised to give Frankie her full attention the next day.

It had been the kind of visit Frankie realized that she longed for—one of those times she had given up with so many makeshift holidays in so many hotels and hovels around the world, mango and sticky rice in Thailand with a wild group of Aussie naturalists, turkey and cock-a-leekie soup in Edinburgh with her friends Gordon and Bryce, who urged her to partake of the traditional haggis—just the thought of the single bite she took made Frankie's guts boil. In the library the previous night, Giselle and Granny Becky recalled the Christmases of their own youth. Becky remembered a platoon of dozens of cousins roaming the neighborhood on Christmas Eve with printed sheet music, singing carols, given so many cookies and so much hot chocolate on their two-hour stroll they were sloshing by the time they fell into bed. Giselle recalled the Réveillon her French parents and grandparents had brought to Canada, a three-hour meal that began with smoked oysters and bran bread and continued with roast goose and three kinds of potatoes, the walk to Midnight Mass and then home for the thirteen desserts, representing Christ and the twelve apostles, and chocolate before bedtime, the tree decked in silver and gold that magically went up overnight, the shoes *Père Noël* filled with chocolate coins.

"Can we do all that?" Frankie asked.

"Maybe not this year," Granny Becky said, giving Giselle the traditional kiss on both cheeks and promising to see her in just a few days.

No sooner were they in the car than Ellabella called back. Frankie pulled the car over and put her on speaker. She wondered what Giselle thought of everything she was hearing.

Frankie said, "So you're a reporter. You can find out anything you want about someone."

"Whoa," said Ellabella. "I can find out anything that anybody else can find out. What reporters can do that sometimes civilians can't, or don't know they can, is file a freedom of information request for documents you don't normally get. But now? You can basically find anything online if you look long enough and follow up with every place the person's ever been."

"So you don't have to take an oath and then they open the vault?"

"Right."

"I want to know about this guy Sailor Madeira. Real name Sandy, well, Santiago."

"You sound like a detective show," Ellabella said.

"There's nothing wrong with him. I don't want you to think that. He didn't do anything. He's just an old friend of my mom's. They went to school together."

Frankie pointed out that she had no idea where he lived, apartment or house or shack. Then she told Ellabella that she wanted her to come along if she was able to get Sailor to agree to have lunch or a coffee. She wanted to dig deeper, Frankie confided, about what had transpired between Carlotta Puck and Frankie's father…and what Carlotta might have done to Sailor so long ago to have sparked a big public fight in front of the Yankee. Ellabella would be Frankie's witness to whatever Sailor said, if he said anything. Frankie doubted the man would have much to tell them. Maybe there was nothing at all to tell. If Ellabella was put off, she didn't give any indication. She said this was the kind of sleuthing she liked, the kind that sounded like dirty fun, much more entertaining than trying to find out about somebody's history with back taxes.

Even before Frankie got to the bridge, Ellabella called back. She had news.

Frankie pulled the car over again.

The first part was that she'd gotten the copy of the *Coast Chronicle* with the story about Frankie. The November issue would go on sale this week. She texted Frankie a copy of the photo on the cover, a photo that Frankie didn't even remember being taken. Draped in strings of water lily and coated with silt, she was standing in knee-deep water, laughing, wild coastal sky all around her, cameras slung from her neck and a salmon in each hand.

See Creature: Photog Frankie Attleboro Rises from the Deep

Giselle asked if this was a national magazine, if it would be seen in Canada. She wanted to tell her friends, if so. "Really, yes and no… Some of these magazines started as regional but the style parts caught on all over the place. So for example, plenty of people in Boston read *Southern Living* and the *Coast Chronicle* is like the one that's called *Yankee*—it kind of slips the boundaries." Frankie added, "But what we can do is buy a bunch of copies and send them to anyone you want."

Giselle called Gil in Scotland to show him the cover.

"Don't bother him," Frankie said, trying to be modest, hoping that her mother-in-law would ignore her, which she did.

"You never saw that cover picture because I took it," Gil said. He explained that when Ellabella talked to him, he showed it to her as an example of how glamorous Frankie customarily looked at the time they fell in love. She was drawn to its humor and impressed by its clarity, amazed it had been taken on a phone. In a pinch, Gil told her, he regularly used his phone to take photos for his articles.

Frankie then switched subjects, asking Ellabella if she'd been able to locate Sailor Madeira.

"Better than that," Ellabella said, but promised the details for the next day.

At Giselle's request, they stopped for coffee.

With the Dunkin' Donuts cup in hand, Giselle shook her head, wide-eyed. "This explains a great deal," she said, nodding at the coffee lid.

Frankie felt secure enough to say, "You are such a food snob!"

"Mais oui!" Giselle agreed, with a grin that made her look twenty years younger. "Not only food. French people are snobs about everything!"

Despite the coffee, once back at the cottage, Giselle confessed that she was too exhausted to begin the Christmas baking. Frankie said that Giselle didn't have to bake anything for Christmas at all but added, when Giselle regarded her with frank horror, "Unless you want to, of course." She gave Frankie a list of ingredients not only for the cream cakes and the *Bûche de Noël*, but for the meat pies, the spiced pork roast, the plums cooked in wine, the croissants… "But it's only four of us!" Frankie said. "Gil and Penn and you and me. My father can't come…" Giselle gave Frankie the same look for the second time. "But of course, your grandmother and Tante Imogen and one of those boys, her sons, Paul, is it? And his intended?" Frankie blushed. She thought, Where would they stay? It turned out that Imogen had already located a kind friend of Beatrice's who had thrown open her four-bedroom summer home for as long as they needed. "I don't really eat meat anymore," said Frankie. "No insult meant by this. It just doesn't agree with me right now."

Giselle sighed but pointed out, "So there will be the pasta with cashew sauce, the trout almondine…"

"That's wonderful. I think I eat fish."

So there.

On her way to the Ballengers' house in Chatham, Frankie located Penn and passed along the shopping list. Coming into the town was always, Frankie thought, like driving onto a movie set that portrayed the Cape Cod of the popular mind, a place where foaming banks of hydrangea verged every sidewalk, where everyone was rich, even the old people attractive and fit, and it was always midsummer.

Some of the brickwork of the two-hundred-year-old Victorian original had been incorporated into the facade of the nine-bedroom manse built for Kitty and Kenny by one of the major Saltwater donors, Eastward Companies. So skillful had the construction been that the place didn't scream new money but instead old comfort and class. Frankie felt as though she'd traveled by tornado to the halls of *Architectural Digest*. "Surely you've been here," Kitty said.

"I don't think I ever was inside."

Kitty led the way to a white suede chaise with exceptionally high cushions. "You're going to need to get up at some point," she said.

"It's still at least three weeks, maybe more," Frankie explained. "Not until after Christmas."

"Do you have names picked out?" Kitty asked as Ellabella came to the room in a rush with a file tucked under her arm. Frankie couldn't help but notice that it wasn't a manila envelope, but a burgundy suede document holder with a snap.

"Ubaldo, actually," Frankie said. "For the saint?"

"That's, well, that's..."

"That's bullshit, Mother," Ellabella said. "Frankie's just being her slap-happy mischievous self."

"I'll get you two some tea. Would you like something to eat, Frankie?"

Frankie said, "I know it's polite to refuse. But actually, that would be great. Anything you've got would be just fine. Except meat. I think I'm mostly vegetarian now. But I was just telling my mother-in-law that I think I might sometimes eat fish, which is ironic, fish being my people..."

"Settle down there, Frankie," Ellabella said.

After Kitty presented them with plates of cheddar and jam and slices of dark bread, she settled down with her own cup. "No, no, no, Mother. We have dark secrets to share about people you know. And you have to leave. Too sad!" Visibly annoyed, Kitty left the room.

Ellabella first showed Frankie the copy of the magazine.

She was shocked and delighted by some of the tributes, among them from her mentor, Abram Murphy, who called Frankie "a bulldog for the shot. Sometimes, I think she takes too many chances. I'm glad she's not obsessed with underwater caves." One of the pictures clearly had been taken by the photographer on her wedding day. It was one that Frankie had never seen, but she quickly decided to call the young woman and ask for a print to be made. A wild, beautiful candid of her, it seemed to have been lifted out of place and time—from here and now to an Ireland of a century past. Her curled hair swept across her face by a breeze, Frankie was looking out to sea, while around her, the boulders and fences and the shoulders of guests blended in a blur of blue and gray. Stripped in just below it was a quote from Mack. "She is like a gold medalist. Not just her photos, I mean the girl. Her eye is impeccable, but the important thing is her heart."

Frankie thought, *If that's true, how does he even know it?*

"People are going to think you like me," Frankie said to Ellabella.

"I do like you."

"You never did like me."

"I liked you, deep down, but I liked being mean more."

Frankie pretended innocence. "Why?"

"It got a reaction. It made me feel powerful. I was deeply insecure."

"You? Insecure?"

"Hello, I'm six one. And a half. My feet are size twelve. In sixth grade, they called me Storky. My family raised me to believe that looking down on other people, in my case, literally looking down, made you powerful. Don't get me wrong. I didn't have to believe them. But the message was pretty straightforward. *Get them before they get you.* My brothers were Titans. I had to be one too. I had to make myself…what? What they call *iconic*, not that I knew that word then. I had to have minions. If just anyone could hang out with us, then that meant we were just ordinary. Just like all the other horses. Not special. Then you enforce that. You know the psychology of it. If somebody's on top, somebody's got to be on the bottom."

"Like being a mobster."

"Exactly. Like an old-time mobster movie. In the normal world, some of those guys would have been losers. But they had guns. Look at Cassie Mellon. She's plain, even now that she can afford to do anything to improve herself. She's not very bright. But she's a thug. She's a natural enforcer."

At college, in a larger world, Ellabella found herself outclassed. Still in possession of her famous beauty and brains, she was no longer one of a kind. There were dozens of her, many of them girls who had risen against significant odds and without the history of emotional roadkill. As years passed, Ellabella confronted herself. For an honors seminar that combined literature, history and psychology, she did a thesis on the social structure of middle-class girl gangs. During that research, she had what she called her moment of grace, recognizing that the emotional pain she had caused for others might have lasted down the years, in directly inverse proportion to the pleasure she got from causing it, which was trivial and transitory. While it was impossible to make amends to everyone she might have put down, she wrote a first-person essay for the *New York Times* ("I Was a Teenage Mean Girl") that not only examined her own cruelty but also the culture that fostered it: how, for their own survival, others often align with the perpetrator of unkind words and acts rather than speaking out and being ostracized.

"I've been mean, too, plenty of times," Frankie admitted.

"But in retaliation, right?" Ellabella said. "That's a different thing. You were protecting yourself and the people you loved. Like Ariel did with that video of me. That was a classic smackdown. I still wake up screaming."

The truest friend, Frankie thought. Oh, Ariel, Ariel.

Ellabella turned back to the folder. It was actually, on reflection, blueberry-colored. "What are you looking at?"

"I'm staring at your folder. It's so beautiful."

"The shoemaker in Dennis makes them," Ellabella said. She pulled out her sheaf of printouts. "Here, you have it. I have three others. Oxblood, this color and yellow."

"I should say, *Oh, I can't*, but I definitely can," Frankie said. "Thank you. It will be my lucky folder, for only the most treasured things."

"So," Ellabella continued, "I did dig some things up, but best of all, we have an appointment to meet Sailor in about an hour at his condo… He knows what we're trying to find out, and guess what. He has some questions of his own." Ellabella showed Frankie copies of some of Sailor's papers, his service record, his clamming license, a single arrest for disorderly conduct many years before outside the Yankee... "But here's what's interesting. Look at the arrest report. Look at the name of the person who called the police. One Carlotta Puck!" She'd further talked to a few old-timers, acquaintances of her father. Sailor apparently did some clamming but mostly lived on his navy pension. He seemed to have some sort of disability, Ellabella added, though she wasn't sure what it was. People also said he drank a little, but she didn't take that too seriously. Everyone on Cape Cod drank like it was a religion, she pointed out. If you counted their nearly nightly dinners out, their gin and tonics at five, their wine with dinner and weekend mimosas, her own parents were heavy drinkers at a minimum, though still well-dressed and culturally appropriate.

"So should we go see him?" Ellabella asked. They set off.

Frankie was consistently amazed that there were streets in Brewster and Dennis she'd never driven down, parks she'd never seen, beaches she'd never set foot on. At the very end of one of those streets that dead-ended at a small cove was Sailor's house, a small, neat saltbox. Frankie lumbered up the steps and into Sailor Madeira's arms. "I know I haven't been by since the funeral," he said. "I just couldn't quite get my mind around the ways things are..."

"Oh, you don't have to explain," Frankie said, holding up a hand. "I'm the worst. It's been years since we really had a visit. The last time, before Mom died, you came over for dinner...?"

"That's right. Birdy made chowder. You know they all called your mom that. Kids in high school called her that. I did too. She made chowder. And those little rhubarb things."

"Hand pies," Frankie said. "One of the many things I wish I'd slowed down enough to learn how to make. I loved those... with cinnamon ice cream."

"I can show you how to make them," Sailor said. "I seriously can. I taught her. I make my own ice cream too."

Ellabella said, "Of course you do. I'm Frankie's friend, Ella. We talked on the phone, Mr. Madeira."

"*Sailor* is fine. Please don't be formal."

As they ventured farther inside, Frankie noticed the hypnotic sweetness of the scent in the room. It was apparently bread season as Sailor had four loaves of what looked to be cinnamon-raisin on cooling racks on the stove, and he told them he had four loaves of sourdough in the oven. "I make everything myself," he said. "I think it's better for you." The place was immaculate, spare but wisely decorated in silver, white and blue. On one wall was a self-portrait in oils of Beatrice which Frankie knew must have cost Sailor a fair amount, unless—and she hoped for this—her mother had given it to him. On another was one of her own photographs, an early one called *The King* of a kingfisher wreathed in bubbles just after going under after a fish. One more photo was a skillful, muted shot of a train yard, taken from a great height, possibly from a crane. Sailor explained that he had taken that one himself. "I was a photographer in the navy," he said. "Although, some of the pictures I took there, in Afghanistan, I wish I could forget." While he'd planned at first to make the navy his career, having gone to Annapolis on an ROTC scholarship, he was injured when a helicopter crashed to the deck of the *USS Fortitude* and, after a month in the hospital, he had limited use of his left arm but would never have any feeling in his arm or hand again. Suddenly, still in his thirties, he was living the life he'd meant to live in his fifties, the life of a much older man, clamming and lobstering, occasionally crewing on a longline boat with a friend for a month here and there, pottering around.

"You never had a wife and children?"

"Well, Frankie," Sailor said reluctantly, "there were people. There were people I cared for, who probably deserved better than I could give. But no one I ever really could say that I loved…"

"Such a romantic. I don't mean to pry," Frankie assured him.

"You're not prying. If you were, I could have just given you a one-word answer. The truth is, I loved Birdy. I had a relationship with Birdy. When I came home, it was to her." Had they done anything? Frankie couldn't decide if she wished they had or they hadn't. Sailor was a good-looking man, with a cleft chin, dark eyes and fair hair, every inch the Portuguese pirate. "There were other things too. Other reasons I came back here. But Birdy was at the top of the list."

Sailor asked how Frankie was doing with all of the changes, and how it was to be so suddenly swept into all the things of adulthood, the death of her mother, the upcoming birth of her child, her marriage.

"I don't know how I'm handling anything, to be honest," she said. "I know I miss my mother."

"I miss her every day. I sometimes felt I got the best of Birdy. I didn't get to be her husband, which is what I wanted. But all the talks we had, we really shared everything about our lives. I brought her my chili, which she loved, and she made stuffed peppers, which no one could make the way my mother made them, except for Birdy. We went on long walks while she took pictures of things she might want to paint. Sometimes, we would stay up late, she would read to me, and I would stay overnight if weather was coming… She would say that sometimes the big house got lonely… There was nothing out of line between us, Frankie, ever. I want you to know that…"

"If there had been, I would not think that was the worst thing in the world. I would have wanted her to have every hour of happiness she could have, Sailor."

"She loved Mack. Once she met him, there was never anybody else. I tried to talk her out of it every chance I could, no disrespect to your dad—"

"I'm not taking it as disrespect. Beatrice had her own life and her own heart."

Soon, impossibly, Frankie was eating yet more bread. With butter. It was cinnamon-raisin, the best she'd ever tasted.

Ellabella said, "You don't make your own butter, do you?" Sailor laughed as Frankie accepted another slice. If she were to be dropped into the water now, she wouldn't need weights to sink straight to the bottom.

Gently, Ellabella steered Sailor toward the matter at hand. She brought out the copy of Carlotta's complaint. Shaking his head, Sailor seemed about to drift into a silence but instead, he spoke up. "I used to take a drink. Twenty…thirty years ago. Not since."

"So you were drinking together, and you had a fight?"

"That's what they assumed."

"But that wasn't what really happened," Ellabella prompted him.

"We had a fight, but it had nothing to do with my drinking. Or her drinking. She just came to the Yankee and found me. It started because I was annoyed, down to the bone, by the stuff Carlotta was doing to people. If I told you, it would sound crazy to you. It wasn't like it was some crime. She wasn't a vicious person. She was desperate, and she knew how to spot people who were the same. Whatever she had, it was never enough. That's not something I should even be telling you. That was later, and that's between her and her own soul. Back then, it was when she got started on Mack…"

"What about my dad?" Frankie said. "She supposedly went out with him?"

"She did, Frankie. She was very…attracted to Mack. Not just to him personally. To the idea of him. I think she saw him as a way to do better. Do better for herself. This young professor, she could be a professor's wife." It went that far? Frankie thought. So far that she had fantasies about marrying her father? "I don't think it was that way for Mack. In fact, there was a fair amount of unpleasantness for him at the college when they found out about Carlotta."

"Why?"

"Well, she was very young. I don't think Mack knew that, not at first. But someone informed them that here he was, a professor in his thirties, going out with...well, I guess she'd turned eighteen by then, or at least she did shortly after they met."

Ellabella, who had by then succumbed to the allure of the cinnamon bread, said, "Who would care enough to rat him out?"

Sailor took a full couple of minutes to take more bread from the oven, then to arrange the racks and grease the next pans. Finally, he looked at Frankie and compressed his lips. "That was Birdy," he said. "Mack and Birdy had met by then, and she didn't want any interference." Frankie tried to imagine a version of her mother, of Beatrice, who would actually inform on her new love and his old flame. That volcanic overspill of passion seemed entirely alien, a concussion of Beatrice's characteristic serenity, the act of a woman Frankie had never known. She didn't know how to feel about it, except to wonder how much of her own personality she would curate for her own child, how much she would allow to be seen.

It was Ellabella who kept pushing, about the argument Carlotta reported as an assault, later telling Frankie she had a strong sense that there was something on the cliff of being said and that she needed to find a way to push it over. They all sat down at a table overlooking a ribbon of the ocean, and Sailor seemed reluctant to talk more. "What was the fight about? I mean, it could hardly matter now, right?"

Sailor smiled wearily. "If it doesn't matter, why do you want to know?" He added, "I don't mean to be so mysterious."

"It's not anything about you that I want to know, it's

about her," Ellabella said. "I mean, about her as it pertains to Frankie." Sailor replied that he wasn't sure that any of what he could say to them had any direct bearing on Frankie's life. He sighed again. "I'm not a very revealing person by nature. Like, Frankie, you thought you knew me pretty well, didn't you? But you wouldn't have expected anything you saw here today, would you? You probably thought I lived in a toolshed." Frankie grinned. She had to agree.

"Carlotta was expecting a baby by then," Sailor finally told them. "She started seeing someone else right after Mack and got pregnant right away. I never figured out why she was so desperate to have a baby right at that time. The best I can guess—armchair psychology—is she wanted something to love. Maybe like she wasn't loved."

"So she met somebody right after…after my dad?"

Sailor got up, stretched, used the apron he was wearing to polish a speck on one of the large windows. "She didn't have to look far."

Ellabella said, "It was you. You're Ariel's father."

In the stillness of the next few moments, Frankie heard the dual tone of one of those strange new ambulances, which always sounded foreign to her. "Does she know?"

"I don't think she does," said Sailor.

"How do you know Carlotta's telling the truth?"

"She just wouldn't lie about something like that," he replied. "And I did a paternity test. At first, Carlotta wasn't even sure she would let me help support Ariel." Sailor hastened to add that he wanted to. "She finally agreed, but she wouldn't let me see her, wouldn't tell Ariel who I was." So he'd sent Carlotta money every month of Ariel's life until she was eighteen and occasionally after that as well.

"I would bet that Ariel never saw a dime of that money," Ellabella said.

"I know that some of it is in a trust for her, for when she

turns thirty," Sailor said. "I used to get copies of the statements, and both Carlotta and I would have to sign to release that money, unless one of us was dead." He said, "Everybody thought that she was dead, for all those years, but I was pretty sure she wasn't."

"Did you hear from her?"

"Never once."

"If you loved her, why didn't you want her to stay?"

Sailor shook his head. "I never said I loved her. She was beautiful and she was smart and she was funny. Someone you love, though, would reach out to you. You know what I mean? That would never be Carlotta. Maybe that part of it, that frightened her. Or it bored her." The night they argued, he went on, was, coincidentally, the last time Sailor took a drink. He remembered. He was at the Yankee but then woke up the next morning under a bridge in Hyannis, his face looking like a mashed banana. His theory was that he got into it with someone who had thirty pounds on him. Scared by the damage, he figured some guy talked some friends into getting a passed-out and injured Sailor off the street. The next time, he also figured, he might not wake up.

"Why would Carlotta leave Ariel, if she wanted a child so badly?" Frankie said.

Carlotta was a rolling stone, Sailor said. She needed constant stimulus and couldn't be content with the same scenes and scenarios day-to-day. He believed that she did love Ariel, but she didn't understand the steadfastness that love required—or the fact that most of the time spent caring for another person was neither exciting nor exalted "Maybe you get a lot of congratulations when a child is born and then when a child gets married, but in between there's a lot of time that's just the boring stuff you do because you love the child, because you have to. Maybe she didn't count on that."

Ellabella said, "But when she found out that Ariel was getting married and that she might have money—"

The phone rang then. It was Penn, looking for Frankie. Mack was in the hospital. He had been underwater in his dry suit, stubbornly intent on repairing one of the pilings of the big pier, a minor thing he could have paid someone else to do, when his scuba malfunctioned. Ariel and Carlotta were in the boat. Nobody noticed anything wrong until an hour had passed and Mack hadn't come up. When he woke up—if he woke up—there would need to be tests for brain damage.

Frankie said, "Brain damage?"

"Something was up with the BCD. I don't know what."

"Mack would never make an equipment mistake. He's obsessed with safety."

Penn told her, "I know. But he did. And we don't know for sure how long he went without oxygen."

8

"This isn't your fault," Gil told Frankie, not once but four times on the phone. He was on his way back from the airport; she was on her way to the hospital. "If someone died every time somebody else had bad thoughts about him, there would be about twenty people left on the earth."

Frankie's tears shut off. "Died?" she said. "Do you think he's already dead? And they're just keeping him on life support?"

"No, sweetheart. It was just a way of looking at things. I'm sure Mack will be fine. The cold water was on his side, for one thing."

Still, Frankie was sure her dad would die or be forever impaired, drooling in a hospital bed on the same porch where Beatrice had died. Frankie's last encounter with him would always be the moment she hung up on him. Yes, Mack was wrong—short-sighted, impossible, tone-deaf, foolish, arrogant. But he was still Mack, still her father, whom she had idolized since she toddled. Gil hung up, promising to get there as quickly as he could.

At the hospital, she jumped out of the car without even pausing to close the passenger door. Through the maze of halls she threaded a path to Intensive Care. "Only family," the charge nurse said. "His daughter and his wife are in there already."

"No, that's his wife and his mother-in-law. I'm his daughter," Frankie said. "Look, here's my ID."

Outside the doors, Carlotta sat huddled on a hard molded chair. "How is he?" Frankie asked.

"He's sleeping. He was conscious for a few minutes, and the good news is he was completely lucid. So far."

"What's the bad news?"

"Well, I don't want to be the one to—"

Frankie demanded, "Just say it."

"He gave explicit instructions that he did not want to see you."

Frankie staggered. She had to sit down. The tables had turned with a vengeance. Who said that? Tennessee Williams? Frankie couldn't remember.

"Could I see Ariel?" She added, "Could I even look in?"

"I don't think so," Carlotta said. "I'm so sorry." She smiled sympathetically. Everything about her demeanor and her tone was respectful, muted, suggestive of truth. Something in her smile, however, assured Frankie that Carlotta was enjoying being the gatekeeper, the bringer of bitter tidings.

"What went wrong out there?" Frankie asked.

"I have no idea. I don't know how those scuba things work."

Frankie still thought that she could sense that insider's glee—the thrill of being at the center of a disaster. But it was probably her imagination.

Over the next few days, Penn brought Frankie news of Mack's recovery.

He had spent a single night in the hospital, under observation, undergoing a battery of tests that had thoroughly annoyed him, according to Penn. (*"Church, cat, spell, bracelet, candle, flight,"* Mack repeated in response to one of the tasks. "That must be the Halloween memory test. I'm not a child, and I'm not senile.") Penn's qualms about the way the accident happened were only increasing. But since it was a subject that neither of them could ever raise with Mack, who was already white-hot with rage at anyone questioning his soundness of mind, they had no choice but to quash their own fears. When Gil arrived, Frankie babbled out a litany of possible hideous outcomes; but Gil just kept saying, look at your father, sweetheart, you don't need a neurologist to tell you he's fine. He's proving that himself.

In the ensuing days, whenever she caught a glimpse of her father striding along, Frankie had to admit he moved like a man twenty years younger. It had been one thing to grandly banish Mack from her life. It was another to learn that Mack was content to banish her as well.

She didn't speak with him. He didn't want her.

So what?

She had her own life, Frankie reassured herself.

To bolster that position, she sturdily made preparations for her first Christmas at home in five years.

For Gil, she'd purchased a very good, very simple Canon point-and-shoot camera as well as a volume of the correspondence of Charles Darwin. Along with this, she was giving him a sweatshirt with a tiny monogram below the right shoulder that looked, from a distance, like hieroglyphs, but when you got closer read *Dad*. She had packaged and mailed Fair Isle sweaters for the sisters-in-law, fishing poles for the brothers-in-law, American Girl dolls for the nieces. For her father-in-law, Thomas, whom she'd yet to meet but who would arrive when Gil returned just before Christmas Eve, she'd gotten the best knife set she could find, realizing only too late she'd have to mail this to Canada as there was no way he would be getting on an airplane with it.

She'd had printed and framed the last photo she'd taken of her mother, a candid of Beatrice, in jeans and an old sweatshirt, standing at the edge of the water as storm clouds, complete with a bright vein of lightning boiled overhead. This she would give to her grandmother and to her aunt Imogen, hoping its beauty counterweighted the sadness. She also had given them warm mittens and socks in hopes that, before the next time she visited, they'd get the message that setting the thermostat at fifty-eight degrees was a little too stoically Yankee for anyone.

For Penn, she'd framed the same picture of their mother, his in a heavy sleek modern silver frame. Remembering her first morning at home, when she'd asked him for truffles for her omelet, she'd also plundered the gourmet-food store in Chatham, making him a lavish basket that included truffles, as well as foie gras, crackers translucent as communion wafers, spiced Japanese plum jam, caviar and a copy of *The Bachelor Gourmet.*

She bought silly Cape Cod sweatshirts for her boy cousins, Aunt Imogen's sons, now men, and one for her aunt's husband, as well as a dark green sweatshirt with a die cut of a nautilus on the front, that was actually pretty, for Paul's fiancée. Giselle was at first a big problem, but then Frankie decided to act on a whim and bought her Joy cologne, the scent that still lingered on Beatrice's cashmere sweaters. In a rare display of sentiment, Giselle would later tear up upon opening the box several days after Christmas, and say that her mother had worn this scent, to which Frankie was able to reply, "So did mine." To her grandfather and her uncle, she arranged to send a vat of chowder and several lobsters—in case Grandpa Frank hadn't had enough lobster to last him the rest of his life. She'd also sent Grandpa Frank a woven silk scarf she hoped would match his gray-blue eyes. She missed her grandfather terribly, she realized, and hoped he could honor his promise to return when her baby was born.

According to her obstetrician, all was well on that front, still a couple of weeks to go…the old joke, *Don't make any big plans for New Year's Eve…* Frankie and Gil had taken the hospital tour, but Frankie had also met several times with a doula, who was the obstetrician's sister, and who helped her prepare for what both of them hoped would be a delivery without need of drugs. She reminded Frankie that she wasn't a midwife, only a source of support, and that if Frankie and Gil wanted the baby born at home, they needed a certified nurse midwife to help. Neither of them wanted a home birth, not at all. But Frankie wanted to accomplish it without pain medication. As she had so many times these past several months, Frankie had to interrogate herself on whether she was doing this because she really thought it would be better for the baby or only because Ariel had managed it. She had no aversion to drugs. She'd given herself any number of injections, including antibiotics and painkillers, and, after ripping her outer thigh open on a reef, had even applied liquid bandages until the coast guard could get her someplace for stitches. Babies weren't in danger from the judicious administration of narcotics, especially if the pregnancy had been routine and the mother had good prenatal care.

She asked the doula, "Do you guys argue about home versus hospital?"

"We used to," the woman said. "My sister was always pretty tolerant of me, a good big sister, and I was that militant hippie who said pregnant women weren't sick and hospitals were for sick people."

"What changed?"

"Well, I still think a home birth is great if everything goes according to plan. But I was helping a nurse midwife who had a bad complication. First off, the baby was breech…and coming too fast. I was terrified. So was the midwife. Then even after the birth, it turned out the mother kept some stuff from us because she wanted to give birth at home so badly. Like she said, this was her first birth so the Rh factor wasn't a big deal, but it was not her first birth. The ambulance got there in the nick of time, and my sister, the goddess Andromeda…"

"Why do you call her that?"

"It's her name. Most people think it's Andrea, but it's not… I'm Cassiopeia. My parents were stargazers," she said. "Andy got the call, and she was on that ambulance. I was trying not to be hysterical, and then it was like, here come the Marines! Everything turned out fine. My sister didn't even say, *Well, told you so.* And I don't think the mother or the husband even knew how touch-and-go it had been…"

"She said it was her first birth because of the husband?"

"Yep. The things people do. The things people lie about." Then she seemed to shake it off, like a wet dog, and said, "Frankie, trust your body. It will tell you the truth. And if it's a false alarm, heck, nobody cares. We're working, anyhow."

As Giselle fussed with final gift-wrapping and baking, Frankie tried to stay out of the kitchen. She felt not so much fat as stuffed, stuffed as the apple-and-chestnut goose Giselle planned for Christmas Eve. The same food that she'd dreamed of in nearly erotic throes only days before was abruptly as appealing as a pot of tripe. "What's wrong with tripe?" Giselle asked when Frankie confessed her disgust.

"Don't even talk about it. I wouldn't feed it to the cat, if I had a cat."

"You will miss out," Giselle said.

Frankie said, "Yes, God willing."

Gil had continued on to Canada after Mack's crisis. In one of their phone calls, she told Gil that they were going to need to rent another storage locker just to hold the pastries. Instead, energized, Penn collected some canvas and baling wire and staked a sort of tent into the ground as a temporary food storage shed. He covered the sandy dirt with a round piece of hard plastic flooring he bought at an RV dealership and knocked apart some wooden pallets to construct makeshift shelves. As an experiment, they set out a single container of old doughnuts. By morning, raccoons had eaten all the doughnuts and daintily replaced the lid on the container. Penn gave up. He bought an impregnable small rubber shed. He and Frankie calculated that, counting labor, the Christmas dinner would cost about three hundred dollars per person.

On the twenty-second, the rest of her family began to arrive. Imogen's husband, Uncle Corbley, announced his intention to read history books and sleep until Christmas. Frankie hadn't seen her cousin Paul, two years older, for at least five years. Accustomed to gangly nerds like her husband and brother, Frankie was astonished by Paul, who was a column of solid muscle, as was the woman he was marrying. When she hugged him, she said she was afraid she would injure herself. "It's all we do," Paul said. "Jen and I are trainers. We work out every morning, except Sunday, for two hours, sometimes afternoons too."

"When we're finished, we're going to start our own studio," Jen said. "We think we'll call it Fit AF."

"As in… Really?" Frankie asked her.

"Fit… Air Force!" said Jen. "Hooah!"

Granny Becky had brought a pot of beef stew, which everyone except Frankie gratefully consumed. She ate oatmeal. Penn said, "Do you have morning sickness still?"

"I just don't like real food anymore."

Next day, booted and coated, led by Imogen, they all strolled through Chatham, wandering among the glittering and glitteringly expensive stores and through the forest of small Christmas trees decorated by merchants. Every tree was so twee, so quintessentially emblematic of the heart of Cape Cod upper crustiness. One was decked out with sand dollars and starfish, one was entirely strung with tiny lighthouses made of stained glass, another with lighted candles to symbolize the New England tradition of promising safe haven with a candle in the window, and one with dog biscuits and golden retrievers (Frankie remembered Penn once saying that every family who crossed the Sagamore Bridge with a moving van was issued a golden retriever and a bandanna for it to wear around its neck.) When they came home, Penn made chili, and Frankie made gagging noises.

That night, she and Gil talked on the phone for an hour. Although she had never wanted to be that kind of woman who was silly about her husband, Frankie missed Gil wretchedly and even her fingertips hurt when he ruefully told her that, instead of the following day, he would not be back until after midnight on the twenty-third. As if this mattered, he had already arranged for Penn to fetch him from the airport. When Frankie suggested that the bear girls had charms that a lumbering wife did not, he was too annoyed to tease her. Gil had not seen his own father in two years and the first time he would see him would be in some tourist muddle at Logan. At least, Gil would be able to make the proud introduction of his wife to Père Beveque on the morning of Christmas Eve.

Listening to him, Frankie admitted to herself, but to no one else, that she also missed her own father. Mack and Beatrice had loved a full-bore Christmas and a First Night on New Year's Eve with illegal fireworks and banging of kitchen pans on the beach before they ever headed out to a late celebration with friends. But this year, Mack and Ariel were taking the baby to visit another beach, in North Carolina, with his family. For the first time, Frankie would not talk to Mack or to Ariel on Christmas. No matter where she had been in the world on Christmas, she'd always spent an hour on the screen with Ariel, once even harmonizing their high-school choir parts of "Have Yourself a Merry Little Christmas," and crying when they came to the part about being together, if the fates allow…

The whole family was settling down to one of those comforting and tedious games of team Scrabble, the kind in which someone was always willing to go down in flames insisting that a word like *oating* was an actual verb, when Carlotta arrived with a tray of gingerbread. Introduced around, she told Frankie it had come from Cape Cakes. "I'm not much of a baker," she admitted. Frankie thanked her, although the gingerbread was coals to Newcastle by this point. Granny Becky asked, "Is everything around here called Cape Cod Something now?"

"It absolutely is," Frankie said. "It's like everybody got tougher all at once and said, *Hey, this is Cape Cod, and we're a building company, so how about we call it—wait for it—Cape Cod Construction?*" She reminded Penn how, in junior high, they used to take pictures with their phones of every sign they passed that conformed to the rule and how Penn had once made a slide presentation for a high-school economics class: Cape Cod Glass, Cape Cod Creamery, Cape Cod Lighting, Cape Cod Landscaping, Cape Cod Seafood ("That's Cape Cod cod," Penn said now). A silence that was not entirely comfortable ensued as people seemed to wonder, almost audibly, if they should turn back to the game.

Carlotta finally wound her scarf around her neck and mentioned that she'd heard from Mack and Ariel. She also said, wistfully, that she would miss seeing Ben on his first Christmas, but was trying to think of her time alone as an opportunity for reflection.

She was clearly angling for an invitation.

Not quite wanting to, but seeing no alternative, Frankie said, "Of course we'd love it if you would come for dinner on Christmas Eve."

Her smile beatified Carlotta's angular face, which, in repose, could look carved by sun and time. Then something that resembled smugness passed over it, and Frankie thought of Sailor Madeira. She hoped that Carlotta didn't presume an invitation to Christmas morning as well. It was not just that Carlotta was not family and that Frankie longed for the rest and release of being nothing more than her unguarded, unadorned self. It was something else, too, something there was no reason for and that Frankie couldn't name. There was still so much about Carlotta that was strange, perhaps only unaccustomed. She wondered if Ariel felt the same way. After all, Carlotta had been back in her life for only a few months. And yet, Carlotta had not gone along with them, despite how much she evidently cheered up Mack's father.

Frankie was accustomed to falling asleep easily and hard. But this night, she rolled this way and that, kicked off her quilt, rearranged her pillows, finally shrugged into her coat to venture outside and walk to the edge of the sand, where the seaweed smelled of sulfur and oregano, following the moonlight as it seamed into the purple plush sea surface. *So far? So early? So soon?* She went back inside, warmed milk with a drop of honey and still could not find sleep, yet she'd never been sleepier.

She wondered if the weight of the pregnancy was what wearied her or the weight of all the circumstances befallen her since she returned home, a cairn of invisible stones not all of her own making. As for those that were of her own making, was she making too much of them? She had eaten meals at more than one hearth around the world where the old man's pregnant wife was nineteen to his seventy-five, the wife the same age as the old man's pregnant married granddaughter. In most other cultures, no one really tried to contravene the primacy of men and their will to do whatever they wanted. It was only the modern gloss of civil seemliness that engendered Frankie's shock. Maybe in global terms, all the things of adulthood had descended belatedly. And yet, if it was true, as Sailor had said, that they had all come down at once, they had come down hard.

And then, as she watched from the window, so did the snow.

Blizzards on Cape Cod were rarer than camels. Frankie had no idea if this one was foretold. She switched on the little weather radio that Gil loved so passionately and heard that the spinning storm was a surprise to everyone, probably including Santa Claus. As if cued, her phone rang. Gil said, "The damned plane can't land in Boston. I'm in goddamned Detroit."

"That's impossible. It's—what?—an hour-and-a-half flight."

"Yes, but it does not feel like that because I've been traveling for eight hours already." She heard another voice. "The one and only good thing is I ran into my father here."

"When do you think you'll get here?"

"We could drive," Gil said.

"It's…no, it's hours, it would be ten hours."

"More."

"And the weather's getting bad here, or worse. Just…call me back in the morning." She added, "Please tell your father hello, that I'm sorry about this."

"He's Canadian. He's seen snow."

"Oh, Gil. Being Canadian isn't an excuse for everything."

"I miss you, and I want to be home with you. Where you are is home."

"You will be. It will all work out."

She didn't believe this at all.

Hers and Gil's first Christmas alone together would also be their only one. She hadn't considered it this way before. They'd barely become a couple before they would be a family, their lives pledged to put another before either of themselves—as they should, as they must. Still, was it wrong to mourn the lazy bounty of newlywed life they'd never really had? Mornings in bed with newspapers, huddling in front of late-night horror movies, dress-up dinners at fancy restaurants…a honeymoon in the mountains.

They were luckier than most.

She did believe that.

Frankie sat down on the big sofa near the window to watch the snow swirl. She got up to stuff pillows behind her back and then pulled a comforter over her. The little potbellied wood stove, which Penn had thoughtfully stocked and stacked with clean, dry wood, still glowed with the previous night's heat. Frankie got up briefly and added a couple of logs.

She fell asleep finally and dreamed.

She was in the kayak with her mother, on the day that the shark bumped them, but in this dream, the shark rose up and snapped Frankie in its gaping jaws, crushing her around the middle, shaking and twisting her with a pain so feral that she thought, *How lucky this is only a dream and I'm not really able to feel this because it would be unbearable.* She looked across at Beatrice and her mother said, "Don't worry, Frankie. Everything will be all right." She was standing up in the kayak and leaning down over Frankie, touching her hair as the shark sank its teeth deeper into her abdomen. "It will be all right," she repeated, and Frankie woke, clutching the edges of the sofa, cold with sweat, but instead of Beatrice it was Giselle leaning over her, gently stroking her forehead and reassuring her. "You were crying out," Giselle said.

"I was having a nightmare."

"I think, no, you are having a baby."

Frankie reached down and touched her belly, stretched, rigid, almost hot to the touch. "Not yet," she said.

"I think very soon, today," Giselle told her. "I think we need some help."

"Not yet," Frankie repeated. *So far? So early? So soon?* Giselle gestured lightly at the window. At first, Frankie wasn't sure what she was seeing. Snow was banked almost to the lower edge of the windowsill. Two feet? Three feet deep? A pristine expanse spread away as far as Frankie could see and a pristine silence as far as she could hear. Only the birds spoke, excitedly. As she watched, snow began to fall again, first languidly, then with vigor.

Giselle said, "Call your brother."

Bundled and disheveled, Penn arrived in minutes, plunging through snow up to his thighs. "We don't even have a snowblower. I'm calling some of the neighbors to see if I can borrow one." He added, "I can't hear plows yet."

"Put on your rain gear," Frankie said.

"I should have. I forgot. You sound like Mom."

"I hope so," Frankie said, and the jaws closed on her again, as if something was attempting to tear her entrails out of her body. She put her fists against her lips and howled. Penn jumped and cringed.

"Is it labor?" he asked.

"Yes."

"Isn't it too soon?"

"Not too very soon," Giselle said. "The baby will be fine. That last was twenty minutes ago. Perhaps fifteen minutes ago."

"I have to get to the hospital," Frankie said. She could feel the pain slip away, roll out like a tide. Then she felt it mustering for its return, circling, gathering, somewhere beneath.

No one said anything.

Frankie called Cassie, the doula, who said she would get in touch with the hospital ambulance immediately. "This is what I want you to do. Get up and take a nice long, hot shower and wash your hair. Put on something big and comfortable, like pajama pants and a big sweatshirt. Have a little tea and maybe, if you can stomach it, just one bite of an orange or one bite of toast. Don't eat more than that. Take a walk around the house. And when the next pain comes, do what we practiced, breathe deep into it, blow into it like a balloon. Rest in any position you think is comfortable."

"My husband isn't here yet. His plane couldn't land."

"Who's with you?"

"My brother and my mother-in-law. My grandmother and my aunt are at a house in the neighborhood but too far to walk here."

"It'll be good. I know I must have scared you when I told you my sad tale, but that was a long time ago, and most babies are born healthy, with no events. That's the truth, Frankie. So the next time you have a contraction, I want you to believe that. Healthy baby. Lucky baby."

"Will you tell the doctor?"

"I will. I'll call her now, and she'll meet you at the hospital. Good luck. This is so exciting! It's so scary but exciting! Christmas Eve! Think of that."

After weathering the next contraction, rolled like a snail on one of the living-room chairs, Frankie collected her things and showered, but she was barely out when another pain reared up, one that gripped not only her lower torso, but blazed down into her thighs. Frankie moaned, then shouted. Someone was banging at the door. Carlotta was outside the bathroom door. Without asking permission that Frankie surely would not have given, she helped Frankie into her mother's flannel nightgown ("Don't bother with the underwear"), a thermal undershirt and her Saltwater Foundation hooded sweatshirt, which Frankie felt it was urgent to wear. When the pain came again, Carlotta stood behind Frankie and held her with one arm securely around her chest and, with one thumb, pressed low at the base of Frankie's spine, which somehow had a soothing effect, as if it moved the pain not into the next house but a few paces across the room. "This was something I learned when I was studying nursing. I didn't get very far, though," Carlotta said. She helped Frankie onto the bed, slipping pillows against her spine. "When Ariel was born, I took a cab to the hospital, and the next day, I took a cab back here."

"No one came with you?"

"You know my mother," Carlotta said and snorted. "And the father...wasn't involved."

"I heard that," Frankie said. For the next ninety seconds, the pain thundered through her, sweat coursing down her cheeks in itchy rivulets from her already-soaking hair. Carlotta massaged her back and then buffed her hair with a clean towel. Frankie took a deep breath and said, "I know who Ariel's father is."

Carlotta said, "Well."

"He said you didn't want him to be involved." She was concentrating every atom of her being on the task at hand, so how could she have room even to think of this? And yet, she did. And why didn't Carlotta ask the reason Frankie had been talking to Sailor about her? She seemed either to know or not to care. "Does Ariel know?"

"No."

"Why?"

"I didn't want him to be involved."

"Why?" Frankie asked again.

"Because he loved somebody else. He could never love me."

The doula called back.

Frankie said, "I thought labor pains started out almost like you couldn't tell what they were because they were so faint and subtle?"

"It's different for everybody."

"This is not faint or subtle."

"It gets bigger."

"Bigger than it is now?"

"I don't want to lie to you."

She was trying to find someone with a plow on a pickup truck, but everyone she knew was out. Penn had located a snowblower, but the neighbor couldn't start it. No one could reach Gil. Granny Becky was furious that she couldn't get to the cabin and called so many times that Frankie finally stopped answering. Paul's fiancée suggested sitting on an exercise ball. Carlotta said that was actually a good idea, but Frankie didn't have one. Snow thickened. Penn brought in more wood, although the house was now using the ordinary heating system.

Then the lights flickered.

Even Frankie, breathless and shaking from the last contraction, stopped and gazed around her in horror.

The lights went out. The heat clicked off.

Everyone in the room listened to the seethe and roar of the wind and the surf.

Forcing the door open, Penn took off for the big house. When he returned, it was in a full rain suit carrying a sack with more boots, more rain jackets, six fat candles and a dozen small flashlights from the stores Beatrice had always wisely maintained. He'd also stuffed in a pound of good coffee. He tried then to shovel, but it was hopeless, he said. Every scoop filled with snow before he could heft another. He offered to do anything else. Carlotta told him to boil water on the wood stove, bring many more warm towels and find sharp scissors and twine, just in case.

"Just like they do in the movies," Penn said. "There are lights in the big house. It will stay warm. They have the generator." To Frankie, he said, "Do you think you could walk there? It's no more than a block or so."

Frankie wanted to laugh. They could tie her to a sled and drag her through the snow like some fallen prospector in an old story about the grim hardships of the Yukon. To try to walk there would be suicide. It seemed impossible to be in suburban Massachusetts yet alone in the indifferent universe. She'd read dozens of accounts of women in labor lashing out at their husbands, frothing and swearing, but she felt no anger, only a fear that the next pain would paralyze her or wrench her in two. The pains had changed in intensity and now seemed to come from a bigger engine. Finally, Cassie got back with a video call. "I'm going to stay right with you now, Frankie." She admitted that Andy, the obstetrician, had not yet been able to get to the hospital. "It's a nightmare out there, Frankie. There are wrecks all over the road." Ambulances were ferrying accident victims to emergency rooms all over the cape. "I can't believe people are actually trying to stick to their holiday-travel schedule in this, can you?"

"How will I get the painkiller?" Frankie asked. She had decided, just minutes before, that natural childbirth was out of the question, a brutal notion. "Who will tell me when I'm ready to push?"

"I couldn't do that even if I really was there, Frankie. Doulas give emotional support. Massage. Advice. We don't do cervical checks or any really medical stuff. I'm studying to be a nurse midwife, but I'm not one yet," Cassie said. "Do you have Tylenol?"

Frankie roared, "Tylenol? Why not gummy bears? I need painkillers, real painkillers."

"Center yourself, Frankie. Dig deep."

Frankie did. She threw the phone against the wall, mustering so little force that it did no more than dribble down to the floor with a forlorn clatter. She was glad she hadn't damaged it. It upset her when people in movies or on TV broke mirrors and plates, angrily swept files off desks, books off shelves, hurled phones, tore up paper. Who cleaned all that stuff up after the crisis? What about keeping things in order?

Speaking of order, what good was Cassie? It would probably be just as effective to have a minister pray over her. Although the room still was toasty, Frankie's teeth began to chatter. She shivered as she felt the approach of the next pain. With extra blankets Penn brought from their father's house, warmed by the woodstove, Giselle tucked her in closer, and Carlotta pressed her strong fingers deep into the small of her back. When the next wave broke and dragged her down, Frankie gasped, "Call my father. Call my grandfather."

A few moments later, she distantly heard her grandfather's voice saying, "Hold on, Frankie. We love you," but was too breathless to answer him. Amazingly, then, spent, she fell asleep. When she woke, she had forgotten where she was. "What time is it?" It was early afternoon, Giselle said. Hours had passed. Then there came a new sensation in the pain, a stabbing, a sinking. When she next looked up, the sky was already darkening. She heard sounds that could have been close or distant, some kind of truck, a plow on the main road, or was it their road? Someone was reaching inside her, pulling and twisting and wrenching, and yet no one was here. Then the whine of another machine. A snowmobile? Through the window, she could see…was it the doctor? A slim form with a medical satchel. To Giselle, Frankie said, "Here come the Marines!"

"Okay, Frankie, lie down and let me have a look. This table will hold you. Good strong table. So let's get you ready for the ambulance," her obstetrician was saying, then murmuring, "It should be here soon. Hmmm, maybe not soon enough. Well, everything is fine, just fine. We've got this. Good sturdy mattress? The Christmas story with a big twist. Not long now… Don't push yet, Frankie."

"I have to go to the bathroom."

"That's exactly how it is supposed to feel, Frankie," said the doctor.

"Do you have kids?"

"No," said the doctor. "But I will in a few months."

The door burst open, and Gil rushed in, with an older man who embraced Giselle. The doctor said, "Really? Is anyone else coming?" And then she continued sharply, "Okay, everyone out of this room except…is this Dad?" To Gil, she said, "Wash up, then, and find yourself something clean to wear." As she closed the door leading out to the kitchen, Frankie glimpsed her brother's pale face, terrified eyes. "I'm okay, Penny," she said and then screamed. Penn fled.

"Pretty soon now," said the doctor.

Frankie floated up, high above, looking down on the snow globe of the cabin, winged by the dark surfaces of water, the flag of chimney smoke and starry chips of snow all swirling, the windows small bright yellow stamps and before the door, a group of dark figures, singing *O tidings of comfort and joy, comfort and joy.* Her family, holding flashlights, singing in the snow. The doctor was adjusting her hips, as though she were a giant doll. "Okay, Frankie. Next time I want you to give me a big push, no hassle, just a nice, big push… That's the way. Superb. You're a champ." With a cloth, Gil wiped the sweat from her eyes. "Again, Frankie…"

Gil said, "Frankie, look at me." She did. "Jump for the mud, Frankie. Jump for the mud."

She jumped, and she did break in half then and heard a sharp cry, not her own.

"Beautiful Frankie, wonderful. Merry Christmas, little fellow!" said the doctor, and then Gil was holding him out to her, and she looked into his unblinking dark blue eyes above plushy cheeks. Oh, she thought, this is not something that I would ever have thought I could feel. She could not make him more perfect, so she would perfect the world so it would be fit to touch him. Gil's face sagged with exhaustion, his glasses were askew, he looked as though he'd had to swim all the way to Massachusetts.

"Frankie, he's wonderful. I didn't think I would ever be a father." He kissed her forehead. "Thank you so much."

"Ubaldo, I think your father is smitten," Frankie said, proud of herself that she had leaped tall buildings and could still flirt.

"What is his name for real?" the doctor asked as she tidied Frankie. The ambulance buzzed and whooped outside the door, and the relatives cheered.

Frankie said, "I don't know." To Gil, she said, "What do you think?"

"Maybe, I thought, maybe Attleboro. Attleboro Beveque… it's very classy, right? One of those New England prep-school names? What will they call him? Atty? Or probably, they'll call him Flip or Skip or Chip or some American thing."

"Attleboro for my father?"

"Frankie, no," said Gil. "Attleboro for you."

"Attleboro Rowan Thomas Beveque. Two names for you, two names for me."

"All of them for him," Gil said. "What do they say? Americans? Attaboy—Atty boy!"

9

"Yo, Frankie!"

She was dreaming, Frankie thought. Most of what she and Atty did was sleep, for hour after luxurious hour, with the sun from the windows full in their faces. He ate and slept; she ate and slept; Gil cooked and ate and slept; her mother-in-law cooked and ate and never seemed to sleep. She made consommé Tosca from vegetarian bouillon, thickened with tapioca and garnished with julienned carrots and quenelles of truffles. She made spinach and artichoke pasta, strata with kale and Muenster cheese, tomato soup with a thick crust of baked Gruyère. She baked loaf after loaf of sprouted whole-meal bread. "Please don't go home," Frankie pleaded. "I will give you my car if you stay."

"I'll teach you to make all of these things," Giselle said. "Gilbert already knows."

But when Giselle left, Frankie was even more contented. Their enclosed world of only three was made of sun and skin and laundered sheets. Its center was the big bed.

That day, when she heard the call followed by a knock at the door, Frankie was almost shocked that someone had found them. Almost frightened by the invasion of her bliss. She knew it was Ariel, hailing her as she had when they were kids, tossing a pebble at her window, then in later years, simply slipping in at the back door.

"Yo, Frankie!"

Would she answer? She longed to answer, but also to hide and pretend, as people did, that no one was home. It was January. She could see Ariel standing bundled in the five additional inches of snow that had fallen the day before, to the delight of the locals, who already were creating legends about this, the snowiest winter of their lives. Ben strapped to her chest in a carrier, his little legs stiff in a snowsuit moving the way that the limbs of one of those wooden starfish toys moved when you pulled the string. She opened the door.

"Hello," said Ariel, grinning as if they'd just had lunch the day before. She looked wonderfully shiny and fit, her thick pale hair cut short and blunt.

"Hello," said Frankie. She didn't know whether or not she wished Gil was there instead of working on his bear-girl article at the library. She must herself look more bear than girl, third-day sweatshirt with wet patches in key spots, rumpled and unwashed hair, sweatpants pulled up over unshaven shanks. "I'm sorry that I wasn't expecting company."

"I'm not company," Ariel said. "I'm never company."

"What are you, then?"

"I'm Ariel. I'm your friend."

"Fine. Do you want some coffee?"

"Sure."

"And you can't leave without promising to take some cakes or cookies from our personal bakery shed. We'll still have these next Christmas. If you haven't tasted Mrs. Beveque's profiteroles, you haven't seen Shakespeare the way it's meant to be done."

"I promise. So can I see the baby?"

Frankie stepped out onto the porch and held up one hand to shield herself from the sunlight. "I feel like I'm in a cave, and I only come out to look for roots and berries."

"So to have this coffee and see this baby I have to come inside," Ariel said. "Is that okay?"

"I guess," Frankie said and then added, "Of course, come in." Attleboro lay resplendent in a shaft of sunlight in the ancestral cradle Beatrice's grandfather had made, the cradle Frankie had threatened to cut in half on the day she came home...which now seemed so long ago.

"Oh, look at this sweet love! Could I hold him? Will you hold Ben for a moment?"

Frankie received Ben into her arms, lowering the hood of his snowsuit and liberating his chubby fists from the sleeves. He stuck a finger in her mouth and smiled. Weakly, Frankie said, "Ari, he's so sweet. He looks just like..."

Ariel murmured, "He looks just like you. Yes. We say so all the time. He has your personality too. He's very stubborn."

Unable not to respond, Frankie kissed Ben's neck. He laughed, a fat, deep bubbling. "He's so smart," she said.

"He knows it's better to laugh," Ariel said and began to cry. "I miss you so much. I'm so sorry. I'm so sorry. I would never have hurt you..."

"You knew how much you would hurt me."

"I knew, but I didn't know. I didn't want to know. Mack seemed so very sure it was fine..."

"Because Mack believes that whatever he does is not only fine, it's ordained. And if he finds out that someone objects, automatically it's that person who has a head problem, not Mack. I mean, if it were wrong, why would he have thought of it? I think Henry VIII used to use that argument pretty regularly about his own marriages. When the bride was maybe sixteen and he was probably fifty. About the same age spread there."

Ariel ignored the vinegar and stroked Atty's cheek; he shifted and smiled in his sleep. "What a big, strong baby, Frankie. I heard you had a hard time." Grabbing a paper towel, she patted her cheeks. "I'm a waterworks lately."

"Me too."

"You're fine now, though?"

"Couldn't possibly be better," Frankie said, thinking she sounded like a complete ass. "But yes, I failed at earth-goddess baby delivery. So where did you hear that it was rough for me?"

"On the news… Come on, Frankie. Penn told me. Your dad was half out of his mind with worry about you. He was up all night, checking the phone. Penn was calling about you every hour." Frankie hadn't known this. She didn't know how much credit to give it. For this, the first month of Attleboro's life, she believed otherwise. She visualized all of them in some fancy catered setting… *Is that the phone? Who'd be calling on Christmas Eve? Penn? Well, he'll be here in a couple of days anyhow… Just don't answer. Oh, whose number? Okay…well, say something to her, I guess. I'm sure she's just fine…* and then back to the second course… "I guess he was worth it, huh? He's just perfect. Can you believe that we both have little boys, at the same time? And they're the same family? Who could have imagined? Ben is Attleboro's uncle. Uncle Ben is pretty little, though! You think we should insist that he calls him uncle?"

Atty Beveque was a big baby, nine pounds exactly. Frankie wasn't sure how that had occurred, having no memory, for the several months previous to this birth, of eating anything except bread and jam, as if she were a storybook character. She'd spent a luxurious two days in the hospital, where Atty was the only baby. All the nurses made a fuss over him and gave him outrageous things donated by this and that store or individual, some intended to shower the first baby of the New Year. There was a Bugaboo stroller and a Montcler snowsuit and big soft luxurious blankets crocheted by local grannies. Frankie hadn't even considered having a baby shower. (Why hadn't she considered having a baby shower?) The only baby clothing she had was her own and her brother's, things Penn had found in the basement and washed and dried for her. Ellabella brought her a case of impossibly tiny diapers. "You'll try cloth diapers for a few weeks, but after that, you won't care if every diaper he poops in takes up a whole landfill. These are biodegradable diapers, so they say. But we'll never know. Some things, I think you have to just step aside." Despite her lack of gear, Frankie still thought she should refuse such luxury items. "Oh, don't!" said one of the nurses, Seneca, a woman so large and imposing and so graceful with her crown of elaborate braids that she made Frankie think of a three-masted sailing ship. "We get dozens of things in here. Like, look, cashmere blanket sleepers! The woman having the baby was mad at her mother and wouldn't keep them."

"But there are people who need them more than we do."

"And we have twenty more for those people too."

That night, more presents piled up as the nurses, carrying candles, sang carols in the hall. Certainly, this practice was in defiance of something ecumenical, but Frankie didn't care. Her throat swelled with emotion at the old words about mother and child and in gratitude for the care extended to her. She ate a vegetarian Christmas dinner twice. The nurses called Atty a natural-born nursing champion. How safe and loved she was, and how safe and loved her child! That any baby could be less than adored, on this night of ancient tales of adoration, was so acutely distressing that Frankie cried herself to sleep with her son clutched tight against her chest. When he was laid in his Plexiglas bassinet, an ornament dangled above his head that read *I Was a Star at Seaside Hospital.*

Home she went then, to a belated Christmas with all her family.

Now, Frankie keenly felt Ariel's gaze on all the pretty trifles. She wanted to explain, but what for? Ben's nursery overflowed with luxe objects. Mack had spared no expense. Not sure why she would put herself through the answer, Frankie asked, "Are you going to have more kids?"

Ariel said, "We hope so. At least one more. Are you?" Frankie nodded, suppressing the gusty sigh that rose up unbidden. The *we* still rankled. "Mack is just great with him. He's the best father. It's like he finally got to a place in his life where he has time to appreciate everything…" Ariel stopped, horrified. The newly dried tears brimmed again in her eyes. "I didn't mean that like it sounded."

"Sure, you did," Frankie said. "And it's true. Everybody deserves a few practice kids before they get it right."

"You know it's nothing like that."

"It's just the truth, Ari."

Ariel said, "No, it isn't."

"Since you're here, please tell your mother thank you for me," Frankie added. "I never got to say that on Christmas Eve, for obvious reasons." Ben beamed up at her, and Frankie resisted the impulse to snatch him up and cuddle him closer. He was clearly watching her reactions, trying to summon her heart.

She told Ariel that she'd invited Carlotta to dinner before everything else happened and about how Carlotta had tried to help ease her pain. Ariel said that was kind and how troubled she'd been when Mack didn't want her mother to join them in North Carolina, a reluctance Frankie now fully understood, even if Ariel still did not. "She's been really helpful with the baby," Ariel said. "I guess she's changed. Can people really change? Maybe she just finally grew up and recognized what a mistake she made." When Frankie didn't join her in speculating, she pressed her lips together and said, "You know, maybe she left because she got sick of people sitting in judgment of her. Assuming she was one way so she'd always be that way. Because people aren't willing to let you be anything except what you used to be." She crossed to the back wall of the cottage and stood looking out that window, her fingers clasped behind her waist. "And I have to believe her, even if I don't want to. Because other than Mack, she's all I have. I'm not like you. I don't have a grandmother and a grandfather and aunts and uncles and cousins. Just her. Especially with your mom gone." She came back and faced Frankie. "Anyhow, part of why I came, now, is to tell you that your grandfather's arriving tomorrow..."

"Day after tomorrow."

"No, tomorrow. Mack moved the flight up because the weather's supposed to be bad again." On the phone, Penn had told her how, when he finally got to their grandfather's place several days after Christmas, Ariel told him how she longed to see the blizzard, how alien she told him she felt on Christmas Eve wearing a sleeveless dress and walking to a fairy-lit restaurant patio ringed by sweet gum trees instead of huddling in her parka on the widow's walk atop the Saltwater office, searching the moody ocean for the lights of ships. She'd done that so many winter nights in her life, many times with Beatrice.

"Penn could have told me about the change."

"Penn promised to tell you. But then your father started loading him down with all kinds of stuff he had to do and get, so he's away for the next couple of days. I thought he might forget. Do you think you and Gil would come to dinner?"

"Thanks for letting me know," Frankie said.

"Okay, I get it."

"Now, I should feed him."

Ariel said, "He's asleep."

"Well."

"Do you have life insurance?" Ariel asked.

"Why? Are you going to kill me?"

"No, it's just, you have to. We do," Ariel went on, that *we* again. "You have dangerous jobs, like Mack. You're always underwater and on boats and flying places in small planes. Both of you," she said. "My mom brought this up, and she's right."

"They gave me some forms at the hospital," Frankie said.

"Fill them out. I'll mail them for you."

For the next short while, then, under Ariel's gaze, she filled out forms. "Gil says life insurance is a scam. That the companies count on most people living."

"That's not a scam, Frankie. That's just an actuarial reality." Math, Frankie remembered, was Ariel's strong suit. "You have to get insurance for the baby too."

Frankie was aghast. "What? Why?"

"Not expecting him to die. See? This kind here." Among the sheaf of papers in the hospital packet were insurance forms from the world's largest baby-food manufacturer. "We got two policies for Ben. Well, my mother got them for him, two hundred thousand bucks each. And the way this works, when the policy is mature, either that's good, your kid already has life insurance and never has to worry about qualifying for it, or you can cash out the value, not the big value but some value. It's like a college fund." Ariel paused. "Unless you're the kind who'd contribute regularly to a college fund."

Frankie knew she wasn't and neither was Gil. Their incomes were too variable and intermittent—and so were they.

So Frankie filled out those papers too and wrote checks.

"You have to make a will too, and the baby has to have a guardian and a backup guardian. You don't even have to have a lawyer to write a will. It's legal if you and Gil just sign it."

Who would be Atty's guardian? Longingly, Frankie gazed at Ariel, cuddling Atty, but she would elect Penn and one of Gil's brothers, probably Luc, as an alternative.

"That was very useful," Frankie said. "Thank you. And now, I guess..."

"I don't have to leave yet. But if you want me to leave, you can just ask me to leave."

I don't really want you to leave, Frankie thought, *and if you're here one minute longer, I'll want to tell you everything that has happened and everything I haven't said for the past four months and maybe even about Sailor Madeira and we'll end up talking for hours*, but instead she said, "Well, I don't want to be rude."

"How long does this have to go on, Frankie?"

"Don't ask me." She shrugged.

"What's it going to take?"

Before she spoke, Frankie took a full minute to compose her thoughts, what she'd planned a dozen times to say. "I can tell you exactly what it would take. It would take my father to apologize for humiliating Penn and…well, me too…at the Saltwater banquet by making it all about you and his new-and-improved child being the future of the organization that my mother started."

"He didn't mean it that way."

"Oh good! Then, it shouldn't be difficult for him to apologize."

"You know he doesn't have the…ability to see it that way."

"Well, you would say that. You're one of his minions now, Ari. Of course he has the ability to do that. He has the skills. He can get adults and children all over the world to understand complex ecological realities and see how those realities indeed affect their everyday lives. He takes pride in giving the complex a relatable face. Mack Attleboro is a scientist who really gets it. That's what he says."

"But he won't know…"

"*Won't.* That's the key word, Ariel. Not *he can't*. He won't. And I won't either. I won't overlook this. I won't let Penn and I won't let myself be one of those pesky little bumps in the road Mack just rolls over. No. No, thank you." She stopped and took a deep breath. "That's what it will take. Some recognition that the family that didn't quite live up to his expectations still exists."

"Frankie, that's a horrible thing to say. You know your dad loves you more than—"

"You're the one saying that. He's not. He hasn't even seen his only grandchild. He didn't even want me there in the hospital! Actually forbade me to see him, when he could have been dying. He hasn't called, hasn't sent a gift. He's sent a messenger. If he even sent you." Something in the atmosphere slipped open and then snapped closed. "He didn't even send you, did he? He wouldn't want to know you were here, would he?" Frankie softly zipped Ben back into his snowsuit, helped secure him in the front pack and then crossed and opened the door. *Go*, she thought, *go fast before I change my mind.* Ariel stepped through the door, looking back quickly, as if to add one more thing, only to turn away again and make her way through the snow.

Then she stopped.

She took a few steps back toward the cabin.

"You know what, Frankie? There's another reason that your dad didn't call. Ben was sick. He was really sick… He was in the hospital for a day and a night. You didn't even know."

"What? How could I have—no one told me, Ariel. Was this when you were in North Carolina?"

"No, since we've been back."

"Well, what was wrong? Did he have a virus?"

"The doctors don't know for sure. That's the best they can tell. He was dehydrated, and then, it all stopped. He got better. He was terribly sick with diarrhea and throwing up. He had a high fever. We were all there with him."

"Penn should have told me!"

"I asked him not to. Maybe that was petty and stupid. In fact, I admit that it was petty and stupid. But if you don't even care enough on your own, and you live right down the street, why should I have to send messages? He's your little brother,

Frankie. And okay, you didn't want that. But now, that's the way it is. Nothing will ever change it."

"Look, Ariel, I'm not some monster. If I knew that your baby was sick, I would have tried to help. I think you know me better than that. I think my father and even Carlotta know me better than that."

"Well, good. But the fact that I couldn't turn to you is not my fault. It's yours."

Frankie said nothing.

"Frankie, I'm going to tell you this one time. I'm not Mack's minion. But I'm not your minion either. Not anymore. I'm not your poor, sad, abandoned pity friend. Did you think I was going to just sit here and wait until you decided to come around to celebrate another one of your many triumphs? People can change. I changed. I made my own life. It's a good life. I'm proud of it. I know who I am. And maybe—don't say anything, Frankie—maybe you should figure out who you are before it's too late." When Frankie didn't reply, Ariel went on. "There's one more thing. Mack rewrote his will. I didn't want him to. It was his wish, after the accident he had. He left everything to me just as Beatrice left everything to him, including the house. Penn tried to joke about it, but I know he's upset. To be honest I am a little too, I know how much you both love the house and how connected it is to your mother. But what am I supposed to do? I have a son to think of now. It's in there that he'll make some kind of provision for you and Penn. But if you want that provision to be anything of substance, try being a decent person."

When Gil arrived back a few hours later, he found Frankie curled around the baby. She scooped him up and handed him to Gil and wordlessly disappeared to take a long and thorough shower. When she had toweled off and dried the snazzy bob cut she'd maintained over the months and put on makeup and new leggings and a long red satin shirt—as if she would soon be heading out for a fancy dinner, she appeared back in the living room.

"You are trying to seduce me?" Gil said.

"Early days for that kind of action," she told him and then asked, "Am I an evil person?"

"I won't touch that one with a barge pole," Gil said.

"I'm serious."

"Do you think I'd be married to an evil person? Or have a child with an evil person?"

"Some sophisticated sophistry, sir."

"Some sensational series of syllables."

"I'm not illiterate, just because I'm not a bilingual writer." When she told him that Ariel had come over and what she'd said, Gil suggested a walk or a ride. They'd just purchased a new car, a small and sleek minivan with all the trimmings, and Gil, who hadn't owned a car since he was twenty, and never a new one, kept inventing errands that would take him to Hyannis or better yet, to Boston and beyond. Once they were settled with their coffee cups and doughnuts in the deserted parking lot at The Beachcomber, high on the dunes above Cahoon Hollow Beach, with Atty nestled in his car seat, Gil turned to Frankie.

"You're not evil. You're good and bighearted and kind. Most of the time. Some of the time, you're complicated." Frankie breathed out slowly. That was code for *you're a bitch*. "These events have not produced the best in you. I don't think there is a person who would have just passed through them without feeling some…some derangement. But this keeps getting bigger and bigger. Now there's the matter of inheritance, which is this subject that somehow always makes people angry. And all I'm worried about is that, finally, it will be your custom. You'll get hard on it."

"I don't even know how to correct the phrasing there in that last part, sweetie, but don't say that outside our house. People will misunderstand. You mean, it will become a permanent way of being. I'll be set in my ways, like old people say. Set, like harden."

"C'est ça."

How was it different, Gil asked then, before all this happened? When her mother was alive? Frankie had to think for a long time before she replied. She told Gil about how things had made sense then. It was as though Frankie had been part of a big, sturdy wheel with Beatrice as its hub, and however it turned, however slowly or quickly, it never lost its orientation or its shape. Now, it felt as though all of those parts were moving without synchrony, failing to mesh, bashing against each other, sparks sizzling into the mechanism and into the air. "I came home thinking that there would be a way to save that feeling, of being part of something strong that lasted forever. I thought maybe I was even bringing home the next generation. But instead, there was a new wheel, and I wasn't even on it."

Gil pulled Frankie closer to him. "No, you're on it, you're just not the center of it." People who have interdependent lives sometimes have to make compromises, he went on, so preachy that, for one of the few times in their short life together, she had to fight the urge to snap at him. It didn't look that way from the outside, he said, but they were probably putting up with all kinds of small and large sins. Saint Gil, Frankie thought. It's easy when everyone in your family takes the usual course and also reveres you and each other. Gil and his brothers were like the March sisters in *Little Women*, except for their being only three brothers instead of four sisters.

"How come you're so smart all of a sudden? And what about all this family devotion? You were the one who once said that family ties were death to adventure."

"I was wrong about that. Or I was showing off. I thought loneliness was romantic, but that was just how I dressed it up for myself. This is a different kind of adventure."

Frankie paused. "That house was in my mother's family for generations. That land was my mother's. Why do I have to be the only one to compromise?"

"I guess because you're the one who minds the way things are." Gil added, "And maybe you're not going to get to be part of that big wheel anymore. You'll have to learn to be happy without it. Maybe we'll have to start our own wheel. Just think, in thirty years, our son will be in the position you are in now."

Frankie thought, thirty years? Thirty *years*?

That night at home, she began to write again. Why was she writing? Was what she was writing any good? Or even worth her time?

She wrote about how being a photographer meant being always a corollary rather than a participant—and that, in some ways, being her father's daughter was the same. Her son's birth was one of the first times she felt at the very center of her own life, as though something was happening that would not happen if she were not truly and fully present for it. It was a strange and powerful emotion, singular despite its universality.

I wasn't intending on having a Christmas baby. People whose births collide with even minor holidays endure jokes for the rest of their lives (Say it's April 1. April Fool's Day! The joke was on your parents… Say it's the Fourth of July…you're a real firecracker!) I could only imagine what he will have to put up with, being born on Christmas Eve. I wasn't intending to set him up for this, but intention is only an illusion human beings have. Of course, I believed what people said, that first babies come late, so he would be born sometime in early January. When he and his brothers were little, Gil told me, they set up the wooden crèche in the French way, so that every day, the wooden figures of the wise men got a little closer to the stable, finally arriving on the feast of the Epiphany, when the wise guys finally got there and explained what the big deal was. Who knew if anyone believed them? Who knew what they believed? They probably weren't kings but stargazers, maybe even astrologers, advisers to King Herod. They were informers. They certainly weren't Jewish and so not waiting for a messiah. They probably rode swift Arabian horses, not camels. They watched the brightest star in the sky, and I too have watched the North Star, usually the brightest, so many times out in the dark when I've lost my bearings, and it led them where they wanted to go. Our son was born not in a stable, but during a snowstorm in a little cottage by the ocean, not far from the hospital. If I was impressed before by the circumstances in which women do this, women I've met when I've traveled, I'm in awe now. I didn't think I was going to die, but at a certain point, that probably would have been okay with me. Nothing is worse, and yet women take this in their stride. Women are serious. Women are undaunted.

She thought of her first published photo, in *Smithsonian*. To be accurate, it was not her first published image: she'd been taking photos in and around the sea for years, with newspapers and magazines like the *Coast Chronicle* paying her impossibly meager sums. But this was real money and a real magazine and the intoxicating notion of millions of people seeing the choice she had made to visually convey the implicit symbolism of a mother cormorant feeding her chick from her own throat—although, back then, she hadn't really understood the full power of that symbolism. It had been, she recalled, part of a feature called "Small World," photographs of every manner of animal cub. Did she understand it now? Did taking her place on this even greater wheel, of women who were mothers, vouchsafe her not only the personal power of growing and nurturing an entire, perfect being from her own body, but also anoint her with boosted artistic chops? Would she be a better artist with better insights even as her time and her capacity to express those insights were constricted exponentially by the very event that conferred the presumed wisdom? Or was this whole line of reasoning just baloney? Was it a chicken-and-egg proposition? Did an artistic disposition predispose you to a tenderer sensibility? Of course not. The human world and even, to a lesser extent, the animal world, was filled with lousy, blunt, selfish, immature parents. Conversely, the human world and the animal world also teemed with terrific parents who (at least, the human ones) saw the truest expression of their role as doing the thing itself, not making some kind of representation of it.

It turns out that I was not up to the task of photographing my own son, Frankie wrote. *I could not see him the way I saw the other creatures I made pictures of. The tide of love I felt for him drowned my objectivity, and I wanted to make him pretty instead of interesting.*

In an odd choice that felt somehow right and even essential, Frankie asked Sailor to take a photo for Attleboro's birth announcements. He had a good camera, a tiny Sony Cyber-Shot that looked like a toy. But what he came up with was a charming picture, the baby giving the world a kind of side-eye from his basket. Frankie would mail copies of the card to friends and editors all over the world and even more gifts would pour in—she had not intended this and wanted to mail a follow-up card protesting that she wasn't trolling for loot—but Gil assured her that it was the pleasure of people to give gifts to babies, most especially perhaps babies born on Christmas Eve. "Those invitations you get, saying no presents…don't you find those both presumptuous and sort of smug?" he said to Frankie, who had to think about it, since she'd received far fewer party invitations in her life than Gil had in his.

A few weeks later, somewhat embarrassed to be treating Sailor like a dad in the absence of her own, Frankie asked him to take a photo of the three of them, of her and Gil with the baby. She insisted on paying him; he insisted she not even consider paying him. They settled on a special dinner after the photo shoot. Frankie wasn't even sure why she wanted the picture taken. It was another of those elemental urges she could neither understand nor ignore.

Since Atty was still so small that he barely had definable features, they discussed how to make the baby a presence. Sailor finally suggested that they undress him and lay him on the thick white quilt that Madame Beveque had made for their wedding and that the two parents wear identical white shirts. Sailor took the blanket outside and spread it out on the snow, taking considerable care to avoid the spots that were melting as the temperature edged up to fifty degrees. He examined the field around the blanket for possible hindrances until he had a blanket of white on a blanket of white and an unmarked view of the sea.

"We… Wait! We can't do this outside!" Frankie was astounded.

"Sure, we can," Sailor said. "Imagine how beautiful and puzzling it will be. People will think it's a made-up background, but smart people will be able to tell that it isn't."

"He'll die of exposure."

"We'll get arrested," Gil added.

"No, he'll be fine. You'll keep him bundled until everything is just right, and then it will take one minute."

That was just what they did.

Frankie had perfected Beatrice's vegetarian chili, which she served with sweet corn bread studded with chips of green pepper and a drizzle of hot apple cider. After the sun set, it quickly got colder, and Gil built a fire in their recently rehabilitated fireplace. Sailor held Atty in Frankie's rocker, which had been her mother's, quietly singing to the baby, "Irene, goodnight, Irene, I'll see you in my dream," a song Frankie remembered Beatrice singing, telling Frankie that it was actually a very sad song about someone who'd lost his true love. As Sailor had lost his true love. Frankie found her camera in her hands for the first time since Atty was born. The flames and the shadows collaborated to make drama of the smooth little face and the lined older face, seeking each other's eyes. With their family portrait, the print of that moment would hang above Atty's bed, fittingly, for it was the moment when Sailor was sealed to their new family. It would be he, not Frankie, who led the little boy to go to the shore to understand the sea, different every hour. When he was two, he would point to the picture taken that night and say, "Baby and Gee Gee," his first word for *grandfather.* When he was eighteen, a smaller version of it, in a silver frame, would be one of the few photos he would take with him to McGill University.

That night, Frankie found herself once more drawn back to Carlotta's mysterious absence: it felt so at odds with the sweet concern she demonstrated for both Ariel and little Ben—indeed, the sweet care she'd given Frankie herself. She told Sailor about how good Carlotta had been, and he was not surprised, but he gave her another possible way of decoding that conduct. "She likes to be at the center of anything," he said. "It doesn't mean that the things she does aren't good. It's more about why she does them."

Frankie reminded him of something he'd brought up when she and Ellabella visited him, something Carlotta had done that was wrong but so strange she'd never pay for it, and he could barely bring himself to repeat it.

"I just can't," Sailor said. "I feel ridiculous bringing it up."

Was that because it ended up meaning nothing, Frankie urged him? Did it have any lasting effect? It did, Sailor agreed, it did.

He couldn't remember where he'd first heard about Carlotta's scam or who it was who told him. More than one person from their shared past had told him, and he was able to look up details on Facebook. Although at that time he didn't participate actively in social media, Sailor was able to track her down by trying a number of family names and finally finding complaints and warnings about someone called Carly Sherry, a combination of her own first name and her mother's.

It was ridiculous.

It was also very, very creepy.

Carlotta apparently lived in New Jersey at that time, mostly near Atlantic City and the hotels and casinos she'd always counted on to make a living. She opened a dog-walking and dog-sitting business, which apparently, through word of mouth, took off like a rocket. From what Sailor was able to gather, she walked ten dogs in two groups twice a day, thirty dollars per walk. If she sat with the pets at the house or apartment while the owner was away, the tariff was something like two hundred dollars a day. Sailor said, you'd think that might be enough.

But then one dog owner complained that when she returned from vacation, Carlotta demanded an additional fee, two hundred dollars or more, and if she didn't get it, she vowed that she would drop the dog off at the local humane society. The owner called her bluff. Carlotta followed through—and the owner had a devil of a time getting his dog released to him.

The owner then took to the internet, where at first no one believed him. It began with the complainant saying, *Watch out for this woman*, then five people, then twenty. The grace note was that no one knew Carlotta's real first or last name. People who might have suspected could simply not credit the possibility that sweet, helpful Carly (or Clara or Sally) on whom they and their pooch relied, could be an unscrupulous dognapper.

"Obviously, a scam like that can't last too long," Sailor said. Carlotta/Carly used a traditional drop-scheme in public places, watching until one of her targets left a package of money in one of those pole-mounted little libraries, where books were deposited for anyone to borrow. She would then call and reveal the location of the purloined pet.

When things started to feel hot in Atlantic City, Carlotta moved to Maine, which might as well have been the moon. In Portland, she started over again, then in Newport. Finally, someone came up with the genius notion to post a picture of

Carlotta, who was very striking and whose naturally platinum hair was a giveaway.

What was strangest about the whole affair was that nothing ever came of it. Apparently, from what Sailor could gather from social media, Carlotta had an explanation for her shenanigans, which was that she only tried to get more money from pet owners she suspected of abusing their pets. If the owner paid up, Carlotta was satisfied that the owner loved the animal and she did not keep the money. If the owner refused to pay, Carlotta either found the pet what she considered a better home or brought the dog to a no-kill shelter—in her mind, having seen her hunch justified. There was no reliable way to prove that she hadn't returned the money she'd supposedly extorted.

"What a strange thing to do," Gil said. "You can't determine… I mean, no one can really say if she did this just for the money or because she loved dogs."

Frankie pondered that. More than strange, it seemed to her desperate, a way to assert dominance. If she had to guess, she would suggest that, for Carlotta, the whole endeavor had less to do with money than power. Moreover, she was pretty sure that Carlotta wouldn't know this. She thought back again to the professor who encouraged her to ask herself what she was really feeling: frustration or hunger? Rage or fear? She then tried to lay that stencil over Carlotta's actions. As Sailor pointed out, Carlotta didn't seem to have friends, in the ordinary definition of the word, people who kept up with her life. Sailor said he was, by nature, a solitary man. But if he didn't have pals he talked to every day on the phone and didn't have a sibling, he had always had Beatrice, as well as a few good acquaintances in the fisherfolk community. Furthermore, he certainly knew that there were farther-flung people he might see only a few times a year, with whom he shared a history and who knew most of what was worth knowing about him, who actively cared about his welfare, who would notice if it had been too long since his last call, who would come to him in a pinch without having to be asked. Still, although for more than eighteen years he had sent money intended to help Ariel each month to a bank account and received a receipt in return, he had not once talked to Carlotta in all the time she had been gone.

Why not?

She didn't know if she should ask, but then scoffed at her own reluctance. The whole scenario was ridiculous, like some kind of paperback Gothic romance spinning around on a magazine rack in the Brewster General Store. In these days of DNA swabs and online revelations, people just didn't keep such secrets. People didn't even honor ordinary boundaries of civility—at least in the United States. And the shenanigans of so-called aristocrats in other countries made even Americans seem discreet by comparison.

"She didn't know as much about Ariel's day-to-day as you did!" Frankie said. "But she controlled the limits of the encounter?"

Shyly, Sailor agreed that yes, she had.

Even more important, at least to Frankie, was the question of how much her own mother had known. Surely, Sailor would have confided the truth about Ariel's parentage to his beloved Birdy? But Beatrice had never said a single word that would have led Frankie to such a conclusion. She must then also have known, as Sailor must have known, that Carlotta was somewhere out there, alive and well.

"You talked about everything," Frankie insisted. "Everything except the biggest secrets in your life?"

"About Ariel, I didn't know if it was my secret to tell," he said. "About Carlotta, I know it wasn't my secret to tell. As for Birdy, I'm sure she knew, or she had a good hunch, but we never talked about it."

Such a level of reticence was foreign to Frankie. In this respect, certainly, she was her father's daughter and not her mother's. For Mack, whose every thought quickly tumbled out of his mouth, who couldn't bear to be alone, for whom company, and indeed, adulation, was as necessary as oxygen, the idea would have been unthinkable. As if to explain further, Sailor pointed out that, in his opinion, Carlotta had never told Ariel. Why, Frankie asked, did Sailor not tell her himself? If not long ago, then why not now? Without Ariel knowing, Sailor had looked out for her, even collecting the trash and cutting the grass at the condominium she owned and rented out. He had no idea if Ariel thought that this was some kind of town service… Before she married Mack, and after Birdy died, when Mack and Penn were out of town and she was alone at the big house, he watched every night, making sure she was safe inside before he went back to his own place. He had done just what the father of a grown daughter might do if he were nearby and the daughter were on her own, everything except tell her how proud he was of her, how much he loved her, everything but rejoice in the grandson he still hadn't held. If it was hormones that brought tears into Frankie's throat, she welcomed them, thinking of this man, this good man, denied the basic gift of claiming his child. But then, did she know that Sailor was a good man? She did know: he had been her mother's best friend, all her life, and nothing about the way he talked or behaved set off the pricking of her thumbs. It was not Carlotta's dicey deeds, Frankie thought, that made her go back and forth about trusting her, but instead what she could only describe as the smell of desperation, the sense that Carlotta changed herself to fill every space she occupied. About Sailor, she sensed nothing resembling that unsteadiness. Having lived his life by the sea, he was nothing like the way her mother described it, changing every hour. He was constant.

"What do you think? Should I tell her?"

"Unless there's a real reason you don't want her to know," Frankie said, and Gil agreed. "Until a couple of months ago,

I would have said I knew Ariel better than anyone on earth knows her. And I'm sure she'd be… Well, if it were me, I would be surprised, sure, but then I would be happy and proud."

"Then, maybe I will tell her," Sailor said. "How should I tell her?"

Frankie told him, "We'll think of something."

10

As she and Gil talked it over, Frankie lay naked under the quilt across Gil's legs, nursing the baby and wishing that nothing might ever change. Even her longing for sex was as distant as the fog bell. She was only this, this elemental moment, and the larger world of editors and womanhood and work and money occasionally bumped her like a blind underwater creature. She understood why women stayed home. When she was a child, years were long, but she had principal tasks to do: she was learning to be the person she would be for the rest of her life. When she was in college, years were compressed into quarters and class hours, assignments given and submitted, projects mounted and hung. When she set out in the world of work, time sizzled past: she loved to tell people that she could not recall a time in her adult life when she had ever been bored. And it was true, so by rights, without tasks, schedules or deadlines, she should be bored now. But instead, there seemed to be no time except gauzy allotments of darkness and daylight, the weather's embroidery on the air and the ocean. All she had to provide was her body and her love, fresh water, dry laundry. She had all the grace and self-knowledge of a strong horse and, like a horse, she craved nothing more. Even the idea of the good it would do to try to negotiate a relationship between Sailor and Ariel seemed monumentally intrusive and exhausting. She would send each of them a note and let each of them act on it or not. She had to force herself to consider anything beyond that.

"Just a note, that would be too crude, would it not?" Gil said. "Sort of silly?"

"You're right, of course," Frankie agreed. Imagine opening your credit card bill and the reminder to make your dentist appointment, and the next card you opened said *Surprise! Bet you'll never guess who your biological father is!*

Gradually, the idea formed of asking Sailor and Ariel over to dinner. Would that be viewed as some kind of setup? What if the news turned out to be unwelcome or upsetting? Frankie had seen TV shows in which long-lost relatives were not just chagrined to be found, but furious. There they would be, in front of witnesses, forced to act out a play that one of them didn't know had been written. Instinct, however, seemed to suggest that the very same witnesses also might end up providing a psychological safety net of some kind...but what were the terms of this meeting? Wouldn't it necessarily mean asking Mack too? Although, wasn't Ariel perfectly capable of walking a couple of hundred steps down a pebbled drive without her spouse? Frankie was by now more bored than saddened by the feud with her father, yet all she had to do was to think for a moment about his blunt, public diminishment of her and her brother, his explicit wish to not see her at the hospital, to feel new rage boil up in her gut. Gil could say what he wanted about how petty and thin-skinned she was being, but Gil hadn't been expected to grin and applaud as he was supplanted in his family's business.

"You know, there's no time frame on this, Frankie. We don't have to get it done right now," Gil said. "It's not like another day or even another year would matter at this point."

But it would matter. Carlotta's return had dug up old histories, and a shipwreck that had lain undiscovered for centuries was still a shipwreck. The comparison was too apt. The few times Frankie had dived a wreck, she was herself a wreck, sucking down her tanks in half the ordinary time, certain that, any second, a fleshless head would knock against her mask. You could imagine the best and the worst result of a revelation, but there was no seeing the unforeseen.

"Let's just move away," Frankie said. "They can all sort themselves out."

Although waiting for anything was alien to her, Frankie agreed to reflect on a course of action. Gil would soon be headed to Canada for EnGarde's yearly seminar, an event that brought journalists and spectators in the thousands from all over the world. Gil wasn't giving one of the big lectures, but there was a star-studded lineup, including Genevieve du Barry, the controversially entrepreneurial scion of the huge conservation family, who was going to discuss her family's plan to buy huge tracts of land and establish exotic game ranches which hunters would pay huge amounts to visit, which she insisted would give support to populations of grizzlies and other big predators better than any amount of park conservation. Gil coaxed Frankie to come along and bring the baby, but she was horrified, almost frightened, by the very thought of venturing into the world outside her cocoon. "You aren't always going to be like this, are you?" he asked her, and while she told him of course not, she had been the lone ranger, out on her own, doing work that she loved fiercely; she was only at the start of her career, she would be back out there…in a year or so. Gil said, "A year?"

"Or two?"

Gil could barely compose his face. He hadn't counted on such a radical overhaul of Frankie's way of being. To be fair, neither had she. And yet, Gil made enough to support them, if they were careful. It would take time to finish her book—not that anyone on earth was waiting with bated breath for its revelations; she didn't even have a contract. When would she begin her lifework again? What had she imagined her next project to be? Beyond a few small things that could be completed locally, she couldn't even guess. Surely, she could take Atty with her wherever she went. Jane Goodall's son was with her in the Gombe. But she couldn't take him underwater in a bathyscaphe...that would mean that she would need to bring a helper with her. A helper, in a camper van? In a tent? Well, sure it was possible, at least in theory... *So far? So early? So soon?*

Did she even want to do what she'd done before she'd become a mother? Life without taking her pictures? It would be a half life. Life without Atty? It would be no life at all.

For a moment, she was almost grateful for her domestic upheavals.

She hadn't returned calls to Ellabella Ballenger, despite multiple messages left. It took Penn reminding her: the two of them were now actually, officially dating. Penn said, "It makes me feel like I did when I was fourteen years old and I stood by the door at school I knew she came through in the morning, and I stared at her like she was a movie star."

"She was kind of a movie star," Frankie agreed. "She still is."

"She's really a good person," Penn told her.

"She's reformed," Frankie said. "She should be reformed. Torturing people in high school? It leaves scars. Ellabella left more than her fair share."

She told her brother about the time, after one of her photos was featured prominently in *National Geographic*, and a photo of her at work appeared in the front of the magazine, she'd received a big and initially cheery-sounding greeting card from an address in Colorado. No signature. As she read the greeting, a sizzle tapped the back of her neck. *Congrats on all your success! Guess this was why you were so stuck-up when we were in school.*

If she had been stuck-up or superior—well, *had* she ever been stuck-up and superior? Did she trade in some measure on Mack's success and visibility? Frankie could think of only one incident, and her face would broil with shame if she even thought about it. In a film class, a guy was holding forth about how he would be the next David Attenborough if he could—or at least the next Gordon Ramsay. "I just want to be the face people see in the grocery store and think *Who is that guy?*" And before she could even begin to stuff an invisible gag in her mouth, Frankie was saying, "If you were, you wouldn't want to be."

The guy disagreed. "I don't just want to be good at what I do. I want the recognition, and I'm not too humble to admit it."

"If you grew up with that spotlight on you, you wouldn't ask for it," Frankie insisted, then suddenly noticed that the whole room, including the teacher, had gone silent.

And yet, years later, every inch Mack's daughter, she had indeed sought out the spotlight. She didn't conceal her identity, her relationship with her famous father. She didn't sell her photos anonymously. They were *Francis Lee Attleboros*.

So everybody had sins. Maybe she hadn't held people's dogs hostage for money but… Carlotta had changed her ways, it seemed. So had Ellabella—and Frankie. The common wisdom was that people's characters were, in a sense, hardwired. But perhaps trauma or experience could temper those tendencies. Only Ariel didn't change. Ariel was rock-steady. (Or did she only seem that way?) One thing Frankie did know: she had seen Ariel in action as a good judge of character. Elaborate denials, evidence to the contrary, nothing fazed her once she'd made her own assessment of a person or a situation. But who, even Ariel, could be suspicious about the motives of her own mother, joyously returned to her after years of mournful speculation? And why was Frankie suspicious? What business was it of hers? Ariel was fully grown, a professional, married, a mother, not to mention no longer part of Frankie's life. No longer, as the person herself had so succinctly put it, Frankie's minion.

"Are you going to be my sister-in-law?" Frankie asked Ellabella when she finally returned her calls.

"Are you always going to be this blunt? Remember, I'm a reticent Yankee." She added that she and Penn were just having fun, enjoying the moment. Frankie said that sounded like something you'd read in an entertainment magazine.

"I want the real deal," Frankie said. "And—wait, no, I don't want the whole real deal. No anatomical information—"

Ellabella said, "Please."

"I was thinking of asking you and Penn over for dinner, for a dinner party." In a rush, before she could recant the revelation, she told Ellabella the reason for her sudden impulse toward midwinter and postnatal hospitality.

"That doesn't sound like a dinner party, that sounds like the Donner party," Ellabella said.

"Hence wanting you there. You can be surrogate family."

"There has to be a more civilized strategy. But before you make a new plan, listen to what else I've found out. Well, sort of found out."

Further and deeper searches led to one after another confusing cul-de-sac where Carlotta was concerned. People often change their names, Ellabella told Frankie, but not their birthdays or their city of origin.

"People change their names when they get married."

"No, they change their names all the time."

"That could get expensive, the court fees and—"

"You don't have to go to court to change your name," Ellabella said.

"You do so."

"You do not. You can change your name, even legally, to Rama Lama Ding Dong if you don't do it to commit a fraud. It's based on English common law. You can call yourself whatever you want. Actors do it all the time. Musicians and artists do it." She added, "Of course, if you want to go to court and pay some fees and enrich the commonwealth and further the salaries of attorneys, you can do that too. They'll take your money."

"What's all this got to do with Carlotta?"

Ellabella suspected that Carlotta had changed her name at least once, perhaps many times, which was how she had become so elusive in a documentary sense. "If it was like it is on TV, the crack internet sleuth—that would be me—would have traced her origins and turned up all these false identities and prior addresses and arrests and who she had dinner with on July 20, 2020."

Instead, Ellabella had a skein of knotty strings, possible enrollments, possible employments, possible aliases, among them Carly, Carla, Callie, Carrie and...Ariel.

"You're kidding."

"What? Kid the future aunt of my future kid?" They both laughed at that. "There's one string I'm pulling, though, and don't ask me about it, because I'm not going to tell you until I really have it nailed down. But why don't you just watch for the right time and snoop around? Where does Carlotta live, anyhow?"

With Mack and Penn away, she was living at the big house full-time, helping with Ben as Ariel resumed her work with the Saltwater Foundation. The plan, or so Frankie presumed, was for Carlotta to move to the condominium in Orleans that Ariel owned, once the tenant's lease was up. Of course, Frankie did have a key to her father's house. But how could she slip in and rummage around in Carlotta's room for some elusive thing when she didn't know what it was? She, who got nauseated even watching people do such things in British mystery shows. (*He's coming up the stairs! Put the box back in the bookshelf! He's going to notice that!*) She thought back to her caper with her mother's jewelry box, which now seemed quaintly innocent. And not everyone would notice something innocuously out of place. It depended on the meticulousness of the person who lived there. Frankie, for example, would not at this point notice a troop of armadillos in top hats crossing her living room.

The idea simultaneously horrified and seduced her. She was perversely proud of Ellabella for her unashamed guile and relieved that Gil had not been in the room for their conversation, for he would never approve.

"I'll do it," Frankie said. "But you have to keep watch. You have to keep watch for Gil and for Ariel and Carlotta. I'm going to give you something to signal me so loud it won't matter if there's a thunderstorm, I'll still hear you."

She produced what she'd found, which was a bullhorn that Mack had used years ago to call swimming races for kids on the Fourth of July at the beach club. Because Frankie was in high school then and wanted it later for her own, he'd ordered it in pink. It still worked just fine.

"How are you going to know when it's the right time?"

"They go to a Baby and Me gym class every Tuesday at ten."

"How do you know?" Ellabella said. "You're not in touch."

"I found the registration paper on the ground by the mailbox. I just put it back in the mailbox. They only went to two of them so far. There has to be more than two meetings. It's at the Y, so they have to drive twenty minutes, anyhow, there and back. Then there's the class. So they're always gone for two hours."

"You watch them pretty closely," Ellabella said.

"I can see them from the second-floor bathroom at my house," she said. "Maybe kind of watching, I agree. But Ellabella, it's my house. Where I grew up. Do you go in your parents' house when they're not there?"

"I live there. Different set of circumstances."

"I don't go in to steal things or hack their computers. I go in to get things that I need, that were mine. Like my good winter boots. Like the quilts my mother made..."

"Aren't those technically Mack's now?"

"Aren't you supposed to be on my side? Why are you upsetting me? I'm already enough upset—I mean, already upset enough, don't you think? I didn't take all of them. She made, like, fifty of them. I just took the best ones. Which I knew she would want me and Penn to have. Some of them were made from quilting squares from clothes we wore when we were little and our baby blankets." Frankie had to push down tears. "Anyhow, Ariel doesn't like anything that was made before last Tuesday. Why should those beautiful quilts just sit in cedar chests forever? They were my mother's. My mother, not hers."

"Frankie, no! Don't cry. Honey, I was just sort of teasing you," Ellabella said.

"You were being pretty much an asshat about it!"

Ellabella apologized. She made soothing noises. Frankie finally gave in, muttering something about hormones. At last, Ellabella continued. "Okay, so tomorrow is Tuesday."

Frankie's stomach bubbled. "What should I be looking for? I mean, I know, documents..."

"Like bank statements or pay stubs or a file with her passport? Pictures? Most people get pictures developed and then they don't ever bother to put them in photo albums. They just stuff them in drawers. Anything like that."

"All that stuff could be in a bank someplace."

"True enough. But think of your most important personal papers. You wouldn't have to have a filing cabinet or a whole suitcase to keep them with you. You'd have a couple of folders or some big envelopes or a cardboard box with a lid and you would mark on it, I don't know, *birth certificate*..."

"I always just left mine here," Frankie said. "That was a different circumstance, though. I never really relocated, just traveled, and the likelihood of losing them would have been so much greater." She added, "Won't she notice they're gone?"

Ellabella's sigh was a long teakettle hiss. "You're not going to take them, Frankie. You're just going to line them up on the kitchen table and take pictures of them, whatever you find, and message the pictures to me and then put them right back."

Frankie's admiration for Ellabella's stealth was towering. "But they don't do that on British mystery shows. Why don't they do that? Everybody has had a phone for at least ten years."

"Not always with a camera, though."

"Yes, with a camera! And still, the innocent person is always breaking into the killer's house and taking some clue and leaving a telltale mark in the dust. Then she has to find a way to break in again and put it back so that when the killer reports it missing and the garda comes, it's right there, and the police just think the bad guy is insane."

"Frankie, you need more sleep."

When Ellabella showed up early the next morning, it was with a tray of coffees, a box of doughnuts and a blue sweater that her mother had crocheted for the baby. It had a huge red letter *A* on the back. As she scooped Attleboro up and nuzzled the back of his neck, Frankie extravagantly admired the little garment. "The scarlet letter!"

"That was intentional. Kitty thought it was funny."

"Well, it is funny. And very Massachusetts. I never saw Kitty as the crocheting type."

"She never was. She mocked people who did crafts, even people who had a sourdough starter. But now she wants to be a grandmother. She took classes. Not at being a grandmother. At knitting and crocheting."

"She's very good at it. This is perfect."

"She's good at everything she does. If Kitty's going to do it, she's going to rule. That was how we were brought up. Captain of the team. No *B*s. Even if you have to kick somebody down the steps to do it. It was worse for Al and Jude and Jazz, but hard enough on me too."

Ellabella's brothers were named Alistair, Jude and Jasper. Frankie said, "I will never get over your brothers' names. They sound like vicars."

"She was going for that. Mom took wanting to be something you're not to a whole new level. If my parents were British, they'd have bought a title by now. Baron Kenneth. Lady Katherine Ballenger. Except she's just Kitty. Kitty on her birth certificate. She doesn't really admit to that. Too shanty Irish. She was Kitty McShane." Ellabella admired the snow portrait of them with Atty, which Frankie had just framed and centered over the headboard of their bed. "So much love in that picture," she said. "I don't just mean you two with the little prince, I mean the way Sailor seemed to feel about it."

"That's exactly what I've been writing about. The thing with photography. You're not really taking a picture of some person or some landscape as much as you're making a picture of an emotion. You're visually describing what is moving to you about that subject at that particular time." She added, "Yeah. Sailor, he's so great. The loveliest man. I didn't ever really talk to him when I was a kid. I was...well, a kid. He was my mother's friend. But all the things he's done...makes me feel like a tourist. I left and wasn't around and didn't invest as much time when I was. He's been here the whole time, though, doing everything he was allowed to. I just, I want to help him with Ariel. Imagine how he's been waiting for that, for over twenty-five years."

Ellabella agreed. More than misfortune, she went on, there was the savor of the Gothic about the elaborate moat Carlotta had built between Sailor and his daughter. That was part of why she remained so interested in Carlotta, even though there would never be a story attached to this mystery. "Something just doesn't fit," she said. "Not just the circumstance. The attitude. The way Carlotta acts, as if, hey, doesn't everybody just drop out for a decade or so and then turn up at the wedding reception?" Nothing that Frankie could find might shed any light at all, she continued, but perhaps what she could figure out was the biggest riddle—the absence of any information at all, as if Carlotta had not just left but instead dematerialized. It was like an episode of *Dr. Who.*

"Why are you going so far with all of this?" Gil asked her one night. "Don't you think it could get embarrassing?" He added, "What if you do all this and you turn up nothing except she was out of touch and got involved with other things for a while?"

"That would be the best outcome. Why would I be embarrassed about that?" Frankie retorted. "Anyhow, people don't just leave their kids and do other things for a while. Innocently? Do they? Can you imagine leaving Atty to…do other things? Especially if you were his only parent? At least on paper?"

"I can't imagine any of that. But what I really can't imagine is how it's any business of yours."

"It's a family concern," Frankie said. But she knew it wasn't just that. She had plenty to occupy her mind and her heart… but she couldn't let this go. In part because she wasn't sure she could, she definitely didn't want to explain to Gil why she was breaking into Carlotta's room.

Gil was writing, which meant he had only half an awareness of anything she said.

So Frankie called, "We're going to take a little walk! In a few minutes. I've got the baby." Attaching sleeping Atty in his front pack over Ellabella's shoulders, she pulled her friend's voluminous down coat around both of them. They sat on the bench outside the cottage as Ellabella described the breaking-and-entering scenario. Frankie shivered, although the temperature was forgiving. She could see Carlotta moving back and forth between the big house and the car, loading up what seemed to be some empty grocery sacks, Ben's diaper bag and a big leather satchel Frankie had seen her carry before. She thought of what her mentor, Abram, had told her once, in reference to being sure to assess potential dangers in underwater settings: *whatever you can see can see you too.*

As soon as Carlotta and Ariel departed, Frankie and Ellabella rushed to the big house. The door was unlocked.

Ellabella took up her sentinel position on the low wall next to the driveway turn in the road. In one hand, she carried her phone and, in the other, the hot pink bullhorn. Frankie slipped inside.

In the living room, everything was tidy, couch cushions plumped, carpets vacuumed, coffee-table books neatly displayed. In the kitchen, every dish was stacked clean and dried in the open cupboards, canned goods and tea tins and jam jars arranged by their contents in the pantry. As it had always been. Frankie made her way to the room where Carlotta was staying. But wait. In the bedroom right next to that one, where Beatrice's ancient great-aunt Coe lived for a couple of years when Frankie was a child, there was a whole other stack of boxes and more luggage. How had Carlotta lugged all this stuff in here without Frankie seeing her do it?

Mack must be grinding his teeth.

Still, her time was limited. She started in the first room, the only one that was obviously where Carlotta was staying.

There was a bookshelf stocked with reference books and novels right beside the door. People always hid things in books. Frankie pulled out several thick books and thumbed through their pages. A telltale gap in *Bartlett's Familiar Quotations* led to the first discovery: six passports, in red or blue jackets—France, the United States, Canada. Flipping them open, Frankie laid them faceup on the bed, using a couple of heavy spoons she'd run down and grabbed from the kitchen to hold the pages flat while she photographed them. Six names: Carly Sherry, Carly Cho, Carlotta Rae Puck, Carlotta Campbell, Carlotta Hollister, Calista Rae Madeira. All the photos of the same woman. She replaced the passports carefully and slid the book back into the proper row. Opening the drawers and cabinets under the bookshelves, she found nothing except some postcards and a few shells. One drawer still contained Penn's stash of extra-long athletic shoelaces, multiple packs of dental floss, stacks of cinnamon bubble gum, Band-Aids and tubes of antiseptic ointment. In the bathroom, a caddy of unopened cosmetics. Next to the bed, a few novels on the nightstand. She opened the drawer. A couple of bottles of pills, of which she snapped pictures, not taking time to decode the labels. Kneeling, she tried to look under the bed but the room was dim, the curtains pulled closed.

All at once, she heard Atty wail. His cries split the quiet morning like the approach of fire trucks. Frankie rushed outside, beckoning wildly to Ellabella who ran to her side. "Take him and give him to Gil and just tell him to change him and feed him. Just say something..."

Back inside, she switched on a lamp and pulled out a small hard-sided suitcase, a leather train case that would have looked at home in an Alfred Hitchcock movie. It was also empty, but as she replaced it, Frankie accidentally dislodged a big envelope that had been shoved under the mattress. Afterward, she liked to think that she would have found it, but had to admit that, in reality, she probably would not have.

She laid the contents out page by page on the dark blue chenille bedspread, photographing. A certificate of live birth, a certificate of marriage, another certificate of live birth, a social security card. She then flipped each page over and photographed the backs. Surveying them, she wasn't sure she'd captured all of them. Should she start over? There was no time. Replacing them, having no idea if there was an order she should have observed, she dumped out a smaller envelope of photos. The oldest, a faded Polaroid, was clearly of the young Carlotta, from the lighthouse in the far background Frankie recognized Stage Harbor Beach. Magnificently fit and gorgeous in a black bikini, she was standing at the water's edge, and whoever took the photo must have been in the water. A photo of teenage Carlotta, her tumult of nearly white curls swept back by an Alice band, holding a baby wrapped tight in a blanket…that would be Ariel. Further pictures of a younger but not as-young Carlotta, several with a group of laughing women in a field that seemed to be at the foot of a mountain, Carlotta in an evening gown, with a tall, imposing dark-haired man, on a beach in what appeared to be a coastal town in Greece? Spain? Holding a basket of grapes in a vineyard. A shot of a woman Frankie gradually realized was Ariel's grandmother, before she paid the tariff on all the booze and cigarettes, a pretty woman whose face recalled Carlotta's except for broader, blunter features, with Carlotta, aged maybe twelve, at her side. With another woman seated on a terrace of some kind, Carlotta holding a dark, long-haired child on her lap, the child maybe two or three years old. With the same woman and child, slightly older, next to a tall lighted outdoor Christmas tree; in an apron and chef's cap stirring a gigantic steaming pot in some kind of industrial kitchen; wearing a nurse's tunic in a lecture class; on a white beach in a shorty wet suit and diving belt, swim fins dangling from one hand; making a comic bow to a scarecrow in a gigantic garden; perched in an apple tree. Despite the chill in the dim room, sweat dripped into Frankie's eyes. There were so many photos that she gave up trying to capture each of them singly and laid them out in ragged groups. Then she couldn't seem to get the envelope flat enough to fit back under the mattress without leaving a visible gap. She panicked and had to tell herself to breathe deeply, out then in, to banish black dots from before her eyes.

Next, she plundered the closet shelves… Penn's books, his old microscope, some BoSox hats, a music box of a boy and girl that Frankie had given him, that played "Moon River." His binoculars and some pairs of Maui Jim sunglasses in their coconut cases. On the floor were two compact cardboard boxes, just as Ellabella had guessed, marked *Records*, in writing that was not Penn's.

The first box was filled with more photos, of various vintage. The next, opened, revealed a flat leather case at the bottom. Frankie reached down and lifted it out, surprised by its weight. Within was a revelation, not a document but a series of velvet boxes, each containing a piece of jewelry that Frankie knew, without ever having seen anything comparable except in a magazine, were vastly expensive—delicate yellow gold and real stones, mostly diamonds and dark blood rubies. One of the rubies in a bracelet was the size of Frankie's thumbnail. She photographed those and carefully closed the cases and the box, clasping the lid. The third box held a green expanding organizer with a series of stick-on labels: Medical, Financial, Travel, Peach Patch Orchard.

"Is there something I can help you with?" Carlotta's voice, calm and low, came from just behind Frankie.

She thought she would die. Slowly, giving herself seconds that stretched and coiled and trebled like hours, she said, "Oh, hi, Carlotta. Maybe you can help me…?"

Draw the line. This is not her house. Frankie turned to face Carlotta. Attired in a white exercise vest and capri joggers, her magnificent, toned arms honey-colored and bare, Carlotta looked like an ad for Cape Cod summers. "Carlotta, have you seen a file here, it looks like this, I thought it was this file, but it's Penn's records, vaccinations and stuff? We couldn't find it in the safe… Hey, aren't you cold?"

"I don't feel the cold," Carlotta said evenly. Her eyes, Frankie noticed for the first time, were amber, almost golden, like a lion's, and her smile decorated only the lower part of her face. She took the green folder from Frankie's clawed fingers, replacing it in one of the boxes. "There was another box in here. I think it was Penn's stuff… I put it in that little closet where the coats are. I don't remember any files in it."

Why, Frankie thought later, had Carlotta even opened that box?

"Did you find it yet?" Ellabella's voice, amplified through the bullhorn, from just outside the door, could have been heard in Boston. It sent an electrical surge up Frankie's forearms and through the bottoms of her feet. Ellabella's accent was plush with entitled impatience, as only a patrician girl's voice could be. *Thank God*, Frankie thought. *Here come the Marines!* "Hurry up! We were supposed to fax that…form…to Penn an hour ago."

"I'll bet that was what he was talking about," Frankie said with a gusty sigh, thinking, *Don't apologize because you weren't doing anything wrong. Don't apologize because this is your home, not hers, where your brother lives…* She crossed over to the coat closet and pulled down the only box she saw. "That's my friend Ella. She and Penn are friends, kind of dating. See you later, then." She brushed past Carlotta without looking at her, trying to keep a calm, even pace.

Outside, she linked her arm through Ellabella's, and the two of them strolled slowly away toward Frankie's house, their heads together, like two friends at an Italian market gossiping about men or weight loss or the high cost of peaches, but actually with Frankie whispering, "What if she'd come while I was taking pictures of her photos? What if she had showed up five minutes earlier?"

"I would have come up with something," Ellabella said.

"I think you need to take that bullhorn everywhere you go. It could be a real conversation starter."

"I'm getting one of my own."

"So there's a whole other stash of Carlotta's stuff, boxes and suitcases, in another one of the bedrooms. If Carlotta was always on the road, did she travel in some kind of moving van?"

"How do you know it's hers?"

"Because I know what that room looked like before, and it wasn't filled with boxes."

"Well, maybe we won't need those. But if we do, we'll come up with a way to get to them," Ellabella said.

Outside Frankie's cottage, everything was silent except the ocean, whispering its promises to itself. She glanced inside. Gil lay on the big bed, the baby asleep on his chest. Frankie consulted her phone. Impossibly, not even an hour had passed since they'd set out. It felt like a full day. They drove to the closest coffee shop where Ella downloaded the photos onto her computer. "This is going to take me a long time," she said with a shake of her head. "I don't know what I'm looking for."

"There are all those passports," Frankie said as they huddled over their mugs, Frankie studying her phone screen, Ellabella her laptop. "Two US. And Canada. France."

"Why so many birth certificates?" Ellabella said suddenly. "And other kinds of certificates. You can't even see the words on a couple of these, Frankie! Great photography, photographer!"

"I was in a hurry! You saw what almost happened. Well, there's hers. Ariel's. Maybe she was married? Don't you have to get a new birth certificate when you get married?"

"If you change your name," Ellabella said. "You don't have to."

"Did you?"

"I did."

"Ella, I don't even know who you married."

"It's okay. We weren't friends then. Although your dad came to my wedding. My husband's name was—well, it still is—Win. Winthrop Merry. Like Merry Christmas. He didn't come from around here. We met in college."

"But still, full Pilgrim, huh? Your name was Ellabella Merry? It sounds like a character from Dickens."

"It sounds like the name of an heirloom tomato." Ellabella sighed. "He's a nice boy. He's a good person. He had a lot, lot, lot of money."

"Did that even matter?"

Ellabella sighed again. "I like money. Our families were nuts about each other. They had one of those crazy houses in Newport. Win isn't a jerk. He's talented. Medical robotics. He's handsome. We loved to dance together. We had fun. I was the one who gave up. In some other century or something, if it was an arranged marriage—and it was sort of an arranged marriage—well, maybe we could have been happy. If there had been no other choice. Maybe I could have figured out how to make it work. Having a choice might be overrated. It was just that I knew I didn't love him. A whole lifetime is a long time to not love somebody."

Frankie got up and returned with a fresh cup of coffee. As she stirred in sugar, she said, "How did you know? And if you had fun and you respected him, what else were you looking for, anyhow?"

Ellabella sipped and, to Frankie's shock, when she looked up from her cup, her eyes were brimming with tears. "What you and Gil have, honestly. It sounds trite. It sounds absurd. But it's like you were made for each other. How you light up when you see each other as if you just can't wait to be with him. It's joyful to see. It's upsetting too. It forces you to take stock. You think, love should amaze you. You think, this is what love could be."

"You had never seen us together," Frankie said, realizing, as she completed the thought, that it was a fatuous thing to say.

"But I had seen others," Ellabella said. "Even my own parents. Win's parents too. My parents have been married a long time, and obviously, my mom isn't the slip of a girl she was thirty-five years ago, but some of the things they do and say, they just break your heart because you can tell those are just for them." As if she were waking up from a brief nap, Ellabella shook her shoulders. "The thing is, it took a whole lot of trouble to change my name to Ellabella Merry and then back to Ellabella Ballenger. New birth certificate. Amended birth certificate. But you don't have to go through all that trouble. We talked about all this before. You didn't change your name, right?"

"No," Frankie said, stopping just short of tumbling over into *of course not.*

"People think that's some big feminist statement," Ellabella went on. "But really, it's just another form of the patriarchy. Your surname is Mack's surname, his father's surname. Attleboro's surname is his father's surname, Gil's last name. If I ever get married again, I'm going make him change our last names to something completely different."

"It'd still be somebody's surname."

"Not if it were Meadowlark. Or Rosa Rugosa. Or Schooner. True, though, even like, the Queen's surname, that was somebody's surname."

"I think they just made that up for Queen Elizabeth," Frankie said. "I think Windsor is just a place, but sure, that place was probably somebody's surname."

"Well, Queen Elizabeth's husband's name was Mountbatten. He was, Philip, Greek and Danish, and I think that name sounded too German right after the Second World War. It just came from one of those crusty old Brits. Elizabeth was supposed to be the quintessential Englishwoman. But not even really English. German and Danish and French."

"Queen Elizabeth?"

"Sure."

"You've made a study of this." Frankie asked, "What's Charles's last name?"

"I have no idea. But the point is that when you get married, you can use your husband's surname as what's called a *legal alias*. Nothing wrong with that. As long as you're using it for good reasons."

They exchanged a look as material as a bridge. Frankie said, "So how many times Carlotta changed her name and how she used it is nobody's business but hers."

Ellabella said, "That depends."

11

Up from the sea crept the fog, filled with ghosts. They were sailors, drenched and gray, trailing seaweed, girls in long dresses, who died heartbroken, hundreds of years before, waiting for sailors who never came back, a pirate in his rotted red boots of Spanish leather, a hapless little child still in her nightgown, a strong-muscled man, his ankles hobbled by chains, a minister in his collar swept away when he came to the water's edge to give thanks to the god of storms for showing his might and majesty to sinners, a boatheader from a whaling vessel whose leg was seized in a sizzling harpoon rope, a teenage boy hanged for stealing salted pork, lovers who would be grandparents now, who got high and ran into the surf holding hands at midnight, the old woman everyone called a witch, wearing the riven rags of her blue winter cloak, and Beatrice, Frankie's mother, in black palazzo pants and a silver satin shirt, glancing around her, confused.

With a cold finger, one ghost tapped on the window glass,

just a foot from Frankie's face. Hearing nothing from within, she tapped again, harder.

Frankie opened her eyes and stared at the woman, who seemed to float up and down in the fog, her eyes mournful blue pits, her long pale hair dripping. *Come with me, come with me…* She screamed so loudly that Gil all but levitated, bouncing Atty in his Moses basket between them on the bed.

"Frankie, you're having a nightmare," Gil mumbled, reaching for her hand.

"No, I'm awake! There's somebody out there!"

"It's the middle of the night." Gil sat up and turned on the bedside lamp. The tapping came again, louder and more insistent. "What…?"

Then there was a knocking at the door, unmistakably human. Gil pulled on his sweatpants and robe and went to the door. "Ariel!" he said. "What's wrong?"

Frankie got up and came to his side. Wearing her boots and a nightgown, Ariel stood in the muck outside the cottage door, Ben blanket-swathed and huddled against her chest. "Frankie, help me," she said. "Ben is sick. He's so sick."

In the bedroom, Atty began to whine and then wail. Gil crossed the room to scoop him up, handing him to Frankie to nurse. Ariel lay Ben on the table as Frankie pressed her baby to her breast. With a touch, Frankie could tell that Ben was incandescent with fever, and he looked not asleep but barely conscious, summoning the effort to cry weakly, streaks of drool leaking from his tiny mouth. "He has diarrhea, and he keeps vomiting…it's been hours now."

Gil said, "I'll call an ambulance."

"No!" Ariel said. "That takes too long. I have to bring him to the emergency room! I don't want to go alone. What if something happens to him while I'm driving?"

"Where's your mom?"

"I don't know!" Ariel said. "She's not picking up her phone."

"She's not here?" Gil asked.

"She had to leave. She left me a note that she'd be back in a few days. I called Mack and he's getting the next flight, but he's in Costa Rica."

"Of course I'll come with you," Frankie said. "Let me just throw something on here and feed Atty, and maybe pump some milk to leave for Gil. It will take five minutes. Do you have everything you need? Is his car seat in the car?" Ariel nodded mutely. Frankie quickly switched Atty to her other breast, relieved when he nursed hungrily and then drifted back to sleep.

Stowing Ariel in the back seat with Ben, she piloted the quiet highway. "This is what it was like before?" Ariel nodded. "Did you call Dr. Daley?" Ariel shook her head. Sharon Daley was the pediatrician for both of the little boys. A wise and funny woman in her fifties with three grown sons and who'd been part of Beatrice's book club, she'd cared for Frankie and Penn, as well as for Ariel, when they were growing up, including through Ariel's own harrowing illness. She'd noticed the similarities in Ben's symptoms the first time he got sick. Frankie said, "Call her right now. She won't mind. She knows Ben, and she knows you. You don't want to have to waste time telling another doctor everything."

At the hospital, with Sharon Daley informed and minutes away, Ariel gave perfunctory insurance information and then she and Ben were ushered immediately through the double doors. Frankie turned to go back outside to move the car. Ariel stopped. "I want her with me," she said.

"Just family right now if that's okay," the nurse said.

"She is family. She's my son's sister," Ariel told the woman, and Frankie watched her eyes flick from the baby in her arms to Frankie in her sweats that read *Surf Samoa.*

Frankie said, "I really am his sister. It's a long story."

"Well, give your keys to the valet, then."

Two hours later, Ariel curled next to a sleeping Ben in a

railed hospital bed while Frankie sprawled gratefully in a reclining chair. Nurses had piled warm blankets over her. If there was anything more comforting than a warm blanket tucked around you by another person, Frankie couldn't imagine what it would be. IV lines ran into Ben's tiny arms and feet; Frankie feared that he'd been all but exsanguinated by the tubes of blood drawn. Dr. Daley stayed, alongside a pediatric intensive care specialist and then a gastroenterologist, who peppered Ariel with questions about Ben's diet, which at not quite six months was still mainly breast milk and formula, with the homemade baby food Ariel and Carlotta made, bananas and avocados and sweet potatoes with a little oatmeal, as well as the green peas he loved to pick up. Until the previous day, he'd eaten eagerly, smiled and laughed, got up on his hands and knees and rocked, bobbed cheerfully to the folk songs and show tunes that Ariel or Carlotta played all day long. He noticed everything outside, calling in his nonsense language to the blue jays and seagulls, slept soundly at night and was hardly ever frightened, reaching out happily to anyone kindly.

His fever hovered at a hundred and four degrees when they'd arrived. But now, when Frankie touched his brow, it was cool and slightly damp. A tube protruded from his nose.

All they could do was wait to see what all of those tests showed.

Another hour passed. Ben woke, alert, seemingly voracious for the tiny cup of cooked cereal he was allowed.

"I'm not surprised he's starving," Ariel told the nurse. "He hasn't been able to keep a mouthful of anything down."

The throwing up stopped.

Ben demolished another cup of cereal.

"Maybe it was just a bug," said the nurse, a giant of a guy from Jamaica. He went on to tell them breezily that he was a true medical phenomenon, a man who took care of babies and loved it, who had three little girls of his own. "Maybe it just will pass over. Give it till tomorrow. The doctors will find the villain."

Later, Gil arrived with Atty, and Frankie went down into the lobby to nurse him. He also brought Reubens and fries for them, and Frankie had never loved him more. When she told Gil she didn't know how she could justify leaving Ariel all alone with Ben, although certainly many mothers on their own had faced much worse, he brushed off her concern, pointing out that it was Sunday and he and Atty would do just fine. Upstairs, apprised of the situation, a nurse offered to locate a breast pump for Frankie.

"What if what the baby has is contagious?"

"You should wear a mask," the nurse told Frankie. "I'll bring one for Mom and for you. But the truth is, if he's contagious, you're already exposed."

Hours later, carrying her breast-milk bottles in a Styrofoam cooler, Frankie went home to shower and change. Her father and Penn would be home by morning; the flight was only six hours, but they'd had to find a way to the airport from the rainforest-river station where they were working with local wildlife warriors on an education project involving the American crocodile. Though Ariel made it clear that she wanted Frankie, not Mack, to stay with her, Frankie knew this was a mistake. If Atty were sick, Gil would be the one that Frankie would want at her side. Why Ariel felt differently was no mystery. When Penn broke his leg in fourth grade, Beatrice had to page Mack at the college, and he didn't get back to her until hours later, after the cast was on. He'd been in the middle of giving a lecture, he explained when he got to the hospital at dinnertime. Beatrice only nodded, but Frankie could tell she was furious. When she sat down, holding Penn's free hand, Frankie watched tears spill from Beatrice's closed eyes.

She decided to go back for just a few hours. After charging her phone and drying her hair, she pulled on some frowsy pajama jeans, a T-shirt of Gil's and yet another airport sweatshirt, only then looking in the mirror and dabbing some concealer on the plum-colored pouches under her eyes.

When she arrived in the lobby, the first person she saw was Sailor Madeira. He was reading something on a slim electronic reader, and at first, he didn't notice her. When he looked up, it was with a tired smile. "I'm not sure what to do," he said.

"How did you even find out?"

"I thought you knew that. Gil called me."

Saint Gil. Was this less or more awkward than the combination dinner-party-and-paternity reveal?

"Well, Sailor, my thought is let's just go up there and see how they are and let the rest sort itself out." She certainly sounded bold and assured. Was she?

"So you don't think this is the wrong time—"

"I think it's a fine time. I think Ariel needs all the help she can get right now...and maybe all the love too."

At the desk, Frankie said, "We're here to see Ariel Attleboro and Benjamin Attleboro."

"Are you family?"

"He's the grandfather, and I'm the sister."

"You're Mrs. Attleboro's sister?"

"I'm the baby's sister. My father is the baby's father."

"So the baby's father is already here."

"He's in Costa Rica. This is the baby's grandfather."

The woman sighed. "So I asked, this is your father?"

"No, this is Mrs. Attleboro's father. But please don't call and tell her that because she doesn't know it yet."

"Oh, I see. It's like a reality show." The clerk slipped her glasses off and massaged the bridge of her nose. She gave Sailor a long, measuring up-and-down appraisal. Then she gave them both clip-on badges.

Ariel was nursing Ben when they arrived at the door of the baby's hospital room. He was almost asleep, taking the little hitch breaths babies take as they drift between worlds of consciousness. Sailor stepped back as Frankie stepped forward. "How is he?"

"He seems fine," Ariel said. "I'm going to feel guilty for rushing Mack to get back here."

"Don't," Frankie said. "Really, don't. This is exactly where he should be at a time like this." She took a deep inhale. "Look who came to see you. And to meet Ben." Frankie motioned to Sailor. He hesitated. She motioned again.

"Sailor!" said Ariel. "I don't quite… Well, it's great to see you! Were you here to visit somebody?"

"No, I just… I've never met Ben."

Ben wakened then, to the unfamiliar voice, looking up at Sailor with eyes amused rather than frightened. He lifted one starfish hand and wiggled his fingers.

"Hi, guy," said Sailor. "Are you better? You scared your mama and your sister. Me too."

Confused, Ariel looked from Sailor to Frankie. "You knew he was sick?"

"I did. What a beautiful baby he is. And personable. He looked me right in the eye, didn't he?" Sailor pulled out one of the molded aluminum chairs and sat down. "He looks like Frankie did when she was little."

"That's what everybody says, even my… Even Mack."

Frankie offered hopefully, "I think I should go to the coffee shop and get us some coffee."

Sailor said, "Not on your life. You're staying for this."

Frankie sat down in the big overstuffed recliner next to the bed. Was this right? Was it even her doing? Why did she want to run to the elevator, across the lobby, out the door and into Gil's arms? She reached down and felt the outside of her big leather bag for the shape of the breast pump. Had she remembered to bring it? She could just excuse herself and attend to what was, after all, an essential matter. But the pump wasn't there, and it was too soon, anyhow.

"I don't know how to begin, Ariel," Sailor said. "Let me ask you something, and you can say it's none of my business, but I hope you don't. How much has Carlotta told you about your father? Your birth father?"

Ariel turned slightly and scanned Frankie's face for clues. Interpreting Frankie's glance as permission, she murmured, "Why? He's never been around. Did you hear something about him?"

Sailor pursed his lips and nodded, and Frankie thought, well, that much is true. Haltingly at first, then with more confidence, Ariel gave the explanation that Frankie had heard all her life, the webby skein of information, more holes than fabric, that they had pored over as teenagers, studying for clues. When Frankie was in college, she and Ariel had ordered familial DNA kits. Frankie's provided no surprises, and Ariel's, she told Frankie, provided no answers. As it turned out, Ariel admitted later that she balked before even mailing the sample. When Frankie quizzed her, she said she wasn't sure why. Of course, had Ariel followed through, this meeting would still have been possible but probably not necessary.

So, said Ariel. Her father was a rich yacht boy from Connecticut passing through for a summer regatta. He stayed with his parents at the beach club, where Carlotta was waitressing. It was a one-weekend stand. In recent months, Carlotta confessed to Ariel that she wouldn't have tracked the boy down if she could have. From everything she could tell, especially as she thought back on their time together, he was a narcissist, obsessed with his fraternity friends. While it was Carlotta's first time, to him she was just one more sunlit adventure attached to the summer before his senior year at Princeton. Did he think of her again, once their car passed over the Sagamore Bridge? Much as she wished otherwise, Carlotta soon resigned herself to the truth that he had not. And much as she—at least initially—wished otherwise, by the time the leaves fell she knew that she would be the one with the permanent recollection.

Tale as old as time.

Carlotta had considered every option.

She could easily have found out the boy's name.

She could have terminated the pregnancy.

She could, as her own mother, Sherry, suggested more than once, have given Ariel up for adoption to a couple who could give the delicate, graceful little child all the things that Carlotta could not give her. Sherry pointed out that she could make some money doing that.

Carlotta knew a few things for sure.

Having a child would probably discourage other men, who might be kinder and worthier than the boy from Princeton, but animal nature being what it was, perhaps not eager to raise another guy's child.

Having a baby would bring the curtain down on her good times.

Having a child would prevent more of the nursing training she'd already begun and which she loved.

But this was not the fault of the baby she'd already begun, and—despite all the choices she'd made before or since—Carlotta loved the bean-sized being that would one day become Ariel, and she immediately knew, almost with a sixth sense, that her daughter would ultimately be someone who would—Ariel quoted her mother here—*matter in the world.*

And so it had transpired.

She was determined to raise her baby on her own, Ariel added, something that her mother had always seemed proud of, although it could not have been the easy choice. She'd also told Ariel, this only recently, that people who knew her and her mother, not everyone but plenty of people, were cruel. An unmarried teen mother and the daughter of an unmarried teen mother, she heard her name bowdlerized as Wholelotta Fuck. Matrons whose houses and rentals she cleaned made arch references to Sherry Puck, nodding, on the verge of an actual eye roll, when Carlotta explained she'd already completed her first year of nursing school. She tried to tune out the weary comments. She struggled. She almost gave up. When Ariel was just a year old, she even filled out adoption papers. But one night, watching Ariel sleep, she instead burned those papers in the sink.

Watching Ariel tell the story, Frankie marveled. This myth had taken on the colors of all the surrounding flowers. Cue the cloud music. Even Frankie believed it was all true. She had to keep reminding herself that this mother was the same mother who'd taken a ten-plus-year leave of absence. Sailor kneaded his temples with a splayed hand; Frankie could not tell what he was thinking. When he finally looked up, she watched him try to smile, fail at that, try to speak and fail at that, and finally reach into the pocket of his soft old corduroy sport coat and draw several pieces of folded paper from a new but unsealed legal-sized envelope.

"Ariel, Carlotta was always a very hard worker. Nobody can deny that. She worked all her life, and she didn't really have a great example for that. I give her all the credit in the world." He took a long breath. "When you get to be the age I am, you're going to have some regrets. Some of the regrets I have I probably didn't need to have. I look back, and I didn't realize what I was agreeing to do or why." He added, "I just don't want to have any more regrets. It's time."

"What has this got to do with my birth father?"

Sailor said, "I wish he could have been there for you when Carlotta disappeared. I wish he could have been there for your high-school prom. I wish he could have walked you down the aisle."

"How do you even know him? Did you…did you work with him or for his family or something?" Ariel asked.

"No," Sailor said. "Let me explain. I was in the navy for many years, until I was injured—"

"Frankie?" Ariel said, her anxiety suddenly like the sound of glass breaking. "What is going on?"

"I was home on leave, and well, your mother and I were sort of seeing each other and… I'm your birth father, Ariel," Sailor said. "I wish I had told you years ago."

"You're my…you're my…" Ariel said. "Let me see that."

She unfolded and perused the paper, while Frankie took Ben into her arms. "This is my birth certificate. Okay, father… Santiago Alexander Madeira. Is that you?" Sailor nodded. "But so what? She could have written down anyone's name."

"There's the other paper. That's a paternity test."

"She made you take a paternity test? So you didn't…you were just like the boy from Princeton… Was there ever really a boy from Princeton? You didn't want anything to do with me either."

"Wait—no, wait, Ariel. I was the one who pushed for the paternity test."

"You… Wait, what?"

"I wanted proof that you were mine if it ever came to that, so that Carlotta would accept support for you. I thought I would have to get a lawyer because she didn't want you to know. She fought that tooth and nail."

"But why?"

"I don't know why. You would have to ask her. I hope you do ask her. I suspected it was because I didn't love her. I loved you, and I wanted to be your dad, but she knew that I cared about her, but I didn't love her."

"Because you loved Beatrice."

"I loved Beatrice. And I was still in the navy when I found out about you."

"And you didn't want to interrupt your life…"

"That's not true. I did want to. I wanted to marry Carlotta."

"But you just said that you didn't love her." Ariel slapped the papers down and climbed off the bed. "You were just willing to do the right thing by her. Am I correct? You got her pregnant and then…"

Sailor got up and approached Ariel, but she raised both hands palm out, to her shoulders, warning him off. "You can put it that way. That's one way to put it. But it makes me sound like a bad man. I'm not a bad man. She's not a bad woman." When Ariel turned away, Sailor almost reached out for her, then stepped back. "The only way that she would agree to let me give her money for you is if I didn't tell you the truth."

"That's insane," Ariel said, and Frankie found herself nodding over and over, as if there were a string attached to her chin. "Why did she make up the boy from Princeton?" She added, "I've seen my birth certificate. I have a copy of it. It says that the father is unknown. Why would she do that?'

"I can't guess, and I won't speak for her," Sailor said. "You will have to ask her that. Maybe she thought a Princeton scholar sounded impressive."

"You went to Annapolis," Frankie said. "That is pretty impressive." She thought, but did not say, maybe it fit the narrative of the callous rich and Carlotta as the plucky downtrodden. What about Carlotta ate away at Frankie so reliably? Was it more than the abandonment? Was it that she now knew about Carlotta's liaison with Mack?

"How did she get that birth certificate?"

"I'm guessing either she got an amended birth certificate, the way you do when you adopt a child and substitute the name of the adoptive parents for the birth parents…or it's some kind of fake birth certificate."

"What? Just to make sure I wouldn't find out about you? That makes no sense," Ariel said. "Okay, so you weren't trying to avoid responsibility. I'm sorry that I suggested that you were. I'm just so surprised. So much makes sense now. The things you did for me. The groceries you brought."

"I tried, Ariel. I paid every bill I could, for twenty years. I paid into a bank account and some administrator sent me a statement, every month. I made sure you and she had health insurance. A college fund, that Birdy took care of. I'm not hoping for any credit here. That's not what this is about, Ariel."

"What is it about, then? Some of this just makes me crazy. You did all these secret things, and thank you very much for letting me grow up with Sherry, who was never sober for one single day of her life—"

"I told you, I have regrets. But Carlotta was around at first."

"The big question is why didn't you tell me? Recently? I've been a grown woman for a long time. Why, in all those years?"

"If I told you, Carlotta said she would take you away. Even after she left and you were grown-up, I still worried she'd come back or you would go with her, and I'd never see you again. I'd made her promise not to take you away, and so I never spoke to her about it again. I just made her sign a legal agreement that said if she ever took you away from here, all the money in trust would revert to me within one year."

"So instead she left me."

"That must have broken your heart, Ariel. I am so sorry. I don't know if this was better or worse. But I'm glad you were in one place. This place. With Frankie. With Penn. With Birdy to watch over you. With me to keep an eye on you. Even with Mack, though he was never around, and when he was, he never paid any attention to you. Or even to Frankie, really. The only one he cared about was Penn."

Frankie spoke up then, although she had intended to be a silent witness and that alone. "If you loved my mother, then why were you messing around with Carlotta?"

"We were both lonely." Sailor added, "I couldn't be with

Beatrice, and I cared for Carlotta. It just wasn't… It wasn't enough." Frankie remembered Ellabella saying that she and Ariel had a *we of me* and that she and Gil belonged together. She glanced at Ariel, grateful for whatever crisis had brought them back together, ashamed for the gratitude.

"That's fine," Frankie pushed on then. "But when it leads to a child no one—"

"She was a wanted child," Sailor said. Ariel narrowed her eyes.

"I was going to say a child no one expected," Frankie went on, although she was lying. She had been going to say *a child no one wanted.* She held Ben, who had fallen asleep, his thick hair damply curled against her neck. The facts kept echoing and rebounding. All of this, Beatrice had known. She had never said a single word of it to Frankie. Not a word, ever. Frankie didn't know whether to hate or respect her mother for her magnificent reticence—a trait Frankie would never possess.

"You could have gone somewhere else and loved somebody else instead of staying in a place where there was one woman you loved who would never love you and one woman who loved you and you would never love her."

"I could have. But this is also my home, Frankie. Birdy was my best friend. And if I went somewhere else, I wouldn't have known anything about Ariel at all."

Frankie nodded, somewhat remorseful. Plenty of people had done stupider things for reasons that were not as solid. This clearly was not the first time this had happened. Didn't every Gothic novel in the world hinge on the unknown father?

"I asked one more thing of her," Sailor told Ariel. "She would not allow you to have my last name. So I asked that some part of your name be from me. I knew I would tell you one day."

Ariel glanced down at the paper in her hand. "Alexandra… So your middle name is Alexander and mine is Alexandra.

Okay. I'm still not sure what… So then Carlotta came back, she's been back for almost six months now," Ariel said. "Did you ever think, maybe now is the time? Did you discuss it with her? I'm in my twenties now. I'm not a child."

"She promised me that we could talk it over. Every time I tried, she postponed it. To be fair, there was so much going on—you had just gotten married, then you had the baby, then Christmas came and you were gone. When Ben got sick," Sailor added, "I didn't know what Carlotta would do. She's always been unpredictable."

"Right. Okay. Look. I mean this nicely, but why don't you all just go away now?" Ariel said. "I need to think. I'm exhausted."

Sailor and Frankie stood up. Frankie handed Ben to Ariel, and Ariel looked up at Sailor.

"No, on second thought, you stay, Sailor, if you can. You can…you can help me with Ben. I think I need a nap." Sailor looked as though he'd been handed a bag of gold. "And I need to talk to you."

"I'll get you something nice to eat from the deli down the street," Sailor said. "After you wake up."

A *we of me*, thought Frankie. Ariel knows about Sailor for fifteen minutes, and she chooses him over me. That wasn't at all the full context of what was going on, Frankie knew that. They needed time, private time, to get to know each other, to ask the questions that needed answering. But hadn't she, Frankie, shared Beatrice with Ariel? And now Sailor too? Wasn't she letting herself feel like a spoiled, jealous child, Frankie thought? She was. Yet the fact remained: she was shut out. And she was jealous.

12

"So now your part is over," Gil said.

"Yes, my work here is done," Frankie said. They were walking the baby up and down in Orleans, up and down from the Hot Chocolate Sparrow to the natural foods co-op, then across to the new store that featured Amish furniture, jams and jellies, luxurious lotions, and then repeating the four-block square. Frankie wanted the Amish brown-sugar scrub in the window, but was ideologically opposed to giving money to people who didn't believe in dentistry. She confided this to Gil.

"That's a lifestyle choice right?" Gil said.

"So's pornography," Frankie said.

"Not…not really in the same way? And probably you would be surprised at how many people you think are upstart professionals…"

"*Upstanding* professionals."

"Yes, who look at pornography."

"Do you?" Frankie asked.

"I have, especially when I would be alone out there for

months. But the truth of pornography is how very, very boring it is."

"I know! The exact opposite of what you think it will be. Literally, you've seen one, you've seen them all." She checked sleeping Atty, and they trudged on. "I can't wait for warm weather. I feel like I'm wearing a rubber fat suit."

"I'm not going to touch that one with—"

"I know. The barge pole. Do you think I look fat?"

"Not at all. I thought you were too thin when I met you."

"You are the most diplomatic husband."

Gil took over pushing the stroller. It was laughable how quickly she tired these days from physical exercise—she who'd spent years burning through thousands of calories every day without ever thinking about whether what she ate was too much or too little, whether it was vegetable or animal, only that it was there. Now, she spent up to an hour every morning listening to recorded books and running on a little treadmill. Frankie thought she was getting soft; she weighed fifteen pounds more than she'd ever weighed, not counting while she was pregnant, and while she had no real objection to buying bigger jeans, her best wet suit wouldn't even begin to zip. When she pictured herself over the past six or seven years, it was as though she were watching an animated cartoon sped up, of a woman who jumped in and out of the sea, jumped in and out of a van, jumped in and out of a plane. Her new satisfaction translated into a sort of languor in her everyday movements. She loved the new-mom life she was living, yet even those moments she'd spent lounging with Ellabella, talking about the past, talking about Ariel, talking about nothing, seemed like a violation of the action-hero creed she'd sworn herself to so long ago that she didn't even remember how she'd learned the vows.

She still wanted to be that jumping, adventuring woman. Soon enough. Not yet.

Up and down they walked. Orleans was one of the few Cape Cod towns that actually had sidewalks. It was this or Hyannis, where all the identical boutique storefronts and beery bars recently made Frankie feel depressed, or a drive to Provincetown, still a ghost town in not-quite-spring.

"As for all the stuff with Carlotta," Frankie said, "it all seems kind of silly in the light of day. The snooping and stuff. For no reason. I guess she had her reasons for the things she did."

"You don't have to agree with them," Gil reminded Frankie. "If I had to venture a guess, it would be that she was *honteux*..."

"I don't know that word."

"Ummm, *timide...ashamed* maybe?"

"Maybe. But that doesn't make sense, does it? I still don't get her reasons for concealing so much stuff," Frankie said. "I mean, who needs multiple passports? And how did she get them all? And I definitely don't know why she took off and left Ariel. That's really at the bottom of it. And why Ari just accepts it."

"Like Sailor said, she was always a— What do you call people who don't want to stop? To settle down?"

"Like a vagabond," Frankie said and smiled. "Like I used to be."

"You see?"

"But if she wanted a child...why would she leave that child? It bugs me. It just bugs me."

"Maybe she didn't realize how much it would require of her," Gil said.

Frankie could empathize. Not long before, she'd been writing in her book—which she now visualized as a linked series of essays about light, about all kinds of light, not just the kind that pertained to photography—how one morning she was just drifting off to sleep, during what she called the *stolen hours*, between five and eight, universally recognized as the time many insomniacs, shift workers, and other troubled sleepers finally receive the golden blessing of unbroken sleep. It was then that she realized that the sun was coming up sooner every day and that sunrise might send a shaft of light around the corner of a drawn shade and somehow rouse her sleeping son. The emotion she had (*What are you really feeling?* that professor had asked) wasn't concern or even irritation. It was terror.

I was looking at some paintings in books. There was Raphael's Aldobrandini Madonna *and also of Botticelli's* Virgin and Child with Two Angels. *Whenever I saw paintings like that, I would wonder why the Madonna was always pictured with such heavy lidded eyes and such a sorrowful expression. Now I know: it was because she was the mother of a newborn, so she wasn't getting any sleep at all.*

"I didn't realize how much work being a mother would be..."

"Frankie, of course, you're a different kind of person. And you're not single either. And you don't have a disabled parent."

"Still, there has to be a reason why I wonder about this so much. Ellabella does too. About those reasons." Frankie began to count up the steps once again. Carlotta cared more for Sailor than he cared for her. And yet, it was Mack she really loved? She wanted a child, but she didn't want Ariel to know the identity of a perfectly good father.

Gil made puffing noises, as if blowing out a recalcitrant candle. "You wonder because you're nosy. They're none of your business."

"Oh, shut up, Gil. I'm tired of you always being the soul of reason."

"You just complimented me for being the soul of reason," Gil reminded her. "The important thing is that you got Ariel and Sailor together. That seems to be working out well."

It was working out well. Better than well. Now that Ben was out of the hospital, home again and thriving, the tests again having turned up nothing except some stomach inflammation with no apparent source, with allergies the exclusionary diagnosis, Sailor was constantly visiting his newfound daughter and new grandson. Mack was entirely on board (probably, Frankie thought without much charity, because it took some of the pressure off him), welcoming Sailor as someone for whom Beatrice had always had the greatest respect, Ariel said (and again, Frankie thought covertly, respect didn't begin to cover it…). Sailor took Ben on long seashore walks in his front pack and even stayed with him while Ariel and Mack went out for a big dinner in Boston with some influential Saltwater donors. The baby turned to him, thrilled, whenever Sailor walked in the door. Sailor did the same with Atty, freeing Frankie and Gil for some time alone to write and also for an evening out. Atty was too little to be very demonstrative, but he delighted Sailor by windmilling his fat little arms whenever the older man approached. Ever careful of her feelings, Sailor told Frankie, "I went from zero to two grandsons in a couple of months!"

Carlotta had not yet returned, nor had she sent word.

One morning when she woke up, Frankie realized what part of the whole tale had put her on high alert: it was the stupid dognapping scam. It was the way that Carlotta seemed to take advantage of the weaknesses of other people. Maybe it wasn't just pet owners. Whether or not she did it for reasons she considered morally defensible was a factor, but not a reason. Maybe it was bigger than that.

Weeks passed.

Increasingly, the light was fuller and benign, not the coldly compelling *lux brumalis*, the light of winter, for which there was no English word, the light that sharply defined every stick and feather.

Though she said Mack discouraged it, Ariel kept coming to see Frankie and bringing Ben, meeting Sailor at Gil and Frankie's house for dinners which, thankfully, Sailor cooked. Gil and Sailor discussed EnGarde's pilot plan for a sort of environmental navy. It would be a seagoing force, separate from the numerous land-based conservation efforts across Canada, with two fully equipped research vessels entrusted to work for marine species preservation as well as intervene in the event of maritime ecological mishaps. Woods Hole and Scripps did something like this in Massachusetts, Sailor reminded Gil, but Gil, who was familiar with that program, pointed out that EnGarde would have a government-grant component so that volunteers would be paid and trained and then receive a lifelong pension based on their length of service, which could be anywhere from two to six years.

Alone with the babies in Frankie and Gil's room, Ariel asked her, "Where do you think she went?" Frankie didn't have to ask who Ariel meant. "Do you think she'll ever come back?"

Of course Frankie knew that Carlotta would come back. Hadn't she left all her private records and most of her clothes in Mack's house? But she couldn't offer this to Ariel as reassurance without giving away her and Ellabella's shabby spy errand. As for that, she and Ellabella intended to see it through. Penn had bagged up all of the things from his childhood room and taken what he wanted downstairs to his lair. He said the plan was for Carlotta to move into Ariel's condominium when she returned, her longtime tenant disgruntled at the news that she needed to move out by early summer.

Penn was clearly eager for her to leave.

"It's bad enough living off Dad's charity, but I justify that. I mean, I earn that through the work I do with him. I don't know how he ever traveled anywhere by himself before I grew up, because the man doesn't know how to find the baggage claim on his own," Penn told Frankie.

"He had minions," Frankie said.

"Right, and now I'm that plus more." The university paid Penn's minimal salary as a researcher and junior faculty, but the Saltwater Foundation paid for many of his other expenses. "But I don't think Mack counted on her being here forever. And I can't see any reason I should have to share this house not just with my dad and his wife but with her mother. It's just too weird. Plus, she watches everything. I can't even have a date over."

"Ellabella?" Frankie said.

"Even Ellabella. Although, she has this same crazy interest in Carlotta that you apparently do. She asks me all kinds of questions about her."

A thought occurred to Frankie then, and Penn, who was his father's son, might just be self-absorbed enough to accept it. "Speaking of Carlotta, I can get her stuff out of here. I told Ariel I'd put it in Ellabella's garage until the renter moves out. There's not that much, is there?"

"There's enough. Lots of big boxes, a few suitcases. It takes up two bedrooms. Mack gets annoyed whenever he passes the door. I put all her—I don't know what they are—essential oils or something in a wine box so all the little bottles wouldn't break."

"Okay. I'll see what Ariel says and maybe get some of it out of there. I'll just leave her clothes and makeup and stuff."

"Sure. Mack will be grateful."

Luck, luck, luck.

Frankie couldn't believe how easy this was. If Carlotta ever asked, Frankie would just tell her that Ellabella agreed to put the big stuff in her family garage. Chez Ballenger Seniors' six-car garage that was heated and climate-controlled so that Kenny's Bentley would never feel a chill. It would all be safe there, and Frankie's snooping could be carried out in peace, hidden from Penn and Mack—and especially Gil's Canadian censure. She wouldn't have to plan any more stealth forays.

Mission accomplished. Family peace restored.

She had just located one of the wagons when she remembered the folder under the mattress. She couldn't just waltz into the bedroom and rummage for it. She began loading boxes into the wheelbarrow and then asked her brother, "Do you have any coffee?"

"I just made a pot."

"Will you get me a cup?"

"Get yourself a cup, Frankie."

"Come on. I have to do all this stuff fast. What if Dad shows up? I don't want to see him. We haven't talked since—"

"Frankie, please. Get over it. I had to swallow my pride and suck up to him, or I would have ended up out on my ass at the college. Not to mention not being part of these documentaries that are coming up…"

"I'm sorry you had to do that," Frankie said. "I think he treated you horribly." She stopped. "But still, come on, just get me a cup of coffee? Cream and sugar?"

Still grousing, Penn went to the kitchen. She could see Ariel, holding Ben, looking out of the nursery window. Ariel smiled, wiggled her fingers and then mimed a phone call. Did she notice that Frankie was moving all of Carlotta's belongings? She clearly still wanted to please Mack and keep her relationship with Frankie on the quiet. How had Ariel explained to Mack the circumstances of the revelation by Sailor? Had she explained at all? Frankie scrabbled under the mattress for the thick envelope.

It wasn't there.

Panicky, Frankie dropped to her knees and peered under the bed.

"What's up?" Penn said.

"Oh, jeez, I knocked out my earring! I just got it back in…" Frankie faked screwing in the little diamond posts that had been Beatrice's. "There. I'd have freaked if I lost that." That was when she saw a corner of the envelope sticking out from the mattress at the foot of the bed, rather than in the middle, where it had been before. Gratefully, she accepted the coffee, sitting down so that her legs obscured the telltale corner of the brown envelope. "Any other stuff?"

"Just all the little containers of homemade baby food they

froze. Superspecial organic and enhanced… They practically prayed over it. About a thousand containers. Mack says he's going to get a freezer for the garage so Ariel can keep them out there. He said, 'God forbid I should want a filet…'" Penn walked out but then turned back, just as Frankie reached behind her, sliding the envelope out. It hit the wooden floor. "What's that?"

Frankie said, "I don't know. I just kicked it out from under the bed," she said, thinking *Be casual. Act curious.* "Look, it's birth certificates. Ariel, Carlotta, Carly…" Penn glanced at the envelope in Frankie's hand.

"Must be hers too. Stick it in one of those suitcases, okay?"

Frankie realized she'd been holding her breath. Why didn't she just tell Penn about all this? Why did she and Ellabella have to keep it between them? Penn was no fan of Carlotta. Yet, once spoken, information leaped like a flame from person to person. "Okay. Thanks for the coffee."

After dropping Carlotta's things off at the Ballenger house, Frankie went home to do what Gil had been asking her to do for days: consider the offer they had for the following year to lead a *National Geographic* expedition for divers, Around the World Underwater. Frankie's friend from *Nat Geo*, Selkirk Bell, would not take no for an answer and had anticipated every one of Frankie's objections. The sojourn was wildly lavish—meant for the kind of people who lived in cramped apartments so that they could devote all their savings to adventure or the kind who were so wealthy they didn't think much about price at all when they wanted something. The pay offered to each of them was substantial, and the tips that the participants would give them were enticing. Selkirk Bell wanted Gil's and Frankie's opinions on the focus, but he had strong opinions of his own too—history, of course, but also wildlife, particularly the salvation of endangered species, and the impact of development on marine life. Selkirk was crafty enough to want to set off with moneyed ecotourists and come back with moneyed ecoactivists, passionate to preserve the wonders they'd witnessed. They would travel with their small group on private jets and stay at the best hotels and would be provided with experienced support staff and a vetted nanny for Atty.

Frankie would help craft an itinerary that would hit the obvious dive-résumé essentials—like the Great Barrier Reef, the divers' equivalent of Mount Kilimanjaro for mountain climbers, but also let her take pictures of places she had never been but had dreamed of. Cape Kri in Indonesia, Saona Island in the Dominican Republic, where the big fish hung out, or the Coralarium in the Maldives, a gorgeous, lavish habitat for coral and other marine life created by partially submerging concrete sculptures of glittering trees and contemplative people. It wasn't a natural underwater site, but it was fascinating as an example of the beneficial possibilities offered by the collaboration of human art and marine ecosystems.

Reluctant as she was in the moment, Frankie knew that they would probably accept. Atty would have had the benefits of an at-home routine in his earliest months. From all she had seen in the world, she knew that, in the absence of disease, a child thrived on as much love and care as the people around him were willing to give, and from what she could already see of his personality, she imagined him happily the center of attention.

For at least a month or more, it would also get her away from here. She still wasn't sure that her cozy home could ever be the safe harbor she had imagined just months ago. Gil reassured her that things would heal, but Gil knew only the good Mack, the approachable and affable Mack, not the proud, needy narcissist who dealt with the damage he did by denying it. For Mack, people's reactions to what he did or said were their own problem.

She wrote:

What does the word home really mean to someone like me? I thought it was a place. I guess I thought it was the place that I was born. But when I got to that place, I realized that a place was the equivalent of a turtle shell, important because it protects the living creature inside it. So home? Home isn't a place but people. For me, this was a revelation. It was both heartening and disheartening because places stay, although they change, and people change too, but people also come and go.

She wondered if her father would ever read those words and recognize how much they applied to him. She wondered if anyone, other than herself and her Grandma Becky, would ever read them.

When Ellabella showed up the next day, Frankie imagined that they would sit in the garage to go over the contents of the folders. Ellabella, however, said that was both chilly and silly. "My mother couldn't care less what I'm doing," she said, reminding Frankie that, in the Ballenger family home, Ellabella had the equivalent of *rooms*, in the British sense: a big bedroom with a full bath, a study with a fireplace and bookshelves, her own second-floor screened porch, as did each of her brothers, although only one still lived there. They separated the paper files from the other possessions in the certain knowledge that they would never be able to restore the original order, but Ellabella had already crafted the pertinent lie. They'd dropped a carton or two, and not wishing to invade Carlotta's privacy by actually looking at private documents, they'd simply restored everything as best they could—apologies! Subtext: *squatters can't be choosers.*

"You are a cool liar," Frankie said.

"It's a gift," Ellabella replied. "There are two secrets to a great lie. The first is that it's the truth turned inside out, sort of what Emily Dickinson had said: *tell the truth but tell it slant.* So you never forget the facts. The second is that you have to semibelieve it."

For their work, Ellabella had cleared a big wooden surface, something between a desk and a picnic table. Once again, they spread out all the documents and photos, more than fifty of them. Frankie photographed each one, painstakingly this time. They took the box out into the garage and slipped it in among Carlotta's other things. After all, she could return at any moment and ask for them. She might have returned already.

Next, they began to study all the documents.

The first thing Frankie noticed was a death certificate.

Milo Collier.

Collier was one of the last names on one of Carlotta's birth certificates.

"She was married. It was her husband," Ellabella said. "It was ten years ago, it says right here. Carlotta Collier, spouse. He was fifty-three. He'd be about your dad's age now."

The cause of death was cardiac arrest. Ellabella tapped the document. "Everybody dies of cardiac arrest," she said. "I saw enough of these in journalism school. It's what happens, your heart stops. But…why? Look here." She pointed out that Milo Collier had been five-ten and, when he died, weighed less than a hundred pounds.

"He had some kind of cancer or something," said Frankie. "A disease where you waste away."

"Yep, yep." Ellabella consulted the document again. "This was in… Okay, this was in Boulder. Here's a copy of this… Wait."

It was a second death certificate. Also in Boulder. A second man, Tim Cho, only forty years old, who'd died of blood poisoning, not quite two years after Milo Collier. Cho was a disabled veteran, a drug and alcohol counselor.

"This makes her look bad," Ellabella said. "But it doesn't mean anything on its own. Kitty's friend, my godmother, Annabella, had three husbands die on her by the time she was fifty, and two of them died of heart attacks. If there was anything funny about it, there'd have been an inquest."

"If there was an inquest, would you keep the paperwork?"

"I myself might. But probably not everybody would. Good point," Ellabella said.

"I have to go home," Frankie said. Her breasts throbbed like electrified cantaloupes. "How about I tackle half of these, and you take half, and we'll compare notes?"

Ellabella nodded and put half of the images into a file she emailed to Frankie. "And I'm going to make a call or two."

At home, Frankie gratefully snatched up her baby and nursed him. "What are you doing all hours?" Gil said.

"You take off all hours just to ride around in the new car," she answered without answering. "I was with Ellabella."

"Not doing the amateur-detective bit again?"

"Don't be silly. And who says I'm an amateur?" They kissed, at first a peck, then in a hungrier way, then like the plane was going down. With Atty asleep in his basket, they shucked their clothes and made love for the first time since he was born. Despite Frankie's worries about sexual desire having gone the way of meat in her life, it was with a shattering fullness that left her breathless. Gil would need to leave soon for ten days at the EnGarde offices in Toronto. Had she really become the woman who wanted to cry because her husband was going away? There were worse fates. And she was luckier than anybody in being able to spend so much time with her baby's father, sharing his care, building the unity of their tiny family, so lucky that she didn't have the kind of job that most new mothers had, that required her to dress up and go to an office every day, leaving her infant behind. Luck, luck, luck. It inspired equal measures of guilt and gratitude. Impulsively, Frankie rolled over onto Gil, pinning him to the mattress.

"Not again!" Gil said. *"Maman!"*

"Oh gosh, don't call me that!"

He said, "It's an expression..."

"Okay... I wasn't trying to ravish you, Gilly, I was just thinking how much I love you and how much I'll miss you in a couple of weeks."

"You should come with me."

"No...not ready for that yet."

"Then, my mother can come to stay with you. She would love that. Or we can hire a helper."

"Your mom basically just went home, sweetie. She's not retired. She has a family bakery to run. But yes, I guess hiring someone for a few hours a day, that would help me work. I don't absolutely need it, but it would help. That's a good idea." *I want my mother*, Frankie thought. Beatrice would not have waited to be asked. She'd have borne Atty up with a waving surge of love. Perhaps, Frankie thought, perhaps Sailor could help her. Odd as the idea seemed, Frankie could not imagine anyone helping her care for the baby with whom she would feel more comfortable. He seemed to have plenty of time. She tried to picture herself asking if he might help her for a day each week, assuring him that, of course, they would pay him. Did her mind balk because he was a man instead of a woman? Or, she would wonder later somewhat abashed, because she was afraid that Sailor wouldn't care about Atty as much as he cared about Ben?

After a while, they got up and shrugged on their clothes and went into the kitchen to forage for food. She'd forgotten about her share of the files when Ellabella pinged in with a call. *Look at your email.*

Frankie did.

A colleague in Denver had helped Ellabella find a couple of newspaper stories (*which I should have found myself*) from several years after Milo Collier's death. The man's sister pointed out that Carlotta, married just less than a year, had inherited a substantial sum at her husband's death. The woman made it sound like millions of dollars, but the report suggested the sum was more like several hundred thousand. Still, all of it had gone to Carlotta. Milo Collier's sister raised questions about the more recent death of another Mr. Carlotta. About the death of Timothy Cho, there had been an inquest and weeks of investigations—that turned up nothing at all amiss. Further, Milo Collier, who made his money investing, had been *sickly* all his life, his friends said. He actually improved when Carlotta, first his nurse, then later his wife, came to live there. The other man, Tim Cho, much less well-off, the one who was a counselor, apparently had no other family except Carlotta. He'd been addicted to drugs in the past; no one could be sure if he had begun using them again. He didn't leave her a bunch of money, but he did leave her a monthly pension. "She was just unlucky in love, all the way around," Frankie said.

"Apparently."

"You don't sound convinced."

"Well, I guess I'm convinced about that part."

"Did you think she, like, offed them or something for money?"

Ellabella scoffed, "That's way too sinister even for me. It was more like she was a nurse, and there's the whole angel-of-death thing, with the guy who was so sick, a mercy killing."

"I see."

Ellabella said, "But she was enriched by those deaths. And you'd be surprised how many people never make the same mistake once." She added, "I'll look into it. This wasn't that long ago."

A few days later, Ellabella called. There had indeed been inquiries into the deaths of Carlotta's two husbands, inquiries that turned up nothing amiss.

That, apparently, was that.

We were both being weird, Ellabella texted. I blame you.

Frankie texted back Of course you do.

Still, Frankie's thoughts wandered to Carlotta and her *two* dead husbands more often than not.

13

Frankie was busy writing about one of the underwater sights:

Even people who make their living underwater sometimes just go swimming for fun. That's what I was doing in Costa Rica, in early fall the year I graduated college, with a friend on a trip my parents gave me as a graduation present. We were diving at Playa Grande in Las Baulas National Marine Park. What I was thinking about mostly was how getting into the water would get me away from the bugs, from the mosquitos and bullet ants, ants that have a sting so horrible that the pain lasts all day, and even the six-inch-long grasshoppers, which are completely harmless but just too creepy. We geared up in the Jeep in record time before we got bitten to death. I didn't even have a camera with me, only a dive bag in case I happened upon something exciting, like a diamond necklace. (You may laugh, but when I was in high school, I found a Cartier Ballon Bleu wristwatch about a hundred yards offshore, just snagged on an outcropping of rock. I saw it sparkle, and I brought it back in and advertised online and in the newspaper. For your information, a watch like that, new, costs maybe six thousand dollars. A week later, a woman claimed it. She couldn't really identify the model, which I thought was suspicious, and I still wonder if I should have let her have that watch… On the other hand, if you asked me what the model was of some piece of jewelry or equipment I had, I might stammer and say, Well, it has a leather strap? It's silver?) So back to Costa Rica. It was just about dusk when we came upon this big sort of rock, just alone in the middle of the seafloor, not connected to a reef. We were wearing headlamps, but it was getting dark, not too easy to see, and we were about sixty feet down, not very far offshore. I didn't really want to explore that rock, but I did want to have a look at it. You probably won't believe me, but I'm a pretty conservative diver. I always try to know as much as possible about what's ahead of me. Back then, I was even more cautious. When it comes to taking risks, there are certain times I'm mindful—in new places, of course, and even in familiar places, at the edges of the day and night. Why? Things happen at those so-called hinge times, at dawn and dusk. Creatures move; bugs come out in hordes; sharks feed; weather kicks up.

So there we were, swimming along, and my friend wanted to explore a reef she could see in the near distance. She kept motioning for me to come along. I gave her the palm-out signal that means No or Stop, but she gave me the Okay sign, and I ended up following her because you never, ever separate from your dive buddy. The only time I'm ever alone underwater is when I'm literally clipped to a safety line, a nice sturdy Jon line, connected to people on the surface in a boat. And in that circumstance, I would also be linked to the person or people in the boat by a two-way radio clipped to my mask so I could talk to them if I had to. That time, we were not in a familiar place, and there was no dive boat above us. Carrying our finds, we had just waded in from the shoreline in that underwater park. Still, I did hang back just a little. It was okay because I knew exactly where my friend was headed. I wasn't going to completely lose sight of her. I stopped and adjusted so I could stand up on the floor of the ocean to have a quick look at that big rock formation. And that's when it happened. I got right next to that big rock, and at that moment, the big rock came to life. It moved. I saw these huge, amazingly huge flippers, as long as my arm. It was one of those times in life when you recognize the reason for the cliché that says I couldn't believe my eyes. I truly couldn't believe my eyes. My brain would not make sense of what I was seeing. That supposed rock was a leatherback turtle, the size of a small car. It was. That turtle easily weighed more than a thousand pounds. It must have been over a hundred years old. Intellectually, I of course knew that sometimes leatherback turtles grow that big, but you don't see them, really. You hardly see leatherbacks at all, much less that size. So it was like seeing a ghost or a unicorn or something. Now, I own a dive rattle that I use for attracting the attention of a dive buddy, but of course I didn't have that with me any more than I had my camera. (Now, I would never go anywhere except my kitchen without my camera!) The giant swam right up to my face, and while I knew it wasn't dangerous, I was still absolutely aghast, sucking air from my tank as fast as it would go. For a moment, I could not move. But when I moved, the leatherback moved right beside me. It swam next to me. I could easily have reached out and touched it, but of course, you never touch a turtle. (You know that, right? You can hurt them or leave harmful bacteria on their bodies.) Why did it do that? Maybe it was because the wet suit I was wearing was red and turtles supposedly are attracted to the color red. I won't ever know why. Meanwhile, my friend was swimming away from me. I could see her, but couldn't easily catch up to her. So I kicked harder and finally, I was able to grab her ankle. Imagine that feeling: I think I must have scared her to death. I was gesturing and pointing like crazy. But in the time it took for her to turn around, the leatherback just flew away into the dark water. It was gone. I don't think she ever believed me when I told her that giant rock had really been a giant creature.

What is the point of all this? It's more than a story about something in the deep that turned out to be something else, astoundingly so. It's not just about the amazement and fear I felt when the turtle swam up to me and looked right into my eyes. It's about recognizing that sometimes, something survives, something important in nature thrives not because we protect it but because we don't know about it. Conservation can sometimes be the most benign neglect. Some things require not our help but our absence. In the previous century, before my parents were born, that old reptile began life as an egg. Who knows how long it will survive, in this century, if we can manage not to find it again? And while I know that reptiles don't experience situations in the complex way mammals do, studies show that they do experience anxiety, frustration, fear and perhaps even pleasure. In fact, who's to say which creature witnessed the other, the turtle or me?

As she finished writing those words, Frankie stopped. She thought of her father and how, as long as Frankie could remember, Mack had been telling people about the Regent Red sea eagle, despite mockery from his colleagues that verged almost on censure. Mack wouldn't give in: he knew what he had seen. Someday, he insisted, he would be vindicated. It was a measure of Mack's dauntless spirit. It was also a measure of his hubris. And it proved that, back when he was barely into his forties, Mack had a screw loose. Ever since she'd become aware of the sea-eagle controversy, since she realized why her father's Boston Whaler was named the *Regent Red*, Frankie had said not one thing about it to her father. Had Beatrice warned her that this was one family subject that might be off-limits?

Frankie seemed to remember her mother saying something like that. Yet, she vacillated. If she doubted Mack, was she a faithless daughter? If she believed him, was she a credulous nitwit? Plenty of things that no one believed in at first turned out to be true...like evolution. Which path proved her worthy of her scientific heritage?

Leatherback turtles, however, were not extinct. They were shy and reclusive, but everyone knew they were still around.

As she wrote and pondered that day, Frankie at first did not notice that Gil, carrying Atty in his front pack, had come into the house, gesturing for her and putting his phone on speaker. It was Mack, calling to tell them that little Ben was sick again, that he and Ariel were at the hospital, and that a social worker was interviewing Ariel.

Frankie said, "Social services?" Gil nodded, his finger to his lips. And they were going to send someone to the house, and Gil and Frankie should let them in.

"Mack, what are they looking for?" Gil asked.

"This is the third time he's been sick like this. Apparently the hospital has to get social services involved. In case Ariel is making Ben sick on purpose or something equally absurd."

"What?"

"They suspect she's giving him something that's toxic," Mack said, and Frankie had never heard him sound so old and tremulous. "Or maybe it's environmental. Ariel told them she was sick like this once, as a baby. The social worker...or somebody...they're going to take samples of the well water and the soil too. I don't know if that's now or—"

"Did you call your lawyer?" Gil asked. "Is it that serious?"

Mack had called his lawyer. Nobody had been charged with anything. The tests done on Ben the last time he was sick hadn't revealed anything abnormal except inflammation of his stomach and kidneys, with no clear cause at all. Idiopathic, Mack said. Before Gil could put the phone down, Frankie was out the door and headed for the big house. Inside, she went immediately into the kitchen and swept all the containers of homemade baby food from the racks of the freezer into a huge trash bag along with all the prepared bottles of formula. Then she called Gil and asked him to come over and wait for social services, explaining that she was too upset to stay. In fact, she was afraid that her face would betray a lie she had not spoken. Lying was never her gift.

Back at her own house, Frankie was unable to stop herself from shaking.

What had she done?

Was she trying to protect her father? Her father's reputation? Her own? Was she trying to protect Ariel? Was it possible that Ariel really was hurting Ben? Abused children can grow up to abuse children; she knew this. But she also knew that abusive parents were often cold and uncaring or neglectful or lacking in compassion. Ariel was none of those things. She was a tender mother, playful and protective, not in the least obsessive. She was as much Beatrice's daughter as Carlotta's. This could, however, be only a facade.

What if what was wrong with Ben came from the water or the soil right here? Was Atty at risk as well? Atty wasn't yet ready to eat any solid foods, and when they used formula, they mixed it with distilled water.

Through the window, Frankie watched as what was clearly a standard-issue van drove up and into the circle drive. Where was Penn? Clearly, he was not at home or he'd have been outside. A woman with a badge got out of the vehicle. Frankie picked up her phone and quickly looked for Simon Land's number. The call went over to voice mail. "Simon, please call me back right away. I need you. This is Frankie Attleboro." She left her number.

In less than five minutes, Simon called her back.

"You're finally ready to leave that Canuck husband of yours for me," he said.

"I absolutely will," Frankie said, trying to flirt, trying to joke, failing miserably, her voice cracking as she began to cry. "If you'll just help me."

"I'll help you any way that I can, Frankie. You know that. Are you okay to drive?"

She was. They agreed to meet in Hyannis, at the Krakatoa Coffee Cup in an hour. Frankie showered quickly, dressed nicely and left a note for Gil. She knew that she couldn't face him. Taking the bag with the food and the baby bottles, she left. She would sit in the parking lot at the coffee shop for thirty minutes, waiting to see Simon step energetically out of his car, his tall, impeccably coiffed and curated form in his camel coat and cordovan wing tips suddenly more familiar and dear than Frankie could bear. They had been friends for more than a decade, not as long as she and Ariel, but since before Gil was even a concept in her life. She stumbled into his arms and, for a moment, wished that she'd listened all those times when Simon had told her how much he was in love with her. He was only a year or two older than Gil and insisted that Frankie was the reason he'd never married, although running Land Ho! Foods since his father's retirement sounded relentless. Once, just before she graduated college, Frankie went with her mother to a dinner party at Simon's waterfront mansion, which was named Tidal. She'd strayed out onto the wraparound porch that thrust out over Nantucket Sound and, a few moments later, felt rather than heard Simon come out to stand beside her. "I could stand here happily for the rest of my life," Frankie said.

"That could be arranged," Simon said.

"How do you ever bring yourself to leave? I mean, how do you go to work?"

"Well, I usually work here. I have to travel, sure. But I don't make the popcorn myself." He added, "When you're a single guy, though, all those bedrooms and beautiful deep tubs and that pool, they're kind of wasted on me. I would probably be just as happy on a houseboat."

Frankie, who'd spent time on a houseboat during a college internship, said, "You have no idea what you're talking about. You're much too entitled to ever live on a houseboat."

"That's why the house is named Tidal," he replied. "It's really short for Entitled."

Months later, in the moments when she believed the salt water that had been her workplace and her playground would become her grave, Frankie would think back to that afternoon, think of putting her face against Simon's soft lapel, with its faint but dark green scent that reminded Frankie of being a kid riding her bike past a neighbor's privet on Two Ponds Road. She would think of that day as the first day she accepted that about one thing Carlotta was correct: some matters lie beyond the things human beings can measure and see.

When they sat down to mugs of hot coffee, Frankie gulping hers down so quickly that Simon winced, she placed two of the little screw-top glass baby-food containers and two of the bottles between them on the table.

Simon said, "Okay..."

"I want—no, I need someone to analyze the contents of these, to see if there's anything in them that could hurt a baby."

"Frankie, what?"

She told him then, not bothering to swear Simon to secrecy because she knew that his loyalty was guaranteed. When she finished explaining everything about Ben, Simon asked her, "So won't the hospital lab, the forensic lab, be doing the testing on this stuff?"

"They would if it was there, in the house," Frankie said. "But I took it."

Simon simply looked at her, his eyes betraying nothing except concern. He finally said, "You could see this as obstructing an investigation."

"You could," Frankie said. "I didn't think of that until after I did it. I guess I didn't think I was capable of doing something like that. Simon, I was just trying to buy time. So I could think about what this might mean. I really wasn't trying to do anything wrong."

"I believe you."

"And the way it is in books, the way my friend Ellabella talks about this, it takes so long to get anything tested in a lab, it could be too late. Ben could die."

Before he said anything more, Simon finished his coffee and slowly, infuriatingly slowly, ate the bear claw pastry he'd ordered. Frankie wanted to snatch it out of his hands and eat it herself…or rub it to crumbs on top of his springy blond hair, just beginning to silver appealingly at the temples. Finally, he said, "Here's what I'll do. I'll test these things. I'll get the results back to you tomorrow. But Frankie, I want you to know one thing. If I find anything abnormal or dangerous, I won't hesitate to give those results to authorities."

"I wouldn't want you to hesitate," Frankie said. "I would want you to do that."

"I think I should take all the samples you have," Simon added.

"They'll all be the same thing, won't they?"

"You don't know that. And otherwise, you'd throw them out, right?"

Frankie hadn't even thought that far ahead. She said as much.

"Will you have to explain this to your lab techs?" she asked then.

"I'll do it myself," he told her. "What, Frankie? Did you think I was just a popcorn salesman?"

"I did, but what's wrong with being a popcorn salesman?"

"I'm a research chemist, Frankie. I created those recipes

myself, with a chef from the Institute of Culinary Education in New York."

"Oh, wow. No wonder it's all so good," she said, feeling sheepish. "This is the worst thing, Simon. It's the worst thing that could happen. I resented my father marrying Ariel. I… resented Ben. I wished Ben had never—"

"No, you didn't, Frankie. And if people really were punished for their worst thoughts, there would be bodies all over the street every day and explosions every night." He paused and then continued. "If I'm going to do this, I have to take this stuff and get back. But you have to promise me you won't blame yourself anymore for this. You're a scientist too, Frankie, and an artist. But more than that, you're a good woman. You would never want anything bad to happen to your little brother or anyone's little brother."

"When people do put things in food to hurt children—I looked this up—it's not clear if they really want to kill the baby or if they just want all the sympathy and attention that mothers get when they have sick children. Most of the people are…are single mothers."

"You mean, like Ariel. She's not a single mother, but Mack is always gone, and she's probably lonely. She probably feels like your mom did, years ago."

"But my mom was different. She was solid. She was stable."

"That's because you only knew her as your mom. You don't know what kind of arguments she had with Mack about him being gone so much." He raised his hands to Frankie's look. "And I don't either. Beatrice never said one single word but how proud she was of Mack's work."

Frankie pressed the heels of her hands to her eyes. She said, "Thank you for doing this. Thanks for meeting me. Thanks for talking to me. I feel crazy. I know that it's foolish to think my selfishness has anything to do with any of this. But when I was a kid, I used to think that all those bad thoughts had wings and they flew around and looked for someplace to strike…"

"Like Pandora's box," Simon said.

"Exactly like that."

"But the last thing in the box was the little angel. Hope."

"I always forget that part." She went on, "Simon, you must have heard about people trying to contaminate food. Don't they do that to try to sue food companies?" He nodded. "So what do they put in it?"

"All kinds of disgusting stuff, Frankie. Scraping from infected wounds. Cat feces. You don't want to hear this. Insecticide. Bleach. Ground-up prescription pills. Lots of times, though, it's just ordinary stuff. Salt or salt water. Way too much of a good thing can be a bad thing."

When they parted, Frankie was reluctant. She wanted to cry out *Take me with you! I want to be rich-rich and go to charity balls and swim in the pool and take pictures of daisies. Take me back to that house with the beautiful porch under the stars! Never mind that bespectacled Canadian guy behind the curtain. He'll be better-off.*

Then she rushed home to Gil and Atty.

When Gil saw her, he shoved a mug of tea into her hands and heated up a piece of quiche from the last of the frozen things his mother had made at the time of the wedding. As he did, he related how he had watched the social worker search every drawer and cupboard, dumping half of the unopened boxes from the pantry into a large white plastic bag and sealing all the open containers, from milk to ketchup to applesauce, in clear plastic bags that they labeled and placed in cartons with cardboard dividers.

"It was awful, Frankie," he told her.

Then Mack and Ariel came home. Mack went into his study and closed the door. Gil said he was pale, his face stubbled. Ariel began throwing clothes for herself and Ben into a gym bag. She would take a shower and go right back to the hospital. She was crying, and when Penn showed up, she asked him where the baby food from the freezer was, and Penn said maybe the cleaner had thrown it out accidentally, but not to worry, that there was more in the carriage house—which he went over and got for her.

"He did *what*?" Frankie said.

"He went and got the baby food, and Ariel thanked him, but she was crying so hard by then that Penn said he would drive her back to the hospital."

"He gave her the frozen baby food they made?"

"I guess she didn't want Ben to have hospital baby food."

"Where is she now?"

"They left. Your dad is going back in a few minutes, I guess. He was going over some checklists left about what was seized. I feel sorry for him, Frankie. He looks terrible. It would be awful if this ended up on the news, but even the gossip… For an academic, gossip is death."

Frankie knew Gil was still talking as he turned away from her to change the baby. But she didn't hear him. She sprinted, if you could call it that, across to the house and took two of the little jars of homemade baby food from the freezer. They looked exactly the same as the ones she had given to Simon. The date on the label, just over a week before, was exactly the same, written with the same Sharpie marker in green. That didn't mean anything. Bad deeds such as these were planned carefully. People sat up, fevered eyes open in the darkness. If they were smart, they planned the next step, and three moves on from that, like chess players. If they were crafty enough, that kind of sleight of hand would be exactly what they would do.

Frankie rushed back to their cottage. After putting the containers in the freezer, she said, "Oh please. Give Atty to me. I feel like I haven't seen him in months."

Her rosy dark-haired son molded himself gratefully into her arms and pushed against her breast to be fed. *Think*, Frankie instructed herself, the baby's suck a force that tethered her to earth. *Think before you do anything else.* If a social worker was interviewing Ariel because they suspected she somehow poisoned Ben, surely they wouldn't let her bring poisoned food from home and give it to him under the doctors' noses. Right? That had to be right.

Poisoned food?

Ariel, she thought. *Ariel!*

Let it be okay, she pleaded with a glowering universe. *Let all this please be okay. Let Ben be okay. And I promise that it stops right here.* How many times had she rolled her eyes at people who prayed for good grades on the LSAT or for their periods to come or to find their grandmother's pearl ring...as if fate were a personal genie to be summoned in a time of need.

Though it was not full spring, the sunset was lurid, the gulls crossing in the air making their raucous appeal. She heard her father's car crunching along the shell drive. Her phone rang.

"Frankie, it's Simon Land. I'm finished with this job you asked me to do. I got to it quicker than I thought. I know how important it is," he said. "Do you want to meet?"

"Do you have the contaminants written down? I can come there and get—"

"Frankie, there were no contaminants of any kind. Peas, carrots, apple. No chemicals, no impurities. This is probably as safe for a baby to eat as baby food can get."

"Did you—"

He interrupted her. "Just to be safe, I did a separate sampling from every one of the ten containers and the three bottles. Same result for every one of them. Nothing." He added, "I want you to know that I'm not a forensic chemist. This is a food-science lab, and it's possible that we don't have the capacity to find something unless it's obvious. I'm just saying it wouldn't hurt to give these samples to the social worker or the police, if they get involved, if you have any more of them."

"I will, if I have to. Simon, thank you so much. I can never thank you enough."

"I hope it puts your mind at ease."

"It does. I feel silly now, as though I've been some kind of village lady in a British mystery poking around in the rhododendrons looking for clues."

"I admire you for it, Frankie. You care."

"I'm paranoid...and way too nosy."

"Nosy, paranoid people care too."

Frankie rebuked herself. How could she ever have suspected Ariel of any wrongdoing? Except when it came to choosing a husband, Ariel was kind and sane.

She left to go for a walk, to clear her head, and as she left the cottage she saw a brand-new car in the driveway at her father's house, dark maroon in color. She inched closer. A Lexus. Had Penn bought a car? Then out of the house came Carlotta, clad in a long silver jacket with matching pants, a string of pearls interspersed with bright blue stones hanging almost to her waist. Her long thick hair was now short, in a fashionable, edgy chop. She waved gaily to Frankie as she removed a suitcase from the car.

Was she back? Was she visiting? Frankie wasn't sure what to say, and she felt vaguely guilty about all those photos she and Ellabella were perusing. She simply waved. Then, repenting, she turned and said, "Well, hi. It's been a while."

A month, but Carlotta, perhaps not surprisingly, simply shrugged.

"So," Frankie went on finally, "I had to move some of your boxes and bags. They're all in my friend Ellabella's garage. It's fancy and climate-controlled so you don't have to worry. I'll help you move your things into the condominium as soon as the renters are gone. I think we may have dropped a couple of your file boxes, but I put everything back as best I could. It'll just be a few days now, right?"

"We'll see," Carlotta said, in a surprisingly acerbic tone. "I'll be staying put here with Ariel and Mack until Ben is better, at least. The poor little guy."

Frankie walked over to the car, detecting that unmistakable new-car scent.

"Do you need any help?"

"I'm fine," Carlotta said.

On the back seat were an Apple computer bag and a caramel-colored Birkin bag—not that Frankie would have known what a Birkin bag looked like if she hadn't recently seen Ellabella's. Why had she ever thought that Carlotta didn't have money, Frankie asked herself, even before she knew about her widow's gifts? She answered her own question: people who lived on communes and picked beets didn't drive a Lexus or buy a new Mac laptop…or did they? Maybe it was a rental car. Maybe it was borrowed. Maybe whatever was in that computer-store box was the only new thing Carlotta had purchased in years. Penn was right: what it was possible to know about Carlotta was exactly nothing.

"You know, I might see if Ariel would sell the condo," Carlotta was saying. "Then I could get something a little more modest. I could sell the land where the old cabin used to be too. That location probably means it's worth good money now. Do you know any Realtors?"

"My dad does," Frankie said, her mind thrumming. Carlotta didn't own the condo, Ariel did, right? And she didn't know about all the things that Sailor had told them. Or did she? "So that stuff I moved, are you moving it back for now?"

Carlotta said, "I'll get Penn to move it. I really am looking forward to having a place of my own, though. I need some privacy, heaven knows. But I can wait a little longer. I probably should get on over to the hospital."

"Ariel will be really glad to see you. She hasn't been able to reach you for weeks now."

Carlotta said, "Hmmm. I'll mention that real-estate thing to your dad today."

"Maybe not today," Frankie said. "If Ben doesn't improve today, they're going to transfer him to some special diagnostic unit at Boston Children's."

"Right!" Carlotta said. "I'm sure he'll be fine."

Why was she so breezy? Frankie chided herself. That was simply Carlotta's way. And…how did she even know how sick Ben was? Who had she been talking to? Did she think that the illness was genetic, much like what Ariel had had as a child, and did she know that Ariel had shared her own history with Ben's doctors? Or did she know even more? That was impossible. She hadn't been around for weeks. Ben hadn't even gotten sick again until after Carlotta left.

Frankie decided to call Ellabella, the only person with whom she didn't feel like a fruitcake for divulging her creepy suspicions.

What was Carlotta up to, after all?

At the time of her wedding, Carlotta had regaled everyone with the story of weathering a massive storm on a fishing trawler. "This was a big boat," Frankie remembered her saying. "A big boat with twenty men and only two women. One was the cook, and one was me. The cook had two sons on the boat, fishermen, one was about eighteen and one was a little older. So this storm comes up, four in the morning, and the old guys say it's as bad as anything they ever saw. Lightning and thunder and wind just screaming. That big boat was bouncing around like a tub toy, and huge waves were washing over the deck. Stuff breaking, stuff falling off the shelves. People were puking. And suddenly this woman, Rena, says to me, 'This is horrible and I'm having a baby.' I think, why would you come out on a fishing boat if you were pregnant? And I said, 'Are you sick to your stomach? Go below and try to lie down so you don't slip and fall.' But she says, 'I'm having a baby right now!' And she was! We're about a hundred miles from nowhere at all, off the Grand Banks, and she's in the bunk, and I'm yelling for people to bring me scissors, and she's screaming, and she pushes out this little baby girl, she's perfectly fine, Rena says, thank you. Two hours later, the storm was over, and she's making pancakes." She added, "All I can say is, she was lucky I once studied to be a nurse."

It was a great story. How Grandpa Frank had loved that story! And like every one of her stories, it offered not one single syllable to explain Carlotta's role in the matter.

That was always the one thing no one could ever really explain.

14

"Lots of people have hidden lives," Ellabella said. "Haven't you ever heard those stories about men who have two families in the same neighborhood?"

"I hear about stuff like that, and I always think the wife has to know, but she's in denial," Frankie said. "I would know."

"Think about it. Mack was always taking off. He could have had a second family in some island nation. Or in Chicago for that matter."

Frankie began to laugh. "That's all I need. I feel like this is a curse of the cat people or something. You saying it is going to make it true!"

Ben was apparently well again, his symptoms having once more disappeared as mysteriously as they'd arisen. He was crawling all over, and Ariel's relief, both at having her baby and her mother back, was like a light around her.

They were lounging in Ellabella's rooms, and Frankie could not stop teasing her about their opulence. "If I ring for tea, will a faithful retainer come? With a heated pot?"

"No, but I'll get us some tea if you want. You look worn-out—not to be insulting."

"I am worn-out. Women used to lose a tooth when they had a baby. I still have all my choppers, but I could sleep eighteen hours a day, like a dog. And now it's time to go back to work."

Earlier that morning, an uncharacteristically balmy day in May, finally able to squeeze into her wet suit, Frankie hired a pilot to go out with her while she began experimenting with the way she would take pictures for a private commission, a pair of triptychs of seals made from consecutive above-and-below the surface shots. Frankie was not a fan of seals: they were inquisitive and aggressive, and where they were, sharks followed. But the collector was very free with his money, gratefully accepting the first crazy figure that Frankie threw out, so she had no choice. There were adult and juvenile seals all over the place, and it was past the time of day that sharks favored for their brunch. The pilot was a very nice guy from Woods Hole who was training in excavating crash sites with a view to identifying the remains of crew members who might have been listed only as missing for fifty years or more. His family lived on Cape Cod, where his mother and father were both ministers. The pilot was considering becoming a minister also. When Frankie pointed out the irony of her using her father's boat while simultaneously not speaking to him, the young man said he would pray for them. Frankie nearly laughed, until she saw in his face that he wasn't kidding.

She would take any help she was offered.

At the same time she was practicing the way she would take the photos, she had decided to do something else she'd promised: testing and rating a new tankless diving system that used a battery-powered compressor to supply breathing air to divers through air tubes. Dubbed Aqua Spiritus, this wasn't by far the first of these systems. But this new one had the advantage of being so light and portable it was almost like carrying a briefcase. The ease of using it—and how it could extend diving times without any threat to the diver—made it a pretty enticing alternative to even the lightest tanks. She ended up loving the device.

When Frankie got back to their dock, she was surprised to find Carlotta sitting on the little side pier, dangling her feet in the cold water. "I have to ask you a favor," she said without preamble. "I want you to help me talk to Ariel about selling the condominium. She's avoiding the subject with me."

"There's nothing I can do about it," Frankie said as she paid her helper extra because he'd agreed to clean the boat for her, a rare luxury.

"I just want her to see my side," Carlotta said. "She's been able to keep the rent from that place for all these years. Now I'm going to need a place to live, and it's only fair."

Fair, Frankie thought, didn't begin to address it. This was another of Carlotta's blithe assertions which, as Penn described them, sounded as if they meant something but really didn't.

"Oh, and Frankie, one of these times, can I come out and watch you again? I'm very good at driving this boat."

"You've driven my dad's boat? On your own?" She wanted to say *Does he know?*

"Sure," Carlotta said. "He was fine with it."

This Frankie doubted at a cellular level, but she said nothing. Mack had a hard time even with her or Penn using his precious boat, but perhaps he was mellowing with age. "Sure," she said, trying to be mellow on her own. "It's fine if you come out with me again." She then, reluctantly, asked Carlotta if she and Ariel could come over for dessert that evening.

To Ellabella, Frankie said, "I am pleading with you to come too. Please just come for a little while."

"What can I do?"

"You're just really good at reading people. I can't tell if Carlotta is on the level or not. She seems like she's entirely ordinary but not one word about where she was for the past couple of weeks. She doesn't say, *I was on a business trip buying rare stones for my new jewelry business...* or *I went to an ashram for a silent retreat.* Nothing. I suspect it has to do with the Peace Patch Orchard that I saw on that file, so I looked it up." She waited. Ellabella seemed preoccupied. "Don't you want to know what it is?"

Ellabella said, "I'm going to guess. It's probably this big vegetable- and fruit-growing commune in Alaska where they grow cabbages the size of pumpkins and pumpkins the size of Mini Coopers. And it's all presided over by a woman who says she came from another galaxy and her three sons, who apparently came from this one because they each have about ten wives."

"You already knew!"

"Just good investigative reporting," Ellabella said. "It took all of two keystrokes." The sons, Ellabella further pointed out, were always getting in trouble for plural marriages and underage brides.

"Well, the only things in Carlotta's Peace Patch folder were some flyers advertising the vegetables—and believe me, those zucchini were pretty obscene—and some stuff about the vegan-food company they're starting. Oh, and a copy of a little essay from a magazine about the ups and downs of communal parenting. That's when your biological mother is only one of the people who raise you."

"A practice that's been around since the Stone Age."

"What's the matter with you? You're acting all...disaffected." She added, "Aren't you even a little bit curious about all this?"

"That's the problem," Ellabella said. "I am curious. But I don't have any real right to be. I'm feeling like a tabloid reporter right now. Digging through her things. After all, she hasn't done anything wrong. She's just made some weird choices. Tons of people have made even weirder choices."

"She's so selfish," Frankie said.

"Which is not a crime."

"But why's she doing all this?"

"She's a rolling stone, like Sailor said. If Ariel's okay with it, we should be okay with it."

"Ariel's only okay with it because she doesn't have my mom anymore."

"Maybe you're not okay with it because you don't have your mom anymore."

"I would like to think I'm not that ungenerous."

Ellabella reached out and briefly hugged Frankie's shoulder. "You're not even a little ungenerous. But you've lost your mom and your best friend and even your dad, kind of, in a year and a half. You've become a mom and a wife. It would be just strange if you weren't shook."

Frankie looked away and studied the fireplace, above which were mounted two of the underwater nude photos Frankie had taken of Ellabella all those months ago.

"Why aren't these down in the main foyer?" Frankie asked. "Right by the opulent tiled entry with the gilded cove ceiling?"

"That would be so Kitty Ballenger, wouldn't it?" said Ellabella. "Trust me, they'll be in the foyer in my own house someday. And like I told you, when my son's friends come over, I promise you I will say, *You know, that's a picture of me, lads!*"

"You can't really see anything. Whoever took that must be a very taste-full photographer!"

"Veddy, veddy taste-full," Ellabella said.

"So you'll come over, right?"

Ellabella sighed.

Frankie said, "After this, I'll withdraw from their business. I know what you mean. Gil says the same thing. He thinks I'm just trying to cook up a storm because I'm so used to being an action hero."

Ariel, Frankie knew, was not a big fan of Frankie's friendship with the reformed Ellabella, but she still wanted Ellabella's reaction. She also hoped that if Ellabella and Gil were there, it might tamp down any fireworks.

That was a bold hope, which quickly turned faint.

Gil announced that he was having dinner with Penn at a taco place in Hyannis, but given the events, wished that the taco place was in Newfoundland. He did helpfully haul out one of the frozen confections left behind by his mother, an almond pound cake for which she'd also concocted a raspberry syrup.

"I was going to make a cake," Frankie said as she bathed Atty, who was fetchingly making bubbles to attract her attention.

"This meeting will be hard enough without you making a cake," Gil said.

"Not nice! I'm getting better," Frankie protested. "At cooking."

"Frankie, I'm a terrible cook! I never expected you to be a great cook because you're a woman or something. All we have to do is survive on the food we make, right? A cake would be extraneous. We have to use up all these frozen bakery things anyhow, they get kind of strange after a few months." He added, "I wasn't talking about cooking. I was talking about the fact that I married into a domestic soap opera."

"All families have drama."

"Mine doesn't. Not like this."

"We're Americans, Saint Gil!" Frankie said. "You caught us sort of at an odd moment."

"I gather. Don't you think that you're sort of setting them both up?"

"Carlotta asked me to help persuade Ariel. I'm not going to do that. But it's possible that Ari will feel like she can tell the truth if I'm here. I guess that's what I think. Maybe I just want to tune in to *The Real Fishwives of Cape Cod*."

They both laughed.

Just before the others arrived, Sailor came to take Atty over to the big house for a while. All over again, Frankie was moved by his capability and kindness with the baby. She caught herself in the wistful wish that Sailor were her father too, as well as Ariel's. Indeed, she thought, he very nearly was.

When Ariel showed up, it was without Ben. "He's home with Mack," Ariel said, as if this was a matter of no consequence. "All he has to do is feed him and get him ready for bed." To Frankie's ears, she might as well have said, all he has to do is build a nuclear reactor. Her father had never, not once, read a bedtime story to her or Penn, although he had, she admitted, taught her to swim and to dive, to ski on snow and water, to see every secret thing that the natural world was hiding. Tonight in the house where she had grown up, in her mother's peaceable kingdom by the sea, two old men were taking care of two little baby boys. Life was a hall of mirrors.

Thawed and slightly reheated, the cake was still dense and delicate and gone within half an hour. Frankie made coffee with cream and offered Frangelico for those who would, even taking a drop for herself. Everyone complimented Giselle in absentia. Ellabella, confounding Frankie anew with her ability to eat like a stevedore and look like a supermodel, consumed three slices and asked if she could take the last piece home.

And then Carlotta began.

"Ariel, I want to talk to you. I think it's time we sold that condominium in Orleans. All that was possible after my mother died, and I'm sure it's been nice for you to have the rental income all these years. And I need to find a place for myself, but I really don't need three bedrooms and beach access—"

"No," said Ariel.

"No," Carlotta repeated. Her green gaze hardened, to something primordial. Frankie thought of the jellyfish that long-ago day in Hawaii, beautiful, ephemeral, deadly. "What? I really don't need as much space as that, Ariel."

"No, I am not signing anything. I am not selling the condominium."

"That doesn't really seem fair."

Rage was a scent in the room, like the aftermath of a fireworks display. Frankie thought, here it comes.

"It doesn't matter that you don't think it's fair. It is entirely my choice. That place is mine. I bought it after Grandma Sherry died, and I've taken care of it all these years. With help from Sailor, I now know, and yes, I know about everything he did for me, and I know that he is my real father, not some mythological Princeton asshole, and let me say this. I do know you've changed. I do want you in my life. But he has been a much better father to me than you have been a mother."

"He told you about that?"

Ariel said, "Yes. He did. It was about time. I want him to be part of my life and part of Ben's life. I already let the renters know that it's their lucky day and they can stay in the condominium for the foreseeable future."

"Ariel, I need a place for myself. And it was my mother's money that bought that condo."

"That may be, but it came to me. I assume you don't want me to talk about this here, but if you need money, at least until you get a job, I can help you out. I'm sure Mack won't mind."

"Ariel, listen—"

"Let's talk about something else."

"We need to work this out, Ariel."

Ariel said, "Okay. Let's work it out. Let's start with why you left me here and took off for a dozen years?"

"The short answer is I didn't know where I was going, didn't know if it would be the best place for a child. I just couldn't take you with me."

"Well, let's have the long answer, then. Was it too dangerous? Did you work for a drug cartel? Did you smuggle diamonds? Did you steal intellectual property? What were you actually doing all those years?"

Carlotta said, "I was thinking of you, not me."

"The way I see it, you were thinking of you, not me. The way it seems, until the last couple of months, everything in your world came before me."

Carlotta got up fast, her hip nudging the table. All the delicate coffee cups, which had been Beatrice's, shuddered like acorns on an autumnal tree. "I don't have to listen to this," she said.

"Just this one part," Ariel said. "I told Frankie off. I yelled at Frankie, who has always been the one person on earth—well, her mother too—who was good and kind to me, who cared about me the way you can only care about somebody who's your own." Ariel turned to Frankie. "It's true. I was cold to you, and I should never have been that way. I owe you and Beatrice my whole life, Frankie. And Mack too, now, and I'm sorry I hurt you. Because I love you, Frankie."

Carlotta, feeling the shift in the air said, "Should I leave? Do you even want me here?"

"I don't want you to leave, Mother. I want us to save whatever kind of family we have left. But on my terms. One thing for sure, I'm not giving Sailor up. He's Ben's grandfather. He's a good man. As for whatever else we talk about—and there's a lot to talk about—maybe this isn't the time or the place."

Frankie thought, please oh please, let's not talk about the dead husbands or the hippie vegetable farm. But then, just at that moment, Carlotta burst out crying. She cried so hard and so genuinely, she was nearly bent double.

"Ari, I'm so sorry. I'm so sorry for being an awful mother and an awful person. I am so sorry I lost you. I just… I was so afraid. It was always Beatrice, Beatrice, Beatrice. She was so much better than me, and she had everything that I wanted and I was so jealous and so afraid. I wanted to be something.

I wanted to be somebody, away from this place. I was afraid I'd end up alone and…crazy, like my own mother. Sherry was a waste of oxygen. Who—whatever set that cabin on fire, it was… She was probably better-off. Please, Ariel, give me another chance. Give me a chance to make it up to you. Please."

After a few seconds that seemed to waver in space like wire stretched across a canyon, Ariel put her arms around Carlotta. "You have time, Mother. You have time to be the person you want to be. We all do. And yes, I loved Beatrice with all my heart. I will always miss her. But Beatrice was Frankie's mother. You're my mother. Life sometimes give you a second try."

Frankie thought of Mack then. For an instant, she longed for her dad. No, she thought. She would stand firm. So would he. Until…until someone blinked. Or until it was too late. She was her father's daughter.

Ellabella caught Frankie's eye. Her look said plainly, *You go, Ariel girl,* but not for nothing was this Kitty Ballenger's only daughter. "So," Ellabella said. "Anybody going somewhere fabulous this summer?"

Life for the next few weeks rolled out an extravagant carpet of daffodils and tulips. Magnolias burst into bloom, their champagne sazzle scenting the air. No Cape Cod spring was ever too drizzly or cloudy for Beatrice, Frankie recalled. She always said the very morning air was like a fancy hydration treatment for your skin.

In due course, Frankie helped Penn and Ariel bring the few things Carlotta needed back into the big house. Most of the rest she left in the Ballengers' garage. She had a line on one of the new studio apartments above the Salty Gal clothing store in Chatham, where she also found a job silk-screening prints of humpback whales and octopus onto seventy-five-dollar hoodies and thirty-dollar baby onesies, but those places wouldn't be ready for tenants for a few more weeks. Frankie noticed that the wine box that contained all of Carlotta's herbs and oils was no longer there. Why hadn't she given some of that stuff to Simon for testing while she had the chance? A fair number of boxes were missing too. Carlotta had apparently showed up at the Ballengers' door one day and told Kitty that she hoped it was okay to go into the garage and fill a few big construction-type trash bags with what she called the junk of a lifetime, stowing the bags in the trunk of her maroon Lexus and gaily waving goodbye. Several nights a week, Carlotta went back to tending bar at the beach club. She was a skillful, quick and personable barkeep, and they welcomed her. She told Frankie that some of the same guys there were sitting in the same seats as when she'd left. On her days off, Carlotta stayed with Ben so that Ariel could make belated headway with the mailings for the Saltwater Foundation. The Lexus was gone, replaced by a ten-year-old Toyota Corolla.

Frankie finished all of her prints for the paper-arts show and made ready for two new assignments—yet another underwater-face portrait of a sea otter and a close-up shot of a bottlenose dolphin. She needed to finish the seal triptychs as well.

Looking back, she would think of this time as the end of innocence—a shock, since she had imagined that innocence had ended the previous fall, when she learned that her widowed dad was marrying her best friend. Instead, her restored life was about to be eclipsed with a darkness unlike anything she ever could have predicted—although she would one day tell her children that she had never really asked herself about the metrics of what people fantasized about doing, what they planned to do and what they actually did, and how vast the gap was between them. Since everyone sometimes yearned to do things that conscience would never permit, Frankie would define this gap as morality.

★ ★ ★

Just before summer began in earnest, Ben got sick for what would turn out to be the last time.

In the translucent dawn of a Saturday morning, Penn called Frankie. He told her that Mack and Carlotta were with Ariel but wanted Frankie. Ben had had two seizures: he was much sicker than he'd ever been before. Frankie was already out in the boat with her helper from Woods Hole, not more than an hour away from finishing every angle of the seal triptychs. She hurried in, and her pilot explained that he would clean the boat but could not return later on that particular day. That was fine, Frankie told him. The project was well overdue, weeks overdue, but it would have to be more overdue than this. Frankie shrugged into clothes and set off for the hospital, only to turn the car around after a few miles. She went back into her house and extracted the two containers of homemade baby food from her freezer. Back in the car, she rushed through the blush summer light to the hospital, with an eerie sense that all of this had happened before, in just this way, and that the outcome was already ordained. If Ben was mortally ill, no matter what Simon Land said, it would be in part because of her evil envy, the cruel thoughts that flew about like hornets, punishing the innocent as well as the guilty. She called Sailor and left a message on his phone.

When she passed through the doors into Pediatric Intensive Care (without asking permission of anyone at all, since she didn't feel like providing a complex family tree), she could hear a loud and sustained moaning, like a woman in labor. It was Carlotta, whom Frankie found sitting on the floor of Ben's room, surrounded by nurses who offered her ice in a cup because she had fainted. Ariel saw Frankie and held up her arms like a child: Frankie enfolded her. They huddled together in the chair. Doctors were working over Ben in another part of the hospital. The seizures had not been life-threatening, but all seizures were serious, especially when they happened to a baby. Apparently, Ben's fever was now normal, but neurological tests as well as the usual blood and stomach contents tests would follow. Mack, Ariel said, was filling out paperwork and making phone calls.

After murmuring reassuring noises to Ari, Frankie went to the nurses' station and gave the containers to the nurse in charge, informing her that the doctors had asked her to bring these, for them and for the police if necessary. "Please hand these to the doctors, not to Mrs. Attleboro or her mother."

When she returned to the room, she overheard Carlotta telling the nurses, "She nearly died from this same thing when she was little. I can't go through this again…"

Frankie told Ariel, "What should I do? I'll do anything you want."

Ariel's face was sculpted downward by despair. She asked Frankie to follow her into the hall. Only her clear green eyes moved as she said softly, "Please, please get my mother out of here. At least for a while. She's driving me nuts. She's driving everyone nuts. Make her stay back at Tall Trees. Just you come back."

"But are you sure you want me to come back? You'll tell me when to come back?"

Ariel said, "Of course."

"So just…maybe call Gil. He'll get in touch with me right away."

"That's good," Ariel said.

They went back into Ben's room.

"Carlotta, can you do me a favor? Come with me, just for an hour," Frankie said. "I need your help taking the boat out. Remember you said you'd help me? I just need to be out for a few minutes, out by the seal nursery, for a project that has to be finished." She added, "Mack and Ari are both here. You don't have to worry."

Carlotta scanned the room, gazing for a long time at a space just above Ariel's head. Later, Frankie thought it seemed as though she'd been adding up a column of figures, and the answer was as close to correct as she could get it. "Okay," she finally said quietly and to Ariel, "Will you be all right?" Ariel nodded, her eyes signaling Frankie.

This would work.

Simply depositing Carlotta at the big house wouldn't work. There would be an argument. Carlotta might call Ariel or call the hospital, both distinctly bad options. No, she would pretend that she was actually so obsessed with finishing her shoot that she would leave Ariel's side with Ben in intensive care. She was betting on the fact that someone so single-minded about her own desires as Carlotta wouldn't find this choice unspeakably callous. And indeed, in the car, Carlotta seemed to recover her customary chipper, chatty demeanor. She told Frankie that she would be fine piloting the boat. Frankie decided that for such a short, shallow dive, she would use the Aqua Spiritus. She explained to Carlotta what it was and how it worked and asked her if she could monitor the compressor once the boat was anchored. It was simply a matter of turning the device on and if it started to sound funny, Frankie said, turning it off. The battery was charged, she was sure of that. Carlotta said, sure, that would work.

When they arrived at the cottage, it was not quite eight in the morning.

Frankie reported in to Gil. The three adults shared a quick cup of coffee and a slice of toast. Carlotta played with Atty for a few minutes, while Frankie dressed and assembled her gear and charged her phone. Just to make sure Carlotta had everything straight, now that she had the tankless diving device in front of her, Frankie went over the operation again. This particular compressor was one that floated, so all that was necessary was to make sure that once it was turned on, the breathing hose was free of knots and directed straight down and true. Frankie and Carlotta practiced. Carlotta caught on easily. Frankie texted Gil. She asked him to say nothing at the moment, but to let her know the minute Ariel was in touch from the hospital. She would explain everything later.

"I don't like this," Gil whispered, having summoned Frankie into the bedroom. "Just stay here until Ariel calls."

"You'll be able to see me from the beach," Frankie told him. "I'm just doing what Ariel asked me to do and trying to use up some time." She kissed Gil and Atty. "Don't worry. I'll be right back."

She turned to find Carlotta regarding her mildly from the open bedroom door. "Are we set?"

Frankie said, "Yep."

Everything is fine. She really thinks you're doing a job and she's helping you out.

With Carlotta piloting the boat, they set off. Although distracted, Frankie noticed how really adept at it she was, perhaps because of her fishing-crew days. When she gestured to Carlotta that she was heading too far away from the planned location, Carla dropped her eyes. "Oh, Frankie, don't get mad, but I got one of your dad's small anchors hung up on the tower rock. Don't ask me how, I feel ridiculous. I don't want Mack to ever find out. I thought, since we were doing this anyway… can we please just recover that first?"

The tower rock, straight out from the dock about half a mile, was technically not a natural formation, although fish and corals gratefully used it as such. It was a tall pile of excavated rocks from around the Tall Trees property that Frankie's family had piled up over the years and hauled out there to make a sort of fish habitat. It was broad and flat enough in parts that four people could stand comfortably on its ledges. At low tide, it protruded like a tiny island with a lighthouse. But it disappeared, entirely underwater when the tide was high, so it was crowned with a tall bright orange pole hoisting an orange and blue warning flag for boaters. The flag boasted a siren and a blinker that theoretically could be activated if somebody did ram a boat into the tower rock. (No one ever had activated it, and it was anyone's guess whether it even worked anymore.) As they approached, Frankie observed that the only chain on the tower rock was an old rusted thing that had probably been in place for generations. Then, on the back side, she glimpsed a newer chain with the orange parachute of the drag anchor. "I'll come alongside, and you grab it," said Carlotta. "We can pull it in together."

As they puttered along slowly, a photo came to Frankie from Ellabella, with the message What about this?

It was a screenshot of Carlotta in court under a headline "Local Woman Questioned in Arson Inquest." The few lines Frankie could see described an inquest into the death of Sherry Puck.

But…hadn't Carlotta run off years before that happened? She'd come back later to give evidence? Weren't inquests usually held right after a suspicious death? Frankie wasn't sure, but that was how it was in true-crime shows, so this would have been more than ten years ago. No wonder this hadn't turned up in Carlotta's belongings, but how had Ellabella missed it while excavating the past? But it appeared that the *local woman* was never named.

In the photo, Carlotta looked only marginally younger than she did right now. Indeed, she was a beautiful woman. She'd told Frankie that she never smoked or drank, never ate meat, never forgot sunscreen and slept nine hours each night. This apparently worked. Frankie thought ruefully of all her own SPF-less years. More to the point, why was Frankie thinking about such nonsense as sunscreen at a time like this? She was alone in a boat with a woman who was potentially capable of cremating her own mother alive.

Frankie texted Am with C right now on the boat cannot talk.

Replied Ellabella, B careful. Sailor looking for you.

Frankie glanced up at Carlotta, who was studying her fixedly. "Did you set that cabin on fire?"

"You went through my things. That was dishonest." They came abreast of the tower rock. "Poor Sherry. A cat would have been a better mother." *A waste of oxygen*, Frankie remembered her saying. *She's probably better-off.* Carlotta gestured for Frankie to stand and reach for the anchor chain as she lowered the bigger anchor. "Let's do this first, and then you can take your pictures. We can talk about the past later."

Suddenly, and so quickly, Carlotta knocked her feet from under her, and Frankie stumbled and struck the small of her back. Carlotta then plucked Frankie's phone from her equipment bag, swiped the screen a few times and tossed it into the water. "You never did put in a code to lock it, Frankie," she said. "Anybody could see what you're telling other people." Carlotta paused as she extracted a smaller, newer chain from behind the console. Frankie struggled to get up. "I wasn't sure I'd have to do this at all. And I didn't think it would be today."

Frankie said, "What are you doing? What are you talking about?"

"There'll be a lot of talk about that tragic family and Mack, such a famous do-gooder in the world—but losing his wife, his daughter..."

"I shouldn't have looked at your things," Frankie said. "That was wrong."

"So why did you?"

"I knew you were hiding something."

"My life is my own business."

"You're right. But then they tried to suggest that Ariel was making Ben sick on purpose. I knew that wasn't true."

"It could still be true," Carlotta said.

"No. One thing I've learned underwater is how to spot a predator."

By then, Frankie was on her knees, shoving Carlotta to one side, reaching out to pull herself onto the pilot's seat. But as she stood, Carlotta punched her in the jaw. Her feet slid out from under her. She would never be able to recall exactly how it was that Carlotta managed to ensnare her legs with the lighter chain. Frankie couldn't stand or free herself. Quickly, as though she had practiced this, Carlotta made a loop she tossed over a big boulder outcropping and pulled tightly, tipping Frankie overboard. Then she held out a hand, and Frankie pulled herself to a sitting position on an outcropping chin of rock. Balancing on the gunwale, Carlotta reached out and cut Frankie's inflatable life jacket and when Frankie tried to push her away, slashed across her palm. Bright blood spurted. How could she be so strong? Think, she said to herself, think. Don't lose control. Don't cry. That's what she expects. Don't say too much.

"Why are you doing this?" she quietly asked. "Ariel will give you money. You have to just stop it now before things get so bad that Ariel will never forgive you."

"You're right about one thing," Carlotta said, reversing the boat and letting it idle. "I do need money. I need a substantial amount—I owe money to some people, sure. But it's not just that, I need to make my own way. I need my own homestead, not some crap little dump over a store."

"Well, we have savings. Gil just got paid for his book. I'll give you money if you let me go."

"No, you won't, Frankie."

"How do you plan on getting it, then? Why not ask Ariel for help?"

"Because that's asking Mack for help. I wish it wasn't necessary to make life so difficult for her. But I'll be there to help her, I'll be the constant in her life, the one she turns to for everything, who she relies on. And eventually, everything will be Ariel's and so then will be mine too." She smiled at Frankie. "That whole place should have been mine to begin with."

"All that was all my mom's, Carlotta! Tall Trees and the land and the money for Mack's foundation, that came from Beatrice! If Beatrice and Mack had never gotten married, he wouldn't have had anything but a professor's salary."

"That's not true. All his shows and lectures, and all his discoveries—"

"Were all things Beatrice encouraged him to do. She even paid for the exploring, at first. He had the talent and style, sure, but he could never have done it on his own."

"Good Saint Beatrice. Well, Mack would have done something big. And I would have been part of that. Maybe even like that couple with the lions or the ones with the elephants. We could have been famous. We could have traveled, had houses all over the world. But Beatrice was the easy way for him." She sighed. "And I was left to take care of myself." Carlotta bit her lip again.

"But you didn't have to be alone. Sailor would have married you! And what about those guys who left you all their money? Your husbands?"

"What, a hundred thousand? Two hundred thousand? That doesn't last long when you travel. Hotels. Planes. Foods. Clothes. It's not cheap to take care of yourself with any kind of style, Frankie. The bills have been piling up. And I wasn't going to live in a little bungalow with my cats."

"Are you delusional? What, are you so privileged that you think you can just take what you want no matter who gets in the way? It was you making Ben sick, wasn't it? Before you even asked Ariel to sell that place." Frankie recalled the day of filling out forms. "You took out a life-insurance policy for Ben. A savings account for his future, you said. You made Ariel take out ones for her and Mack as well, you had her make a will. All so that you could have it all *if* something should happen."

Lunging forward, Frankie felt the chains bite. "And you…you made Ariel sick too. When she was little. Didn't you? Why? That wasn't for money!"

Carlotta just shrugged.

"Are you insane? People don't get away with stuff like that. They'll find out, Carlotta."

But she had gotten away with it.

Carlotta said, "No one will find out. I could have been a scientist, like your precious Mack. Another thing denied. But I had his attention, and Beatrice's for a time. I was the one people were talking about, the poor beautiful Carlotta and her sick daughter—it was a tragedy, they all agreed. And it was nice to be thought of, and for more than just my looks. But sympathy doesn't pay the bills." She grinned. "As your husband is soon to find out. Such a tragic family story…"

It suddenly hit Frankie. "That thing with my dad's scuba. You were behind that."

"It almost worked. Frankie, it was a dry suit. Not a CT scanner. Hardly a big challenge. But I'll get another chance, and then Ariel will really have no one to turn to but me—you'll be gone, and so will Mack."

Then Carlotta was standing, pulling down the inflatable dinghy that Mack kept lashed to the roof of the cabin portion on the *Regent Red*. Frankie watched as she ably extracted the small portable motor Mack kept in a metal casing and fitted it on the dinghy. She had done all this before. It went like clockwork. Then she began rummaging in the tool chest next to one of the water wells on the deck, whistling as she worked. "So how this will look is that intrepid Frankie went out alone… Such a risk! I tried to talk her out of it, I'll be sure to tell them. But that was our Frankie, so ambitious. Why am I even bothering to tell you? You're not going to be around to share the story. Oh well. The dinghy and your life jacket could just drift to shore on their own. High tide is in an hour or so. Everything on this rock will be submerged. Including you. Everyone's so busy, family emergency and all, no one will notice for a long time."

"You're not thinking straight, Carlotta. You're panicking. You're making mistakes. You won't have a nine-thousand-square-foot house. You'll have, like, a sixty-square-foot cell." Frankie paused, then tried to say in a brighter tone, "Why don't you marry some rich guy? There are plenty of rich divorced guys and widowers around here."

"That could be a lot of trouble. He could live forever and get really boring," Carlotta said, and Frankie thought, not with you around. "Life that's the same every day is so boring."

"Please, Carlotta, stop this. Ariel is your baby. Ben is her baby." Frankie said then, trying to keep her voice level, "No one has to know about this. You can just go on and be a better person."

"Yes, get a job. Live in a one-bedroom someplace and be the grandmother, the mother-in-law that's tolerated, that no one really wants around. Sorry, no thanks."

"You crazy bitch! Don't you believe in karma? Don't you believe this will all come back to haunt you?" She added, "What was all the weeping and screaming in the hospital, Carlotta? Was that all just to cover up the awful thing you're doing?"

Carlotta bit her lip. "No, that was all real. I genuinely do feel sad for Ben, for Ariel. Hell, even a little bit for you, Frankie."

Carlotta pointed the dinghy toward shore and revved the little motor. "But this must be your karma. Wonder what it is you could have done?" And then she took off.

Frankie felt the cold gradually. She was only wearing her shorty wet suit. She had not been able to grab even her mask and snorkel. Someone will come, she thought. It's morning. Gil will hear the dinghy come in and see Carlotta. Or a fishing boat will pass by. Anytime now. But the horizon remained unmarked, the unruffled water rose, to her hips, to her waist.

Blood from her slashed palm ribboned faintly through the water. Well, Frankie thought, a shark would at least be quicker. She began to cry. *Gilly, help me. Mom, help me. Dad! Ari, help me!*

So far? So early? So soon?

She was too frightened and too young, she later thought, to take stock of a life that was barely underway or to ask or offer forgiveness. And to whom? And how, if not in prayer? There would be no one beside her. Only the sea she had loved and feared since she understood its power, claiming her body, claiming her life, as it had claimed her imagination. She tried to take some solace in this. The tower rock with its rusted chains would become a storied place, a haunted place, her own restless spirit sighted there at the close of day by generations of teenagers… *She was so young. You can still look up her photos. She had a little baby…* The water crept up to her thighs; the day was extravagant with thready clouds against the boundless blue. The tankless diving rig floated just out of her grasp. She flailed, scooping water toward her until she snagged it. When she went under, perhaps there would be a way to breathe from it. She flipped the switch to On and put the regulator into her mouth. It worked, it worked! Then a wave swept the rig out of her fumbling hands. She watched it float free.

The water rose to her belly.

At first, though she would vacillate on this point, she was mostly sure that what came next was only an artifact of her anguished mind. Neither then nor later did she believe in folktales spun about matters outside human cognition. Still, what Ariel later told her was hard to deny: in Ben's hospital room, Ariel heard Frankie's voice as clearly as if Frankie were speaking into her ear. *Ari, help me!* And Ariel answered, and Frankie heard her. *I'm coming, Frankie!*

As the water reached her chin, Frankie picked up the sound of a small motor. Extending herself beyond what she thought was possible, she reached up out of the water and grabbed the pull cord on the flag and, to her befuddled shock, the alarm sounded and a beacon began to flash. She fell back, flailing, her mouth filling with salt water, her senses flooding with flashes of light. Then Ariel was beside her, on her knees in the dinghy, tipping it half under the water. Ariel, frightened even to wade in the water, reached out for Frankie's head, holding her face up so she could keep drawing in air as the water closed in on them both.

"I've got you," Ariel said. "I called the coast guard. I've got you."

Then, suddenly, there also was Mack's boat, Sailor driving it, the wake swamping them as he zoomed closer. He would later tell them that he had somehow caught up with the drifting *Regent Red* from Penn's small dinghy, now roped to its side, which he'd found bobbing at the dock. Using bolt cutters to snap the chains, Sailor hauled both of them onboard. The coast guard cutter showed up then, booming out an offer of rescue, speeding alongside, but Sailor didn't slow down. He aimed the boat straight for the beach, driving it right into the sand. The cutter followed with Mack's inflatable in tow. Gil splashed into the water and they all half carried, half dragged Frankie and Ariel to shore.

Then Sailor took over, answering the coast guard officers' questions as best he could, offering phone numbers, asking the two men to send the police. With Atty on his chest in the front pack, Penn brought out piles of Mack's clean T-shirts and massive white robes to the outdoor shower where Frankie and then Ariel rinsed away the salt water with hot streams. Sailor bound Frankie's cut hand, which would be stitched the next day by a cosmetic surgeon, who told her she was lucky, if you could say such a thing about a thing like that, because she didn't seem to have nerve damage. The scar would be there all her life, and she would make up tales about it for Atty, Giselle, Emile and Grace—she had used her hand to force open a crocodile's mouth; she was wounded by a rapier in a sword fight; she cut her hand on a rock climbing Mount Everest.

Sailor made tea with brandy, just like a BBC mystery. When he handed her the mug, Frankie took his hand and held it to her cheek.

She heard Ariel say, "I killed her… I know I killed her."

Sailor said, "Ariel, wait."

That was how Frankie learned what had happened.

Rushing down to the dock, Ariel came upon Carlotta just as she got to shore in the dinghy and, terrified by what she was doing, she pulled her mother out by both arms, saying, "Where is Frankie? Where is she?"

In response, Carlotta shoved Ariel to the ground and attempted to run past her, but Ariel grabbed her ankle and they fought, Carlotta punching Ariel in the chest and the stomach so hard that Ariel gasped for breath but wouldn't let go. Finally, Ariel actually socked Carlotta, and down she went, hitting her head on one of the boulders that lined the path to the pier and going still, blood from a wound pooling around her neck.

That was when Ariel heard the alarm from the flag on the tower rock.

The dinghy was foundering, water already sloshing over the sides. Without even stopping to grab a life jacket, Ariel threw herself into it.

What Sailor told them next would always seem part of the extended myth of that day. He showed up at the pier and saw the blood splashed everywhere around the boulder…but nothing else. No one there, no one nearby. At a loss, he untied Penn's little rowboat to catch up with the *Regent Red*, which he could see drifting. He thought someone in the big boat might be injured.

Later, they would find the dining table in the big house covered with expensive electronics, including Penn's virtual-reality headsets, and Mack's laptop and his camera. A video camera, two phones, and Mack's newest laptop would be missing. She had apparently run out of time.

Each of them talked separately to the police that night and the next morning.

Carlotta's Toyota turned up eventually in the Berkshires. It was registered to Roland Wheeler, of Provincetown, who'd died in 1948 at the age of three. Vanishing was Carlotta's gift.

At home that night, Frankie nestled on the sofa with Atty beside her, hungrily accepting potato soup and bread that Sailor brought to them, while Gil kept touching her as if to make sure she was real. His eyes brimming, he apologized over and over. "I should never have let you go. I had a terrible feeling. I could have left him in his basket and gone after you. He would have been fine, but what if he was not fine? I could never have forgiven myself. You needed me, and I couldn't help you. Until I heard Penn's car."

"You did the right thing," Frankie said. "Atty comes first."

After a while, the pulse of the long day slowed. With the sound of the surf shushing her, Frankie slept for eleven hours, a sleep leavened by dreams of Beatrice smoothing back her hair, as she had before sleep when Frankie was a child. *Must you really be gone?* Frankie asked her. *I must*, Beatrice said. *But now you will be okay. If that weren't true, I wouldn't tell you so.*

When Frankie finally awakened, Mack was sitting in the chair beside the bed. In his faded Duke sweatshirt with the ripped neck and frayed cuffs and his jeans with the raveled hems, with his stubbled chin and reddened eyes, he looked old. "How is Ben?" she asked.

"He's fine," Mack told her. He took her uninjured hand in both of his and began to cry. "Frankie," he said, "I couldn't live without you."

15

From Edinburgh, in their rented van, the eight of them traveled first to the Highlands, where they walked and biked through ancient woodlands that thundered with startling waterfalls. In a tiny nearby town, they took over all the rooms at the single inn and ate bowls of fish chowder with chunks of bread and glasses of ale, except for Ariel, who had just learned that she was pregnant and was sticking to orange juice. In the morning, the baker gave them an insulated bag to keep their thick scones warm and thermoses to keep their sweet tea hot, which they promised to return on the way home.

They biked slowly through Cairngorms National Park, home to wildcats and golden eagles. Near dusk in a deer park, where dwarf birch waved their branches like ribbons, Frankie photographed huge and very endangered Scottish red deer. They couldn't move too quickly, because the babies had only a limited tolerance for outdoor life. Frankie had to sacrifice her plan to go out among the orcas and minke whales when Atty became miserable with teething and would rest only when she held him.

On top of this, Mack was eager to get out to the island, and since they would pass this way again on their return some weeks hence, she hoped for the greater likelihood of seeing the whales in even warmer late-summer weather. Near Branha, they came to the cliff where, on the night of the banquet, Gil had instructed Frankie to jump for the mud. If she had not trusted him then, there would have been no Attleboro Rowan Thomas Beveque, no courtship tale unlike any other for their children to tell their own children one day.

Rob Roaken from the reserve invited them back to his house. "As is only right," he said, "since you're beholden to me for your marriage and your near deaths." He, too, was newly married and, of all people, to a photographer. That night, in honor of the great conservationist Mack Attleboro, they again dined in the inside-out tents Roaken had constructed. This time, instead of keeping the storm from soaking them, the tents were filled with cool air but no night bugs. They ate Scotch pies and potatoes and turnips whipped with sage and cream and finished with deep-fried Mars bars, which turned out to be just what they sounded like. Ariel ate four of them. At the close of the evening, Roaken's wife, whose impossibly beautiful name was Fairy Clanahan, handed each of them a small etched glass with a splash of champagne. On her command, she instructed them, she wanted all of them to take a sip and then throw the glasses up into the air and let them smash on the rocky ground. Mystified, this they all did. The glasses were made of sugar and exploded with a snowy dusting in the night as if the eight of them, laughing, were caught in the middle of a cloud of crystals. The photo of this was spectacular, so beautiful that Frankie had to admit that she could not have taken one to equal it.

The next day they hiked again, through scenes so glorious they didn't suggest suitable adjectives. Although Penn did everything except carry her, Ellabella bitched every step of the way, saying into her voice app, "This is the Scotland of Wallace and Rob Roy. On this historic Culloden battlefield, the English finally defeated Charles Stuart, Bonnie Prince Charlie, in 1746...and I don't know why they bothered."

Finally, after driving east and then south on the glorious roadway thousands of feet above the sea that was called Bealach na Bà, they crossed the bridge to the Isle of Skye, with its Hebrides microcosm of moors and mountains. Mack was back after more than twenty years and kept seeing things that he remembered. All of this was on Mack's dime, the trip his idea and his treat. He was more relaxed and genuinely cheerful—not merely with Mack bonhomie—than Frankie had seen him in years.

In Portree, Skye's version of the big city, they checked into a fancy hotel with a view of the red and black Cuillin Hills. They dined on mussels in garlicky white-wine broth and drank golden Skye Ale. The next day, they were foolish, buying sweaters and china teapots. They walked through Dunvegan Castle, where the chiefs of the MacLeod clan and their descendants had lived for eight hundred years, and they saw the tattered yellow flag that, in battle, would keep the MacLeods from harm. It could be used only three times, and it already had been used twice.

One afternoon, outside a deli where they had just polished off sandwiches the size of their heads, they met a bridegroom and his brother walking up the hill to the church for his wedding. Both young men were handsome, virtually identical, their blue eyes bold, their dark gold hair crisp in curls, and they wore full Highland, down to sprigs of purple thistle in their buttonholes. As they walked, they linked arms, smiling and singing.

"It's like goddamn Brigadoon," muttered Ellabella, whose feet still hurt.

"We might end up wishing it could disappear too," Frankie told her.

She knew that her father was determined to make one last try to find the place where he had almost certainly not seen the extinct sea eagle, back when Frankie was in kindergarten. He wanted her (and her alone) to come with him on the appointed day, into that same drowned forest he was almost sure he could locate. And if he couldn't, he was going to find locals who could, perhaps the same old men who'd first told him about the eagles, although those men assuredly now, like Robert Louis Stevenson's weary traveler, were long since home from the hill, having lain themselves down with a will.

Before they left Massachusetts, they'd made a pact not to discuss Carlotta.

It almost worked.

At dinner, the night before they would search for the drowned forest, Mack said, "I owe all of you an apology for being such a fool. Penn, if you can find it in your heart to consider it, the future of the Saltwater Foundation is yours and yours alone, with whatever help Frankie wants to offer. I would hope that Frankie and Gil and Ariel and little Atty and Ben will help steer this organization into the next decades, extending the vision of my darling Beatrice who loved nothing more than the sea, except her family."

Ariel raised her orange juice. "To Beatrice, goddess of the sea!" They all drank, and Ariel began to cry. "I have to talk now! Beatrice was my true mother, even though she wasn't really mine. If I turn out to be a good mom, it will be because of all the things Beatrice taught me, about being loving and patient. For years, she protected me from the worst of what Carlotta dragged home, but when Beatrice was gone and Carlotta came back, I thought she wanted to do better. It turned out that she wanted to do worse. So I was a fool too. I gave her a second chance she didn't deserve, and I almost lost the dearest people on earth. But I'm not ashamed of believing in second chances in life."

Frankie then said, "Well, I was a fool from the minute I drove up Two Ponds Road last summer. What I thought I saw, a silly old man and a greedy girl, wasn't right at all. I was seeing two lonely people I love. They weren't letting stereotypes stop them from giving each other a second chance at happiness. Please give me a second chance too."

Gil said, "I'm happy to report that I am innocent of all charges."

"Let us all praise the decency of Canadians!" Ellabella said, raising her glass. Frankie raised Atty's little fist, pointing out that he was Canadian too. They stayed in the restaurant until the staff began giving them mournful looks and they found the unfortunate need to sing "The Skye Boat Song" through twice as they left.

Through the owner of the inn, Mack arranged an informal car rental from a local garage, as he and Frankie planned to stay overnight somewhere on their hunt. The rest of them would use the van to visit the storied Fairy Pools, where waterfalls that seemed to froth blue or green depending on the light crashed down into icy small ponds. Ellabella found a reference to the Battle of Coire na Creiche, between the MacLeods of Dunvegan and the MacDonalds of Sleat, a feud so violent that the horrified King James, son of Mary Queen of Scots, interfered to force a lasting truce between the clans. *"The pools ran red with blood,"* Ellabella read from a guidebook. "How picturesque. Yikes."

"But Americans know all about that," Penn teased her. "Think of Antietam."

Gil said, "Think of Oakland a few years ago."

"You Canadians!" said Ellabella. "Decent, peaceful and—"

Frankie finished, "And so morally superior!"

The island was bustling with late-summer tourists, and Frankie privately thought that Mack was naive to think that a charming *Masterpiece Theatre* inn, preferably at a vicarage, would turn up at his fingertips. But she said nothing. She'd slept in cars plenty of times, and who knew if the visit would turn out to warrant an overnight, anyhow?

They set out just before dawn, driving slowly for a half hour, stopping, then driving again. Frankie would cry out, "Wait, Dad! Stop! Look at that." She told Mack, "I didn't remember how emotionally exhausting this place could be for a photographer." The mossy valleys and black rock spires were comically enticing, the mist-wreathed peaks beckoning her lenses. She hadn't taken so many land images since her father's wedding.

"A nature writer called it the *landscape of grand gestures*," Mack said. "Frank Lloyd Wright…what did he say about God?"

"He said, *I believe in God only I spell it Nature*," Frankie said. "I love that."

Mack and Frankie parked off the road just north of Bradford. Frankie hefted her camera bag, and they began to walk. When they came to a cliffside clearing, they sat down on slippery flat rocks and, looking out over the Crowlin Islands, they drank their thermoses of sweet tea and ate cheese-and-tomato sandwiches on dense brown bannock bread. When they started to walk again, it was out toward the downslopes that led to the beach. Outside a thatched cottage so pretty it might have been part of a Disney movie, they met a very old man selling tiny wych elm saplings in a little biodegradable kit for visitors to plant.

"There are not many forests of any kind left on Skye. The Vikings got rid of most so people couldn't use the wood to build boats, and the big landowners got rid of the rest because they could make more money off sheep than off folk."

"True," Mack said and observed an impatient moment of what he probably hoped would seem like sympathetic silence. He bought a dozen of the little kits, which the man explained required only that the planter kick a shallow dent in the ground and set it upright.

"Most of them won't make it, but some will," the man said. He told them that his name was Barry. "True of everything that lives, I would say."

Mack began again, "There's a sort of marsh by a loch, where the water has drowned some old trees. Do you happen to know where that is?"

"Four lochs nearby and two of them got a little wood and a marshy bit like that. One to the left's called something I don't know and I've lived in this same place all my life, and the other to the right is Glen Haar because it's called after the sea fret."

"The cold mist that Mom used to talk about, that brought the ghosts," Frankie said.

"There's a story that there's an eagle back in that old woods, a really big bird, a red eagle..."

"Ah, yes. Extinct for a hundred years it is. It's only the bird doesn't know that."

Mack said eagerly, "You've seen it?"

"Not I. I don't like going about in a dark forest that isn't underwater, much less one in a swamp so deep it can cover a tree. No, I leave that to mad people."

"But people say they've seen this eagle?"

"When they're drunk, which is usually," the old man told them. "That bird shows up as regular as Nessie during these long summer nights."

"Ahhh, well. One more thing. Around here, would you know a place where my daughter and I could get rooms for tonight?"

"Crowded this time of year," Barry said. "But my wife and I keep two guest rooms, and we could give you your tea and breakfast."

His eyes flashing triumph at Frankie, Mack all but leaped into the air. "That's perfect," he said. "We'll pay you for them right now. Can we put the car by your house, you think?"

The rooms were side-by-side, linked by what Mrs. Barry called a *necessary*. They were miniature spaces, and Frankie marveled again at the expanses Americans considered necessary. The bathroom back at her cottage, with its sixties vintage tub, was as big as one of these bedrooms chez Barry. She sat down on the bed, then lay down just for a minute, then slept for two full hours. Much as he wanted to shake her awake, the new-and-improved Mack Attleboro settled for rattling around the area, planting several dozen more trees he purchased from Barry.

That wasn't why her father was excited, however.

He and Barry had taken a drive and come across a place he vividly recalled from decades ago—the ruins of a tiny stone chapel that sat in the middle of a family graveyard with a few stones scrubbed blank by the toning sea winds. Mack remembered it because one row was made up of headstones so tiny that they must have marked the graves of babies. It was not only quite a distance off the road, but tucked into a small cul-de-sac. Barry had pointed out that that portion of the structure that might once have been visible from the main track had been leveled in a fierce storm twenty years before.

"Barry had a couple of kites in the trunk of his car from when one of his sister's grandkids visited," Mack said. "We tied those on the road sign and on a fence post right by the place where you should turn in." Shoving a mug of tea into her hands, while he abstractedly reached for and ate the two pieces of shortbread on the saucer, Mack continued. "We have to go there right away, Frankie."

"Just let me get something else to eat, Dad."

"You already wasted hours sleeping! Come on, Frankie. You can eat later." So she collected her wet suit and goggles, her primary on-land camera, her second-best underwater rig and a backup point-and-shoot, stowing these in her big backpack, and Mack packed his with Frankie's new and even-lighter floating surface air-diving system. With packages of cookies in the pocket of her hoodie, Frankie followed her father out into the misty afternoon, drove to the spot marked by the kites, both in the shape of dragons, which lay forlorn in the still air, and then set out walking down the path to the shore that was little more than a sandy track along the sparse forest of stunted trees. As they crisscrossed small spits of land and plopped through deep muddy puddles, Frankie heard a ping signaling a text coming in. She was stunned that there was service at all.

It was from Ariel. Did you ever hear of Cadbury Flake Bars? Buying new suitcase to bring home 2000 of them.

She laughed out loud. Mack said, "What?"

"Oh, it's just she's such a joker…your wife!"

She had never used those words, and the sound of them felt like a clap of thunder between them. Mack's wife was Beatrice, Frankie's mother.

But no. Not now. Not anymore. It was sad. It was tender. More than either of those things, it was simply true.

Pivoting, Frankie, who knew almost nothing about birds in the UK (or anywhere) said, "Dad, look! That is the biggest brown gull I've ever seen in my life! What are they feeding them?"

"It's not a gull. That's what's called a skua, or a bonxie, but around here, a skua. It looks like a gull, but it's kind of a small raptor. They are really ferocious. They've been known to attack people." He pointed. "And there… I can't believe this. That's a whooper swan." Frankie shot furiously and silently. "It's not that they're incredibly rare, it's the same as a trumpeter swan in America, but usually, at least with my luck, you never see anything unless it's thirty degrees and sleeting. There's another skua. That word means *dumpy*."

"Sounds like the name of the little-known eighth dwarf, Dumpy."

"Not very appropriate, Frankie."

"Dad, oh please! You of all people lecturing me on how to be politically correct? I meant the storybook kind of dwarf, not pituitary dwarfism. What if I said Barry the Scot was… gnomish?"

Even she could spot eider ducks with their puffed furred throats, and huge rooks with their intelligent eyes and magnificent polished black feathers. All at once, they came to the marsh that Mack recalled, where birds of all sizes and sounds flew as if in an aviary above what clearly were the bare white branches of ancient trees, trees that had not seen sunlight perhaps for a thousand years. Even if it was desolate, the drowned forest clearly was stable, because Frankie could see two huge messy nests, far back in the gloom. And it was gloom, despite the sun overhead. The forest seemed to linger in its own rosy-gray twilight. What was clearly a river coursed through it, and this made Frankie bold. She wanted to see the fabled creatures that brought fishers from all over the globe to Scotland, sea bass and rainbow trout and mighty salmon.

"Are you going to go under?" Mack asked.

"Just for a little while," Frankie told him. "You keep looking." Mack had the Canon binoculars Ariel had given him for Christmas, and he settled himself happily on a tree fall. "If you see the dive system disappear, you know something ate me. Maybe the Loch Ness Monster after all. Keep whatever parts you find."

"Nessie is a vegetarian," Mack told her affably. Frankie could hear the strain in his voice. How badly he wanted to see the bird that haunted his dreams. How bravely he was trying to signal that it really didn't matter very much. Frankie sank into the marsh, where the visibility was cloudy. She propelled herself forward, the hose lengthening smoothly, the breaths uncomplicated and easy. She tried to make herself quiet, and was rewarded when an Atlantic salmon that must have been nearly three feet long glided with spangled sides. She snapped pictures of rosy trout and striving frogs. Then, just as she was encountering a bank and was about to stand, an even-larger salmon leaped, twisting in a sudden slant of sunlight. Frankie knew that they rarely jumped once, so when the huge thing came up again, she was ready to shoot fast and repeatedly. A fish angel, Atty would say one day, when he looked at that picture.

Mack and Frankie roamed through the mud, with her taking pictures of all they saw. Finally, hours had passed. The marsh was darkening, and Frankie knew the hardpack path back would be rubbled and hazardous. "Dad," she said softly. "Are you hungry?"

Mack said, "No."

"I am."

He looked at her with such a grave, enormous openness then that she had to avert her eyes. What could she say? Anything she said would be clumsy. But she wanted him to know somehow that she was refusing to see him as Old Eagle Eye, the admired but eccentric figure of fun. While she didn't quite want him to keep on believing or, heaven forbid, talking about it so long as he had no proof of its absence, the extinct red eagle was still out there, more noble in size than any modern eagle, flying silently, landing with mortal swiftness on its prey. Why, Frankie wondered, had Mack's mind conjured up the Regent Red sea eagle instead of some other big bird of prey? The obvious reasons were that he knew it had once lived around here; he had seen it in a long-ago drawing, perhaps even a specimen of taxidermy or a photo. She knew that Mack did not believe he was lying or imagining things...and it was still even possible that, two decades ago, there had been still individual birds. Who could prove that there were not?

"Dad, I think we need to head back before dark. Mrs. Barry promised us a big tea, lots of sammies and scones, huh?"

"Do you think I'm a child, Francis, who can be distracted with the promise of a sweet?"

"Okay, have it your way. I was trying to be nice. I feel terrible for you. There. This has to be a pretty crushing circumstance."

"And now the carrion birds can all gather around Mack Attleboro and pick the carcass of that silly old man. My esteemed colleagues. I've forgotten more than they'll ever know. Everybody can laugh now, let the old grandpappy tell his crazy stories by the fireplace…while his pretty wife waits for him to die."

"Dad, stop!" Frankie said. "Dad, nobody feels that way."

"How do you know? You say I was never around for you. You're the queen of never around! You came home for four full days when your mother died."

Frankie asked herself, what are you really feeling? Under the shock? Under the rage? Hurt, oh hurt, like a blow to the heart. "Let's go back now. I'm tired and I'm hungry, and I don't want this to go any further…"

"Why not? Didn't you laugh right along with all the rest of them?"

Frankie carefully replaced her cameras, just as she remembered seeing figure skaters, whether trembling with hope or bowed down with despair, never neglect to replace the guards on their costly blades. Then she turned and began to pick her way through the mud, brushing the gnats from her eyes and her mouth, back up onto the track. Her father didn't move. She kept walking.

At last, she turned back. "Let me tell you this. I never once laughed at you. Neither did Penn. Ever. But you are one of the most self-centered and selfish people I've ever met in my life. No, that's wrong. You *are* the most self-centered and selfish person I have ever known."

She walked on, grabbing and breaking off a dry branch to use as a walking stick. Behind her, she heard Mack roughly stow the tankless diving compressor—if he wrecked it, he could buy her a new one. Then she heard a hard splash, a grunt and a scream. Mack burst out of the water. "It's my knee, my knee! What the hell?"

Frankie rushed back, shoving her shoulder under Mack's arm, half-hauling him to the track as he winced in pain. "Lean on me, Dad," she said. "Here, grab the stick."

"I can't, Frankie," he said. "Call an ambulance."

She did nearly laugh then. "Dad, where would I tell them to come? The ass-end swamp in the middle of nowhere at the end of no road? No, we're going out of here the way we came, and as soon as I get a signal I'll call Mr. Barry and ask him if he knows somebody sturdy who can get us to a clinic someplace." Excruciatingly slowly, they hobbled along. Mack was strong and lean, but he was sixty-one and, though Frankie could not imagine how, had never injured himself beyond a cut or a scrape or some evil sunburns and once appendicitis that had him and Penn racing for the nearest hospital in Venezuela.

There was no Highland urgent care, but Mr. Barry's son, a large-animal vet, iced and bound Mack's knee,

A neighboring doctor of the people variety dropped by with some painkillers. "I won't need them," Mack said.

"Ah, you'll surely need them," the woman told him. "By ten tonight, you'll want to take them all at once, but don't." She also provided Mack with an aluminum crutch.

With Mack ruefully acknowledging orders to elevate the knee for a couple of days, Frankie texted Ellabella and asked her to gently explain matters to Ariel, further and explicitly stating that there was no reason, none at all, for anyone else to come and experience Mack in what possibly was his worst mood ever. After raiding the local book trailer for a dozen books about wars, fishing, spies and mountain climbers, Frankie wordlessly gave these to her father, then shut the door between his room and the necessary. Mrs. Barry agreed to bring Mack plenty of tea and sandwiches on a tray. She asked Frankie to join her and Barry at their own table for a venison stew, and Frankie, who hadn't eaten meat in over a year, asked for seconds.

Through the night, she heard Mack moaning in pain, gruffly telling Ariel, then Penn, that he was just fine and, no, there was no reason to ask Frankie. She heard him roaring as he washed himself in the sink and made not one move to help him. Ariel sent a text asking if Frankie had checked on Mack, asking what if he got a blood clot and died? Checking on him won't do any good, then, Frankie replied.

The next day and night were proof of the theory of relativity. Time seemed to flow backward.

Frankie walked and took photos. She walked and ate meat. She walked and called Gil and made goofy noises to Atty, which Gil said the baby responded to by trying to lick the telephone. She was truly grateful to have weaned him earlier in the summer. She walked and picked purple blossoms to put in a jar in her room. She walked and recognized that she had grown to be like the seals: clumsy out of water but togetherness now as essential to her survival as her own breath, graceful underwater but no longer built for solitude. She walked until she was exhausted and finally purloined one of the books, a grisly Scots mystery, from Mack's bedside, noting he was not dead. She read all of it and hoped the doors were locked, because the victims were Highland lassies, then purloined another book. When she fell asleep, she dreamed that her fingers and nose were blue with frostbite.

The vet came back the next day and told her Mack was a very strong man, but he'd given himself a mighty wrench. He wrapped the knee again, while Mack cried out. The doctor called and told Frankie that Mack should visit the clinic, only a forty-five-minute drive. She thanked the doctor for the information.

In the predawn darkness of the third day, Frankie woke with a scream to a muffled sound, sure that she was about to become the next of the bludgeoned Scotswomen. Instead, Mack was sitting on the foot of the bed, and Frankie could not even see his face. But she heard the thickness in his voice and realized, to her horror, that Mack was crying.

"I am the most self-centered man on earth. I have been a foolish old man. I've been prideful and unreasonable."

Frankie said, "Dad, is this about the eagle? Is this about the wedding?"

"It's about everything. I didn't stop to consider how what I wanted would affect you. Any of you."

"Dad, go back to bed.

"I apologized, but I didn't learn."

"Oh, Dad."

"Okay, Frankie, see you in the morning."

"Okay, Dad. Do you need anything?"

Mack said, "Yes, I do. But I can tell you in the morning."

Over breakfast, he told her what he wanted. Frankie said, "Dad, no. A hundred times no. Not if you were to offer me ten thousand dollars."

"I'll give you ten thousand dollars."

Frankie gazed at him, her spoon suspended over her bowl of porridge with currants. She had asked about the black pudding, as well as the white pudding, and was back on the vegetarian wagon.

"You'll give me ten thousand dollars to take you back to that same place where you just almost crippled yourself."

"Yes," Mack said. "And if you won't go with me, I'll go alone."

Could she report him? To whom? The polis? The large-animal vet? With his leg encased in a bin bag, Mack had screamed and sworn his way through a Euro shower only an hour before. Even the placid Mrs. Barry had rolled her eyes. A couple of painkillers had restored him, but his dark eyes were glassy, his face loose and pale.

"Dad, we'll come back here next year. I swear on Atty's head, wherever I am and whatever I'm doing, if there is any way on earth I can, we'll come back, right here, and if that bird was ever here, it will still be here. And if it's not here, it will still not be here."

"It has to be now. I'll never be able to come here again," Mack said.

"Don't guilt-trip me, Dad! Until you fell over, you were fitter than men half your age."

"This is how it starts."

Please, Frankie implored the universe, whatever divine hags of Scotland or English Attleboro shades happened to be hanging around with nothing but eternity on their hands. *If this were a romance novel*, she thought, *I could marry the large-animal vet, whose name actually was Harry Barry, although in the novel, he could be named Beathan MacDonough MacLeish. But this isn't a romance novel and I want to see my husband and my baby and my brother again. Please don't make me go back into the dismal swamp with my father, unstable in a couple of ways right now, who will fall in the swamp and need to be airlifted to Glasgow.*

She waited.

The universe shrugged and said *Whatever.*

Frankie sent a text to Ariel. Please tell Mack he has to come back right now.

She waited.

She heard a small whistle, then saw her father consult his phone and put it back in his shirt pocket.

She ate some more of her porridge and cold toast. Finally, Frankie asked, "Can you make a bank transfer from Scotland? Can Ariel do that?"

Mack said, "Of course."

"That'll be ten thousand bucks, sir."

To her horror, Mack pulled his phone out again. He didn't even hesitate. A few minutes later, all their things stowed in the trunk, they took one last drive to the road by the ruined chapel.

"Before I get out of this car, Dad," said Frankie, "I want you to promise me one thing. You remember how you used to go over the safety rules with us? Twice? Before we skied? Before we went on a dive? I'm going to go over the rules with you."

Only Frankie would actually wade into the swamp. Mack would remain seated on a stump, safely out of the mud.

"Say *check*," Frankie instructed Mack.

Mack said, "Check."

"No matter what happens, when I say it's time to go, we'll go. Say *check*."

"Check."

"And you'll believe me when I say this next thing, Dad. This bird is your white whale. I get that. I even sort of respect you for it. But even if you never see it, even if you come back every year until you're eighty, you will still have done more for helping people understand how to protect wildlife than almost anyone of your generation." She added, "Say *check*."

Mack said, "What do you mean, almost anyone?"

Frankie was relieved by his flash of arrogance. "Say *check*."

"Check."

Frankie handed Mack the crutch. With her father hobbling painfully and the air temperature hovering around forty degrees, they set off along the track. Immediately, rain began to fall, light but needling, little slivers of ice down her neck. Ahead, the drowned forest raised its fingertips toward the dull sky.

On they walked until the water overtook Frankie's wellies. She slipped them off, adjusting her high-top water shoes and handing them off to Mack, who sat down gratefully on a thick fallen log. Puckers of pain pinched the corners of his mouth. She extracted her camera from the bag (this time, she'd brought just one, the digital point-and-shoot) and secured it by the strap around her neck. A slug dropped onto Frankie's hand and a luridly colored salamander scuttled away. *And a thousand thousand slimy things lived on, and so did I*, Frankie thought. *What fun. Back at that cozy inn, they are all eating scones, mushrooms on toast, and pots and pots of hot tea. My son apparently loves baked beans, and my baby brother is pulling himself up and about to take his first steps any second. And here I am trapped in a freezing swamp with the ancient mariner.*

What she would remember later was that she heard a commotion overhead and felt a sudden rush of wind. Her instant thought was that a branch was falling through the weighty wet air. She ducked and rolled to one side, instinctively protecting her camera and her head. Instead of a branch, what came to rest in the notch of a thick treetop ten feet from her was a bird. It was absurdly large. Frankie had only seen one Steller's sea eagle up close, at a raptor rehab, and this bird was bigger by a third than that one. Its feathers were the color of blood. In its nearly white talons it clutched a thick pink trout that it began to tear at, all the while regarding Frankie with a bored golden eye.

She whispered, "Dad."

"You don't have to be completely quiet," Mack said in an even tone. "This individual has probably never seen a human being so you're only strange to it, not necessarily a threat. It's an apex predator in its territory."

"Dad," Frankie said again, overcome.

"*Rufa aquila regens*. It must weigh forty pounds."

Frankie raised her camera from where she lay and began to shoot, making rapid adjustments for the low light, capturing the wingspread—nine feet?—as the bird lifted off and with a single stroke of its wings, came to rest deeper in the swamp, on the lip of one of the huge messy nests.

"So maybe this is a female, maybe a male," Mack said. "They both bring food. There are chicks in there. Big ones."

On her knees, then up to her waist in ice water, Frankie crept closer. The bright red fledglings, three of them, fought noisily with each other for the fish their mother dropped into their mouths.

"It's beautiful," said Frankie. "Dad, it's here! The Regent Red sea eagle. Your whole life! How can you be so calm?"

Mack said, "I'm trying to think. I don't think we should tell anybody about them."

"Dad—what?"

"They survived because no one knew they were here. Except people around here. And me. Probably nobody believed the people around here either. Like Barry said. A giant red eagle is the same as a pink elephant."

"Dad, this is like finding the coelacanth," Frankie said and thought of how, nearly a century later, people were still entranced by the story of how the spotted jawfish, believed extinct for sixty-five million years, was discovered off the east coast of South Africa. The flightless takahe in New Zealand, the tiny South American monito del monte, ancestor to kangaroos. "This is the moment of your career as an apex predator. Not to mention the best up-yours moment ever. Not to mention just…wonderful."

"So perhaps it has to just be a moment of my life and to hell with my career. I saw the birds. I know they're here because you saw them too. That's enough for me."

"Not so fast," Frankie said. "It's not enough for me."

Frankie would later write:

While they were filming The Red King documentary, my father and I talked about that very moment. I confided that I admired him so much that I almost went along with him. But I was Mack Attleboro's only daughter. And through his sheer stubbornness, he had shared this wish, this obsession, this gift—and now it was mine too. "Don't go all existential on me, Dad," I said. "You've been waiting your whole life to make them stuff their words back in their mouths. You're the right one to have found this eagle because you're the one who cares so much you'd give up the chance to have your own TV show to protect the animal." I don't even know why I brought up a TV show. But life is such an ironic evolution, isn't it? I had to really work to convince him. I had to convince this guy, who went around for decades bragging about discovering something nobody else believed, to finally brag about it when it was real. I had to show my pictures and the short video to our family so that Mack could see their reaction. When the video showed the second eagle coming with another big fish twisting in its claws, Ariel was fighting back tears. She said she felt that this sight was a message from nature, that it could heal and comfort itself if we would just stand back, and she added that this was the strongest conservation statement she'd ever experienced. Still, Mack decided to go back with Ariel and Penn and make a very specific and gentle effort to tag several chicks, not to interfere, but to offer our help. The Regent Red sea eagle was not extinct, but it nearly was. And that was how it was decided that we would close every episode of The World According to Mack with that sentence: Nature will always have the final word. It's in its third season now, and even though it's wearing Gil and me out, it means that there's a whole new generation of kids falling in love with marine wildlife, a whole new generation growing up wanting nature to have the final word. All because I wouldn't let my eccentric father decide to keep quiet—to keep quiet for the first time ever—after risking his life and his reputation for something only he believed in. Mack Attleboro is a character, but he's a character who has character.

There was more. Frankie never wrote about it.

That cold night, as they made their way back to the car, Mack hobbling on a leg that was now stiffly swollen to three times its size, Frankie said, "You deserve to celebrate, Dad."

Quietly, Mack said, "I feel like praying."

"We'll have a Scottish coffee, though, huh? With lots of whipped cream. I don't think I should take you to a pub. But what the heck, I guess after a day like today with a leg like that, it will probably at least get you a few hours of sleep. The pub is apparently right by the hospital. It's called The Old Boar, and Barry says they have some mean bubble and squeak."

"Okay," Mack said. "That sounds great."

They did go to the pub, and they toasted each other. Frankie ate heartily, and Mack picked at his food, talking about contacting the university and his friend Gunther at Woods Hole and discussing with Penn how to proceed. Finally, he said, "I am happy, Frankie. It's just that…tomorrow is your mother's birthday."

"Last year, that was right before you got married."

"I still thought of Beatrice."

Now Frankie thought of her as well. Since she had driven up Two Ponds Road, it had been a year exactly, four seasons of life and life and life, a chambered pomegranate bursting with new love and old secrets, with recognition and renewal, loyalty and loss, so many things that were not supposed to happen.

"Frankie," Mack said, "one more matter."

"What, Dad?"

"I changed my will."

"I know about that. It's okay."

"No, I mean, I changed it again. Ariel and I did. I would never take Tall Trees away from you and Penn. It's yours forever."

"It will be all of ours, Dad. Down all the years. The children's too and their children's. You didn't have to do this."

"I did have to."

"You didn't. I thought it mattered so much. It turns out other things matter more. But I'm grateful."

Her father dropped his fork with a clatter, and Frankie almost got up, fearing he was stricken again with the pain. But he only reached for her hand, threading his thick fingers through her slender ones.

That night as Mack slept, for the vet would check his knee just once more before they departed in the morning, Frankie wandered out into the cold night, over the tufty ground where the sea fret billowed up from the shore.

When Frankie felt her mother's hand come to rest lightly on her cheekbone, she was startled, but only for a moment.

Beatrice said, *Frankie, what do you want?*

Frankie said, *I want you. But in real life, I want months and months when nothing at all happens.*

Then Beatrice told her, *Oh, little girl, that's not your destiny. You're a person to whom things happen, and some of them you cause yourself, and some of them are gifts.* Said Frankie then, *There isn't always a gift in a loss, or a life in a death.* Her mother agreed. *But since you can't rub away the hurt, you need to temper it, the way you temper a color that's too dark, by adding a different tint.*

Time, said Frankie. *You mean it's tempered with time. That's what everybody says about time, that it heals.* Again, Beatrice agreed.

I'm just not good at this big life, Frankie said. *My life before was really only me. Now, every move I make could hurt the others. It takes so much more courage. I don't have the hang of it, and nothing will ever be different.*

It will, Beatrice insisted. *It's already different. You lost some freedom. You found love. You found motherhood. You found your father. All that in one year.*

Frankie said, *Don't forget the eagle.*

The eagle, of course. The eagle is real, but I spell it angel. And most importantly, you know how to talk to yourself about life now. You are the one who's saying all this. I'm not even really here.

Yes, you are, Frankie said.

Only in you, said Beatrice. *So trust yourself. Trust time. And salt water.*

★★★★★

Acknowledgments

Please allow me the briefest moment to give credit to the people involved in publishing this book. First, to my ever-patient agent, Jeff Kleinman, who forgives me my moods and wishes only that I would stop sending him nine one-sentence emails in a single half hour; you are creative, innovative, and supportive beyond measure and I am grateful. Nicole Brebner, Meredith Clark, and all the top-notch team at MIRA, Harper-Collins, I thank you for seeing the sparkle in this strange story. Credit is also due to my family, especially my daughter Merit, who actually sometimes listens when I read my words to her, my daughter Marta, who loyally likes everything I write and cook, and my sister-in-love, Pam, unflinching in any storm. Thanks to my book-club sisters, who have no idea why I still insist on doing this, and to all my gallant writer pals, especially Ann Wertz Garvin, who do know why, sometimes to their rue. Thanks to my beloved friend Deb, for reading this and recognizing its dicey origin; everything you say is funny or beautiful. I owe a debt in absentia to brilliant photographers David Doubliet, Jennifer Hayes, Brian Skerry, and Joel Meyerowitz, whose works I studied to help me see, under water and above it. And thanks most of all to readers for sticking with me: writing a story for you is like hearing a sudden peal of laughter at 4:00 a.m. in the pouring rain. You're not quite sure where it comes from, but you're grateful that it's there.

This is a work of fiction. Even those places that seem to share a name with actual places have been seined through the storyteller's net to become unreal versions of themselves. Despite this, I acknowledge that there are undoubtedly mistakes, and that all of them are mine.